THREE NOVELS

[KENN]

THREE NOVELS

John Henry Mackay

translated by

Hubert Kennedy

[ENN]

Copyright © 2001 by Hubert Kennedy.

ISBN #:   Softcover   1-4010-3542-6

All rights reserved. No part of this book may be reproduced or transmitted in any form or by any means, electronic or mechanical, including photocopying, recording, or by any information storage and retrieval system, without permission in writing from the copyright owner.

This is a work of fiction. Names, characters, places and incidents either are the product of the author's imagination or are used fictitiously, and any resemblance to any actual persons, living or dead, events, or locales is entirely coincidental.

This book was printed in the United States of America.

To order additional copies of this book, contact:
Xlibris Corporation
1-888-795-4274
www.Xlibris.com
Orders@Xlibris.com

KENN]

CONTENTS

INTRODUCTION

The Scotch-German author John Henry Mackay wrote on a variety of subjects. This is well illustrated in the three short novels presented here. The first, *The People of Marriage* (1892), appeared only one year after his instantly successful book *The Anarchists* (1891). Although in a fictionalized form, *The Anarchists* was a work of propaganda. But from the beginning critics have called it a novel; Mackay himself always insisted that it was not. Thus *The People of Marriage* is Mackay's first novel (though "long novella" might be a better description). Nevertheless, it too had a pronounced propagandistic tendency, namely in the cause of free love. This subject is no longer as topical as it was in 1892—today's interest will probably be more in the denunciation of small-town life that Mackay presents in his scathing picture of Saarbrücken, where he lived for a while in the home of his stepfather.

The second novel in this volume is Mackay's only thriller—*District Attorney Sierlin: The Story of a Revenge* (1928). All propaganda is lacking here—this novel was written for money. *District Attorney Sierlin*, which is set in Berlin where Mackay had been living for many years, was one of his few commercial successes. Before publication as a book, it had been serialized in the well-known Berlin paper *Vossische Zeitung*. The sustained tension in the story is well suited to serialization and Mackay's characters are psychologically interesting. The novel reflects his lifelong fascination with the "perfect crime."

The third novel, *The Imagined World*, was written shortly after *Sierlin*, but was never published in Mackay's lifetime. If it had been, he would probably have given it a subtitle to describe its content as he did for all his other stories. I have taken the liberty of adding the subtitle given here. Although lacking the excitement of the earlier novel, it has elements that reflect Mackay's own weltanschauung—and, indeed, sexual interests—that make it fascinating for anyone interested in Mackay's biography. These aspects will be further discussed in the afterword.

John Henry Mackay was born on 6 February 1864 in Greenock, Scotland, the son of a Scottish father (John Farquhar Mackay, a marine insurance broker) and a German mother (née Luise Auguste Ehlers). His mother returned with him to Hamburg, Germany, on the death of his father when Mackay was only nineteen months old. Thus he grew up with German as his mother tongue. He later learned English—and translated a volume of American and English poems into German—but did not write it well. His mother married a second time to a Prussian civil servant who already had a son. Mackay did not get along with his stepbrother and spent his later school years away from home as a boarding pupil. After one year as an apprentice in a publishing house, he was a student at three universities (in Kiel, Leipzig, and Berlin), but only as an auditor. With a generous allowance from his mother, he traveled much and began his long career as a writer.

Overnight fame came to Mackay in 1891 with his propagandistic *The Anarchists*, which was translated that same year into English and later into eight other languages. But he was already known as a lyric poet. The composer Richard Strauss, whom Mackay met in 1892, later set four of Mackay's poems to music—his "Morgen" has remained one of Strauss's most performed lieder. Mackay was also known as an anarchist poet, but he wrote in a variety of literary forms, including novels, plays, and shorter fiction of all lengths. His first full-length novel, *The Swimmer* (1901), was one of the very first literary sports novels. It has all the excitement one expects from a sports novel and is also notable for its psychological insights. In addition it is historically important for the picture it gives of competitive swimming and diving in the first period of the organization of those sports. (An English translation of *The Swimmer* was published by Xlibris in 2001.)

The death of Mackay's mother in 1902 brought on a depression from which he only recovered with his dedication in 1905, under the pseudonym Sagitta, to the new cause of homosexual liberation, especially the right of men and boys to love one another. Mackay himself was attracted to boys in the ages 14–17. His literary efforts in this direction were ruthlessly crushed by the state—though Mackay continued to write and publish underground.

Mackay was also the rediscoverer of the philosopher of egoism Max Stirner, whose biographer he became. During the years of World War I, he was unable to publish but did complete his second large work of anarchist propaganda, *The Freedomseeker*. By the time it appeared, however, interest in Mackay's brand of individualist anarchism had nearly died out. Nor was he able to reclaim the attention that his earlier works had brought him. The runaway inflation in 1923 wiped out the value of the lifetime annuity Mackay had bought with his inheritance from his mother, so that he spent his last years in relative poverty. He died in Berlin on 16 May 1933.

Hubert Kennedy

THE PEOPLE
OF MARRIAGE

SMALL TOWN PICTURES

KENN]

I do not laugh at them because they are what they are;
I laugh at them because they think their life is
a model and example, and that it is worthwhile
to live as they live.

John Henry Mackay

1

The dust of the burning coal filled the air far and wide. A thousand chimneys emitted the yellow, black, gray, and white smoke up into thick billows that imperceptibly dissolved into the gigantic cloud of haze that overshadowed the whole width of the river valley for miles.

It lay over the small town like a thin veil. At times a fresher breath of wind coming from the south of the valley lifted the veil. But it did not last long and the veil fell again over the unattractive features, hiding them as if in pity.

Actually there were two towns here lying side by side. Only the river, a sluggish, yellow river, separated them, and two bridges connected them: an old, massive stone bridge with powerful pillars and blocks, which had silently borne everything that was drawn over it, and a new one of modern steel, which groaned and shook when large trucks ran over it, coughing out hideous masses of dust from under their heavy wheels.

A stranger hiking on the heights of the valley, who saw the red and black gables at his feet, would not doubt that they all belonged within the municipal limits of one town. Those, however, who lived under these gables were of another opinion. And that was what mattered.

Since time immemorial the sister cities were at daggers with one another. The little frictions never ended; the final landmarks of the great decisive battles, however, were the empty eye sockets of the gas lanterns on the "old" bridge. Under the barrage of stones from the youth of both towns, who imitated the chirping, no, the howling of their elders, the lanterns had caved in from the throws that, alas, had missed their more noble targets.

These battles ended in dialogues of both classical brevity and beauty:

"Just wait till I tell my father!" from one side.

"And I'll tell my mother, who'll take your mother!" from the other.

"But my father is stronger than your father."

"You dumbbell, just don't come over."

2

The society of the town was made up of three easily recognizable elements: the businessmen, the officials, and the military.

The first had been settled here for many years. They were the original body of citizenry. They had married almost only among themselves for so long that they had in a certain sense become *one* big family, which sought as long as possible to continue in their inherited views and customs, and they spoke among themselves in the strong accents of the regional dialect.

Piling up millions upon millions they had erected here a modern fortress of capitalism, against which an attack seemed impossible. Never had it ever been tried.

Thus they—the absolute rulers of this town—had long stamped their mark on it; the mark of a sovereign, rigid will, opposed to progress.

They were the "natives."

Then the state had established large undertakings and an innumerable host of officials of every kind had flowed together here, bringing with them from all parts of the empire new languages, new customs, new cooking recipes. New life did not come with them. Powerless for any initiative, they had will-lessly adapted themselves as wheels in the great state machinery that employed them. But the air began to buzz with new titles, from the morning walk to the office until the last—always very late—evening beer in the "Münchener Kindl," and the grumbling native residents drew back more and more under the thick skins of their secure privileges.

If they had been here ten years, all these strangers, without being further transferred to another town, then they became "locals." Until then they remained what they were: "outsiders."

The town lay not far from the national border. Since the terrible war with the "hereditary enemy" the military had continually moved in until two regiments had their quarters here. Everywhere on the widening town limits arose whitewashed barracks of wood and large, red, rectangular brick piles of atrocious ugliness, from behind whose surrounding walls the raw curses of brutal non-commissioned officers and the stamping feet of heavy and panting human masses sounded, and the streets of the cities, which had been so peaceful until then, shook under the clatter of rustling cavalry sabers.

But even more frightful was the devastation that this new force caused in the hearts of the daughters of the businessmen, and if the fathers of the great families only grumbled, the cousins were infuriated to see one after another lovely blossom be plucked by the impudent hand of a noble second lieutenant, who knew not only how to disdain purses, but also how to empty them with grace.

And was not all in order thus? Capital united itself with the power that protected its privileges.

In between an indolent petty bourgeoisie and a powerless class of laborers had thus accustomed itself to live, from day to day, gossipers and ne'er-do-wells. They hardly asked for anything else than to always be allowed to grumble about something or other.

Those were the people of the town.

One still sensed nothing of cultural needs here.

Outside, however, there where the chimneys smoked and the fires flamed up, where the earth was mined down into its depths in a restless struggle, there where colossal masses of workers lay chained to one another by the sweat of their terrible work, there the ideas of the times fell on fertile soil.

3

The traveler arrived with the express train that came in at eleven
o'clock in the morning. He waved the baggage carrier away from
him as he stepped out and carried his bag himself down the stairs
to the exit.

Four or six porters were there to receive travelers. He looked
over the signs on their caps and, not seeing the name he was looking for, named it himself: "Old Post Hotel."

They grinned and looked at one another questioningly, while
their eyes twinkled. Finally the oldest of them said: "There is no
longer an 'Old Post' here; it closed six years ago. If the gentleman
would like to stay near the railway station, our place is down there,
with all new furnishings—"

The stranger hesitated a moment, but when they all now
reached for his handbag, he gave it with a shrug of his shoulders to
the speaker, gave him orders to take care of his other baggage right
away, and walked down the street that led into the town.

It was a sultry and dusty day. He was tired, for he had traveled
half the night, and he was dusty from the long journey. He was
hungry and thirsty, and his tongue stuck to his gums.

Yet after he had taken a bath and changed clothes, he felt as
fresh and healthy as ever. He descended the stairs and wrote in the
hotel register: Franz Grach. When he found himself for a moment
in the porter's lodge, he suddenly recognized the house again.

He avoided the table d'hôte. The long, white tables with their
rows of people smacking their lips and chattering were repugnant
to him. He had a table set for him in a side room.

Once he let his knife and fork sink, so sharply and suddenly
did a scene from his youth stand before his eyes—something that
had happened here in this very room many years ago.

Then it had been, not the clean breakfast room of a modern
hotel, but the sad backroom of a second-class inn of bad reputa-

tion. The furniture had been changed, just as the proprietor and the guests, and yet all came to life again for the stranger:

They were all still young, hardly any of them had reached his twentieth year. All had sat on the same school benches, and now in many cases separated the greatest part of the year in schools abroad, they had come together again during the vacation for happy days and boisterous nights—a wild company overflowing with youthful spirit and liveliness, always inclined to every crazy prank, whose number for years remained limited to seven or eight men.

On that evening after a long hike they had all stormed in here, just as they shoved into all taverns where "there was still light." A fat waitress had come in with them from the front room, no one else was let in through the door, and one of those scenes arising from the cloud of beer and the smoke of tobacco was played out which appears to elders so repugnant, but to youth so charming.

He still remembered even the details, as it stood before his eyes again after so many years: how he himself, pressed into a curtainless window niche, had watched it, his legs drawn up and his glass on a chair beside him, recognizing already in his drunkenness what he was seeing, observing what was going on around him, and victor thus also over the hour that had drawn him along: how "Tubby" worked at the piano keys and his dreadful bass voice mixed in with the clear shouts and noise of the others; how the whole group suddenly was dancing around the stout woman and "Tiny"—a lean man with watery blue eyes, full of learning despite his youth, and full of shyness because of it—and the wedding of the unequal pair was proclaimed.

Glasses clinked; voices shouted through one another; heavy feet stamped the floor; smoke piled up against the ceiling; one man, in a dim memory of "Nana," emptied his beer into the piano; another ripped the red-striped covers from the tables and wrapped in them whatever came to hand, while the remaining—with the tough stubbornness of the half-drunk—did not stop, but insisted on carrying out their wild idea—and already the boundary had been crossed, where what could be forgiven stopped, to give way to senselessness, when with a great leap he had sprung from his window niche into the middle of the shouting group and cried out to them:

"Have you all gone mad!"

And he shoved the waitress out through the door, oblivious of the shouted protests, put his hat on, and the whole company stumbled after him to another bar, to another foolishness, filling the quiet street with new songs and noise, so that peaceful citizens were aroused from their sleep and woke up their spouses with the question whether something was on fire.

No, this time it was only the children of their own love.

4

Should he look them up, his comrades of those days? The desire almost came over him as figure after figure now popped up before him.

What had become of them? How had they turned out? Where had they landed?

For most of them it was not difficult to guess.

For the majority it was already determined in their youth that they would live a prescribed life: live life down, as he called it.

After a university degree—a door through which one must irreversibly pass if he wanted to enter this life—had forced them to fill their heads with an unbelievable pile of modern trash, they were allowed a few years to get rid of this rubbish.

They had to forget what they had learned. After those years of unbounded freedom at a university, however, the father inexorably stuck them into the bed made by the grandfather and well-warmed by himself, and—"they never again saw the world."

They chose one among the daughters of the land—one for each—and began to multiply in rearing and respect.

They joined the "Harmony" or the amateur society "Urania" and danced in winter in the "Casino," as long as they were still young.

When they grew older there began the only feeling of worth that a philistine is capable of: to be a citizen of the state, to swell out one's breast. They believed they took part in the destiny of the country when from time to time they cast their ballots into the urn and in the evenings over beer carried on endless debates about the most indifferent and unimportant questions of domestic and foreign politics—the playground of all men without spirit and strength—until the hour struck when fear of their wives drove them home and into the common bed.

They had become the *people of marriage.*

No, he wanted to see none of them again. They would just offer each other a sad disappointment and talk in such a changed way about people and things that they would no longer understand one another.

5

While the newcomer drank his coffee and blew the clouds of his cigar into the air, the fleeting remembrance had already disappeared, and other thoughts pertaining to the current day occupied him.

A letter had called him again to this town, which he had not seen for more than ten years. It had reached him after many detours, and after he had read it his first feeling had been to throw it into the corner.

He laughed at first; then he became angry.

But at the same time he thought of the many acts of kindness he had received many years ago from the mother of the woman—she was long since dead—who had written to him, and of her greatest kindness: that she had mostly left him undisturbed. He measured his time and money, saw that both sufficed, and had made a quick decision to travel here.

He had been left on his own very early, almost still a child, and was taken in by a distant relative, in whose house he lived many years, not dependent on her grace, but still depending on her kindness. She had an only daughter, who was her idol; he had no claim to the sentimental tenderness with which the spoiled, moody child of a short and very unhappy marriage was showered.

Almost from the moment he left this town his life had fundamentally changed, its circles and relationships become so different that he seldom had occasion to think back, all the more since the leisure of a comfortable, lazy stop and look around was never allotted him, and hardly a day had gone by that would have left him time to be absorbed in innocent dreams of the past and the present.

Only twice had he written the name of this town in the address of a letter: the first time when his relative died and he sent friendly words of condolence to her daughter, the second time when he sent brief congratulations on her own wedding.

Then this letter came, unexpected and unwanted.

It lay before him, and he read it yet again carefully, word for word.

From the pale-pink paper arose a strong scent of a peculiar perfume. The writing, which covered its four sides, was slanting, sensual, and womanish-weak.

He read it for the fourth time, and for the fourth time he sought behind the lifeless words for the living soul of her who had written them: he did not find it.

This was what she reported to him.

First, she was very unhappy; second, she was so unhappy that she could "endure" it no longer; third, her husband was the reason for her unhappiness; fourth, she had heard that he, her brother, the "friend of her youth," had written a book in which he had "liberally" expressed himself about marriage; fifth, he might "rescue" her; sixth: she was very unhappy; and seventh: she was so unhappy that she could "endure" it no longer.

That was all very silly.

He told himself rightly that unhappiness did not call for help that way.

But he also told himself, and he did so again and again, that women of her kind were not capable of finding an individual expression for their feelings—even their truest ones. As she was taught to speak, so she spoke: always in the same expressions and turns of phrase of her specific circle, the men this way and the women that way, and they were always as similar as was only possible.

And therefore were they also mostly so boring.

As they spoke, so also they wrote.

It was as if they were afraid to use a new word, and if there once came to them, not a new thought, no, only a view of their own about something or other, they carefully hid the criminal emotion behind their customary usage.

Could it not be so here?

He strained his eyes to be able to see behind the words. What lay there? A wife thrown to the ground and trod under foot? Or a lazy, dissatisfied women of the world who was simply bored?

Did he not find one word, one single unwieldy word, touching in its helplessness, deeply affecting in its simplicity?

He found none. And yet he answered the call of this flat and trite language.

There are people who we cannot believe are capable of being unhappy.

For him, she was one.

And yet here he was.

In the final analysis he had come for himself, in order to be quite sure he was not guilty of the accusations of his own heart.

6

The last clouds of smoke from his cigar vanished onto the ceiling and he looked at his watch.

It was after two. A long afternoon now lay before him. So he went to his room, threw himself onto the bed, and for over an hour slept a leaden and dreamless sleep.

He started up astonished, as he awoke. He had to remember

where he was, and it was with a feeling of displeasure that he walked down the stairs. It was as if he had to fulfill a disagreeable duty, and he wished to have behind him what now stood before him.

Then he walked out the door.

The heat had increased even more. At this hour of the afternoon life stood still.

A long street stretched out before him—the main street of the sister town, the longest and liveliest in the two towns and the center of the trade and traffic of both.

How often as a child had he strode it up and down again, and up again!

Little appeared to have changed in the external appearance of the town. A few empty spaces had been built up, where earlier circus and carousel owners had spread their transitory canvas over stony meadows, and only the side streets still offered an open view to the river. The newly erected houses showed the effort to keep step with the modern style. Cornices and balconies were hanging all around on them, and in their ground floors were shops and beer halls with high window panes and bright signs, whose letters in shining gold displaced the poor, faded, and old-fashioned inscriptions of the old establishments.

The swindle of business, which murders work, carried on its mischief the whole length of the street.

Poor workers! Sundays they walked here in their heavy shoes from far and wide, from the villages and boroughs, the men with their crude staffs and the women with gigantic, misshapen umbrellas. Still half-covered with the sweat and dust of the week, still entirely depressed under the burden of their slavery, they came here to buy what they needed, that is, to barter for three, four, five, and ten times its value what they themselves had created in another form: work. Self-conscious, unsure, pleading, and shy they entered into the "shops" and let themselves be taken in by glib-talking Jews—and Christians who were worse than the Jews—so that they were quickly fleeced.

The open shops had increased in a shocking degree in these few years. But the cheerless, dull impression of this street had remained, and from dawn till dusk it resembled in its unattractive, dusty grayness an aging, uncombed, and unwashed woman.

Grach let his glance wander about. Everything seemed to him curiously changed: foreign and yet familiar. But everything had become smaller, shrunk together, and like old people, sunk into itself.

The child sees the world larger, the man sees it smaller.

The clerks loitered in front of the shops, the servant girls stood at the fountain and shouted at one another. Why did they shout so loud? Were they arguing? No, it was only a "good-natured conversation." But this dialect was so broad, it was suitable only for a loud speech and difficult to understand for the stranger. Grach made an effort to catch the words and sentences of the passersby and understood most of what they said. Had he himself spoken like that once?

And the way the people greeted one another! They looked over the street with anxious care, bending their arms out at a sharp angle, and then drew or tore off their hats, either straight up into the air or down almost to the ground. "Your servant," they said doing it, "your servant"—and a long title followed.

The undisguised curiosity with which the people looked at and after him began to anger Grach. Their glances became irksome to him and he imagined that they must recognized him. He had forgotten that no stranger escaped these glances.

He walked faster. This side street must lead over the bridge to the other side of the river. He took it.

A young lady came toward him, her eyes modestly sunk to the ground, her parasol the length of a small cavalry lance pressed against her breast. She tripped along, laced up and decorated with ribbons and padding. Against his will he had to laugh, at first silently, then heartily and openly.

Just so, just like this had everything been at that time already: this anxious insecurity in relationships, this cowardly regard for privileges carefully wrapped thousands and thousands of times in padding, this narrow-breasted stiffness, this cardboard dignity—how he knew all that, how he recognized it all again!

And he laughed about all this, he had learned to laugh.

And again he laughed as he walked over the bridge, the old bridge, and saw that all the panes in the gas lanterns were whole and undamaged.

What, were they no longer fighting their battles of honor? Had a truce been declared between the exhausted sisters? Or—was there reconciliation—peace—but no, it was just madness to think about it!

A comical town! A comical, small town! Grach muttered to himself.

7

The "castle" reared itself before him on high terraces, a massive, old structure with many additions from more recent times. Ancient ivy hung down from its walls, from one garden into the next, until it almost touched the roofs of the houses at its foot.

The castle was no longer well defined. Its separate floors with their many wings and innumerable rooms were rented to several families, to the richest of the "natives" and the "locals" who possessed no houses of their own.

The stranger, who was no stranger here, slowly climbed the steep path up that went by the old, gloomy church—it stood in curious underground entrances, long since shut up, connected to the castle—up to the wide, deathly quiet square that, so to speak, extended the wings of the castle to the edges of the height. Grass that a burning sun had singed yellow grew here between the coarse and irregular paving stones; the youth of the town never played here, on this wide square that seemed built for romping around. Only rarely did one of the white curtains behind the high windows move and a hooded head peer through between them, only to disappear immediately again, for the empty solitude of this wide space was seldom broken by a figure that made its way over to the other side. Most people walked along the long front of the building to then suddenly disappear into one of the doors. Often during the day it happened during one of the afternoon hours that wagons—modern, elegant carriages with exquisite horses—stopped at the doors.

Grach had to smile again as he walked over this broad, dead square on which the sun carried on its shadow play undisturbed, which he had never entered as a child and which he would never have believed that he would ever enter.

But here—according to her address—she must be living now.

He walked slowly. And yet he had become curious to see her again. It had been such a long time since he had had any glimpse into the home life of the German bourgeoisie. He was a stranger— and everything had become foreign to him that came from there.

8

He rang the bell at the door he believed to be the correct one.

The sound of the bell echoed shrilly. Then came shuffling steps and a servant in livery, but with a blue apron, opened the door. It was not the visiting hour. But that was for the questioner now of course quite indifferent.

"Is Frau Boehmer at home?"

"Whom shall I announce?"

"Is Frau Boehmer at home?" he repeated once again.

"Yes—but—I don't know—Madam—"

"Tell her a gentleman wishes to speak with her."

"Madam is in the garden. I will announce to her—"

The servant had completely lost his composure and dignity through the energetic tone of the visitor.

"Then I will look for Frau Boehmer myself in the garden. Where is the garden?"

.ENN]

The servant did not dare any further objection. He threw off his apron and walked ahead.

"Here, please."

They walked through high and cool halls, over large stone tiles with which the floor was laid, past broad and distinguished old stairs with low steps and whose banisters were painted with white, clean oil colors.

Then the terraces of the garden opened before them, which quietly lay there as if slumbering in the burning afternoon sun, opening a wide view into the valley from the east to the west, where the chimneys smoked and life hammered out its existence.

From the well-cultivated, luxuriant beds arose the scent of ripe blossoms. The gravel of the raked path was so fine, that it soundlessly accepted the steps of those walking over it.

"I've changed my mind," said the stranger suddenly, "you go ahead and announce to Frau Boehmer a gentleman wishes to speak with her."

The servant allowed himself a shrug of his shoulders, but he walked on.

Grach remained lingering before a tulip bed and thoughtfully looked down into the purple, wide-opened flowers.

9

The servant returned.

"Madam requests—" he growled.

From an arbor in the rear of the garden there shimmered a white dress.

There, leafing through a fashion magazine that she obviously threw aside with displeasure, lay a young women of uncommon beauty stretched out in a rocking chair.

She glanced toward the man approaching, but make no indication of rising.

Only when he stretched out his hand to her and smilingly

said, "I received your letter, Clara, and have come myself to answer it"—did she spring up with a cry of surprise in obvious embarrassment.

"No, how you have changed, Franz!" she cried a couple of times; but then, after she had sat down, and while she looked him over with that testing curiosity that is characteristic only of a woman, there followed a flood of questions, for which no answers were awaited, since they were posed without any thought being given to them and without the least feeling of her heart in them.

At the first word that she spoke, he noted that this woman had not advanced one step intellectually, and—just as before—he listened good-naturedly and patiently a long time to her curiosity. He hardly answered anything and contented himself with a yes or no here and there, or at most a brief word to break his silence.

Thus it happened that after a half hour she had asked about everything, but had learned nothing from him. She used to complain afterwards that she told everyone everything, but no one related anything to her.

Then it occurred to her that she did not yet know where he was staying.

"You will stay with us, Franz? Certainly, won't you?"

Up to then she had avoided looking at him completely, but now their eyes met. She lightly blushed, when she received his answer.

"Under these circumstances?" he said, seriously and questioningly at the same time.

As she now sank back into her rocking chair, at first holding her hands out before her defensively, then striking them together in front of her face in pretended pain, he would have bet a hundred to one that she only in this moment exactly remembered what she had written him.

She did not return to her question. Her thoughts were already occupied by something else.

"Oh, let's not yet talk about my unhappiness—you are staying here longer, aren't you? A few days, weeks. You do have to see all your old friends and school comrades again, do you recall little Ehrling whom I sat beside in school and who came to us so often—you just must remember?—married a district court president and already has three children, and your fat friend Rempe, with all his dueling scars—but you don't know about that, you knew him only in school and they didn't yet fight there, yes, what did I want to say… yes, fat Rempe got the rich Krüger girl, her with the bangs and silk dresses. Oh yes, much has changed here—"

She was afraid to question him again, for she feared his look, his serious, almost hard voice with which he had just said, "Under these circumstances?"

And so she talked on: about tall Lenz, who "—oh yes, that's what I wanted to say—" had to duel over a woman and got a bullet in his abdomen; about the fate of the large Neuhaus family that had so many sons—one poisoned himself and another went to America because their father was so hard, but it is still a real affliction when sons don't obey their parents; and about—and about——and so on, a banal, unpleasant prattle that numbed and anguished the listener, and tortured his nerves.

In the end he no longer listened at all. While she thus sat before him in the luxuriant beauty of a mature woman, he recalled that it was he who had awakened the bud of this blossom with the first kiss.

10

Her beauty had kept all its promise. Already as a child she had been really striking, although the child had been neither graceful nor elegant, nor even of any particular physical attractiveness. But the blond hair could hardly be richer today than it had been then, and the moist gleam of these blue eyes, which today appeared to him only a sign of dreary boredom, had been for him and others at that time—for half the class was in love with her—a fantastic ideal and a true, feminine need for devotion.

Not for long.

But there was a short time in his youth—it was two years before their separation—when the constant living together with his half sister under the blind eyes of her mother had been very dangerous for him.

His senses awakened and longed for her. Her constant presence brought them into uproar and kept them awake.

He spent the whole summer in a tormented excitement, in a constant conflict that, for his energetic nature, was harder to bear than everything else.

She was indifferent to him. Everything she said left him cold. Her behavior toward her mother revolted him more than ever, even if he also never actually concerned himself about what went on between the two persons. Her flirting with his comrades, who made fun of the vain girl, he found laughable—and yet he was obsessed with her. He dreamed of her. He believed he held her in his arms. He snatched at her hand when they were alone, and he was quieter if she did not withdraw it from him. He was more often with her than before. Her mother was pleased that the previously cool relationship between sister and brother had improved.

An uncanny ardor went out from her that made him frantic. Days could go by without her being dangerous to him, but then an hour always came in which he had to jump from her side because he could no longer bear to see her without clasping her to himself.

He was in fear of himself; but in dread of her.

A late evening brought the solution. They were sitting together in the arbor by a dimly burning lamp. Her mother had retired, yawning and sighing. It was an evening full of wonderful softness in the air. The gleam of the stars was moist and deep.

She dared to remain. She was playing with fire in consuming curiosity.

He was reading in a book and held his head sunk down, so as not to have to look at her. He still had something to study and believed that she would go.

She did not go, however, but rather bent forward further, asking a question in her soft voice that she had inherited from her mother.

Their foreheads almost touched. Then he grasped her head in a sudden move and covered her face with uncounted kisses: he kissed her eyes, her cheeks, her mouth, her neck.

She resisted, but only weakly. Meanwhile—secretly overcoming a half serious, half joyful shock—as she asked herself with a woman's superiority whether she should allow him, she felt how he suddenly released her and shoved her away.

If often afterwards—thinking over this sudden change in his nature in that minute—she wanted to imagine that it had been a moral motive that tore him so suddenly from her, then she was completely mistaken.

A scent had gone out from her, as he hung on her lips and ran his hands through her hair, that had suddenly sobered him. The very same scent that from a distance had acted on him like a narcotic and drew him, now shoved him away when it worked on his senses in close proximity. It was a downright aversion that gripped him—inexplicable, but compelling.

Still more desirable than anything, she was now as indifferent to him as formerly.

He swiftly gathered his books together and rushed into the house with a quick "Good night!"

She looked after him and did not understand him.

Her enchantment was completely broken.

She noticed it immediately the next day.

She did her utmost to win him again. But nothing succeeded.

In the course of the next two years in which they continued to live together, they almost forgot the scene of that evening.

He too became indifferent for her.

She was thinking already of her future husband when she saw the men who pressed around her because of her beauty.

She chose one of the oldest among them and almost the richest.

She only thought of her half brother again when the tedium of her days caused her to seek new sensations and curiosity demanded new nourishment for her gossiping tongue.

11

The enchantment was broken.

She was only just a study for him, as she sat there before him: her small feet stretched out in the elegant shoes, tired from doing nothing, joking, flirting with the opulence of her surroundings, for she found that he had really not gone very far, to judge from his simple, almost old-fashioned clothing.

Yet she began to notice that he was also observing her, although he was not looking at her and obviously was not listening to what she said.

She became uneasy.

"But you are not listening to me at all, and I'm sitting here and telling you all the important news that has happened here in the past ten years—"

He looked up. And again she blushed under his gaze.

She again sought to distract him.

"And next Wednesday is 'Harmony Evening' in the casino: music and dancing. You will see everyone there that you know, our whole society—"

For the first time she spoke of her husband.

"To be sure, he has forbidden me to go there, he says that it is too much for me," she stamped her feet, "but now that you are here, he *must* allow me, he *must*, he *must!*"

She paused for a moment, somewhat exhausted and heated from the long speech, but already continued.

"Or better yet, we'll give a party, a big party in your honor—" she clapped her hands from pleasure and obviously waited for a similar outbreak of delight from him.

But he recognized now that it was high time to put an end to this comedy.

He drew his chair closer and bent forward somewhat, so that he was sitting directly before her.

She felt, now it's coming.

He began almost jokingly.

"I believe you are bored, Clara."

"Oh yes, I'm bored—" she sighed.

"Well, you should look for some activity—"

She did not answer. He smiled imperceptibly and continued: "Or some diversion—"

Then she looked up and directed her swimming eyes at him.

"Diversion—but how? What is there here for a diversion?"

"Travel."

"Travel—I can't do that. He just never has time."

"Who?"

"Well, he, my husband."

"I wasn't thinking of him. I meant, of course, you should travel alone."

"Alone?!" she repeated with an expression of astonishment, of shock. "How can a married woman travel alone, without her husband?"

"Just why can't a married woman travel alone, without her husband?" Involuntarily he used the same words as she. But it was done without any mocking intention.

He waited for her answer. She evaded him.

"Yes, I know that you have such odd views about marriage. How is your book about it called? A girlfriend—the wife of Redlich, you don't know her, they have only been here three years, her husband is a captain—yes, she told me. She also wanted to lend me the book, she definitely promised it to me, but she has still not brought it to me, for she first has to ask Professor Hastrich from the Gymnasium. It belongs to him."

It took an effort for Grach not to burst out laughing.

That one could also buy a book was obviously not known to this woman, and she, who was accustomed to sleep on damask and eat off silver dishes, did not hesitate to let the dirtiest books from the lending library slip through her white hands. On the table before him were lying several examples of this kind.

The sun was burning through the leaves of the arbor. Its heat had reached its highest point. He was thirsty. He asked for some wine and water. While the servant brought it, they kept silent. When she saw that he did not respond, she said: "Could you not tell me what you have written in your book about marriage, only very briefly—I so seldom happen to read a book—"

He bent toward her again.

"I believe there are as many various inclinations and needs as there are people, and I wish every person to follow his own inclinations undisturbed, for the simple reason that I can be able to follow my own undisturbed.

"I do not presume to understand people. We understand altogether little of one another. But we impudently intervene daily and hourly into the lives of our fellow human beings, under the mendacious pretense of wanting to help them.

"I would like for each to be happy in his own fashion here on earth.

"That approximately is the basic thought of my book. You have not read it; therefore I had to outline it for you quickly.

"But what they probably told you about is the chapter that I titled 'The People of Marriage.' Without any classifying and schematizing I posed the question in it, whether it was not a larger part of the people in our time to which this designation rightly applies: the narrow-minded people in opposition to the broad-minded; the people who never come into conflict with their surroundings, since they consider every fate—all that comes to them from the hands of men—as laid upon them by God; the people of small contentment, who find their daily happiness in narrow spaces, always at one table, always sharing the same bed; the people who do not know what it means to give a promise for life, because they do not know what it means to live; the people of stagnation, not the people of action; numbers, but numbers that become mere counters, and whom I hate on that account!

KENNJ

"The people of the common herd!—The people of marriage!"

He had spoken almost slowly, calmly, and without any visible passion.

But while he was speaking, he had forgotten to whom he was speaking.

When he stopped and noticed it, he was annoyed. He had been used to speaking as he truly thought for so long a time, that he had forgotten to model his thoughts to the ear of his listener.

He need not have been annoyed. For he had spoken to deaf ears.

"Forgive me," he said—he believed he had spoken at length—"forgive me for speaking so long. I would not like to be misunderstood in what I must now say to you."

Again, without willing it, he forced her to blush. Until now he had hardly opened his mouth, she had chattered without ceasing—and he asked her for forgiveness.

She began to hate him.

She had hardly understood anything of what he had said. She had listened to him almost as little as he to her. Her thoughts were now occupied with how she could best get rid of him.

For her, there were no important and unimportant people. For her, there were only people who listened to her. The men especially! From them she was indeed used to nothing else than that they lay at her feet.

Therefore she was offended by this calmness and assurance.

"Oh, I am so unhappy!" she cried and covered her eyes with her hands. "I don't know what I should do."

It was her second means to be done with him. Her third and final means was tears. But she did not want to reach for it until all other means were exhausted.

"Well, Clara, if you don't know what you should do, then who would know?"

She looked at him with her clear eyes like a helpless child.

"But you did come here to help me."

He stood up. This woman understood nothing, she could and would understand nothing.

He had to force her to look the facts in the face, from which she was fleeing like a coward, tearful and without moral strength.

He remained standing before her.

"From your letter I had to assume that you had made the irrevocable decision to separate forever from your husband, since you had recognized that continuing to live with him is impossible. I came to help you in carrying out this decision, but not to influence you in your decision. And also not, as you earlier sought to make yourself believe, in order to see again this town, which for me is entirely uninteresting, and old acquaintances, of whom I know nothing more and who want to know nothing more of me, or to go to your balls and into your society, for I frequent bourgeois circles not at all. My time is carefully apportioned."

He was walking around in haste. She was afraid of him.

"But you called me with the cry for help. Does one let a sinking person go under before his eyes when he hears a desperate voice? And if"—he interrupted himself with an involuntary smile—"I did not see you struggling on the open sea, I did see you wrestling with the dismal current of this—backwater."

He was warming up.

"Your deceased mother was very good to me. She offered me, an orphan, a roof and a table for many years. And then we two spent our youth beside one another, if not with one another. That is not so easily forgotten. That's why I have come, only for that reason."

He had torn a rose from a bouquet and during his speech had scattered its petals about.

"How he treats flowers!" she thought. She had yet only one wish: no longer to hear this mercilessly clear and cutting voice. But this voice continued.

"I came here in the firm belief of finding you ready to take the decisive step. I find you completely vacillating, without any decision—so tell me, just why did you call for me?"

She saw herself driven to the final point and relinquished it so as to rescue herself by going on the attack.

"You talk so much," she complained, "of the sorry state of affairs in marriage. Won't you tell me then, just how you imagine marriage? If you intend to do away with something, then you must be able to set something else in its place."

She had once heard this last sentence somewhere and it seemed to her good and suitable to apply to him. No woman is entirely without cunning. She too was not.

Grach immediately answered.

"I know but one relationship that I can call worthy to exist between one person and another, thus between man and woman: that resting on mutual independence; for it is at the same time the only one that makes mutual respect possible. The master despises the servant, and the servant hates the master."

She looked straight ahead with eyes lacking in understanding.

"And in marriage?" she asked uncertainly.

"The husband secretly pities the wife, while the wife secretly laughs at him."

She furtively looked at him from the side.

How does he know that?—was her first thought.

"But there really are so many happy marriages—"

"How many do you know?"

"No—but—"

"Well, I deny it. There are infinitely few. What is called happiness is contentment. And what appears contentment is only habit—the habit of weak powerlessness that shrinks back from breaking its chains and in cowardly yielding gives way step by step. Bit by bit it sacrifices its own dignity, its own liberty, and—what is the saddest of all—its own happiness, so as to become what a foolish public calls a good husband, a devoted wife."

"But then how do you imagine—" she began to repeat.

"'The relation between man and woman in freedom?' I hardly understand such a question. Rational people come together if they love and separate if they no longer love. It may be that they remain together until the end of their lives in love and unity. Often that is not the case."

She too now stood up.

"But for God's sake, that is in the highest degree immoral, what you are saying!" she cried. "It is just indecent!"

He only laughed, loudly and heedlessly.

He had trusted her with enough cleverness to ask what was to become of the children of the free relationship. But he deceived himself this time too. Like all blockheads, she called on morality for help, where her understanding no long sufficed.

He calmly said to her:

"Yes, about decency and honesty my views are widely separated from those of your class, which you share, as I see. I know that there are still many, many people who hold a union to be decent only if they have mutually allowed the same things: registry—church and parson—honeymoon; call it decent when two people remain together who cannot stand the sight of one another anymore and have recognized that not the least feeling holds them together, but only just the word given. But I also know that there are people who call base every embrace that does not follow from mutual love, and I too belong to those people. I would like to say one thing to you and all who defend marriage and who complain so loudly and emphatically about our views of free love, one thing I would like to say to you all, you people of marriage: Do what you wish, but show us through your own happy marriages that we are in the wrong, that you are in the right with your sanctification of marriage! Then we will perhaps believe you, not before!"

He reached for his hat and walking stick.

"Adieu, Clara," he said and gave her his hand, "goodbye! I've seen that you are not unhappy. You are of course discontented—you are certainly not free. But who can help you in this if you don't do it yourself?"

She was completely confused. She still wanted to say something back to him, she had the burning wish to humble him yet, but she found no word more against his cold superiority.

Not even her final means seemed practical for her to use now.

Oh, if she had known this ahead of time, she would never have written to him!

And she fought with her tears of rage and anger, as she had to give him her hand against her will. He, however, seized it and shook it in a friendly way. Then he left along the gravel walk with his quick strides, through the high and cool hallway past the white stairs and over the wide square, which was as deserted as several hours earlier.

As he reached its midpoint an older gentleman was approaching from the other side. He was walking already bent over.

Grach saw him enter the door that he had just left. Was that her husband?

If his gaze could have penetrated through the walls, he would have seen the following picture: Frau Clara Boehmer was hanging onto the neck of this older gentleman, kissing him stormily, and begging him for permission to be allowed to visit the ball at the "Casino" on the next Wednesday (in an entirely new dress), while inwardly she had decided to tell him nothing at first of the visitor that she so quickly and in such a relatively good way had gotten rid of.

12

Grach was walking without really knowing where. While he was still sunk in the thoughts that had come to him in this hour and which he now thought further on to their end, while he was thus looking down toward the ground in thought, he was walking quite instinctively the path between the gardens and their walls that led up to the summit of the mountain, where he so many times as a child and as a boy had gone in play, running, learning, talking with his comrades—and also alone, sad or cheerful.

He did not see where he was going. Only into the open, out, away from the foolishness of this narrow place, which had just now kept him bound up for hours!

He felt battered.

For years nothing had wearied him so much as the conversation this afternoon, no conference, no discussion, no debate.

It was as if he had had to drink sugared water in great quantities, one glass after another. It seemed to him that he had groped about in a sultry and unstable fog, as though he held something soft and runny between his fingers, which was shapeless and took no form, however he tried to mold it.

It had been the morality of the bourgeoisie that he had just struggled against, that sated, complacent, contemptible morality that was based on no thought, that daintily licked at every truth, and that drew down everything and everyone into the dust of its mediocrity. He hated them, these people, he felt for the very first time how much he had always hated them: their views, their customs, their habits, their hypocritical crying, and their superficial, humorless laughter.

What did this woman really want?

Did she not have all that any one could desire in external fortune?

She was beautiful. She was still young. She was rich. But she had a husband who at times probably allowed himself to have his own opinion—a husband who did not satisfy her in the way her nature demanded. Well, why did she not leave him, if she could "stand" him no longer?

Nothing held her back except the childish views of her class about honor and decency.

The world lay before her. Why did she not go into it, get to know what for a searching person must appear so interesting, so mysterious, and so infinitely attractive?

Why did she not enjoy the beauty of this world, of which she knew nothing?

She was unable to be alone. Too shallow to be sufficient for herself even for an hour, she could not endure an hour without the society whose life was her nourishment. Powerless to create new connections through her own personality, out there in the wide

KENN]

world she would die of boredom, consumed by longing for the petty bustle of her earlier days.

Therefore she had to remain where she was, on the place where her own free will had set her, from which she did not possess the strength to leave.

She must continue to bear her "unhappiness."

He did not believe in this unhappiness. In truth he had never believed that this woman could ever be unhappy.

Besides, she would gradually conquer her husband. A genuine woman, which she was, would wear him down: slowly, little by little, with all tenacity she would rob him of his strength lock by lock until he lacked any willpower against her.

The husband was more to be pitied than she.

For him, however, she was finished business. It had been stupid for him to have come here. He did not belong to the people who are ashamed to look their stupidities in the face. But he did believe he could now say that he would not so soon commit a new one.

He would most prefer to depart that very evening. Yet he did not know when the trains left. And besides—he was here now. The heat of the day slowly began to slacken. He wanted to spend a few hours yet on this peak, with the view of the town at his feet. He would find a green and cool little place somewhere.

And with a characteristic jerk of his shoulders, he shook the experiences of this afternoon from him: from his forehead and from his breast.

Now he was done with them forever.

13

"A comical, small town!" he had already said to himself three hours ago.

But viewed from this height the town appeared neither small nor comical. He thought it must be ghastly to live and die in it.

Certainly—one no longer knew what his neighbor cooked and

ate. But they still always concerned themselves about what he did or left undone, down to the smallest details.

Therefore no one dared to move, and with every action that he made he looked first at the others to see if they had ever done or would ever do it.

There were men of genius in this town, but their genius was completely one-sided. It was directed at only one thing: to stash away the largest amount of money possible. A worse use could hardly be made of it than was the case here. It often simply lay there and then increased—as a result of the privileges that protected it—of itself. It drew all the strength and all the energy of this whole land to itself. It was a cold, gruesome, senseless monster, insatiable and greedy.

It gave nothing, even to those who possessed it. For they had no spirit. They had not a trace of spirit. Every year they made a four-week trip and sent their sons for a few years into the freedom of life.

In addition, every few weeks they gave a big feast for their whole family, at which things were pretty lively. They spoke the local dialect and enlarged the family history.

But that was all. They did not have the least understanding of pleasures of the finer sort. They had no theater, no concert hall, and they never bought a book. Art was without a home here as much as science.

It had still been like that ten years ago.

Whether it was still so today, Grach did not know. It was also indifferent to him. In the newspaper of the one town—that of one was conservative, the other liberal, and naturally they were constantly in each other's hair—not one word had been changed in comparison with earlier. He had glanced through it during his meal.

No, it was not a comical town, at least not for him who was forced to live in it.

It was also not really a small town, for it filled, as he now saw, the whole width of this valley. It had grown larger. They had—sadly enough—built two new churches to add to the three old ones.

This valley was not without its charm. The lazy river cut through luxuriant meadows and the hills were thickly covered with fir and deciduous trees. From one of these dark knolls the narrow turrets of a modern castle towered into the sun-hot sky. There dwelt the king of the region. He knew that's what he was: he talked down to his workers (using the familiar pronoun "Ihr") and cared for them like "a father for his children." Things went well for him doing it; less so for his "children." Never mind!

Again and again Grach's eyes wandered right and left to where, at the limit of his gaze, the clouds of smoke billowed up to curious, strange, shapeless figures.

They seemed to be ideas struggling for a form. And in spirit he saw the day when these ideas, not in a clear afternoon in the hot sun, no, in the cool evening, at the beginning of night, embodied in sooty, strong figures drawn from both sides of this valley came and shook up this quite decrepit commonness, this whole nest of officials, titles, and ranks, this whole uniformity of opinion, into such confusion that the peaceful sleepers of these good towns would no longer know the next morning on which side of the river they really were.

Then the bitter struggle for supremacy would perhaps finally be at an end.

But then it would also be too late.

- -

A comical small town!

No, it was neither a comical nor a small town.

In spite of the heat Grach shivered.

The sun pained him, and his ungrateful thoughts likewise pained him.

Did he not have grounds to be thankful?

Thankful that he no longer needed to live here?

He turned away and climbed farther up the path. A tin sign struck his eyes: "Garden Tavern." That was what he was looking for, trees and shade and quiet.

He climbed up a stairway and walked through the entrance.

Then he suddenly hesitated.

A woman was walking in front of him.

14

He recognized her immediately.

He had met only one woman in his life who had this firm, proud walk, this erect and yet graceful bearing: Dora Syk. She must have heard his steps, for she turned around.

They simultaneously held out their hands to one another and grasped them with a strong, friendly pressure.

The pleasure in seeing one another again was on both sides equally great and sincere. But equal too in both of them was a certain embarrassment: they were on foreign ground here and at first did not rightly know how each was to make clear to the other why he was here.

There where her true home was, in the great, wide world, in the bustle of the gigantic city, in its unlimited circumstances, whose physiognomy varied with the changing day, in the great intellectual movement—there they had first met, had seen and spoken with one another, and were quickly torn apart again. They had not forgotten one another, but also had hardly thought of one another any longer, perhaps only for the reason that they no longer had time for it.

She often heard his name—he was mentioned many times; her name too had long been known to him before he saw her, for it had been well known for a long time. It had happened when she was twenty-one years old and her first work caused a sensation. About six years ago.

"Franz Grach—"

"Dora Syk—"

To see one another again *here* was for both of them a quite extraordinary surprise, and while they searched for words to ex-

.ENN]

press this, they both suddenly began to laugh and gave one another their hand, as if to make certain that they really were here.

"Fräulein Dora Syk!" he cried. "So this is why one heard nothing more of you—"

"It is very odd that we meet here," she said as she drew back her hand.

"Not so very much in my case: I am here in the town of my youth. That is to say, I was reared here."

"So. And now I am rearing here."

He started back.

"That is horrible. Whom are you rearing then?"

She laughed heartily. "Children," she said, "girls twelve and thirteen years old."

"In the upper schools for girls?"

"Yes, the same," she replied, and a laugh lingered around her mouth. "I admire the faithfulness of your memory. How long has it been since you were here?"

"Almost a decade. Listen: The Lord bless your going out—"

"And your coming in—right, just as it's written over the door."

"Just don't laugh, Fräulein Syk! I know what it means to be a teacher in that school—it is unworthy of you."

"No," she quickly said and became serious, "it is not unworthy to earn one's bread. But one thing is certain: it is crippling, for it is useless, totally useless. Because I am hindered from saying what I would like to say, even if not forced to say what I will not say. Unworthy? No, the silence of the powerless is never unworthy."

He saw her in the midst of this group, which he knew—the persons could have changed, the tendencies never: the director a Pietist, the male teachers become half women in their false position among pure petticoats, the female teachers old maids, the ones embittered, the other emancipated in the bad sense of the term—and he was not listening to what she had replied.

"How can you live here?" he cried almost vehemently. 'How can you take your place among these mummies—"

"Very well. They hate me so much that we almost never speak—"

"What indeed should you talk about!" he cried. "And don't try to fool me that it is different with this charming youth, I know them, this immature company. They are worse than the boys: they flirt already, with dolls still in their arms, curious, sweet-toothed, and already with that dreadful talkativeness of their elders, that empty talkativeness that knows nothing to say and always babbles, babbles—oh I have just now heard it for three long hours!"

She walked calmly on, but she no longer answered him. Her example, he thought, this splendid example of strength and health, of lack of prejudice and of beauty, of the taste and health of harmony, her example—should this at least not have a silent effect? And he asked her about it.

With some impatience she rejected his further questions. Not even her example, she said. The ground was not prepared.

He suddenly noticed that she was suffering and he became quiet.

15

During their short conversation they had entered the garden. It stretched out over the whole top of the hill. Its trees were splendid. They formed thick and protective roofs over the tables and chairs that were placed all about the climbing terraces.

A large hall stood at the highest point of the hill. Rough and made of hewn wood, its purpose was to offer refuge to large groups in bad weather. For, on Sundays and holidays hundreds and hundreds of people enlivened the quiet of this almost lonely summit; on weekdays hardly any guest came here. The rich nature could heal undisturbed the damage done by trampling feet that paid no attention to the paths, by rough hands that wantonly rummaged about and beat down this green splendor.

No large city possessed a garden larger and more beautiful in its raw and uncultivated wilderness.

Grach stretched out his arms from pleasure.

"This is splendid!" he cried.

She smiled.

"Yes, it is splendid!" she also said. "Hardly a day goes by that I don't spent the final hours of the afternoon here. No one disturbs me here. I can sit where I wish, I can walk, I can read, I can do what I want. It is as if all this whole summit is mine."

She slowly led him up past the restaurant where the owner of the garden lived with his family.

"We could sit down anywhere, Grach," she said. "Do you wish to look at the town? Or shall we remain here on this terrace where it is coolest?"

"Here," he requested, "let's stay here. It is solitary here, cool and beautiful."

So they sat down opposite one another at one of the tables. A girl came with a bottle and a glass. When she saw the usually solitary guest in the company of a second person a look of speechless astonishment appeared on her fresh, young face.

"No beer today, Katie," said Dora Syk, "I have a visitor today. A bottle of Rhine wine and two glasses."

The girl only hesitantly left.

"She is completely perplexed, the little thing. That has never happened to her in three summers. And, to admit it to you, I too am somewhat astonished. So, did nostalgia drive you back here? You wanted to wander once again on the fields of your childhood?"

"Oh that," he cried almost gruffly, "I have committed a stupidity, a great stupidity."

He briefly related to her what he had just experienced.

16

The wine sparkled in the glasses before them. They clinked them together.

"But I am reconciled to my stupidity," he cried in honest joy, while he looked at her.

She was worth looking at.

Firmly leaning back in her chair, with her feet planted on the floor and her hands folded in her lap, she sat in the motionless rest of people who work much and this rest, which they need, is also truly enjoyed when they get it.

She had taken off her hat, and Grach admired the simple art with which she wore her hair tied back into a Greek knot.

All the lines on this beautiful figure were grand, bold, and free; the folds of her dress fell down long and naturally, decorated by no artificial means.

Her hands, on which she wore no rings, were large and white, and likewise were her teeth, not "pearl" teeth, but teeth of perfect uniformity.

The symmetry of calm, great beauty was embodied in her. And just as it was impossible to imagine it could be disturbed by anything—by an awkward, clumsy movement, by the wildness of an upsetting pain, by the madness of an unbridled passion, the ugliness of a humiliation, or a violent arrogance—was it just as impossible to believe that age could bend this tall figure, that affliction could crack this simple dignity, that disease could break this embodied health.

There are profiles that appear to be scrawled, bungling amateur efforts, distorted caricatures in their width or length, clapped down by an unpracticed hand, and then smudged by crinkling the paper; and there are profiles that appear quickly sketched by an artist's hand in deceptively beautiful lines full of softness, grace, and charm, or drawn in one great, wonderful stroke in a rare hour.

To the latter belonged the profile of Dora Syk. An onset, a daring line, swift, energetic, masterly—blameless: this was the profile that Grach, in awakening passion, was again and again secretly copying with his eyes as he observed her.

Never before was the infectious harmony of her nature so striking as now. The busy working day had clouded his vision at that time. Now she was sitting before him, looking straight ahead while he spoke.

And more than anything else the expression of incipient weariness spreading over this beautiful countenance conquered him. Not a trace of ugly bitterness, only a quite gradual loss of energy.

A still almost imperceptible loss of energy.

But he saw it.

This lovely mouth was beginning to close in the harshness of pride—when might it once speak in the sounds that it was used to, the sounds of recognition, of freedom, and of the understanding of love? These deep eyes were already beginning to have shadows around them. Accustomed to looking into the farthest distance, to drinking in the variety, the fullness, the richness of an exterior life, they were beginning to grow dull among the hazy clouds of this miserable valley, the smoke of the fireplaces of this pitiable town, the stuffy air of an unventilated schoolroom.

He thought of other things as he related to her why he had come here. He was becoming uneasy.

17

"People of marriage!" she said as he ended. He looked up. She had therefore read his work. He did not know that for years there was no man whom she had admired for the quietness of his courage and his unshakable energy as she did him.

"People of marriage!" she repeated, without any depreciation or scorn, but rather with the calmness with which the researcher names the object of his study. But she still appeared unable to laugh over Grach's hasty tale. She was just too close to these people for that.

More and more Grach was convinced during the conversation of the next hours how very much she had known how to keep close to everything that this time in goodness, importance, and greatness was accomplishing. Almost nothing remained unknown to her: she had read every book, had observed and judged every event with her own sharp vision, had drawn every new perception into the circle of her understanding.

They spoke of everything as it came to them. On many things their views differed, but on everything each listened to the other's opinion, and on nothing did they keep their own silent to the other.

He sounded her out. But it was just as he thought: she stood here all alone, without friends, without connections, without the understanding of any other person. She read much. But she was perhaps the only one in the whole town who read anything other than newspapers and the novels of the lending libraries.

No one here even knew who she was. She had come here as a foreign phenomenon, and they avoided her in shy regard, while they heaped on her all the gossip of their misunderstanding and hatred because she was "different."

Who indeed should know her name here? Here the only famous names were those named on street signs and in the newspapers of the day.

She was suddenly forgotten, and the sound of her name had already almost died away. Was she submerged in this swamp so as to die here? The thought made Grach shudder.

And again he observed her with the look of love, while he listened to the sound of this deep, beautiful, alto voice. She spoke slowly of the serious matter that had formed itself in her mind, with emphasis on every word. However she lightly and unaffectedly answered his questions about her personal life, with a quite small tinge of mockery and melancholy in her voice.

It was pleasing, this voice. Involuntarily once he had to compare this simple and lovely speech with the chatter that had tortured him the whole afternoon. Even in all the incidental things there was no greater difference imaginable than between these two women.

What a wonderful woman! What a wonderful woman! he thought again and again and did not let his eyes go from her. More and more he began to understand her. Yet did he deceive himself? Was she happier here than she had been earlier? Or was this resignation only the result of an external force.

No, he could not deceive himself!

She was suffering.

A splendid and almost inexhaustible fullness of vital energy had up to now kept her erect. Nothing had yet affected her, not to mention disturbed her.

But the external haze was beginning to turn her pale. She required life, as a plant requires water.

For three years already she had perhaps enjoyed no drop of external happiness—that happiness which is a daily need: a satisfaction for body and spirit.

And yet she still stood erect! But already from today to tomorrow the first of those dark hairs could fade, for the first time a cry of wildness, of rage, and of complaint could open this mouth, and then it could close forever into silence, this so bright and clear spirit could grow gloomy in the night of this life. And then it was too late!

No, that should never be!

He laughed suddenly, loudly and bitterly.

She looked up astonished.

"Why are you laughing like that?"

Everything boiled up in him.

"Dora Syk," he cried, and laughed again as before, "Dora Syk—and teacher of the second class in the girls' school of Abdera! Now if that is not a joke one may laugh at, then I don't know what is!"

She turned pale at first, then a deep displeasure came over her forehead. For the first time a sound of sharpness was mixed into her voice.

"You misunderstand my position completely, Grach." She looked at him steadfastly. "I did not come here only to be able to live for a while in a secure, externally secure position, but rather I came here because I—I repeat—for a while, needed inner calm. That is sufficient excuse for my flight, if it needs any at all."

But Grach was so aroused that he took in only half of what she said.

"What," he cried impetuously, "a woman like you has altogether no excuse! The only possible one could be that you are truly living your life here. But among these mummies and money purses, in this stagnating heap, you *must* suffocate sooner or later!"

Her answer followed immediately. She was irritated.

"You are always going on the unfounded and quite false assumption that I want to bury myself here forever. I have no intention of doing that."

He had jumped up and was walking up and down.

She was again completely calm. Even during her last words not a trace of her calm attitude had changed.

"I know what I have to do and not do. And if you really must know, well yes, I think that I will soon return to the wide world of my home."

He was standing by her side and she heard his heavy breath.

"Do it now today!" he vehemently cried, and with a trembling voice that he himself could hardly hear he added, "And—do it with me!"

He looked down at her. She did not move. The soft twilight that lay under the hanging branches prevented him from seeing how the color of her face changed.

She did not answer. His hand was lying on the arm of her chair.

Then she looked at his chair. He understood her and slowly sat down.

She picked up the glass standing before her and emptied it in one draft.

His heart was beating.

Then she looked at him and smiled. She still did not answer him a word. But he knew now what he desired to know.

He took her limply hanging hand. He did not kiss it. But with both of his hands he enclosed it intimately, with a tender and at the same time firm pressure.

"Dora Syk," he said softly, and his voice still trembled, "the world is so poor in happiness in our day. Shall we not once seek to be happy together?"

She looked at him. In his eyes burned the hot, mute, desirous request.

He had conquered. He saw it in the expression of her eyes, the smile of her mouth, and he felt it in the warmth of her hand, which he did not release.

She drew it back. She did not want the mood to overpower her.

"Pour me another glass, Grach.—So.—And now let us talk together rationally, now, as people who are no longer young should talk about such things."

Her voice had only superficially its joking sound.

She made another pause before she began.

"Yes," she finally said. "You are right. I must get away from here. I want that myself. And you are also right in this: it should be soon, it should be immediately. My vacation begins only in eight days. But a substitute can be found for me. It is the first time that I'm calling on help of this kind, and since it will also be the last time, I have no cause to wait for a consent. It is enough if I give the director notice of my departure.

"My affairs I can also directly put in order. But before I leave with you, you must accept the following conditions:

"I love my freedom above all, as you do yours. We will therefore be completely, in every connection, independent of one another. We will mutually spare one another all foolish intrusions into time and mood. If we do not wish to go a path together with one another, then each will go his own. And—what is most important—we will separate in the first hour when we—begin to bore one another."

She bent forward and looked at him with her beautiful, wise eyes.

"If you want to accept these conditions, Grach, then give me your hand once more."

He reached for both her hands.

"Dora Syk," he cried in youthful enthusiasm, "heaven knows, but you are just the most splendid woman that I have ever met in my life!"

Then she burst out in a loud laugh, and the spell between

them was broken. Question after question and answer after answer followed now in a colorful whirl.

They wanted to go to Paris. That very evening. With the express train at ten thirty. They would be there tomorrow morning. He doubted if she could be ready by ten o'clock. Certainly, three hours were enough for her. She didn't have to take her leave from anyone here.

But they should not remain here any longer. What time was it then? Already seven! Yes, it was already dark under the trees. But she did want to say farewell to the little girl who had served her so often and with whom she had exchanged many a friendly word in the loneliness of the many hours she had spent here.

She went into the house and asked him to wait.

After ten minutes—ten minutes in which he had sat there, numb from his good fortune—she returned.

"Poor little thing, she almost cried. But I said to her that she should do as I am doing."

Then he could hold himself in no longer and took her in his arms. She let him kiss her.

Earnestness, dignity, poise—charm, goodness, harmony, the wit of refinement—an extraordinary intelligence, an immeasurable heart: How did he suddenly possess all this without earning it?—

The last glass stood before them. The yellow wine shimmered in the twilight.

"To our love!—Dora!" he cried.

"No, to the freedom of our love, which makes it so beautiful!" she slowly said before she drank.

18

They left the garden

They spoke no more. They walked on silently.

But as they heard a child's clear voice singing—shrill and off-key—they lightheartedly chimed in:

"May blooms only once in the year—

"Love—only once—in life!—"

They looked at each other and smiled.

"It is not true," they told themselves with this smile. "It blooms a hundred times and always anew, often together, often the one without the other."

And they told themselves, "But never has it bloomed as lovely as this time."

Again they heard the voice and the words.

"It is not true—"

"It is always not true—"

At the intersection they stopped. She said to him aloud, "I'm going to my house now. I'll get there quicker if I go alone. I'll be at the railway station at ten o'clock."

She did not give him her hand, she parted from him only with a nod of her forehead.

He understood her. He had taken off his hat and he bowed as she left. He understood her: it was not from cowardice that she did not want to be seen with him in the streets of the town. Only *now* she wanted to remain undisturbed by the impudent looks of the curious, whose words could no longer touch her from now on, whose actions could no longer hinder her from now on.

But he could not refrain from looking after her. Only one woman walked like that: she. Without the swaying of the hips, without the rocking of the shoulders, she walked, even in haste as now, always with the same calm, even, firm, fearless strides, that more than anything showed the healthiness of her being.

These strides led down the steep street; then the hanging branch of a tree hid her head and right afterwards a house hid her figure, which the lowering shadows of evening were already blurring.

As long as his eyes could still see her, he looked after her. Not sooner did he let go of what he was still able to feel with his senses.

Even through the dimness of the distance he still sought to follow her.

But he was already long alone.

19

He looked at the time: seven thirty.

Thus not three hours had passed since he had last stood on this square!

He almost began to doubt the reality of his good fortune.

Was it not all a dream?

How wonderful: He was standing again as a man in the places of his childhood. Only moments before he had seen them again, moments later he was to leave them behind again and—presumably—forever.

Short moments in a long life: not even the time of a day had gone by. When it was over, then the hands of *his* world would hold him again.

It was all wonderful.

There was perhaps only one person in this town of pettiness, of self-satisfaction, of narrowness, only one single genuine, self-owning, free human being with whom he would be able to live together—and he had found this person! A strange coincidence!

Found here—not in the fullness of time, which in the small space that they inhabit forces them to pass by one another sometime, no, through the strangest coincidence in the world, on the border of this space, in the freedom of nature, in the quietest hour that disturbs no one.

He had recognized that the main part of what people call luck, may be gained by experience and persistence: tranquility, clarity, security, and a certain independence.

The greatest coincidences of luck had passed him by and there was little that he had not had to achieve by his own strength. Therefore he felt all the more deeply how tremendously great the

coincidence of this luck was, which had met him here, shimmering and blinding from out of the dark space, close before him——

And an insane bliss came over him! The twilight was increasing and the coolness with it. The citizens were returning home
from the gardens with their families—for the evening meal, then
to the tavern. Lights were flaming up at his feet. The outlines of
the houses and streets were running together, and only the pointed
towers of the churches still rose up sharply. Most brightly shone
the lights across the way on the other hillside, where the railway
station was. Flickering lines ran from there out toward both sides
and were lost in the side valleys.

But at the end of the valley the mighty flames of the raw iron
furnaces blazed up into the darkness, gigantic cones of fire, there
where day and night a never-resting labor was engaged in a victo-
rious struggle with a merciful nature and in a fruitless battle with
merciless, inherited, all-powerful, moldy privileges.

A little cat with white fur slipped across the path. It turned
past a child that was sitting on a bench in front of one of the
scattered houses, and then ran with quick leaps to Grach.

He saw the child. He reached into his pocket, gave the child
all the money he had grasped, and lifted and kissed the startled
child on the mouth, just as if he had to quiet the expectation of his
happiness, which he could no longer bear.

Then he hurried with quick strides, as if on wings, down the
narrow path between the gardens and the mountain.

20

There it was again, the large, deathly still square, now wrapped in
the darkness of evening. There it was again, the old church, which
he now strode by and where as a child he had so often been forced
to enter and spend deadly hours of boredom in its pews. There it
was again, the old bridge of stone and the old river.

He stood for a long time bent over the railing. A feeling of reconciliation began to creep over him.

He no longer hated it, this town; he no longer hated them, these people.

What were they to him, that he should hate them? Nothing.

They might live and die as they wished, it was all the same to him. Didn't they themselves suffer most under the fact that they lived so thickly together, each in the neck of the other, and thus slowly tortured one another to death?

And why should he not allow them the harmless pleasure of self-satisfaction? The vanity of this inflated smallness was surely not worth more than a laugh.

She had lived and suffered here, three long years. He was ashamed at himself when he compared his own ill-humor over the one day today with her dignified, melancholy calm and her gentle, strong seriousness, which did not seek to change these people, but rather to let them go their way, but shoved them aside when they became a burden to her.

Poor town! he smiled to himself. And he was taking from it its most precious asset.

Two hours yet. Still two hours?

He crossed the bridge and turned into the main street. Then he entered a large, public restaurant and seated himself quietly in a corner.

He ordered something to eat. But when the meat stood before him, he suddenly lost his appetite from the warm odor, and he shoved it away again.

Internally—he felt it now distinctly—he was still highly excited.

He looked around. Near him was a large, round reserved table that began gradually to be occupied. More than one face seemed familiar to Grach, and suddenly it occurred to him: this was indeed—doubt was no longer possible—"The Rogues," the greatest men of the town, wise in counsel and careful in action, whom he saw there before him. Why they were named "The Rogues" he no longer knew—probably had never known earlier—but the name popped up in him again with all clarity.

And yet the times had changed: for earlier these authorities had met every evening in the "The Little Work Basket" and now—what a difference—here they were sitting in the jaws of "The Crocodile"!

Inwardly he was laughing secretly and heartily. Mirth won him over. Now he could eat, while he took in individual words that flitted over to him.

They were talking about municipal affairs. Naturally. Grach knew that talking about politics was prohibited here.

Suddenly he heard a voice that he knew. He looked over more sharply. Did he know that face? No, it was not possible.

This narrow-minded-looking man, who was drinking his beer in small, deliberate drafts and smoking his cigar in small, deliberate puffs, who just looked like he knew no greater happiness than to sit here and listen, this man with the heavy movements and the satisfied voice, with the obvious high regard of every one of these pedantic old men—that was by no means his old, jolly Fritz, always in the mood for every stupidity, whose roaring voice had so often shaken the streets in the latest of all late hours!

Grach called the waitress over and softly questioned her.

"Yep," she said "that is Herr Town Councilor Beuer."

Then he quickly finished off his beer, paid, and left the restaurant. He had a sudden fear that Beuer would recognize him too and speak to him. That would have been for both of them just too depressing.

21

He went to his hotel to pack his things and pay his bill. Then he climbed up to the railway station and bought two first-class tickets for Paris. He knew when he was allowed to be extravagant. Today. In the waiting room there was an old newspaper seller—he also recognized him again—and he bought from the old character a timetable and a newspaper.

Now he was walking up and down the platform with long, irregular strides.

He knew she would come, for she had said so. Sooner would the world go under than that she would not keep her word.

And yet restlessness tormented him, the restlessness of waiting.

The tenth hour had not yet come by a long way. The large hand of the white clock had hardly reached the number six. He knew that she would also not come sooner than she had said; and yet his restless glance turned again and again toward the black, yawning opening of the stairway, up which people climbed from time to time: officials, travelers, baggage carriers, a colorful mixture.

The summery evening lay sultry under this broad hall, which the rumble of the trains and the hundreds of cries sounded through and made shake. The trains rattled in and out. Only the track for the express train that was to halt here for three minutes remained free. The rails gleamed white from the wheels grinding on them.

Grach had forgotten everything that he had seen here today— except her.

Now he was still thinking about her and his happiness.

There was little he called his own. Every one of his boyhood friends in this town surely lived better than he, and among all these people there was probably none that would exchange places with him.

And yet he was a blissful man. For he was a free man.

No one could give him orders, and he had to obey no one. He could come and go as he pleased, the whole world was his.

Not to hate and not to mock, not to envy, no, they were to be pitied, those people down there in the town, who knew only one happiness and only one contentment: money, money, money to heap together in tiresome acquisition, to which all pleasure was lacking: the pleasure of true enjoyment!.

ENN]

And he turned away from them.

With every minute that the tenth hour drew nearer, he became calmer. His strides became slower.

When the hand of the clock had reached the awaited point, he leaned with crossed arms against a pillar and no longer took his gaze from the entrance stairway.

Many and various people were still climbing up in the next minutes before him and going past him. Perhaps a hundred. His eyes stopped on none of them.

But then he saw her: slowly and surely her tall, proud, beloved figure, now in a gray dust-cloak, arose from step to step.

Her gaze was lowered and she still did not notice him.

He went to meet her.

DISTRICT ATTORNEY SIERLIN

THE STORY OF A REVENGE

CHAPTER ONE:
DISTRICT ATTORNEY SIERLIN

1

On an evening in March District Attorney Sierlin of the Berlin District Court was coming home as usual when, near his house, a young man approached from behind him and—as it seemed to him—slowed his steps in passing. But since he neither looked at him nor glanced back, he believed he had deceived himself.

Two days later, and almost at the same hour and on the same spot, the same thing happened: again it seemed to him as if the steps that he heard behind him became slower on approach and passing. This time he fixed the person in question with his eyes and looked at him closely. But neither did he recognize in him the person of the day before yesterday, nor did he have reason to concern himself again about the stranger, for he disappeared in the overcast and rain-threatening evening. He had already forgotten the incident as he opened the door of his house, which was separated from the street by a small front garden.

He only remembered the meeting again when, on the next evening around an hour later, but again in the neighborhood of his house, it occurred a third time. Again the quiet suburban street was empty of people. The few houses on it—villas separated from one another—lay still as ever. So too the little park opposite them—the pride of the residents and the joy of their children who played there in summer.

Again on returning home District Attorney Sierlin heard the

steps behind him and their gradual slowing on coming closer. Again the young man—the same as yesterday and two days before that—was walking without looking at him or concerning himself in the least about him, but again—as he could not help noticing this time—closer to him than was necessary, given the width of the sidewalk. This time he threw an examining side glance at him and stopped, so as to look at him more closely, until he disappeared around the corner. It was a still young man, in his twenties, simply but thoroughly decently dressed, without a topcoat, with a soft felt hat. He kept his hands—as on the first two times—buried in the pockets of his jacket.

A bank clerk or some such, he thought looking after him, whose profession lets him out at the same time as me and who probably lives in the same locality. But this must really be a detour for him. And why does he always walk so close by me?

The young people of today have bad manners, he concluded on opening his house door. If I meet him again, I'll give way and step to one side, so as to make him aware of the impropriety of his conduct.

Since the young man remained away, however, on the following days, he had no opportunity to carry out his intention, and the fleeting and indifferent meetings completely disappeared from his consciousness.

2

They would have disappeared forever, if he had not seen about eight days later—and likewise on returning home—a figure sitting on one of the benches that had been placed at regular distances on the edge of the small wood on the other side of the street (and indeed on the one that was nearest to his house and stood nearly opposite it). He believed he recognized again the young man whom he had met several times here in the last week. It seldom happened that the benches were used already at this time of the year. It was still quite cool, and spring started especially badly this year. Strangers almost never came for walks in this out-of-the-way region, and those who lived here had grown accustomed to viewing these grounds as belonging to their houses and therefore, to a certain extent, as theirs alone, so that unknown persons who strayed here would stand out.

So what could move a person to sit down on one of the benches on such a cool and damp day as today was incomprehensible at first view and could only have a basis in a passing indisposition or a great fatigue. If there was an intention here, of what kind might it be? A housebreaker who was looking for an opportunity to spy out the region would surely begin otherwise and in a less crude way. This young man on the bench over there also did not at all look suspicious. Yet, that it was the same man that he remembered again, District Attorney Sierlin was no longer in doubt: it was the same brown suit, the same soft hat, and the same posture of his hands buried in his side pockets. Before he entered his house he stopped for a moment to throw yet a second glance over at him: to observe whether the one sitting there would, for his part, look across at him or stand up and walk away. But the young man, who was sitting there under the bare trees, separated from him only by the roadway and about half the distance to the next villa, seemed to him this time too not to have seen him and not to see him now. His face, as far as it could be discerned at this distance, was turned up and his gaze went away from the houses and up to the sky over them. It was the attitude of one deeply sunk in thought, of someone completely removed from his surroundings.

He was free today earlier than I was, District Attorney Sierlin said to himself as he mounted the steps, but he seems not to have a desire to go home, but rather would prefer to catch a nice cold. A crazy oddball! And, as usual, he announced his arrival by calling for his dinner.

Since it did not come immediately, while he was waiting in the dining room for his family he walked for a moment to the window and looked across. The young man was still sitting on the bench in the same unchanged attitude.

He also does not appear to be hungry. But I am!—District Attorney Sierlin thought.

He walked back into the room, since the soup had just been served.

He had already forgotten the repeated meeting as he was sitting at the table and having his wife and his children, two boys in ages nine and thirteen, relate the trivial, but for them so important news of the locality and the school.

When he went to the window again after the meal, this time without any intention, the bench opposite was empty. He did not notice it.

3

Not so on the next day when, a whole hour later than usual—for he had been delayed by a meeting—he turned into his street.

This day sitting in the open was even less inviting than the day before: it had rained, the benches were still wet, and drops were coming down from the branches of the trees.

But there he sat. The same attitude: gaze up, hands in his pockets. A crazy idiot!—muttered District Attorney Sierlin to himself when he saw him again sitting there thus—one should lock him up, the fool, so that he doesn't get tuberculosis. Although he told himself that this stranger and his conduct were nothing to him, he did not forego casting a glance over there after the meal to see if he was still sitting there. It was pure curiosity. How long could such a person in such weather hold out on a bench in the open air?

As if the man observed had only waited for this moment, he stood up, took a few strides, and then crossed over the roadway, coming directly toward his house door, but without looking up.

He looked just like someone who had decided to carry out a long-nourished decision.

District Attorney Sierlin, at the window, was not in doubt for a moment that this decision meant a visit to him. This was the reason for the first meetings, for this sitting and waiting on the bench yesterday and just now. At any moment the door bell would ring and Marie would come with the question, whether Herr District Attorney was available.

He did not know the man, and he would of course have him turned away. But he now had an explanation for his curious behavior. A petitioner, of course, who had finally got up his courage. But for official things—and it could only be a question of such—he was only available during working hours in his office, and even there only in certain, previously granted cases.

He stepped back from the window and waited.

He waited in vain.

It neither rang, nor did the maid appear.

Had he again lost his courage, or was he still standing hesitantly before the house door in the rain that was now beginning to come down again strongly?

He opened the window and looked out.

The street was empty; the unknown man had vanished.

He had surely seen the impropriety of his conduct and had given up wanting to speak to me in my house, he though, as he closed the window and wiped the raindrops from this forehead and beard. I'll hear from him officially.

4

But eight days passed without District Attorney Sierlin hearing or seeing anything of the unknown man, and when he now thought of him at all, it was at most at the moment when he entered his house and involuntarily cast a glance toward the bench. It was

ENN]

empty, however, and remained so, although now the loveliest days had come.

The man only occurred to him again when one evening he heard quick and firm steps behind him. Against his will he half turned and saw who it was. But instead of walking by close to him, today this young man seemed to want to avoid him—he walked as far from him as the sidewalk allowed, almost on the curb, and quickly went on by. He did not at all look as if he wanted anything from him or was struggling with a decision. He also did not seem lost in thought as when he was daydreaming on the bench. He walked just like someone who has no other wish than to go home as quickly as possible. Just as little did he seem to have caught a cold—so fresh and healthy was his appearance and so firm his walk. He had again not paid him the least attention, just as if he had not seen him. I must have been mistaken, District Attorney Sierlin told himself.

Curious and now striking, however, was the fact that this incident—the hasty passing at an almost deliberately chosen, rude distance—repeated itself the next two days. It was all the more striking since precisely on these two days he came home at entirely different hours—uncommonly late. It was already dark both times when—almost in front of his house door—he saw the young man hurry past him and disappear around the corner. Since he then again remained away and these last meetings had been quite momentary, he now also did not yet lay any more weight on them than some fleeting thoughts about the curious ways of chance, and he forgot them all over his work, which was piling up daily to unbearable proportions.

In the meantime April had arrived, this year too a variable and dampish month. The bad weather, however, did not hinder the unknown man from sitting on the bench every evening—and indeed for a whole week—staring ahead or looking up into the gray and cloud-laden sky. This too would have left District Attorney Sierlin indifferent, if he had not begun to be angry, at first indeed with himself. For one thing, his first glance on returning home was toward the bench; and then, almost against his will, he could not help walking quickly to the window after his meal, to see if that man was still sitting there, to find every time that the bench was empty. It was just as if the man sitting there shortly before had only awaited the moment of his homecoming in order to stand up and leave.

It was striking, and it struck him.

He was already thinking that the next time he would go to him and ask him if he were waiting for him or anybody else. But he let it pass each time. It was beneath his dignity. And it would have meant attaching an importance to an affair that had no importance.

He might sit there until he turned black or caught a cold, which would then force him by itself to give up his foolish and irrational behavior. The bench was there for everyone. Only he now grew angry every time he saw him. He grew angry even more when suddenly he did not see him again for a whole week. Did he catch a cold? Well, let him have it.

Then two weeks later, the third of this April, the quick walking past began again, and indeed once more on three days in a row. Damn it, what was that supposed to mean? He listened when he heard the hasty and firm steps behind him, stopped, let him go by, and did it on the third time in such a provocative way that any other man would have stopped likewise in order to look at him. But the passerby neither looked up, nor acted as if he had noticed him at all. He looked straight ahead and walked on even faster, if that were possible. He could not follow him—here in his own street? It would have been the first time in his life that District Attorney Sierlin had followed a strange man! He grew even angrier.

But he decided, not to let himself be angry, when he then saw him sitting on the bench again for a whole week—evening after evening. He resolved neither to look across nor to glance out the window. He had formed his judgment: The man was obviously

KENN]

not entirely responsible, but a harmless fool, whom one had to let have his way.

Therefore he concerned himself no further about him. He also did not speak about him to his wife. It would have seemed ridiculous to him; and she, in her unbecoming curiosity about strangers would surely have sought to attribute some kind of reason for the behavior of the stranger and on her side daily make him aware of him.

In the meantime he was now even reminded of him within his own four walls.

One day little Kurt said at the dinner table, "Daddy, there's such a funny man always sitting in our wood, he always looks like this." He made a goggle-eyed look.

Then he immediately shut up in fright, when he saw with what firmness he was reprimanded, as if he had said something impertinent. "Let him sit! What business is it of yours! And don't have anything to do with strange men, I've told you boys that already!"

At the astonished look of his wife (and before she could ask, just who are you talking about?), he didactically added: "Everyone has the right to sit there. It's public grounds. It does not, as you seem to believe, belong to you alone, but to the whole community in which we live."

He was angry again, but did not wish to show it and spoke of something else.

For that matter, the children had no more occasion to obey their father. The stranger stayed away and, as it appeared, forever.

Spring was now truly here, the trees were covered with green, and the little park was no longer unfrequented. The children playing and chasing in it had probably driven away the man seeking solitude and quiet.

So thought District Attorney Sierlin when he still occasionally thought about him (which hardly happened anymore).

5

District Attorney Egon Sierlin, now in his mid-forties, had had an unhappy youth among many, mostly younger brothers and sisters, now scattered around the world, and a late second marriage of his stern father had not make it sunnier.

Although only moderately gifted, he still made his way: through only half-enjoyed studies and laborious years as a junior and assistant magistrate, through all the examinations passed—more or less satisfactorily—until he had risen up to his present position as second district attorney in the district court of the capital.

As soon as it was possible he had married—after a brief acquaintance and without love (of which he was indeed hardly capable), and entirely in a conventional way. With the money that his insignificant, but good-natured wife had brought he had bought the villa in the suburb, and his salary now allowed him and his family a sufficient way of life, free of worry. In his marriage he was neither happy nor unhappy. With his opinions, the rearing of his children was not always quite as easy as he had thought it would be—also a symptom of this corrupt time, in which nothing was sacred any longer.

For it was his opinions that basically had led him so far: they were what, in spite of relatively little change, had led him at the university into a student corps to which he belonged today as one of the Old Boys. They let him endure and overlook many a humiliation during those years. They strengthened his backbone again and again, and in them alone he found the true satisfaction of his spirit. His opinions were inborn, firmly rooted, cherished in every situation of life—any doubt about their God-given nature would seem a crime to him. And no such doubt had also ever come to him.

He was tall and strong, with a healthy color in his face, in which the dueling scars of the once feared swords had left their sharp traces behind. His voice, so often heard in public, had a somewhat grating sound; his bearing was firm; and his behavior was never other than absolutely correct. He knew the laws of society as well as those of the state, whose attorney he was, and he scrupulously followed both, the written as well as the unwritten.

He was little liked in his circles. He did not enter others. Feared in his profession, he actually had hardly any friends. He was called, not incorrectly, a bloody climber, and he knew that he was called this. But that was easy for them to say—they were more careful in the choice of their parents than he had been.

That he was ambitious, ambitious beyond all measure, could not be doubted. He wanted to be. His ambition should carry him much higher still.

He believed he had every reason to be satisfied with himself; and if he was not always satisfied, then it was only because this ambition of his, in his view, did not lift him up quickly enough. His goal was a position in the Supreme Court of Justice in Leipzig. That his talents just did not suffice for that—his industry stood beyond all doubt—his inner voice did not always tell him with the necessary clarity.

It would probably otherwise have trickled at times a drop of bitterness into his otherwise so contented and—by many of his colleagues—envied life.

6

A couple of weeks after that brief conversation at the dinner table, which was long forgotten by all (the stranger that the talk had been about had let himself be seen no more, and the beautiful month of May had come to an end), there happened something that for the first time gave District Attorney Sierlin serious pause for thought.

He was standing outside the court in conversation with a few other gentlemen—waiting for his streetcar—when a young man walked by him so remarkably close that he almost grazed him. He had to look up and after him.

He broke off the sentence he had begun. He was in a good mood, for he had just pushed through the death penalty against a robbery murderer, whose defense attorneys wanted to see given a lifetime prison sentence. (Being a humane person, he was against such a "prolongation of the death penalty.") He interrupted himself, as was said, for he was looking after the person who had just then almost touched him: it was the same young men that he had so often seen weeks before in the neighborhood of his home. To be sure, he was wearing another, lighter, and now gray suit, but the attitude—the hands in the side pockets—and the soft hat were unmistakably the same.

The arrival of his tram spared him from giving an explanation to the other gentlemen, who, for that matter, were hardly listening to him (for they did not at all agree with him), and he could only just take a hasty farewell.

This renewed meeting with the young man—after weeks and in such an entirely different area—would have hardly made him think and would have been forgotten, like all the others, if he had not seen him sitting on the bench in front of his house about an hour later (the length of time of the tram ride and transfers).

It was such a surprise that he stopped as if thunderstruck. He did not trust his eyes. How did this man get here? Here *before* him?! He stood there and looked across. This time he would indeed hardly have controlled himself, but rather after a short reflection had gone over to him and asked for an explanation of this repeated and so altogether singular meeting. But hardly had he recovered from his first astonishment than he saw him stand up and walk away. The bench was suddenly empty again—the man who was just now sitting there walked down the street and disappeared around the corner. He walked as fast as if he were in fact pursued.

Only the new surprise hindered District Attorney Sierlin from immediately following.

He entered his house, was unusually quiet during dinner, and after the meal was ended, he went directly to his room, pleading pressing work after a fatiguing day. There, as he knew, no one was allowed to disturb him.

7

He lit a cigar and settled into his easy chair, which he always sat in when there were difficult cases to think over.

For the time being he was still inclined to believe in an illusion, so unbelievable the second meeting inside of an hour and on entirely different, widely separated places. For one thing, however, he had no illusions and could not have any; then too he knew that he was not mistaken. It had been the same attitude, the same face—which he now already knew well enough not to mistake it any longer—a smooth-shaven, narrow face with a curious, hard line around the mouth. It was the same, somewhat strong back of the head, with blond hair. He knew the face down to the color of the eyes. Only he had never seen their glance. He had still not met their gaze. It was as if they avoided him in their fixed, forward-looking stare on the bench, in looking beyond him in passing.

There was, therefore, no doubt about the identity of the person.

He forced his thoughts into their usual, cool reflection.

This was a case—doubtless. Cases were there to be clarified. He, to clarify them.

He quickly recapitulated:

First: A young man, completely unknown to him, was here some weeks ago in front of his house, had walked past him closer than was necessary, yet without looking at him, greeting him, or otherwise noticing him. That could—in accord with bad manners—have been a coincidence.

Second: This same man had then often sat on a bench opposite his house and once, directly after he had arrived home, had walked up to his house without, however, entering or otherwise making himself noticed. That could be explained, even if no longer by chance, then still by other grounds, which he had already at that time figured out—a decision to pay him a visit, a sudden failure of will at the last moment, guilt feelings and fear.

(In contradiction to this was the unconcerned attitude, which instead of attracting his glance to himself with a mute request, rather—and almost ostentatiously—showed that he did not see him and did not wish to be seen or addressed and questioned.)

Third: The very same young man had during the following weeks often sat on the same bench for hours and in the most unfavorable weather, day after day, always in the same dismissive attitude, and had always disappeared as soon as he arrived home. That was remarkable. It was at the least striking.

Fourth: Always the same man had then again several times at the same place and almost (but not always) at the same time walked past him, but then not slowly and near, but rather at an again striking distance and always so quickly that he would have had to run in order to overtake him. In his usual way he had ignored his challenging glances, his stopping and looking after him. That was striking, even very striking.

But all this together would still not have yielded sufficient and convincing grounds for the assumption that the man concerned was pursuing, with his curious activity, a determined intention and one that concerned him. It could be the behavior of a harmless fool, that of someone who felt guilty, someone suffering from an idée fixe.

He had already considered the assumption that it concerned precisely him, but again and again let it drop.

Until today. Until just now—two hours ago.

For, that there was a connection between the first meeting at the court and this second one, and that a quite determined intention was being pursued with it—on this there could now hardly be any further doubt. This now raised two questions:

How did he get here so quickly and *before him*?

What did this man want and what was he aiming at?

The first was easy to answer and in only one way: Since he himself had taken the first streetcar that came and in transferring had the not exactly frequent luck of immediately finding the one expected, which hat brought him to the neighborhood of his house; since in this second car besides himself only an old lady was riding (whom he had helped to climb in)—he would have seen him if he had been in the same car. There was no other, quicker connection except by auto (or airplane, but this latter did not yet belong to the daily and regular connections). Besides, today he had come home more quickly than usual, through quiet streets, and would have been able to notice if anyone had followed him.

Therefore, in order to have reached the bench before him, this young man must have taken a taxi—there was no other possibility.

The second question thus arose:

What could have moved this young man, who was indeed decently dressed, but altogether did not look as if he had money just to throw away, what in all the world could have moved him to go to such an expense, an expense that bitterly pained him, the well-off District Attorney Sierlin, every time that he had to reach into his pocket for it—eight to nine marks?

Just in order to see him, or better, to be seen by him? And then as quickly as possible go away again?

The question was not so easy to answer.

Naturally the explanation could only be found with regard to his official activity.

It was only one among the many cases that a district attorney met everywhere and which he therefore had to reckon with.

Threatening letters were the order of the day in his profession. He had long given them no more attention, and they did not end up in his wastebasket just because he added them to a collection that already counted in the hundreds, and which he was thinking about evaluating sometime later for an article on this side of the human character. Threats were very seldom, almost never carried out.

Even if all kinds of things happened: Twice already he had a narrow escape from the toss of an ink bottle (and its contents) at him during a trial; even oftener had the condemned criminal tried, before he was led away, to leap over the barrier at him (but which he was hindered from doing each time); he had been abused and insulted in the open street—he had the fellows or their enraged women arrested or, disdainfully smiling, he had walked on. Only once, likewise in the open street, had he been assaulted—a powerful blow had knocked the attacker back. Whether the shot that once nearly struck him—late in the evening as he was coming home—was really intended for him—that had never been clarified, due to the prevailing darkness and the emptiness of the street.

His profession brought dangers with it. He knew them and was a match for them. He was not cowardly. He was proud of his courage. He did not let himself be intimidated. Not he. He went his way and would continue on it. Crimes and their perpetrators always found in him their most stubborn prosecutor. He would be finished with those directed against him personally, just as with all the others with whom he had to do professionally. (Moreover, since that unexplained shot he always carried a loaded Browning in his rear trousers pocket.)

The district attorney would soon be finished with this case too. In no time.

As soon as he had found out what it was all about.

But that was precisely what he did not know.

This young man threw no ink bottles; he did not step directly in his path; he uttered no insults. On the contrary, he seemed to go out of his way. He did not once look at him. He observed him in no kind of way. He gave him no occasion to proceed against him; none even just to speak to him.

Still he wanted now to find out at last what he wanted from him. The next time he would simply go up to him and ask.

In any case, he wanted to settle the affair personally. He would have made himself ridiculous with his tale of a man whom he only saw—and saw again and again—and who never did anything to him. (District Attorney Sierlin feared nothing in the world more than to appear ridiculous.)

But he was angry again, when he saw how much time he had sacrificed on this evening to such an indifferent case (which besides was really no case at all). He threw away the smoked-out cigar (the third already since he was sitting here) and went across to help his children with their school homework. He spoke with his wife and, after the children had been sent to bed, drew the astonished and delighted woman to himself again for the first time in a long while.

8

Across from the district court stood a small café that was frequented almost exclusively by jurists who came here for a refreshment during the recesses of the proceedings—judges, defense attorneys, lawyers, assistant judges.

Now, since the days were beautiful, they mostly sat in the small terrace on the street, with its fifteen little tables, back to back, so as to get a breath of fresh air at the same time.

Naturally they all knew one another. Each knew who the other was and only said what this other person was allowed to hear or—should hear. The conversations thus carried more of a general than a private character.

District Attorney Sierlin was also one of the regular guests of the café.

He had not succeeded in the recent weeks in carrying out his intention: to stop this unknown man (who had not shied away from using a taxi to catch sight of his face for a moment) and question him about his reasons, although he looked around for him every time he now drew close to his house. He had disappeared once more.

Now he suddenly saw him here one day—in his café. He saw him and recognized him immediately as he entered: how he got up from the place where he was sitting and walked out past him. His first feeling was again to step in his path and speak to him. His second, that here on this spot, where all eyes would turn to him, it was simply impossible. He had already been greeted. Very painfully affected, his thoughts were not on the conversation into which he had immediately been drawn.

Now what did this mean again? How did this man come here, and what did he want here? Of course any decently dressed person could patronize this bar, even if it seldom happened that other guests than those "from over there"—jurists—visited it. And what did this hasty getting up on his entrance mean?—this indifferent walking past him?—what was all this again now?

He was anxious to see if this incident was unique and therefore could possibly have been by chance, or whether it would repeat itself.

It repeated itself. It repeated itself in the next two weeks at least six times and always in the same fashion: When he entered, the man already sitting there stood up, walked past him and into the street. District Attorney Sierlin thought of following him out. But this too was impossible: the street was swarming with acquaintances. He must avoid even the slightest sensation or scandal anywhere. He must act as if he did not know this man and had never seen him—walk past him the way everyone walked by, in a careless, foreign, indifferent way.

He became even more angry than before. He became boundlessly angry. He felt how the blood rose to his face when he approached the café and, already at a distance, saw him always sitting at the same little table on the terrace near the entrance, at the little table where a place was immediately made free—just as if he wished to offer him that place. It took an effort to retain his self-control, shake hands, and answer questions. But what was he to do? He could not once show in his looks the ill humor, of which he was ashamed and which gripped him anyway, which he could hardly get rid of any longer.

He was coming close to avoiding the café. But that too would be noticed. And then: go out of the way of this man—let himself be disturbed by him in his habits? That would be an even prettier state of affairs!

But the brief relaxations between strenuous and exhausting sessions truly became embittered for him through this man, whom he did not even know. What did he know of him? That he possibly lived out there, like him; that he had unlimited time at his disposal (for what time alone was spent just in sitting around in this café!); and that he obviously had money (where did he get it from?).

District Attorney Sierlin visibly lost his never especially good mood.

He came home ill-tempered and angry (even when he had not seen "him"); he was uneasy and no longer slept well; and he grew angry for no reason and really over everything: over his wife and her chatter; over the boys, who did not get ahead in school correctly; over too lenient judges and all too bold defenders; over hardened criminals; and—over this strange man, whom he saw or did not see, for he never knew when he would see him and when not. Sometimes he came; other times he stayed away.

It was about time for the court vacation to began. Then he would have rest above all—from this fellow too.

There were only eight days to go.

He wanted to go with his family to the Baltic Sea, right away on the first day.

9

On the evening before the general departure a small change occurred in the travel plan. A letter came from relatives in Kiel, in which he was urgently reminded of a promise given long ago to visit—at least this year "to give them a couple of days." It could hardly be avoided any longer. The visit had already been put off so often that a renewed rejection would be an insult. Better, therefore, to do it right away, so as to have it behind him then for a long time. It was therefore decided that he would go to Kiel in the morning with the earliest train, his wife would depart for the spa with the children only on the morning after next, and he was to join them there in about a week. She was pleased—a dress that was not yet ready could then still be tried on and taken along.

Marie, who had her free evening today, was called by her mistress and instructed: "Marie, when you leave, do order a taxi for tomorrow early around seven at the taxi stand. The master is leaving early tomorrow with the first train for Kiel, and we are staying yet a day. But don't forget it and make a note of the number. Do you hear?"

Marie did not forget.

Punctually at seven o'clock the next morning a taxi stopped before the house, and the master rode to the train station.

Arriving there, he first sent a telegram to his relatives to announce his arrival for early afternoon, and then, handbag and umbrella in hand, he went up to the window to buy himself a ticket.

About to take the necessary bills from his wallet, he heard—close in front of him—in a calm, clear, and firm voice the same words that he himself was on the point of saying the next minute, the words: "One—Kiel—second-class—please."

He looked up. Before him was standing a young man in a gray suit who had just pocketed money, received a ticket, and then walked away.

The place before him was free. But District Attorney Sierlin took no step forward. He did not budge. He was looking after the man walking away. He could not believe his own eyes.

Only when he was shoved from behind—not very gently—and a gruff, entirely different voice asked whether he did not want to finally move ahead, since others also wanted to travel with the train, did he rouse himself from a kind of stupor, throw his money down, likewise receive his ticket, and stumble onto the platform.

The train was standing waiting. The passengers were already in their seats. A few stragglers were hurrying to their cars.

KENN]

He too had to climb aboard if he still wanted to go along.

He did it, found a second-class compartment, threw his bag and umbrella onto the rack and himself into a corner. The train pulled out.

He sat in thought. Now he had him! He was with him on this train!

After a while he jumped up, walked through the two second-class cars, and looked into every compartment—the man he was looking for was not in them. The train was lightly occupied.

He was again in his corner. Besides him only an old gentleman was sitting at the window. He started to brood.

Then he stood up again and walked through the whole train—from the last car up to the first of the third-class cars, again and again by those of second class; he tore doors open and shoved them closed again, omitted not a single compartment, even looked all around to see whether the toilets were empty, here too opening doors excessively, only to slam them shut again—astonished looks followed the man chasing up and down the aisles: the man sought was nowhere to be seen. He must not have come aboard. It was impossible. Where could he keep himself hidden?

The sweat was standing on his forehead when he was again sitting in his seat.

Why had he not come along? Where did he disappear to? And *how* did this man know that he wanted to take this first train and travel to Kiel? For he *must* have known it.

He brooded further.

How could he have known about a trip that had been decided on only in the last moment and which no one knew about except his wife?

For he had not just dreamed it—earlier! He really had seen him before him! And not only seen—he had also heard his voice, which suddenly sounded so remarkably familiar in his ear, as if he had already heard it once. But when and where?

District Attorney Sierlin was tempted to laugh out loud. If that had *also* been a coincidence, then there were coincidences in life that were more than remarkable. But it had not been a coincidence and the affair was not at all laughable. On the contrary, it now began to become serious. He must now finally get to the bottom of it. If he only had him here now, here on the train, where he could no longer escape him! But—he was just not on the train. He was gone. Vanished in an inexplicable way—before his eyes.

Then he felt how precipitously a rage was welling up in him, over which he was no longer master.

Now this man was pursuing him, this man whom he still did not know, of whom he still knew nothing (not even what he really wanted from him)—now he was pursuing him even on his vacation! He bought a ticket for the same train and then did not travel with it! He was traveling on another train—after him!

For he did not doubt for a moment that he would meet him in Kiel.

He sat in his corner, stared straight ahead, and jumped up at every stop, to go to the window and keep all those getting off in view. A question of the old gentleman, whether he did not feel well, he answered so curtly and unpleasantly that it was not repeated.

The breakfast that his wife had so carefully packed for him remained untouched. A feeling of unease came over him so strongly that he was unable to touch anything.

When the train pulled into its final station, he leaped off in one bound as the first one off, hurried to the gate, and stationed himself beside it. He let all the passengers, one after the other, go by him, until the last had disappeared and the platform was again deserted. Only then did he too leave the railway station.

During his stay with his relatives he was not a pleasant guest. He had never been loveable, but this bad humor, this restlessness and bluntness exceeded all measure. They were happy to be rid of him after only six days, since he himself said that he had to cut his visit short. It had also been downright striking to all that he very often gave absurd answers and on walks and in public places was always looking around, as if he were seeking someone who was following him (although here, except for them, he could not be acquainted with anyone).

10

District Attorney Sierlin was greeted with jubilation at the little railway station of the Baltic Sea spa and led in triumph to the hotel. He was glad himself, for he was fond of his children, and they, in spite of his strictness, were fond of him—at least little Kurt was. His wife too was eager to be able to relate to him who of all their old acquaintances were also here and what new acquaintances she had made in these five days. She did it in her usual fullness, which easily degenerated into prattle.

But only when they were sitting and eating at their usual table on the veranda, which in honor of his arrival today had been festively decorated with flowers, did she do what she had forbidden her children to do—did it quite unconsciously out of one of her typical and sudden ideas, which she herself could not account for.

For already on the first day of their arrival the children, quite excited, had come with the news. "Mommy, just think," said Kurt, "the man from our garden is also here."

And the older boy added, "And he is staying with us in the hotel."

She started up. "Which man? Who are you talking about?" and received the answer from both together:

"Why from the man who was always just sitting in front of our house. We talked about him already, that time when Father got so angry and said we should not talk to him. We did not talk to him here either."

She had long forgotten the conversation at table and therefore only said, "Then don't do it again. Best that you don't speak of him at all, if your father just gets angry."

However, as they were dining she had the strange man, who was sitting two tables away, pointed out to her and she confirmed it for herself: He does not belong to us, to society, and also not to this hotel.

She then ignored him, and the children, who did not see him much, had soon forgotten him in building a great castle in the sand, which had to be built anew every day and yet was supposed to be ready when Father came.

So she said now, thoughtlessly and entirely by the way, "There is also a man here whom the children think they have often seen in the park. He's the one already talked about. Do you know the man? He is staying in the hotel."

The children, now relieved of their prohibition, eagerly fell in and pointed toward one of the other tables. "There he sits—with his back to us."

But they were immediately reprimanded by their mother. "Don't point with your finger at other people!"

It was good that District Attorney Sierlin was intensely occupied at this moment with his somewhat tough steak and that the knife didn't want to cut correctly. He had to bend deeply over his dish.

When he looked up again, his face was red from the effort of cutting, and again (like the earlier time) there was a certain vehemence in the tone with which he rebuked the children, who were anxiously waiting for his answer. "I already told you many times that you should not concern yourselves about strange people who are none of your business. Do what I say!"

The children were taken aback and stared straight ahead, while the thoughts of his wife were again already far away (she was now trying to get the attention of some newcomers she had recognized as acquaintances from Berlin).

District Attorney Sierlin had need of all his not inconsiderable self-control to keep his bearing until the end of the meal and to answer further questions. He succeeded in not looking over—and he did not look. He knew quite exactly who was sitting there a few tables from him with his back to them. He knew just as exactly who now—while the children were occupied with their dessert

and his wife, half turned away, was speaking to other acquaintances at the next table—walked by his table, in a detour that was
entirely unnecessary to reach the exit, and closer than was likewise
necessary and that the separation of the tables allowed. He felt
him in his back.

But he still controlled himself. He did not look up. Here too
there should be no scandal.

Nevertheless, when they were above in their room somewhat
later, he surprised his wife with his intention of going out alone for
a half hour. He justified it by saying his head felt heavy after the
trip and he wished to make himself acquainted a bit that very day
with the layout of the spa. He promised to return in half an hour.

Outside, alone in the half-dark and empty corridor, he stopped.
The veins were swollen in his forehead and his hands were balled
into fists.

Then he slowly climbed down the stairs to the lobby of the
hotel. All the tables in it were occupied by guests, who were drinking their coffee here after dinner—chatting, laughing, flirting. He
looked them over with a quick glance.

The two adjoining rooms, a reading-and-writing room and a
billiard room, were empty. From a room farther back sounded
dance music. He also entered it, watched the dancers a while, who
were doing jazz steps and the fox trot to the sounds of a piano and
a violin. Then he returned to the lobby. At the entrance to the
hotel was a small bar. But only two older gentlemen were sitting
there on high stools, their knees drawn up as if they had stomach-
aches, drinking a reddish mixture.

He left the hotel without having found what he was looking
for.

Outside in the cool and damp air, he felt how his face was
burning.

He climbed down the wooden steps that led over the dunes to
the beach. There he walked along it, at first by canopied beach
chairs and fallen-in castles, then on the damp and firm sand, on
and on.

Beside him the surf of the sea was singing its eternal song. He did not hear its voice. He did not see the shining of the stars in the night sky, nor the silver shimmer of the waves. He also did not feel how they were wetting his shoes in their impetuous impact—he walked and walked.

The beach was empty of people. No one came toward him. No one followed him.

Slowly his rage subsided.

A wicked and ferocious joy arose in him: He had him! He finally had him! Here! Here, in this little spa where he could not escape from him! And he was staying with him under the same roof!

What was the harm that he had escaped him this evening? It was perhaps a good thing. He did not know *what* he would have done with him if he had come under his fists already this evening.

But tomorrow, tomorrow early (if they were alone)—then he would take him to task so that his sight and hearing would vanish, his sight and hearing just like his following and slipping away!

If they were alone—for here too, where there were already so many acquaintances, the affair must be settled without a scandal. But this time it would be settled!

He grew calmer and turned back.

Once he laughed out loud, with a discordant, shrill laugh: That was the limit! The fellow had followed him here! Traveled after him! And, in order to be certain, was already a couple of days here before him! That was the limit!

But now it must end. One did not trifle or make sport of him, District Attorney Sierlin.

Already tomorrow. And then he would not be embittered another day here.

When he again entered the hotel, the lobby was empty and the dance music hushed. Here everyone, spa-fashion, had gone to bed early.

Above he was already impatiently awaited. He had stayed out

over an hour without knowing it. The children were already long asleep in the next room.

It took a while for him to fall asleep. He slept uneasily. He attributed it to the trip, the first night in a strange place, and the stimulating sea air.

He got up unusually early; he dressed unusually quickly. Below, in the vestibule, he was the first guest. He wanted to be.

He walked directly to the porter's loge.

There he asked first for letters, then for the register, signed it, and finally, as if by the way, as he pressed a mark coin into the porter's hand: "Tell me, Herr Porter, yesterday evening a gentleman was sitting near our table"—he briefly described him—"who was supposed to have already been with you a few days."

The one questioned immediately got the picture. He suspected something strange (district attorney—so early—tip) and hastened to say, "The gentleman has just left not more than half an hour ago to return to Berlin," and he pointed at the same time to a name in the register in its next to last page.

District Attorney Sierlin felt a rush. Departed? Just now! Escaped again!

But he did read the registration (in a clear, businesslike, impersonal handwriting): "Adolf Braun, businessman, from Berlin. Expected stay: undetermined. Goal of the trip: Berlin."

He slowly closed the book and left the loge.

The porter looked after him: certainly a criminal case. He was a good judge of human nature. (Who else should be, if not a porter of a large hotel, who for twenty years had seen people from all foreign countries and their experiences pass by him!) But that this young gentleman, who always went his way so quietly, had been so friendly and generous with his tips, that this man should have committed an offense or even a crime—he could not get into his head. He shook it.

For District Attorney Sierlin relaxation was missing, at least in the first two weeks. He withdrew from all company if possible, something he otherwise had never done, took long and solitary walks in the dunes, and returned from them in no better mood. With his wry face, his short and sharp questions, and his often entirely meaningless answers, he also spoiled the stay for his family.

Only in the third week did he become more approachable, sought old acquaintances and made new ones according with his rank, and sat with them evenings by beer and skat.

He was as before. His usual characteristics came out even more strongly.

It was at this time that Assistant Judge Kreidewien from Lübeck, who was feared (especially by young ladies) for his malicious remarks, coined the term "somewhat too human" and immediately applied it to him. "This Berlin district attorney is," he said confidentially to an acquaintance (who he knew would promptly pass it along), "this insufferable gentleman is 'somewhat too loud,' 'somewhat too determined,' 'somewhat too little distinguished.'"

Otherwise the last weeks went by like the first, in a hurry. They bathed; they made up sailing parties; they lay in the sand and were lazy according to their needs.

Of that "fellow" there was, of course, no more talk, already for the reason that he had disappeared from sight.

After he had racked his brains in vain over how he had learned about his stay here and why he had followed him, District Attorney Sierlin resolved to think about him no more. He only partially succeeded, but yet did from time to time.

After six weeks the whole District Attorney Family returned to Berlin. Wife and children in the best frame of mind. The master of the house was not quite as relaxed as he should have been for the hard and irritating work of the coming winter semester.

11

The trip had gone satisfactorily, a taxi had taken the whole company from the train station to their home, where they were awaited and greeted by the fat cook and Marie, the housemaid. There they were on the point of taking their baggage into the house—the wife already in a lively conversation and the children only waiting for their father, who was settling accounts with the driver—when a young man, politely avoiding them, walked through between them and the last pieces still lying around on the sidewalk and, without otherwise concerning himself about the arrivals, walked on looking straight ahead.

The two children poked one another, looked after him, and whispered to one another, as their father, finished with paying, turned around. "What is up with you two?" he asked when he saw their excited faces. He repeated the question more sharply when he received no answer.

Heinz, the elder, got up is courage. "The man from the bench, Father," he said and looked down the street.

District Attorney Sierlin whirled around in a bound. Nothing in the world, not the presence of his wife, nor that of children and servants, nor the whole neighborhood would have kept him in that instant from chasing after the one talked about.

But it was too late.

The street was empty.

To run after him now. Leave everyone and everything behind—impossible! And—he would be gone!

He grabbed with a quick hand for the hand baggage still lying there, indicated to the children to take the remainder, and shoved them before him into the house.

Above, in his room and alone, he stopped and stared ahead.

A peculiar feeling crept up in him. He did not recognize it. It crept up from his stomach and settled in his breast.

How was a man so proud of his courage to recognize it?

It was the feeling of an undefined fear.

12

He overcame it quickly.

Even if he had known what it was, this feeling—never would he have allowed himself to call it by its true name.

He was District Attorney Sierlin, who feared nothing in the world but God alone; who had nothing to fear since his life lay blamelessly open to all eyes; and who lowered his eyes before no man.

And he, was he to let himself be intimidated by such a vagabond—this scoundrel who was up to God knows what? No! Never!

He would see him again. He did not know when and where, for there was no telling what this man would do. But that he would see him again, that he would meet up with him again one day, his feeling told him now with absolute certainty. But then—God help him!

He did not know who this "Businessman Adolf Braun" was. He had never heard the name. It meant nothing to him. He did not know what this Herr Braun (if it was not perhaps an assumed name, which was likely) wanted from him. He did not know why and for what secret reasons this fellow spent such an enormous amount of time, money, and patience—yes, patience too!—to place himself in his path and then leave the path open again. He only knew that he would see him again.

It was he now who was on the lookout for him. On the street, in the café, in the streetcar, every time he returned home. It was he who listened to see if the known steps were sounding again behind him, so as to turn around quick as lightning and confront him.

But once again he saw nothing of him and heard nothing. One week passed, a second—nowhere even a trace. It was as if now, precisely now, he wanted to stay away forever. But he did not believe it. He would return. Entirely unforeseen, one day when he was precisely not thinking about him.

The riddle that was hidden behind this person and his behav-

ENN]

ior did not let go of him. Again and again he tried to solve it.

How did he know about his sudden trip to Kiel? The place and even the name of his hotel and when he meant to arrive there? From where? From where did he learn the day of his return, down to the exact hour and minute? It was incomprehensible. It made one lose his reason. What confederates did this man have then, to know things that besides his wife and himself no one could know?

He still refrained from speaking about it to her. She was not the wife to share his thoughts with, and she would have been the last to keep these thoughts to herself.

He only asked her once, by the way, "Tell me, Bertha, who actually knew beforehand of our stay at the sea? Who knew of my visit to Kiel?"

She looked at him in surprise with her lovely, empty eyes. The behavior of her husband was becoming more and more peculiar. He had never been loveable, that was not in his character, but recently he had changed so much that it could hardly continue like this. (She had already for a long time been complaining bitterly about it to a trusted circle of her women friends.) And now what was this supposed to mean?

So she only answered, "Who knew of our trip? Well, our acquaintances." (She named a couple of names.) "But why do you want to know? It was really no secret."

He did not give up. A suspicion had arisen in him. "And Marie? Did she also know nothing about it?"

Now, however, her patience was at an end. The servant question had always been a dubious topic between them. Not that she, like so many of her acquaintances, would have been jealous of the younger of them—she had no reason to doubt the faithfulness of her husband. His morality forbid him any escapade. But he had already driven away so many capable hands through his suspicious and overly strict nature—now he was beginning with Marie too, who had already been with them a whole year, this so hard-working and capable, in every respect so trustworthy girl. She would not find a second one so easily.

She remonstrated and began to sing her praises: how trust-worthy and honest she was; how well she had kept the house in their absence; how she never had visitors, not even when they were away (proof: the witness of the cook). And she concluded, "Natu-rally Marie knew where we were. She had to write to me if every-thing was in order."—"No," were her last words, "no, Sierlin, you are not going to drive her too out of the house with your—your—unkindness, which is getting greater really every day!"

He had to admit defeat and kept silent.

But a couple of days later—he could not calm himself—he interrogated Marie when she brought him his tea (his wife was not at home). The old cook—taken over with the house as part of the inventory—did not come into question; she cooked well, but was more than stupid and of a downright touching simplicity.

He therefore questioned Marie. "Tell me, Marie, you knew about our trip. Whom did you speak to about it?"

He wanted to catch her by surprise.

But Marie did not let herself be caught so easily. She was a Berliner and so had a ready tongue. She guessed right away where this was heading. This nasty fellow whom she hated—she was attached to his wife, since she was stronger and more clever than the wife—wanted to discover her relationship with her beloved Ede. But he would have a hard time there with her. She did her duty, was honest and hardworking, never received her boyfriend in the house (as did all other girls in her position), and what she did elsewhere was none of his business. To dictate to a poor girl what she was to do and not do in her free time—that would really be a pretty state of affairs!

She therefore steadfastly looked at the questioner with her bright eyes and said snappishly (and how snappishly!), "To whom am I supposed to have spoken then? It's none of my business. And I don't concern myself at all with the affairs of my master and mis-tress. Madam would have—" (never asked me something like that, she had wanted to say).

She was cut short.

[KENN]

District Attorney Sierlin completed for himself what was not said and dismissed her. What if she came at him with his wife? And besides, there was just nothing to get out of her (if she knew anything at all, which now once again appeared very doubtful to him).

He was defeated for the second time and no wiser than before.

He brooded further. But the more he thought about the affair, the less understandable it became for him.

If only a certain bit of sense was in all this nonsense!

The story became uncanny for him, all the more as to all appearances it had come to an end. It was a story almost like out of a criminal novel. But even an expert detective (and he held himself to be such) would have been at his wit's end here.

He could do nothing but wait until he got him under his hands. Under them, these hands of his, the riddle would unravel itself; he himself was incapable of solving it—as he admitted to himself.

13

Never in his life had District Attorney Sierlin worked so hard as now. He sat late into the night over his files. His voice grew harder and more cutting, his call for justice louder than ever, and the sentences he demanded as prosecutor exceeded all bounds. It did not escape the more sharp-eyed how a certain insecurity lay hidden behind this audacity. It showed itself also in the incessant confrontations with the defense attorneys, which did not end.

They shook their heads over him.

Autumn was here. The days were becoming cooler and in the park the trees were beginning to turn yellow. The benches, occupied in the summer by mothers and nursemaids from the neighborhood and played around by children, were empty again.

On one of these evenings, toward the end of the month of September, District Attorney Sierlin was alone in his house. His wife had gone into the city with the boys to visit acquaintances and then the circus. Marie had her free evening and had left after she had prepared dinner for the master.

He had intended to be very industrious today and work on a particularly difficult case (spousal murder by poison?), with whose clearing up he hoped to gain honor.

But the work did not go so well. He felt again this inner uneasiness, which seldom entirely left him anymore. At first he walked up and down and then to the window to look out.

It was still light, but a fine fog lay in the air and lightly veiled the trees and benches across the way.

On seeing them he had to think again of this damned fellow who had caused him so much trouble the whole summer, more than any other man before (and only through the mere sight of him), this fellow whose hidden intentions he still had not found out; and who was again away for weeks and was probably unreachable now forever.

He sat down again to his work, but things went even worse than before, so that he again took up his wandering through the room. His thoughts were no longer so occupied by a case, they stayed with it no longer as firmly as before. He was clear about this to himself and at times not unconcerned. Nerves? Ridiculous. What was that? Nerves!

As he walked to the window for the umpteenth time—he didn't know how many—it seemed to him that a figure was now sitting over there. But it too was veiled as in thin smoke and even the outlines of it were hard to recognize.

But District Attorney Sierlin knew immediately who it was. He and no other! He cringed in fright, as if struck by a blow.

Then he got control of himself.

Calm down, stay calm!

He went into the hall and reached for his hat and cane. Everything, everything now depended on one thing, to surprise him, so that he could not escape again. He slipped down the back stairs of the house that led to the courtyard. He listened at the kitchen, where the cook was occupied with washing the dishes. It did not occur to him that his caution was entirely unnecessary, for she was as deaf as she was stupid. He left the house through the rear door, crossed the courtyard, and went along the path behind the neighboring villas to where the street began. It and the little park on the other side now lay before him.

The fog proved useful to him. It was impossible to see him from the bench as he now crossed over the roadway and entered the park. He went deeper into it, so that he could just make out the benches through the bare bushes.

Slowly and carefully he approached the bench he was seeking. Now he saw it and the man who was sitting on it. If he now rushed him from behind and grabbed him by the shoulders before he was able to spring up, he had him!

But something held him back: it was the attitude of the man sitting there, now only steps away from him. It was the same attitude as earlier, the unconcerned posture of someone entirely sunken in thought, whose gaze went far over the surroundings into an unknown distance. Only he no longer held his hands in his pockets. He was smoking—his knees crossed over one another, he propped himself on them with his left arm, while his right hand held the cigarette, whose smoke went into the air.

At the sight of this, a new thought came to him as he approached. He suddenly changed his plan. He reached into his pocket, drew out his own case, took a cigarette from it, and then—quickly approached the bench. The other man still seemed not to have noticed him. District Attorney Sierlin sat himself on the fog-damp bench, leaned somewhat closer, and said, holding out his cigarette (not politely requesting, but rather as if self-evident), "Um—you have—a light?"

The one who was now sitting within reaching distance of him appeared at first not to have heard him. Then—slowly turning toward him—he looked fully at him *for the first time*, so that their glances met. He stood up just as slowly, threw his half-smoked cigarette with a single motion into the bushes, and calmly walked away.

District Attorney Sierlin remained on the bench.

He knew now where he had once already met those eyes and that glance.

CHAPTER TWO:
ADOLF BRAUN

1

Adolf Braun was the son of "poor but honest folks."

He had attended primary school, completed his three-year apprenticeship in a dry goods shop, and in the following years held more or less poorly paid positions, until he had the good luck of obtaining a job in the largest of the branches, so that he could now support his old parents, with whom he lived. He was very happy about it.

He was what one called a "good boy": friendly and open, willing and unobtrusive, a brave comrade and a loyal friend. In his free hours he devoted himself to sports (like almost all young people today), but not exclusively, and just as often also to a good book at home (like few young people today). Not chasing after the girls, but also not running away from them. Still unattached.

If his character, basically a quite uncomplicated character, showed a particular quality, it was that of a marked feeling for justice. He could hardly bring himself to do an injustice (which, not thinking deeply, he recognized only in its consequences, not in its basic cause)—he could hardly bear to see an injustice done calmly. Just as little could he bear to have one done to him.

That had already in his time in school led the not yet thirteen-year-old to a difficult situation. He was unjustly accused by a fellow pupil to the teacher. A bloody fight was the immediate consequence, an enmity to the death (on his side) the further consequence. For he never forgave his opponent and rejected all later reconciliation attempts of the regretful party with a harshness and vehemence that was unusual to his otherwise so good-natured disposition.

Overall, he was anything but quarrelsome. On the contrary, he was sociable, and so his life would have turned out peaceful and inconspicuous like that of most people, probably without any special incidents, if a horrible—horrible for him—occurrence had not changed his life from one day to the next.

2

He was accused of embezzling money in his shop. It was not a matter of a very large, but also not of an unimportant sum. In his desk papers were found—register receipts and stubs—whose existence in this place could not be explained. He did not know how they could have come there—to his desk—to which only he possessed the key.

On the grounds of this suspicion he was arrested and committed for trial.

He was dumbstruck.

He could do nothing but assert his innocence over and over again.

It came to the trial.

He defended himself poorly. His official defender, a still young and inexperienced man (he lacked the means to hire another), was even worse.

Asked what he had to bring to his defense, he could only stammer again and again that he was innocent. That was the way it had been that time in the school, before the accusation against him turned out to be false.

That one could take him to be a thief already rendered him beside himself and robbed him of every consideration that alone could have helped him here, even if it could hardly have saved

him. Basically he possessed a decent and extremely sensitive soul—
a difficult inheritance for a man in a raw and indecent time.

In spite of everything the judges and jury did not appear unfavorably disposed toward him. His good reputation up to then,
the fact that the case was unclear, the improvability of where the
missing money had gone—all spoke in his behalf.

Until at the close of the brief trial, the last one and late in the
day, the public prosecutor arose and began to speak. Only now
did Adolf Braun awake from his numbness. Only now did he hear
what was being spoken around him and understand the meaning
of the words. They were hard, false words, as if learned by heart,
which this monotonous, grating voice threw out into the room so
self-confidently. Words in which he, the one speaking them, did
not believe himself, could not believe. Adolf Braun wanted to jump
up, interrupt him, refute him. He could not. His throat was choked
under the fearful injustice that was happening to him here—with
these words. Then it was too late.

Only when the judgment was pronounced and he was to be
led out did he find his speech again. He turned around, looked at
him who had just spoken and whose words alone had led to this
judgment, looked him firmly in the eyes, and said once again and
for the last time, "I am innocent!"

And he added, clearly and distinctly so that it was understandable into the farthest corner, *And you know it!"*

3

He was sentenced to a year and a half in jail. He had served one
year when his innocence came to light. The actual perpetrator was
discovered. He confessed it. A retrial was introduced. As could not
be otherwise, Adolf Braun was exonerated and released with the
usual couple of phrases of regret.

He was standing in the street.

His parents had both died during this year. He had hardly

seen them anymore—his father as last, when he came to announce the death of his mother, whom he soon after followed. They had never doubted their son, but they were in misery and had died with broken hearts.

He was standing in the street. The relatives that he still had received him, to be sure, but in such a way that he never returned. He was rehabilitated, of course, but he had still been "there." His friends were scattered to the winds, for they were all young, young as he—had been.

The terrible year began, in which every single day was a new and hopeless struggle for bare existence. He had made an acquaintance in jail: Eduard Pritzow. Not quite as innocent as he, but no worse than reckless and unscrupulous. They met one another again in freedom and loyally shared misery and hunger, all disappointments, and every kind of humiliation of this year—from the regretful shrug of the shoulders on to the cheap and empty words of comfort. They helped one another, however good or bad it went, with the little that they occasionally earned and so became friends. It was Eduard Pritzow's attachment and robust humor that kept Adolf Braun going in this year and kept him back from the final action.

No! What really kept him going, what was alone able to keep him going during the year behind walls and this year when freedom was almost worse, in the endless hours of dejection, of despising mankind, of despair, was something quite different—something that no man knew or even suspected.

For young Adolf Braun became a different man in these two years. Better said, that side of his character which had already shown itself in his early youth awakened to its full strength, took power over his whole being down to the depths of his soul—so much so that it became one with him, like his hand, his eye, the heart in his breast.

An injustice had taken place. It had happened to him. Every injustice must be expiated. This one too. The expiation lay with him. It had been laid in his hands.

But on whom should it be carried out, this expiation? The man who wanted to ruin him in order to save himself (and who had succeeded in ruining him, but still without saving himself) was now sitting where he had been. The judges, the court—together with the jury they formed an impersonal and therefore unassailable mass. In fact, they were not really the ones who had judged him: they had acted only on the order, or at least under the direct influence of this tall, lean man with the slashed face, the hard eyes, the hooked nose, and the sharp voice, this man who did not believe himself what he was saying, who had hated him without knowing why, and whom he now hated in return—far, far more than that man or any other man could altogether be capable of hating.

He alone was the guilty party. He alone had plunged him into misery. On him alone must the expiation be carried out.

And it would be carried out!

Slowly in the numberless hours of sleepless nights in a lonely cell, slowly in many, many inactive-creeping days of hunger and despair a plan arose; it matured, grew and grew, gained shape.

In the first year after his release its execution was not to be thought of. But his plan was only put off, not given up for a minute.

He had to wait and he waited. A relative of his was still living—abroad, of an advanced age, and wealthy. He knew that it would have been just as pointless to turn to the miser during her lifetime, as he was certain after her death to be one of the relatives among whom her inheritance would be divided according to her last will.

He did not deceive himself. She died some nine months after his release. Two months later he found himself in possession of the inheritance that fell to him—not quite four thousand marks.

4

He kept five hundred marks and put the rest in a savings account.

He took, as the sole tenant, a quiet and clean room with a nice, old woman, fitted himself with clothes, and helped his friend Eduard get on his feet.

He calculated thus: he had one year's time. It lay before him. Then his money would probably be used up, certainly by then if the carrying out of his plan required unforeseen special and large outlays.

Therefore he had to succeed in this one year: bringing his enemy to a fall. If his enemy were still standing, then his plan would have failed. But a year was long (he knew how long it could be!).

Adolf Braun set about what he called his work—what was to become and should be his whole and exclusive occupation in this year.

He knew his enemy's name of course: District Attorney Sierlin. He also knew where he lived. Once, on a day of hunger-madness, he had been out there, before his villa in the quiet suburb, determined to choke him with his bare hands, if he should meet him. He did not meet him that day.

Now he no longer thought of killing him himself. That would have been something easy and monstrously simple: to lurk after him and then shoot him down. But such a punishment would have been much too easy and painless. And then, it should be carried out without he himself running into danger. He did not want to go back there once again (and forever), where he had suffered all that a human being was capable of suffering.

No, his revenge should be non-bloody, certain, and invisible to human eyes. It should work like poison—not like a merciful, quick-killing poison, but rather like a creeping, unrecognizable, inexplicable poison, which should eat into him like a malicious sickness: harmless in its first action, horrible in its last.

That was what he had in mind.

The enemy should see him, his victim. See and see, again and again—everywhere and unexpectedly. See, see, until he could no longer bear his sight, until he—

5

Adolf Braun set about carrying out his plan. Not that this plan was laid out before him in all its particulars—these would result of themselves, develop out of it. They could not be determined beforehand.

What he suspected more than knew was this: What was necessary for a successful completion was an excessive amount of patience, iron nerves, and a will that could not be shaken. (In addition to time and money—but he indeed had both.) It meant, therefore, that he should so steel his body, which had been weakened by the depravations of recent years, until his nerves were ready for any demand, any exertion, any shock. They must obey his will unconditionally at any time. If he felt that they were yielding in the least, he had to allow them rest and begin again to train them for the goal. And so he prepared himself.

He lived several weeks exclusively for his health. He ate well, slept much, made long and distant hikes in the fresh air and avoided every, even the slightest dissolution. He trained as only a sportsman trains.

After these weeks he had recovered so much that he dared trust himself to the first, small attack.

The enemy should at first only be reminded of him: see him (even if he most probably did not recognize him). So, toward evening on three separate days, after he had either inconspicuously followed him from court to the streetcar, or now, when he knew approximately when he usually came home, had lain in wait for him, he first walked up from behind him, then closely past him— always without observing him in the least, as if he did not know him and had never seen him. On the third time he felt that he had been seen.

Then in the following week he sat evening for evening on the bench that stood diagonally opposite from the house. He often sat there for hours. It was still cold—he did not feel it; it rained—he hardly noticed it. On one of these evenings, shortly after the enemy had entered his house and had appeared at the window, he strode toward the house, walked by it and away. He was almost certain that now he had not only been seen, but also had been noticed.

He took his place again—in a carefully studied attitude: looking straight ahead, as if in a dream; withdrawn from his surroundings, as if in thought. It happened that he actually forgot the place and hour and missed the arrival of the other man. That hurt nothing. If only *he* was seen. If only attention had been called to *himself*.

He convinced himself that it was. He noticed it in a slowing of the steps of the man awaited when he entered the street; he felt more than he saw the glances that flew over toward him and then in affected calmness turned away again. He also already knew the children, as they him. At times they played in curiosity around the man sitting there without moving, though they did not dare to come very close to him.

He also knew the majestic and snobbishly dressed conceited turkey—his wife—who rushed out and in again; the nimble and robust serving girl, who flitted about here and there; he even knew the stupid, good-natured face of the fat cook, who appeared at times in the house door—he acted as if he cared nothing at all for any of them.

He sat there, always in the same, indifferent attitude, with his gaze ignoring the house and its residents, and his hands deep in the pockets of his jacket.

Then to be quite certain, again on three successive evenings of the week after the next, he walked past the man coming home so strikingly fast, and this time on the curb, so that he had to be noticed in this quiet, hardly frequented street. He was noticed. He detected it in the sudden stopping of the man as he passed; in the challenging looks that met him from the side, without his seeming to notice them. He did not know if he had already been recog-

[KENN]

nized. That he had been seen and noticed and that the man had *begun* to be angry about him—of this he was certain.

With this he had obtained for the time being what he wanted. He allowed himself to enjoy a pause. These first, harmless skirmishes, with their often hours-long lying in wait, the pursuing that required the wakefulness of all his senses, and the sitting on this bench in all kinds of weather—all this did not tire or weaken him, to be sure, but still put him in a new and somewhat excited mood. To this came the stretching to the limit of all his strength of will every time, so as control himself in passing—not to attack the enemy and strike him down.

He forced himself not to do this. It was not part of his plan.

When he believed that they had calmed down enough (the two of them), he took up his work again.

But he now did it no longer out there in the suburb, but in the vicinity of the court.

There he saw "him" every moment, without, however, being seen by him. He did not want to be seen for the time being.

Yet, on one afternoon, a wonderful May day, the opportunity was too favorable for him to let it pass unused. His enemy was standing with several other gentleman at the tram stop, waiting for their streetcar. He pulled himself together and walked so remarkably close by him that he had to be seen, although he himself threw no glance to the side. On the quick turning of the other's body, on the almost unnoticeable start, he felt that he was being watched.

He walked a few streets further, climbed into the first taxi available, and let himself be driven out. Short of the goal, he climbed out and set himself in his old place on the bench.

It lasted a good half hour before he saw the familiar figure turn the street corner. He saw him suddenly stop, noticed that he had again been seen, quickly stood up, and walked away.

He knew: now he was *thinking* about him.

6

That is what he must do. He must not think about him just once
and then forget him again—no, more and more often. Still more
often! And then—always and always!

Again a small pause was allowed. He spent days, summery
June days, full of brightness and warmth, in the swimming and
open-air baths, allowed himself complete rest again, strengthened
his nerves, and then set himself again to the service of his cause.

Opposite the court was a small café. It was frequented almost
only by jurists—"the gentlemen from over there"—who were accustomed to take a quick refreshment here in the breaks, before
their duty called them again.

Adolf Braun needed to make no effort to find it. He suddenly
belonged to the regular visitors of the small café, sat on the narrow
terrace, drank his coffee, and leafed in the newspapers. The waiters
soon knew him—he gave the best tips and had the characteristic
of always paying immediately, as soon as what he ordered was
placed before him. He also drank quickly, but often sat much longer,
then suddenly got up and left the restaurant. They thought he
was a student of criminology.

From his seat Adolf Braun could well survey the street and the
entrance of the large, red building across the way. He saw his enemy approach, let his newspaper sink, stood up as soon as the man
entered, and walked by him and on out.

He saw by his startled movement that he had been recognized. He saw it in his abrupt turning away and correctly concluded what he had told himself: that the man, here where all eyes
were directly on him, would not let it come to a scandal—that
every sensation should very carefully be avoided.

The man was reminded of him. He was reminded of him again
and again. Somewhat slumbering thoughts were again awakened;
a remnant of discomfort strengthened to a germinating disquiet.
The sight of him must make him angry. It should anger him.

ENN]

Again he had gotten what he wanted for the time being. He might stay away again for a while, swim, and lie in the sun.

7

But not for long. For vacation time was approaching and District Attorney Sierlin would naturally go out of town. The vacation should not pass without the man seeing him at work. Now he needed help: he must be informed about the movement of the enemy, so as to follow him—on his heels if necessary.

Now was the time for his friend Eduard to be brought into the action.

They saw one another, not regularly, but still from time to time. They always knew where they could meet.

So he invited him to a restaurant. He had told him nothing of his inheritance, but rather that he was now receiving from a relative, who was touched by his misfortune, a small monthly allowance, until he could find work again. Under the circumstances, he was in no hurry to find a job—to whom could this be more evident than to Ede? (Ede himself was doing all kinds of occasional jobs, by which he tried as much as possible not to get into trouble again with the law—the "girls" took care of the rest, and in case of real need he knew now that he always had the support of his good friend Adolf.)

Naturally he also knew nothing of Adolf's plan. On this evening too he only learned that his friend had again seen the district attorney who had played such a dirty trick on him, and that he wanted "to make him angry a bit." For this he needed his, Ede's help. He must see how the man lived and what his living habits were.

That was grist for Ede's mill. To make disagreeable people angry was always a pleasure; but to be able to make a D.A. angry was a *delight!* So he listened eagerly to the words of his friend and promised every support desired. He was also of the opinion—quite correctly—that when the D.A. became so angry that he would want to investigate who was making him angry and get back at him, then it would no doubt be better that they continue to see one another in an inconspicuous way and in a less frequented place than this busy restaurant.

It was therefore agreed: Ede was at first to flirt with the D.A.'s serving girl and see if he could not learn various things from her.

Ede did it with his little finger.

"Listen," he said already a couple of days later, as they met in the new tavern (a quiet bar up in the north of the city and with a telephone). "When you have still more such jobs for me—I'll gladly undertake *them.*"

For Marie was a cozy thing and just suited him. He had insinuated himself as a peddler of illustrated family magazines and weeklies. On her next free evening they had already gone walking and to a café, and next Sunday they were going dancing. He got out of her what he wanted to know, it was child's play—she already had a boundless trust in him and babbled out everything on her own, even before she was asked.

"And she's pretty," concluded Ede, "pretty—like—oh you know—" He made a broad movement of his hands. His friend laughed and pressed a ten-mark bill into his hand—"for immediate expenses."

Adolf Braun was therefore certain now of learning all the particulars that he wanted to know, and he let the vacation come on.

8

Naturally he did not travel with him in the train to Kiel

That affair had been very simple.

As he entered the large restaurant in which he ate every evening at a certain hour (and in which Ede and he always met at first), the old waiter who usually served him said that a gentleman had called.

That was the sign that he should come immediately to the

other restaurant in the north. He rode there. "Listen," said Ede, "I have just met Kitty. We made a date for Sunday. She told me that your D.A. is traveling early tomorrow with the first train to Kiel, she had to order a taxi for seven o'clock. It's perhaps nice for you to know."

How nice it was!

The next morning, an hour before the departure of the only train in question, he was standing in the background near the ticket window. There was no crowd. The moment he saw the man he was waiting for come into the hall and walk toward the window, he quickly stepped in front of him (and without being seen by him) and, with the counted out money in his hand and now standing in front of him with his back to him, asked for a second-class ticket to Kiel. He spoke deliberately loud and clearly. The next moment he was through the gate and onto the platform. But there, instead of going to the waiting train and boarding it, he made a quick turn to the right and entered the office of the station master. There he discreetly waited until his turn had come and the train had left, before he asked to get his money back for the ticket: because of sudden, strong pains that had come on, which in the view of the doctor made an operation necessary (it was probably appendicitis), it was unfortunately not possible for him to undertake the trip. After a bit of back-and-forth, he received his money back. (Even if in this cause no money was allowed to be spared— it did not need to be thrown away.) Outside again he saw the last smoke clouds of the just departed train.

He looked after it with a satisfied smile.

9

Two days later the two friends said a touching farewell to one another after an enjoyable evening. Adolf was, as he said, invited to spend a few weeks with his uncle—the same one who was supporting him. (Eduard did not need to know more than was necessary to know, and so also not where he was really going.)

He had naturally learned from him (as he had from Kitty) where the rest of the D.A.'s family had traveled yesterday and in which hotel they planned to stay. Kitty had written the address down, so as to be able to contact them if "something should happen." Naturally she showed this address to her sweetheart.

Adolf Braun departed the next morning.

The first people who met him in the hotel lobby were Frau District Attorney Sierlin with her two children, who immediately recognized and looked after him.

He appeared to see them on this day as little as on all the following. All he did was: ask the headwaiter (with the help of a good tip) to reserve a certain table in the veranda for his meals.

Otherwise, he swam, lay on the beach, led the idle and healthy life of all the guests here—observed by no one, observing no one—and waited.

On the sixth day the table festively decorated with flowers—the second table from his own on the window side of the veranda—showed him that the enemy was to arrive today. He immediately went down to the office and settled his bill, since, as he said, he had to leave early in the morning with the very first train.

When he again came into the veranda, the enemy was already sitting among his family over his soup. Adolf Braun took his usual place, also today with the others' table at his back.

Also this time, to be quite certain of being seen as he left, he stood up shortly before the end of the mealtime and walked in a small, but completely unnecessary detour, so close by the table of the family that he had to be seen. Although no one sitting there looked up, he still felt that *one man* had noticed him. That was all that he wanted.

He went directly to his room and to bed.

The next morning, while everyone was still asleep, he left the hotel and departed.

[KENN]

10

Not back to Berlin. Why? He was now here at the sea, and if his enemy could treat himself to a stay by the sea—he could too. He too would have need of his nerves during the coming winter, and the sea, never seen before, exercised a calming and magic influence on him. He could lie on the beach the whole day and listen to the sound of the waves.

So he simply rode a few miles farther to another spa on the coast. He again gave himself up to his first impressions, lazed about, omitted no mealtime, and slept many hours—in salty air and sweet sun. After four weeks—one before the end of the vacation—sun-tanned and healthy as a fish in water, he returned to Berlin, where he was greeted with jubilation by Ede.

He had also had a good time with his fiancée (as he now always called her). If he had never gone to her in her house—on her own wish, but even more because of his friend's so emphatically expressed wish—they still had seen one another rather often and for whole days, and that she now held the first place in his roomy heart could no longer be doubted by those who heard him talk about her.

Adolf Braun naturally learned the day and hour of the D.A.'s return home and was at his post in good time.

When the taxi drove up, he walked between it, the baggage that had just been unloaded and was not yet all carried into the house, and the two boys, while he, for whom alone all this was aimed, had his back turned, still preparing to pay the driver. The children had seen him. That was enough. They would repeat it.

This meeting too, like the two before it, had been exactly considered and well thought out.

11

Now it had come far enough that he wanted and must let himself be recognized.

He was convinced that his enemy still did not know who he was, not to say, what he wanted.

Otherwise he would have acted differently—with greater sureness and probably also seeking to come into some kind of contact with him: to speak to him or step in his path.

How should he indeed have recognized him again? At that time, during the trial, he had only leafed in his file and had hardly looked at him. The moment of leaving, however, had been too short, even if it could not have failed to make a certain impression. Besides, he himself had changed: he wore his hair no longer in a brush style, but longer and parted. He now had a moustache, and was broader in the shoulders.

Everything was ready. Half the appointed time had already elapsed.

He had gained in this time what there was to gain. He had been seen and noticed. The man was uneasy, irritated, furious (to what degree could not to be determined). In any case curiosity, mistrust, suspicion had been awakened.

The skirmishes had to stop now.

Instead it must come to the first attack, before the real battle then began (in which it would be proved, which of them was the stronger).

He felt how much his opponent was burning for this first encounter.

He wanted to avoid him no longer. He should find him.

The park was again almost deserted when, about two weeks after the vacation, he took again his old place on the bench in an early hour one afternoon.

The first two days in vain: one evening the awaited man came home quite late, when he had already given up hope—he learned it afterwards through his friend; the other day from an unknown reason.

But on the third day, toward evening, he saw him coming home around the usual hour. He had not yet sat down, but was standing to one side at a considerable distance, observing. Thus he could not be seen.

Now he took his place, looked into the air, and lighted a cigarette. Then another one and still another. He waited.

After about a half hour he saw the enemy, not coming out of the house, but rather approaching him from the left side. He must have used the rear exit—and he knew why.

He rushed to take out a fresh cigarette and start to smoke. This too was part of his plan.

Soon he noticed the enemy had stepped out from the bushes behind him and was carefully coming to the bench. He saw him sit down.

He did not move.

And then the voice, which he had not heard for years, but which was not forgotten, struck his ear as he asked him for a light.

He turned toward him, slowly and apparently indifferently, and looked for the *first time again* into the hated face that was now so near him, he looked for several seconds into the cold, somewhat protruding eyes, stood silently up, disdainfully threw his cigarette away, and departed.

He did not know where he was going.

He only felt how he was trembling. He was trembling, his nerves were threatening under the monstrous effort to control himself so as not to strike (no, to spit) into that face so hated and detested like nothing in the world, in a way he had never ever come close to hating anything—his nerves, otherwise like steel, were threatening to give way.

Only gradually did he become calmer.

He knew that he was recognized now. A startled look in those greenish eyes proved it to him.

The preliminaries had ended.

The battle could begin.

His enemy had iron nerves. But his steel ones, which never again, as just now, would be allowed to twitch, would wear them down slowly, but surely.

[ENN]

CHAPTER THREE:
THE BATTLE

1

District Attorney Sierlin remained alone on the bench.

He was now no longer in doubt about where he had already seen this young man, who was just now sitting here, where he had seen that look.

But he still did not remember when it was—two or three years ago?

The day, however, he now recalled exactly.

He stood up and walked deep into the park. He was searching his memory for details. It had been the day when, on getting up in the morning, he had had the first, serious argument with his wife. She accused him of not getting ahead fast enough; he accused her of hindering him in all—her—possible ways. All kinds of unspoken things came to light and were aired in loud, vehement words on both sides.

He left the house in an already upset mood. His mood did not become better in the course of the day. This so much discussed case, this tapeworm of a case (arson in connection with attempted murder), came to an end that day. Not to a good one for him, because it ended with an outright acquittal of the accused, although he had given his entire eloquence to bring about at least fifteen years in prison.

After a rough day there was still another case coming to trial—a quite indifferent, everyday one: simple, but unproven embezzlement. He had an easier game here: the official defender was a dunce, the accused himself could not offer for his defense anything other than what was to satiety heard again and again: "I am innocent!" The jury as well as the judges had only one wish, finally to go home as soon as possible. He himself had looked through the files only cursorily and had no clear judgment over the guilt or innocence. But these cases of embezzlement by young employees were increasing in recent times in such a shocking way that finally an example must be made. He therefore spoke more vehemently than he really meant to in such a basically indifferent case. He spoke of the increasing depravity of our youth, their impudent arrogance regarding divine and human laws, and the prevailing confusion in the concept of property. He asked for an eighteen-month jail sentence. It was given.

He also remembered, as he walked about in the park, how the accused, before he was led away, had shouted some words at him, something like: he was innocent and he, the district attorney, must know that he was.

Naturally that had left him quite cold at the time. The case was concluded and was forgotten among a hundred others.

He would also have hardly remembered it today, if a motion for a retrial had not been made, which ended with the complete acquittal of the man sentenced. He was not involved in that because he was away on an official trip at the time.

All the same, it was a blow for him (among others), over which he comforted himself with the old saying: all men made mistakes, even district attorneys.

The blow was made up for, and the memory of it too sank with the files into the Hades of legal practice.

It was forgotten down to the name of the one unjustly sentenced at that time, on whose person he had hardly cast a glance during the trial. A young man like a hundred thousand others.

District Attorney Sierlin stopped and saw that he was still holding his unsmoked cigarette between his fingers. He was all alone here.

All at once, while he turned here and there, it was as if he heard the voice from that time again, and now also the words he had thrown at him: "I am innocent! And you know that I am!"— and the words that had left him so indifferent at that time gained in this minute an entirely new meaning for him.

A feeling of unease came over him.

He began to sense why this young man had been after him for a half year.

But what he really wanted from him—to this question he still found no answer.

2

Nor did it find it that evening when, in his study, he was still thinking about the whole affair.

This man could not actually imagine that he had been guilty of the judgment against him? The judges had sentenced him on the verdict of the jury—not he.

But such people often come to the strangest notions. (Especially when an injustice has been done to them, as doubtless was the case here.)

He had them dig out the files of the accusation for embezzlement and the retrial: "The case of Adolf Braun."

That lasted several days.

He learned nothing new: A young businessman, Adolf Braun, twenty-two years old, good references, not previously convicted, was sentenced to a year and a half and after one year, in the retrial, in which his innocence was proven, was later acquitted. Well now, with that he was rehabilitated.

District Attorney Sierlin made some notes for himself regarding the person and dates and sent the files back.

Yes, why was he pursuing precisely him? What had he done to him? He had indeed only carried out his duty and even, with the lack of clarity in the case, had asked for an especially low sentence.

A man such as this, whose mind had been confused by the injustice suffered, naturally did not comprehend that he had been simply the victim of a judicial error (like so many others).

But he obviously hated him and was spending a quite unbelievable amount of time and money on only one thing, meeting him again and again.

Only this hatred had first expressed itself a full year—he saw in his notes—after his acquittal, and such a stubborn and irrational hatred must be directed against precisely him from another, particular reason.

Had he, this man, really been able to assume that he should ask for his acquittal? That he only did if there was no other way, if rock-solid and unshakable proofs of the innocence of the accused were present, and if he himself believed in this innocence.

In this case however—

Suddenly District Attorney Sierlin found himself no longer on such solid ground in his meditations. As far as he was able to remember (but the case had been so long ago and was such an ordinary and uninteresting case), in the face of the accused man's own defense (which was nil) and that of this idiotic lawyer (which was rather an incrimination), he had not held him to be guilty, but also not innocent. Thus had it doubtless been.

But how did that concern him? The decision between guilty and not guilty did not lie with him, but rather with the jury and judges. They had spoken the last word here.

What therefore—he asked himself again and again—what object for his persecution mania was this young man looking for in him so as to procure a satisfaction that, for that matter, had already been given him through the acquittal in the retrial?

Now he himself had become the innocent victim, and it was high time to think how he could get this incessant molestation (which by this time was beginning to be unbearable) off his neck once and for all (for a sure feeling told him again that it was not at an end with this meeting today on the bench). It had to end. But how?

ENN]

The jurist in him naturally thought of protection through the law. But what means did this offer for an action? When he asked himself this, he had to answer: actually none at all. For what punishable action was present? None. The man had done nothing to him (nothing up to now). Recently he had even gone out of his way. He was just there. Always there. In the most impossible places; at the most unexpected times.

That was not only disturbing and annoying, it gradually got on the nerves.

He could turn to the police and say that a suspicious personage was loitering in the neighborhood of his house, and ask them to keep a watchful eye on him. But this denunciation would just be much too general and then also was no longer applicable. For he, the man in question, had avoided this region for months for a change, and then he himself did not believe (and had never believed) that in his case one had to do with a thief or a burglar. In addition, the police could not station one of their people day and night in front of his house.

If he would only show the least sign of abnormality! Then one could more easily seize him. But no, he neither threw furious glances around him, nor did he mumble incomprehensible words to himself. Up to now he had never even looked at him (except for this one time), not to say spoken to him. He no longer got in his path; he avoided his path. He was—District Attorney Sierlin had to admit it—calmness, sureness, unconcern, and imperturbability itself. It was this that so upset him; he felt how he was gradually losing his own calmness.

No, there was no getting at this indifference and passivity through force.

If he would meet him again only one single time alone, all alone!

But where?

Should he look for him at home?

Not only did his pride forbid him that, but also it would not be in conformity with his official position (as he believed). And then he was certain not to find him (such young people as this were never at home); or, if he found him, to be turned away.

Write to him? Make him aware in this way of his error? He would never receive an answer and his letter—a private letter!—would get into hands that could use it against his person. He knew how careful he had to be in his position.

He could turn the tables on him and now set into motion from his side regular surveillance and following. Lacking to him personally was the time (over which the other had an unlimited amount at his disposal) and the means for a surveillance by a private detective. These people cost money (much money, as he knew only too well), were not at all sure in regard to their discretion, and then—what would be gained in this case? Nothing. For this man—his feeling told him this again and again—was anything but a criminal and legally untouchable.

District Attorney Sierlin suddenly shrank back from his own thoughts. Where were they leading him? All that was indeed completely indisputable and only showed again that this case possessed an importance for him that was in no way due it—as he had to tell himself after more sensible reflection.

He wanted to wait calmly for the next opportunity to approach him again, one different from this first (on remembering it and the insult suffered the blood rose to his head), and then explain to this poor and no longer responsible young man with all possible friendliness (but also determination) how very much he was in error. Then that man would go his way, and the affair would be settled without attracting any attention. Yes, he wanted to do that and in that way only be done with it.

From the path of his duty, however, this man was also not to bring him away one foot with his madness. He would do it, as he had done it up to now: a protector of justice, a prosecutor of injustice!

He threw himself again into his work.

But he had become irritable, moody, and hard to bear. His

family at home had to suffer under this at first; then the accused in court.

Heads shook more and more over him.

3

It was as if the other man knew his intentions.

For District Attorney Sierlin saw him no more: neither in the neighborhood of his house, nor in that of the court; neither in the café, nor on his homecoming.

And yet he felt more clearly than before that he was still always behind him and on his heels.

Not that he now still saw him clearly and recognizably. But somewhere—in the distance—he was popping up and disappearing again. The man who had just got off the streetcar and walked by him—had it not been he? The shadow that turned around the corner, that shadow of a man, of whom he only saw the back—wasn't that he again? Late one evening on returning home from his evening beer—could he really have deceived himself about the person who had been waiting across the way in half darkness and who had disappeared when he wanted to get a closer look at him? He no longer knew what to think. He wanted to grasp, but grasped only emptiness: shadows.

One day he had Brendicke called to him. Brendicke, court summoner from time immemorial, was an old scamp. Generally known as a shrewd and cunning fellow (although he looked quite harmless with his red nose and his stout little belly), he was just as generally known by the gentlemen of the court as thoroughly discreet. He was submissive and was always there if there was something to be gained. Periodically drunk, but useful in service.

Brendicke appeared.

"Listen, Brendicke," he was instructed, "there is a certain Adolf Braun, businessman, but probably without a position at present; born at such and such a place and such and such a time—have you written it down? Good. Just confirm if this person is registered and where he lives. Try to find out—"

District Attorney Sierlin did not need to finish the sentence. Brendicke knew enough.

On his next free afternoon Brendicke set out for the resident registration office and confirmed that Adolf Braun, businessman etc., was regularly registered and lived at such and such an address (up in the northern part of the city). An hour later he was standing in front of his door. An old woman opened. Brendicke asked whether there might a room for rent. No, she had only one room and that was rented.—Pity!—And it would probably not be free soon.—Tenants often do not stay long, but move on.

Yes, but not her tenant.

Now he had the old woman where he wanted her. Happy to be able to empty her overfull heart, she began to sing his praises in every tone.

What was he thinking—her tenant leaving her?—Such a reliable, fine, young gentleman?—Every evening home by ten at the latest, no visitors, also no women; and the first of every month the rent on the table!

She opened the door to his room: a simple room, but kept clean in every corner—bed, table, wardrobe, an old easy chair, and a table with writing material and books.

But then she became distrustful and already regretted having said too much. She shoved the stranger out. "Look down the street at Plünnecke's, perhaps they have something free."

Now Brendicke did not do that at all, but returned immediately and gave his report.

To his astonishment, the D.A. was not particularly pleased by the good news that he had brought. But he took as honestly earned the three-mark piece that was pressed into his hand.

4

Even more than in the summer Adolf Braun made an effort to steel his nerves for the battle that was now to begin. He regularly went to bed at ten, slept fast and long, and nourished himself well.

He exchanged sport in the fresh air with boxing in the arena. His teacher was soon proud of him and prophesied that, if he continued to train, in a short time he would be able to take on a strong lightweight boxer. He only laughed at that and continued to train. He especially practiced certain defensive maneuvers; he also became familiar with some jujitsu.

His only acquaintance remained his friend Ede. They usually met in the small bar up in the north, where no one knew them.

There was not much more to report during this time than that the D.A. (who had always been a disgusting fellow, as Kitty said) was becoming more unbearable, and that she now wanted to give up her position very soon (but she was again and again hindered from doing so by her fiancé, for she was still needed).

If Eduard saw his friend enter in a good mood, he greeted him with the words:

"Well, did you make your D.A. really angry again?"

If he was not in a good mood, he sought to cheer him up by relating to him all kinds of things that his fiancée told him, and he made suggestions for his part (all impossible to carry out and which Adolf, smiling to himself, never took into consideration).

He never told him the goals that he was pursuing, and little of the ways in which they were to be gained.

He kept silent. But he constantly looked for always new ones. He constantly thought of only *the one thing*!

5

The autumn was uncommonly beautiful and dry. One could still sit comfortably in the open air.

District Attorney Sierlin went on an outing with his family one Sunday afternoon. They still managed to find a table in a densely crowded garden café. As he looked around, he saw "him" at another table in conversation with the others sitting there. He had difficulty distracting the boys so that they did not look over. When he got up under some kind of excuse, the man he sought was gone. Follow him? Where? But in the evening, while returning home, from the platform of the suburban station just after they had left their train and as the train was again leaving the station, he saw him enter the same compartment that his family had just left. Spring after him? Leave everyone standing? Too late!

He had been to a concert with his wife. As he left it and waved to a cab (for it had begun to rain and his wife feared for her dress), the cab was entered by a young man who rode away before his very eyes.

Every fourteen days he had his "evening out" in the back room of one of the larger restaurants. As he entered the front room (he was not alone, the other gentlemen had already joined him), he believed he saw him sitting at a table. He came back. The place was empty.

It was always too late. As often as he tried to corner him—the circumstances always forbid it or he was gone … disappeared … as if sunk into the earth.

But it never ever stopped. He never knew whether or when he would meet him. He was never sure not to meet him.

This man possessed a tenacity, an indefatigableness, an endurance that surpassed everything!

District Attorney Sierlin began to comprehend something of the extent of the hate that was pursuing him, even if he still had no idea what this hate wanted.

He struggled between anger and rage as often as he saw him (or believed that he saw him), and again there arose in him at times this damned feeling that he still always shied away from naming.

6

One day he could stand it no longer.

It was now already in October. He was with his wife in the theater and they were sitting in the parquet. Shortly before the curtain rose a still empty seat in the row in front of him was taken by a young man, who was then sitting almost in front of them.

The whole evening he had this brown and firmly muscled neck, this strong head covered with blond hair, before him and had to force himself to keep his fist from dashing down on it. He heard and saw almost nothing of what was happening on the stage.

He was determined to ask his wife before the intermission to remain sitting, to follow him when he got up, and to confront him. It did not come to that. When the intermission began and the lights came up, the place before him was empty.

The second half of the evening too was spoiled for him. He thought only of him who had just been sitting there.

He could stand it no longer.

He had to talk with someone about the affair. Not to get advice—only to hear what another would do in his place.

For a long time he thought over the question: With whom?

It could only be a jurist like himself. None of his superiors. Naturally none of the gentlemen with whom he had to act officially and constantly. (And self-evidently also not a lawyer—a district attorney who went to a lawyer—it had never happened!) It could only be a friend and a colleague. But he had few friends. Actually, he had only one, and whether he was still truly his friend District Attorney Sierlin was not so sure. In any case he was his mentor in the student corps. An Old Boy now, like him; and when they met in society, they chatted a while with one another, Counselor-at-Law Eberhardt and he, in a quite friendly way.

They also never met officially and therefore also never came into conflict. For Counselor-at-Law Eberhardt had not appeared in court for a long time. He only represented (somewhat haughtily) a large notary office with first-class clientele, in which he condescended to appear on special occasions. He lived in a flat in the Tiergarten district and was known as a rich bon vivant in the grand style.

His pronounced characteristics were joviality and humor—two things that District Attorney Sierlin possessed not a trace of. With his always obliging nature he charmed everyone, and in spite of his corpulence and his gray years, he still stole into the hearts of younger (even much younger) ladies even today.

His wine was famous; his bons mots went from mouth to mouth; the evening parties (for gentlemen) in the comfortable and artistically decorated rooms of the childless widower were considered small events of the season, to which his numerous friends thronged.

Counselor-at-Law Eberhardt was not only a witty person, but one of outstanding talent and would have gone far, if he had not been so comfortable and had preferred the independent life.

So District Attorney Sierlin decided to visit him, although in their hearts they could not stand one another (he called him a man without moral principles and received in return the designation of insufferable, bloody climber).

For Counselor-at-Law Eberhardt was, as was said, the only one who came into consideration; then too he was a man of absolute discretion, in the tender affairs of the heart no less than in the serious ones of his profession.

He announced himself, therefore, and was greeted with kindness, urged to sit in a leather armchair, and provided a Havana cigar.

He was asked about the health of his family, then of his own, and finally, cautiously, about the purpose of his visit. "But you wanted

[ENN]

my advice, dear Sierlin?" The questioned man chewed on his mustache. (A horrible habit, thought the smooth-shaven counselor-at-law—it balls itself up later in the stomach to indigestible lumps.)

"Well, yes, a quite foolish story … really not worth talking about." He waited for help. It did not come. He had to go on alone and gave a quite general picture. "There is a man who for a long time has been following me everywhere." He related several cases.

Counselor-at-Law Eberhardt quickly got the picture.

"So, a pursuer. Why is he pursuing you?"

District Attorney Sierlin chewed further. No, he was not helping him. On the contrary. He hesitated. "The man was innocently imprisoned. He thinks perhaps that I helped put him there."

It was curious, what a sharp expression the friendly blue eyes under the clear lids opposite him could take on, those eyes that not for a moment left him, whereas the voice kept its soft sound as he now asked, "And did you help put him there?"

The answer was brief and sharp. "I only did my duty!"

He always does his duty, thought the counselor-at-law to himself. But one can do his duty this way and that. He always does it—"thus." One day he will run into trouble with his damned duty-doing.

But he only said, "What is he doing to you?"

Now District Attorney Sierlin was almost irritated. "That is just it. He is doing nothing to me. At least nothing that I could catch him with. I see him, wherever I go and stop. Then he is suddenly gone. In the long run it is unbearable and must be put to an end."

The listener kept silent for a long while. He leaned back in this chair, crossed his somewhat too short legs, blew out the smoke of his cigar, and finally said good-naturedly, "Well, my dear Sierlin, now you must just explain that to me somewhat more in detail. Excuse me—but I still don't understand it rightly. He pursues you and does nothing to you. He is there and then always gone again. I really still don't see clearly—"

Driven into a corner, he had to talk about it again. He gave a concise picture of the whole affair. He mentioned again the numerous meetings in the street and in the café. He now also spoke about the meeting at the sea spa and on his return—about all those mysterious and inexplicable meetings whose explanation had already cost him so much racking of his brain, and which were still incomprehensible to him.

The clever, blue eyes again did not leave him for moment.

He concluded: "The fellow is gradually embittering my life. I won't have it any more. It must stop. I won't let myself be taken for a fool any longer by such a rude fellow. I—"

He was interrupted. "But why don't you simply ask him what he wants from you?"

"I just can't do it. I wanted to a hundred times. Either it won't do or he is gone before I can get close to him. The man is mad. He should be locked up."

Counselor-at-Law Eberhardt now finally turned his gaze away and onto the well-groomed nails of his soft, white hand.

The conversation now became entirely question and answer.

"When was the sentence?"

"Two and a half years ago."

"For what?"

"For embezzlement."

"The retrial?"

"A year and half ago."

"And the result?"

"Acquittal. They found the man who did it."

"What do you know about him?"

"Little."—Name, residence, exterior circumstances (money, always has time, decent clothing) were mentioned.

Pause.

Then further:

"How could he have known where you were traveling to this summer?"

"I don't know."

"But he must have learned it?"

District Attorney Sierlin shrugged his shoulders.

He had still not said anything about the trip to Kiel. Now he brought it up and the meeting at the ticket window.

Over the features of the listener there was drawn for the first time a weak, light, amused smile. It was not seen.

"You know, dear Sierlin, the story seems to me just somewhat too improbable. You start on a trip quite suddenly, of which no one but your wife knows. You go to get a ticket and the same man, of whom you speak, is suddenly standing before you and asking for precisely the same, and then does not travel with you. No, you must be mistaken."

District Attorney Sierlin started up. "But I *am* not mistaken! I have seen him, as close in front of me, as I now see you in front of me!"

He received no answer. Still he now noticed the light smile. He wanted to become vehement. But one was not vehement regarding Counselor-at-Law Eberhardt. He therefore controlled himself and only asked, "What would you do in my place, Eberhardt"

This time the answer came without hesitation. "Nothing at all! Let him go on. Ignore him the way he—according to your description—ignores you. And—don't take it evil of me, dear Sierlin—just see the affair also from the other side. A quite obvious injustice was indeed done to the man. He is embittered. It is surely going badly for him. If you see him again, speak to him. In a friendly way. Try to explain his error to him. And if he is in need, help him. Speak humanely with him. Not—pardon me if I say it—not in your at times somewhat hard way. For really it's quite nice of him that he is doing nothing at all to you. Many another—"

The listener shook his head.

He had not been understood. Everything that he had said had been spoken in vain.

"No," he said and his voice was much softer than usual, "no, that's not it. The man doesn't want any help from me. He wants something quite different. What—I don't know. And I can do nothing against him."

"But you are not afraid of him, are you? Afraid of a man who has done and is doing nothing to you," he heard said.

He stood up and raised himself to his full height. "Afraid? Do you believe that I am afraid of any man in the world, Eberhardt!"

Likewise arising slowly, he said appeasingly, "That you have no fear, I know. We were both in the corps and I was your mentor."

After a brief pause, he continued: "I would like to advise you. But how can I? According to all that you told me, you have no hold of any kind on him. He lies in wait for you and runs away when he sees you. He travels after you and departs when you come. A somewhat remarkable kind of pursuing, dear Sierlin, as you will admit. All that lets one conclude that they were pure chance meetings rather than intentional ones. And should not—even if admittedly in the case of some of them a certain, even if quite explainable intention may have been present—should not the majority only exist in your imagination, dear Sierlin?"

He concluded: "In any case your appearance seems to be just as unpleasant to him as his to you. Still, a guarantee of sorts for the future, that you will no longer meet him, or that, if you should meet one another, you will immediately have him out of sight again."

He had not quite come to the end, but a hand was outstretched. "Excuse me, if I have kept you so long, Eberhardt."

"Not in the least! So, if you want to follow my advice: Let him run. If it is really supposed to be a race—I still don't rightly believe in it—then think: One will always get tired first. He will quickly get tired, and sooner than you. This—mysterious unknown man."

They took their leave somewhat suddenly and briefly. "If you need advice again, you know—"

Alone, Counselor-at-Law Eberhardt carefully brushed the ashes from his cigar and thought: A beginning persecution mania! Only the devil can make anything of this story! A pursuer who runs away!

He laughed to himself. Fear? No fear? it was written on your face, my dear, in spite of your big words!

Then again seriously: That's a result of his damned climbing. "Every accused man is guilty, even if he is not." A lovely maxim! But I never liked him, my good Sierlin, not even when—against my will—he wanted me for his mentor.

He, who was the subject of these hardly friendly thoughts, was standing meanwhile in the street, undecided where he wanted to turn.

Then he called a taxi driving by.

He did not notice that he was observed, just as he had been observed on entering the house.

This conversation had failed in its purpose.

He was thinking only of the last words of his friend: Get tired. One will always get tired sooner than the other.

He straightened himself up.

I am not the one! he said to himself.

But he was no longer so sure of himself.

7

"Don't see him! See him as little as he seems to see you!" he had advised. "If you don't exist for one another, it would be impossible for you to cause one another pain."

District Attorney Sierlin realized that the only thing he could do was to follow this advice.

He should have done it long ago, from the very beginning. He should never even notice this man, who was nothing to him, never waste a thought, not to say a glance on him. It had not been worthy of him to stop in the street to look after him, to start or to eye him when he stepped in his path, to spy out the window whether he was still sitting there. It was not right, and besides had been pointless to speak to him on the bench and get brushed off. He could have told himself ahead of time that this man was a lout, a quite shameless fellow, a—

He would therefore see him no more.

That was all the easier, since it was indeed always only a matter of a moment of popping up and disappearing. This coward just ran directly away from him. From now on he would no longer leave even the trace of a thought behind him.

District Attorney Sierlin deceived himself.

For now it was no longer a short moment that he met and saw him. It was as if this enigmatic man had guessed all this thoughts: now when he no longer wanted to see him, when he was no longer to exist for him, he seemed suddenly to aim at being spoken to.

He no longer ran away.

He was sitting in the streetcar almost opposite him, but he did not stand up as usual; he remained seated. He was standing in front of the shop where he was accustomed to buy his cigarettes and was looking over the wares in the window, apparently attentively, when he came out again. He came toward him somewhere, always in a quite unforeseen spot, slowly and thoughtfully. Always it would have been easy now to stop him and start a conversation.

And this man saw now how he was giving himself pains to look away from him. It was not easy, and District Attorney Sierlin felt at every new attempt how the blood rose to his face and his heart began to beat harder—the man was suddenly no longer looking away from him, but rather at him. His eyes slid over his figure from top to bottom before they—like those of an indifferent stranger—again turned away from him.

He looked at him, and through and beyond him, just as if he were not a living being, but rather a dead object without any interest—as if he had never seen him in his life and did not know him. He never looked him in the eyes. It was impossible for him to meet once again the gaze of these eyes; and—he was almost pleased.

No, it was impossible to treat him as he was treated—like air. He had to see him. This was worse than anything. There was such a boundless impudence in this behavior that he could bear it no longer.

He must speak to him. He must finally know what was behind it. It was impossible to follow any longer the advice of the counselor-at-law.

But, after their conversation, he was more than ever determined to avoid any scandal.

However—that too was easier said than done. He never saw him alone. There were always people around them or nearby—those eternally curious Berliners, intent on the least sensation, even if it was only a fallen horse, with their insolent way of talking and their bad, but often so pertinent jokes and remarks.

He therefore gave up his vain attempts to look away from him, rather he returned the glances—returned them again in a provocative, expectant way and—now—inwardly boiling with rage. For again he did not succeed, not even in this way, in catching the glance of those eyes, as on that day of recognition on the bench. They never rose higher on him than his breast. Then they turned away, not disdainfully or even only uncomfortably touched—no, only indifferently, indifferently, infinitely indifferently.

And always the calmness and composure of this young man were unshakable. Nothing seemed able to upset him. He sat there; he stood there; he walked by him and on farther—and no motion betrayed that he was here, precisely here, only for one definite goal: that with all this only *one* goal was being pursued—a quite definite goal. He was always the same—in his attitude, in the expression of his face, his firm and self-confident walk, the walk of strong and unconcerned youth.

Always and unassailably the same—whereas he, District Attorney Sierlin, was little by little becoming another person. Earlier in his life and striving he had been a conceited, hard, and pitiless man. He had been self-confident, rigid, and unbending in his principles and the three thoughts he held to be correct. Now he was vacillating, uncertain, and restless.

Not that he had in any way changed his views. He was of a

much too shallow and basically insincere nature to recognize a once formed view as false and to throw it resolutely overboard and put another in its place.

What so boundlessly angered and enraged him was his powerlessness. For what reason were the laws there, if in such a case as this one—a case such as had never come to his attention before, such as had probably never before occurred—if they did not protect him here? How was it possible that he himself found no advice among his associates—from his only friend?—that he had not once dared to defy the judgment of society, in the fear of making himself ridiculous and left all alone. For he would make himself ridiculous. After the conversation with such a clever and personally experienced and skilled man as Eberhardt, he was no longer in doubt about it (for that light smile had not escaped him). He was no longer sure. He had nothing more on which to support himself, as he had had up to now in every situation. The laws failed, the written and the unwritten.

He was exposed to this man who had run up, this monomaniac, this—

It was unbearable.

It could not go on. It could not go on like this.

No, he could not and should not be like air for him any longer. He should become a man of flesh and blood, whom he now finally wanted to grasp. He wanted to grasp this body, hold him between his fingers, shake him until he finally gave up his secret—that secret: what, *what* did he want from him!

He wanted to hear this voice again, this forgotten voice, which he had heard only once (that time, and which in a remarkable way was now quite audible to him again over the years). He wanted to hear it again, and—oh!—make it speak. Wanted to feel the gaze of these eyes again into his and then meet them so that they should never look down again.

Was he not a man in comparison to this lad? Was he not District Attorney Sierlin? Only the next opportunity needed to come, then the matter would end. Once and for all.

He waited for it, this opportunity. Even if it was among people—no matter. He would no longer pass it up.

He wished to see him. He it was, who was now looking for him again.

But the days went by; almost two weeks went by. He saw him nowhere.

He had remained in the city to shop for a few necessary things. It was a Saturday, toward evening, and very lively on the streets and in all the shops. In the department store too. As he went to pay at counter 43 on the fourth floor of the large store, he saw how a young man in front of him pocketed money and with the receipt in his hand turned toward the delivery desk. He quickly threw down his amount, received the sales slip, and saw the same young man receive a small package and disappear into the aisles between the piled-up goods. He left his purchase behind, hurried after him, saw him disappear among the thronging people, then pop up again and turn into a less visited department, that of pictures and photographs.

He appeared not to be in a hurry. Now he was standing still before a picture and seemed to be carefully examining it.

The moment had come.

District Attorney Sierlin stepped beside him, stopped, and said, more to himself than as addressed to the other (who did not move), but distinctly enough that it must be understood, "I have something to discuss with you. I wish an explanation from you. I—"

The man spoken to appeared not to hear a word, as if he were deaf.

He walked on farther, without having given a glance to the side, and remained standing at the next display before another picture, apparently also giving it his entire attention.

District Attorney Sierlin was beside him again. He was trembling.

Somewhat more loudly (for they were no longer entirely alone) and even more distinctly he said, "You appear not to have understood me. I would like to have an explanation from you. Do you understand me now? Your behavior—"

The man addressed for the second time now finally appeared to have understood that someone was speaking to him. His glance went sideways onto the figure standing beside him, from his feet on up to his breast. In the otherwise so unmoving face there now showed for the first time an expression, a clearly recognizable expression. It was the expression of an unconcealed aversion. Then he shrugged his shoulders, turned away, and joined the stream of people in the next aisle, which carried him on and away.

District Attorney Sierlin remained behind, as at that time on the bench. Across his face, flushed with blood, the scars were drawn like white chalk marks.

8

Counselor-at-Law Eberhardt was sitting at home at his desk— occupied with answering a letter written in a tender hand (an invitation for this evening to a small, discreet dinner)—when his servant announced a visitor: District Attorney Sierlin.

He angrily covered the unfinished letter, but met the arrival with his usual kindness. His sharp eyes immediately noticed the change that the last month had brought to his face. He saw the distortion in the smile, the insecurity in the quavering eyes, the fidget in the hands.

But he said nothing. He waited.

"Pardon, Eberhardt, if I burden you once again with this— uh—this foolish affair—" The counselor-at-law made no attempt to suppress a certain questioning astonishment in his look.

"You remember—this fellow—who pursues—" Quite suddenly his visitor jumped up, grabbed him by the arm, and drew him to the window.

With a completely changed, a husky and hardly still controlled

ENN)

voice the counselor-at-law heard him say further, "There he is. He is standing down there!"

He looked out. "Where? I see no one."

The voice beside him became a whisper, and there was in it now nothing but naked fear. "I tell you, he is there! He is standing down there and is waiting for me. He is again after me."

Now Counselor-at-Law Eberhardt knew what the matter was and what he had to do. He tried to put a bright tone into his answer as he drew his friend back from the window.

"If he is there, we will seize him. Come!"

He quickly preceded him into the hallway, helped him into his fur coat, and made himself ready to go out. The other man followed as if he had no will of his own.

In the street he asked lightly, "Now, dear Sierlin, where is your so-called pursuer then?"

Far and wide no one was to be seen.

Only an auto slipped between them and the bare trees of the Tiergarten and disappeared in the next second.

"But he was still here when I came to you."

The counselor-at-law said appeasingly, "You know, Sierlin, let's take a half-hour walk through the park. The fresh air will do us both good."

They silently walked over the roadway and onto the paths on the other side.

It was the counselor-at-law alone who spoke. He asked nothing. He spoke of other things, distant things, as if he had entirely forgotten the point of the visit. He received only short and meaningless answers from the gloomy man walking beside him. They were now at one of the ponds and walking along it. Its surface was covered with a light crust of ice, which the dark water broke through here and there. The bare trees gave a free view toward all sides. All the paths were deserted. So far they had met no more than three people.

Suddenly Counselor-at-Law Eberhardt felt himself frantically gripped by the arm and held fast. The husky voice beside him whispered, "There—over there on the bench—there he sits!"

On one of the benches on the other side of the lake a figure was sitting—as it appeared, that of a still young man. His face was not recognizable, for it was buried in his hands, which were propped on his knees. He was sitting motionless. Since he could not have fallen asleep in this cold, he must be deeply lost in thought. He was wearing, as far as this could be recognized from here, a sort of winter jacket and brown leather gloves on his hands.

The counselor-at-law was in fact astonished. Involuntarily just as softly, as if he could be heard, he asked, "Are you quite certain that it is he?"

The grip on his arm relaxed. He heard the husky voice again, trembling now from suppressed rage: "Certain? Quite certain! He has followed us."

Followed? he thought. It was absolutely impossible. For a half hour they had wandered in all directions through the park, had just now turned back, had often stopped, had looked around—no person had followed them. Besides, how was the supposed pursuer to land quickly over there where he was sitting now, his face in his hands?

He expressed his thoughts.

"No!" he received as answer, "no, you don't know him. But now—now—" District Attorney Sierlin looked as if he would hurry over there.

But he was held back. "So he runs away from you again when he sees you. He has younger legs than you. No, let me speak with him. He doesn't know me. Stay calmly here. Walk around here in the meanwhile, or better there behind the bushes, and wait until I return!"

The counselor-at-law was gone before he even received an answer. With short and quick steps he hurried down the path, crossed the iron bridge over the lake, and walked toward the bench on the other side, where the figure was still sitting in an unchanged attitude. Close before it he stopped. Then he walked up to him.

The young man looked up.

Counselor-at-Law Eberhardt looked into a young, smooth-shaven, except for a slight mustache, sun-tanned face, with light-brown eyes, looking at him hardly astonished.

He liked it, this face, he liked it at first glance. (He liked it much better than that of his friend.)

I will be easily done with him, he thought, a simple, nice young man.

Aloud, he said, while he sat next to him and lightly raised his hand, as if he would lay it on the arm of the other in the next moment—he said aloud with his soft voice, this famous voice, with which he knew how to ingratiate himself into all hearts (and especially into the young ones of the opposite sex), the voice that no one could so easily withstand, "My dear, young friend, I would like to speak a word with you. But since it is really too cold to sit here longer, won't you have the goodness to walk up and down a bit with me."

He stood up.

The young man did the same. In his eyes there now entered a questioning expression.

But he only said, as he now removed his hat and bowed politely, "Then you will surely allow me first to introduce myself. My name is Adolf Braun."

Counselor-at-Law Eberhardt was known for not being easily upset. At this moment he almost was. In any case he was not immediately clear whether what he had just heard was politeness or a boundless impertinence. He decided for the time being to assume it was the former and therefore, lightly touching his hat with his finger, but involuntarily stretching up his short figure, casually said on his side, "Counselor-at-Law Eberhardt. And now—if it is alright with you—"

With his hand he made an inviting motion down the path.

Before they walked, the other took his place to his left with a quick movement (as is entirely proper for a younger person).

They walked along beside one another.

The soft voice began again: "I have, namely, a friend, an old friend, whom you likewise know. Between you two there has apparently arisen a small misunderstanding, which I would be honestly pleased to clear up in the interest of both of you. With a bit of goodwill, in a short time it will—"

He paused and considered how he should continue.

When he was about to start again, he heard the same calm and polite voice that had just introduced himself say, "May I ask, Herr Counselor-at-Law, of whom you are speaking?"

Again Counselor-at-Law Eberhardt was close to being startled. Was this young man playing a game with him? Was it naiveté or impudence? He was strong, this man here.

But he did not want to lose his mood and so began again. He spoke now in the considered and self-sure tone in which he had earlier spoken with his clients, when they sought to lie to him, in that tone colored with light irony.

"Naturally you may ask. As much as you wish. But why? You know as well as I who is being discussed. We both know that you were innocently sentenced a couple of years ago, then acquitted. That makes a man, such a young man as you are, bitter. He fancies that he has unjustly been cast into misfortune—intentionally unjustly. He seeks for the opponent, throws all his hate on him, and commonly hits upon the wrong man. As you in your case—"

The man walking beside him was listening with blameless politeness. Without interrupting, he had listened to the words, his head somewhat tilted to the side, as though not one of them should escape him. Now, when he was silent, he calmly asked, clearly emphasizing each word, "And on whom am I supposed to have thrown my entire hatred?"

They did not stop, but continued walking. The counselor-at-law was not the man to let himself be pressed to the wall by any person. He said briefly, and his voice now sounded sharp, "On the district attorney in your case, an old friend of mine, as I have already said!"

Since he received no answer, he continued in the same tone,

"You will hardly want to maintain that you do not know Herr District Attorney Sierlin?"

The answer betrayed not the least interest. Rather a certain indifference.

"I know the Herr District Attorney—from that time—slightly—from appearance—"

"No," said Counselor-at-Law Eberhardt, "no, my young friend, you know him not only slightly, but quite exactly. You often see him, for months already. You lie in wait for him. You travel after him. But let us rather leave that. I beg you for only one thing: tell me what you are aiming at. And why do you disappear every time and always in such a mysterious fashion when you have seen him?"

The other did not answer, as if he were too astonished over what he had heard to find an immediate answer to it.

He only shook his head as if in surprise, and Counselor-at-Law Eberhardt in fact did not know what he was to think of him. But he was not an old jurist for nothing. He softly said, "Perhaps you will tell me why you did not travel that time when you bought a ticket for the same train and for the same destination as my friend? Why you then departed immediately when he arrived at the spa?"

The questioned man stopped. He stood before the questioner and looked at him. In his look was neither hate nor bitterness, in his voice no longer any trace of politeness, as he now answered, "Because I cannot bear the sight of that gentleman!"

His look was returned. And he who returned it recognized how very much he had deceived himself when he held this young man to be harmless. In these young eyes lay such an unbendable will, such a firmness of will, and at the same time so much suffered pain, such a hopeless loneliness, that he kept silent. The same feeling of sympathy that had so strongly gripped him at first sight, came over Counselor-at-Law Eberhardt again. It was an unhappy human being who was standing here before him: not a crazy man, not an evil man—someone deeply offended, defrauded of his happiness in life.

He sought for a word to comfort him—to convince him that he meant him well. He did not find it. When he found it, he did not get to speak it.

For he saw him—again quite unexpectedly—put his hat on and bow politely, and he heard him say, again with the same indifferent voice as before, "And now, Herr Counselor-at-Law, you will allow me to view as ended this conversation that you brought about."

Counselor-at-Law Eberhardt retraced his path more slowly than he had come, and with not quite so light and enthusiastic steps. He was thinking: either this man, who has just now left, is an actor such as I have seldom seen and has nerves of steel; or my old Sierlin has completely misunderstood everything, is seeing ghosts, and is actually in the first stage of a persecution mania.

But then he laughed to himself. The humor of the situation he had just experienced came over him. He repeated to himself, "Allow me Herr Counselor-at-Law—to view as ended—may I ask—" All a bit learned. But from where did he get it, this simple fellow?

He had not yet formed a conclusive judgment over his new acquaintance when he saw the figure of the man waiting on the other side walking up and down, and his whole anger now directed itself toward him.

He saw the long legs behind the bushes.

Like a stork in salad—he further thought. Damned fellow! He had never been less able to stand him than now.

He gave himself little effort to hide his true mood as he briefly reported to the man regarding him expectantly what he had experienced, and then he concluded: "He does not at all deny knowing you. Why does he go out of your way? Because he can't bear the sight of you." (Counselor-at-Law Eberhardt would not have been able to suppress this last expression for anything in the world).

I rather should have, he thought right after.

For the laughter in which the other broke out was so horrible, that he was startled. It was shrill, morbid. And it was embarrassing—here in a public path after all, where an acquaintance could

come by at any moment. But the other appeared not to be thinking about that. He only cried, no, he screamed over and over and
made a regular dance around him, "That's the limit! The limit! He
can't bear the sight of *me*! Hahaha! He, this fellow who has put
himself everywhere in my path for almost a year—he can't bear the
sight of me!"

The horrible laughter started over and over again.

Even Counselor-at-Law Eberhardt, who was known for *never*
getting angry, began to get angry: over this Adolf Braun, who had
led him around by the nose and from whom he had learned not
the least about what he wanted to know; over himself, because he
had taken an obviously false tone with him; and over this tall, half-
mad fellow at his side, who howled and laughed in turn, and listened to no more consolation.

It had to stop. Besides, an only half-finished letter was lying
in his house, which must go out immediately, if he did not want
to deprive himself of the small, discreet dinner this evening.

He therefore said with the greatest possible determination,
"Calm yourself, my dear Sierlin. You will gain nothing in this way.
We are not alone here. As far as the matter itself is concerned, I
regret I can give you no more advice. For I don't understand it. I
absolutely do not understand it. And now"—he reached for his
hand—"pardon, I must go home—a pressing engagement."

He left the man standing, suddenly mute and staring straight
ahead.

While walking away he was thinking: "That will come to no
good end for you, my dear Sierlin. You're already a bit crazy. It
should not get any worse with you. The other man, however—
whoever holds him to be crazy would err greatly—he knows what
he wants. But what does he want?"

But then his thoughts went toward the coming evening. They
were already with the little girl from the Metropol Revue. She was
also a bit crazy. In another way. But that was precisely what was
attractive about her.

9

Not only would anyone who had doubted Adolf Braun's clear intellect have been deceived, but also whoever would have believed that his work—this work carried out with such unexampled tenacity—had been easy. Its entire difficulty could only have been judged by someone observing it. But no one saw it.

Especially this last quarter year, from the end of the vacation until now, had required an excess of energy, self-control, and patience, compared to which the first months of spring and summer—with their meetings at definite times and in predetermined places—had been the purest child's play.

Now, when every single one of these meetings no longer was based on definite hours, but happened quite without choice (and was supposed to happen this way), one hour of coming together cost many of waiting—hours to stage one minute or even only one second of seeing, being seen, and departing.

And how many of these hours were in vain: the man sought did not come, stayed away, or was, even with the sharpest pursuing, all at once out of sight!

When he learned certain clues from his friend Eduard (who was constantly kept in the know by his Kitty), it was easiest.

For example, she had to procure a theater ticket, met her boyfriend in the morning, sent him to the theater box office. He naturally noted the row and number of the seats and brought them to this friend, who that same day bought a seat in the row in front. Thus he was sitting almost in front of the enemy and his wife that evening. But he himself had likewise no real pleasure in the performance. He plainly felt the boring looks in the back of his neck, but betrayed himself by no movement.

The meeting in the tram too was by far not as convenient as in the summer, for District Attorney Sierlin now came home at quite irregular times, and often, in order to see him (and be seen), he had to stand and wait for hours at a tram stop.

But when a whole day passed like that: with waiting for him, looking for him, walking and riding after him, until the opportunity finally arose (or did not), then it was not entirely easy, especially during wet and cold weather. Then even he, who was hardened against everything, against all weather and every feeling, was ready to collapse from fatigue in the evening.

It was after the return from the trip. He saw what an effort his enemy made not to look at him. How he looked over him, as though he had not seen him. He saw what exertion it cost him. He saw how his look became uneasy before he turned away. He saw his slight cringe.

He himself now no longer looked over and beyond him. He looked at him, indifferently, unknowingly, and then immediately away again. But he never looked him in the eyes. Their glances never met one another. That too was intentional.

He noticed how the other was again and again on the point of coming up to him and speaking to him (as that time on the bench), and how he again and again gave up the approach. He must have chosen to ignore him. He could not let that succeed!

During this time he was often at home, especially in the evenings, and seldom saw his friend Ede. After a hard day of successful or useless waiting (regardless of the weather), he allowed himself these evening hours of rest by the warm tile stove in the old easy chair.

There he sat many hours and brooded. For everything, everything, that he did was carefully thought out ahead of time, from the very beginning and, as far as was possible, down to every detail.

It was his work, on which he labored as only an artist does. It formed itself, took shape, grew and grew.

Just how was it that he had first come to these thoughts, which he himself had at first held to be nonsense and impossible to carry out, and which now had after all become reality, such as he had not hoped or dreamed? How did it happen?

Years before, even before his misfortune, as he was drinking a glass of beer with a colleague who was much occupied with the questions of hypnosis and suggestion, of spiritualism and such things—quite foreign to him—the man had told him of the influence on the human will by another human will, and they had immediately made a test. In the—not very frequented—restaurant a gentleman was sitting a few tables distant from them, reading the newspaper. His colleague began to fix his eyes on him—boring his unmoving gaze into the neck of the stranger. A quarter—a half hour long. Adolf Braun saw how the stranger gradually became uneasy, how he looked around, how he laid down his newspaper, and how he finally stood up to leave in an ill temper.

Persistence, patience, and a strong will—those were the requirements, his colleague said.

For fun he had then occasionally tried it himself, but without any particular success.

From this seed had then developed, first the thought, then the decision to his plan.

Many hours he had sat there, brooding and brooding, until he was that far.

And he was still sitting there, brooding on and on.

Or he read.

Since he had time and money, he was again reading a lot, as he had done as a boy. Now these were mostly the better criminal and society stories, which he brought home in stacks from the lending library.

The first were to help him find new tricks. He saw himself lamentably disappointed. They did not nourish his own inventiveness, and he set them aside again to say to himself with satisfaction that no one except he had come upon *his* method. No one besides himself. It was absolutely new and original.

The others, the society novels, served to acquaint him with the life of the circle that his enemy frequented. He wanted to know how one acted there and how one spoke. He learned whole phrases by heart, spoke them to himself, and even if they did not become part of his flesh and blood, he did have them at hand just in case.

He studied his own face in the mirror. Like an actor, he gave it every possible expression, to learn how to control each one. Then he put on the old and tested mask again—the mask of indifference, of inapproachability, of absence from everything that was happening around him.

Persistence, patience, strength of will—he incessantly told himself that these alone could lead him to his goal.

He possessed all three. He never became tired. He was never discouraged. He began tomorrow where he had left off today. He was like the hunter who pursued his game until he had bagged it.

He knew every move of his opponent. He saw now how it was no longer possible for him to look away from him, when he again sought to approach him.

He let him struggle a bit more—escape a few times yet, before he let it come to the first serious confrontation.

He knew exactly that his enemy would also still avoid arousing any kind of scandal (although he was nearly bursting with rage).

Thus it came to the meeting in the department store. On that day Adolf Braun had been, unnoticed, on the heels of District Attorney Sierlin for hours: he had followed him from the court to the department store, where, always hidden by the throng of people, he had to make three small purchases before he succeeded in meeting him at the payment counter. But then everything proceeded as planned.

His studies—for these were regular studies—had also on the day of the visit to Counselor-at-Law Eberhardt led him after him and into the neighborhood of the house in which he lived. His enemy had not deceived himself, when he believed he had seen him. He had followed him. But what then happened on that afternoon was a pure game of chance.

He had—he himself did not know why—abandoned waiting

in front of the house for his return. It was not fatigue, but a certain feeling of satiety—really for the first time—that came over him.

Thus he had then walked deeper into the park and sat down on one of the benches. It was cool, but all the same—one could sit here.

As always, he was thinking only of the one thing. He wished it would now soon end. But he still saw no end.

All at once he saw across the way two gentlemen walking up and down. On the other bank of the lake. He knew the one; the other he had never seen. He remained sitting. But he propped his face in his hands. If he had been seen, that was good. If he was not seen, that was good too. He wanted to wait.

Then he saw the strange gentleman—a short, thick-set man in a fur coat, with a round face and blue eyes—in front of him.

He pulled himself together. He knew it was now a matter of words. He selected each one. He thought of his books and what he had read in them. Much was suitable.

He was very satisfied with the result of the conversation and with himself.

That had again been a bit of good luck!

He knew now: his enemy was already seeking help.

No help, not God's, not man's, was to help him!

He decided to leave him in peace again until Christmas.

Then the holiday was to be spoiled for him.

10

On Christmas Eve, District Attorney Sierlin himself shopped every year in the suburban market for a Christmas tree, carried it home himself, and decorated it there.

Adolf Braun had learned of this practice in the well-known detour through his friend.

He had at the same time been pressured: "You will spend the

evening with us, won't you Adolf? With me and my fiancée, whom I have you to thank for—and whom you still haven't met."

He declined. He would guard against meeting her. Not yet. Only then, when everything was past. She would have been able to recognize him—from his sitting on the bench, his hanging about the house in spring.

Ede was deeply offended.

"You're a very funny fellow, Adolf," he said. But he had to resign himself. He knew how impossible it was to influence him in many things.

The day before Christmas was clear and frosty. Adolf Braun was already at his post in the early afternoon—in the market where the fir trees were on sale. He walked among the trees robbed of their earth, again and again felt the urge to buy one, and saw the last shoppers come. In a few hours the place would be empty and a forest no longer.

He waited, as he had now waited countless times before—for him.

But this time he was not up to par. There was not the tense attention in his features, with which he otherwise observed everything that happened around him.

He was standing at times minutes-long, as if lost in thought. Then he started up and reminded himself of his duty. He was not here for dreaming!

When it became evening, no more buyers came and the unsold trees were again bound together and thrown onto a pile, he left.

He walked the whole, long way up to the north of the city by foot. He interrupted his hike once, entered an empty tavern, and ordered something to eat. Only late in the evening did he reach his house.

His old landlady was away—with relatives, to celebrate the holiday with them. He had given her a warm jacket; she gave him a little tree with three thin lights and a plate filled with pastry.

She set her old heart on the young man, treating him like her son (who had fallen in the war). In the morning she had said to him, "You will go out, won't you Herr Adolf? This evening?"

He had soothed her. Yes, he would not stay at home.

Now he was here anyway.

He stood at the window and looked over the roofs—roofs—roofs—

They lay in rows, black under the milky sky.

No sound of life came up from below—no sound, no light.

He had not seen him today, his enemy.

Another day was lost.

But for the first time he was almost glad.

It was as if a voice were speaking in him: Give it up. He has been punished enough.

But as he was standing in his room again and, as so often, before the pictures of his parents in the cheap frame, his face again took on the old expression, the hard expression that at times instilled in even such a hardened person as his friend Eduard a feeling of discomfort (since it seemed not at all to go with his usual so amiable and friendly nature).

Even the words that he was speaking to himself sounded harsh. "No! For I'm not revenging myself. I'm revenging you!"

*

He had been seen.

District Attorney Sierlin had just paid for the tree he bought and taken it under his arm, when he saw him standing at some distance.

His first impulse was again to run after him. The opportunity seemed favorable. Then he suppressed it; this evening should not also become spoiled for him.

But he could not refrain from spying over, now, when he was not seen and could hardly be recognized through the trees. In the face of the man standing there, staring down at the ground, he saw an expression that he had not yet known, and it seemed to him more foreign and uncanny than ever.

Furtively, so as not to be seen, he held his tree firmly under his arm and slipped away.

The evening was spoiled for him anyway.

11

The short Christmas break was long past. The court sessions had begun again and it was nearing the end of January.

It was as if a turn in events should come in with the new year: District Attorney Sierlin saw his pursuer no longer. He saw him neither on the street nor in the neighborhood of his house. He saw him nowhere, as often as he also looked out for him.

But on the inside he did not become calmer. On the contrary, he thought again and again about this case. On one hand, it tormented him that he could not get behind those unexplained meetings and their purpose. On the other hand, a secret rage was gnawing at him, he was so helpless, so inextricably helpless against this fellow—he never named him otherwise. He was the weaker—in every respect. He did not deceive himself about it.

Something vehement and overwrought had come into his whole being. He had always been "somewhat too," as that malicious Lübeck assistant judge had recognized. Now he became "all too much." He walked with even longer strides. He spoke with an even louder and more provocative voice. His moods changed from one minute to the next. His associates trembled before him—at his moods, his domineering nature, his outbreaks of unmotivated vehemence over every little triviality.

In his official acts his motions went to the farthest limit, the lawyers more than once gave up their defense and left the room.

He was avoided wherever possible. He noticed it and became more and more irritated with every day.

It was the last session of the third week in January—a case

against the accountant of a large business, who was on trial for embezzlement.

He was speaking and was almost finished with his speech for the prosecution, when he was interrupted by a rude and improper shout from the visitors' gallery. That happened now often and he no longer concerned himself about it. This time too. The presiding judge intervened, had the disturber—a drunken bum—thrown out and threatened to clear the gallery if the incident was repeated. Calm was restored and they were waiting for the continuation, or rather, the end of the speech.

But District Attorney Sierlin appeared unable to find the thread again. The small incident appeared to have excited him. He leafed restlessly through the papers that lay before him. Only after a while did he find his speech again, and everyone was astonished at the small measure of punishment that he then—after such a vehement prosecution—almost hastily asked for.

This time he took an taxi, rode directly home, went to his room, and closed himself in, without having eaten.

In a fleeting glance at the visitors' gallery he had seen a well-known face. It was a serious and reserved, young face, whose eyes went in another direction than at him. But he recognized it. He knew it only too well.

District Attorney Sierlin walked to and fro in his room for more than an hour.

How did the "fellow" get there? Stupid question! The gallery was open to every citizen.

So this was the new trick that he had brought out against him! And again, he was powerless against it, as against his earlier ones, against all of them without exception. Powerless and helpless.

With his family, he sat taciturn over a meal grown cold; taciturn and reserved he remained all the following days.

He no longer looked around him when he was on the street; he no longer looked over at the empty bench, as he had so often done. He knew quite exactly that he would see him *there* from now on.

KENN]

He did not want to see him, but—had to.

Whereas he usually almost never looked up at the visitors—they had nothing to do with him and his duty—he now looked them over with his first glance, as soon as he was in his seat. If he did not see what he was looking for, his speech became calmer and more determined; if he saw him, he lost clarity, urgency, persuasive power, and he felt it, even more since the others in the room felt it—the judges, the jury, the defense lawyers (who immediately caught on).

He no longer walked into a session without thinking: Will he be there today—the fellow?

Often he was not. But again and again he saw him there, not always in the same seat, but always in the midst of other visitors—still and discreet, without looking over at him, and without any particular interest, as it appeared.

Yet he was there.

It *must* come to an end. Justice suffered under the presence of this man in this room. One day, as he was leaving the court building, he saw him coming out. He had already seen him earlier, up there, and he had been able to finish his speech only with an effort. He had spoken worse, more disconnectedly than ever, and yet was better prepared than he had usually been recently. He was beside himself with anger, with resentment, with rage.

He looked around him. Among the people around him there was, by chance, no one he knew. Now!

He followed him. He caught up with him. The street was nearly empty.

He was beside him. He was trembling so much from suppressed rage that he had to control himself not to take him by the arm and forcibly hinder him from walking on.

He gnashed out half-loud words, while he walked along beside him: "This must come to an end! Do you understand me? This has been going on now for almost a year. But it *must* not go on like this! Don't you hear what I'm saying to you? I'm speaking to you, you insolent lout you! Stand still! Stop right here and listen to me, do you understand?"

But he, beside whom he was striding and to whom he was speaking, had continued walking and walked on as if he did not hear or see him. He held his hands in the pockets of his jacket, and his glance was indifferent and directed straight ahead. Only it seemed as if he was now seeking the middle of the sidewalk, to get to where the number of passersby would be greater.

District Attorney Sierlin suddenly sprang in front of him and blocked his path.

He gasped, "Don't you understand me, you damned lout? You are to stop and listen to me—listen to what I'm saying to you!"

Now the other finally stopped. He would have had to touch him if he had continued walking. He let an icy glance glide up and down the man standing before him, then turned to one side with a quick movement and shouted with a voice so loud that it would have to be heard by everyone nearby and distinct in every word, "Stop molesting me or I will have you arrested!"

The people around them stopped and looked with curiosity at the two of them. What did this older, obviously so excited gentleman want from this much younger man with the open, nice face?—the young man who was now walking on, as calmly as if nothing had happened and as if he had only shaken off an irksome and improper advance—what did he want from him then?

They only dispersed, with satirical remarks, when the older man had also turned and disappeared.

District Attorney Sierlin was as if stunned. His only thought now was not to be seen or recognized. He turned involuntarily into one of the quieter side streets. The glances of those left behind burned like fire into his back.

Now he was alone, as far as he could see. Suddenly, however, he began to run. He ran through streets that he did not know, on and on, hurried farther and always farther, as though he were chased like a criminal.

After an hour he found himself, bathed in sweat and out of breath, in a quiet tavern of a strange neighborhood before a glass of beer in a corner.

If he had a sense of humor (such as his friend Eberhardt possessed), then he would now, as he collected his thoughts, have become conscious of the grotesqueness of the scene just experienced: this unbelievable impudence, him, wanting to have *him* arrested! This impudence, which could already no longer be taken seriously, since it collapsed in its own enormity. But alas, District Attorney Sierlin possessed no sense of humor, and so he was overcome now by only one feeling: of having been made ridiculous, ridiculous to others and—to himself. He had been hit in his most sensitive spot. And if he had been recognized—what then?—

Here he was not recognized, could not be recognized. Besides, he was and remained almost alone in the tavern. He remained sitting and sitting, without the ability to get up, drank one glass after another, without any effect, and did not know when and how he got home.

Glances had also followed Adolf Braun. But he did not see them. What did other people and their glances matter to him!

He too possessed little sense of humor. If he had ever possessed it, then it had been lost with the unconcerned cheerfulness of his youth.

Today however he was again cheerful. As he had not been for a year.

He walked home and decided to spend the evening with Ede—to celebrate to a certain extent. For in him was a pure and great joy. He had succeeded once again! Things had gone exactly as he had wanted. Hopefully his enemy had been recognized and was now the talk of his circles!

How furious he had been, this Herr District Attorney! How he had behaved—like a half-crazy person! And how he had run away, when he saw, what he had caused. Adolf Braun laughed and laughed.

He felt that today he had come a new and good way forward with his plan—and now hopefully it was coming to an end.

It had now become so comfortable, this plan: no more watching, no more waiting, no more reflection—he only needed to sit up there in the well-heated room among the other people, and already his opponent was upset. Naturally he could have done that from the very beginning. But it was not part of his well thought out plan, and that it had been better to reserve the knock-out blow until the end he now recognized with satisfaction.

Now only diligently to further attend the sessions; further generous handshakes with the ushers there, who all knew him already and constantly found a seat for him; then another encounter, or for that matter even several, if possible again in the open street (he was armed and prepared for anything). The end could not be far off.

Ede had a jolly companion for this evening, and they could not stop laughing. But what the real cause of his dear friend's joviality was, he did not learn today either.

CHAPTER FOUR:
THE VICTORY

1

District Attorney Sierlin was apparently not recognized, for nothing happened.

Only one thing: Now, as often as he was speaking and raised his glance up, he saw two eyes in the gallery calmly and firmly directed at him, eyes that—even from up there—had always looked away from him. Now they looked at him—not impudently and provocatively, no, on the contrary, with undisguised and therefore really flattering interest they followed his presentations, they seemed to approve and praise them.

If up to then the presence of this fellow had angered, disturbed, irritated him—the gaze of these calm, interested, insolent (beyond all measure!) eyes upset him completely. But he could do nothing against them—the benches up there were for everyone, and there was nothing in the behavior of the one sitting there that would have given a possibility to intervene. He disturbed the proceedings in no way. He only sat there and listened—discreetly, one among many, and did not move from the spot as long as the session lasted.

District Attorney Sierlin was boiling. It was now already the fifth or sixth time in this month, February, that he felt his last bit of self-control disappearing under these glances. It cost him the most tremendous self-command to stand up and to speak, as soon as he knew "he" was there, listening and—looking at him.

He *should* let himself notice nothing. He *should* not betray himself. It would be meaningless and pointless. He knew it. As he had no one he would have been able to confide in without having to hear, "You are just deceiving yourself. So just don't pay any attention to him. I really don't understand,"— just as no one would understand him, but everyone would think *him* mad on the relating of this whole unbelievable story (and especially its details), so too he felt that he should not reveal it. One single time, to the counselor-at-law, the friend of his youth—yes. But he was not so stupid as not to sense how very much he had gambled away—and forever.

He was boiling. What anger he had had to swallow this year— it went beyond his strength. He was surrounded by an invisible, fine-mesh net that was drawing closer and closer around him. He had no more rest. He had no more peace. He also had no more joy, not even in his children, who only disturbed his thoughts, the thoughts that never got away from this fellow, this dog, who was after him. He was boiling with rage. Even the thought of his duty no longer held him erect. He felt more and more that he was losing the ability to carry it out. He spoke badly under those eyes— too mildly, too generally, so little to the point. Or he started up, became his old self—and spoke vehemently, persuasively, with chest tones, and—still did not get to the point.

He had already thought about having himself be transferred— with an unbearable feeling of shame and humiliation. Flee from this fellow? Give way? Openly admit his defeat regarding him? Unbearable and—impossible!

For one thing, his wife would rather leave him than leave Berlin, the beloved city with its swarm of relatives and acquaintances.

And then, was he certain that his dog would not follow him to his new residence and also molest him there? This man could be trusted to do *anything*. There was nothing that he now thought him incapable of, when it came to angering him, pursuing him— hunting him.

(Hunting—what a terrible word!)

He could retire. He had not yet thought of that, for that would be the end. To retire—at his age? With his abilities? Not only unworthy, but likewise completely unthinkable.

District Attorney Sierlin was boiling with inner rage. He boiled the whole day during proceedings.

He boiled while he himself was speaking.

He boiled as often as his glance only touched on the gallery.

He boiled during the ride home in the unbearably overcrowded and uncomfortable streetcar, in which he never found a seat.

He boiled as he left the transfer stop and crossed the street to buy some necessary things in a shop on the other side.

His mood—at the boiling point for many hours—did not improve when he found the street blocked. Two autos had run together and a crowd of people was around them. It was the usual picture: drivers shouting at one another, accusing each other; two policemen with open, thick notebooks; a swarm of breathless curiosity seekers—Berliners.

He did not want to stop. Rather he wanted to go around the crowd of people. While he was doing it, he saw how a young man approached and also stopped—apparently likewise curious—to see what has happening. He did not appear to see him.

But District Attorney Sierlin saw him no longer either. For suddenly everything became red before his eyes. He controlled himself no longer. He was seeing nothing more. He was thinking nothing more.

With a suppressed cry of irrational rage, he sprang at him and grabbed him on the chest. But before his fingers could claw in, he received such a terrible blow of a fist in his face that he tumbled back. He did not fall. He could still just hold himself erect. But he was staggering here and there.

He wanted to go at him again, when he felt how he was firmly held by the arms and kept back. Then everything went dark before his eyes.

When he came to himself again, he saw himself walking be-

side a policeman, on whose other side two others were striding—
an older gentleman with a gray beard and a young man.

It was only a few steps to the next police station.

There he recovered his senses enough so that he was able to go
first to the man on duty and give his name and profession.

Sergeant Major Groterjahn looked up astonished and stood
up. It happened that he knew District Attorney Sierlin by sight.

He saw how excited he was.

He did not yet know what the matter was, but he said politely, while he pointed with his hand into a side room, "If the
Herr District Attorney would perhaps take a seat there while I
take down the statements."

He was not further astonished, when the Herr District Attorney answered only briefly, "No thanks. I will wait outside. Have
me called, when it has come to that," and walked out.

Then he signaled the policeman to him, had him give a brief
report, and, after the personal information had been taken, next
turned threateningly to the younger of the two standing before
him: "You have assaulted the gentleman who just left the room
openly in the street? Why did you do it?"

The one rebuked stood there calmly. He did not smile. He
was not in the least excited and answered almost politely and not
at all insulted, "I believe rather that the gentlemen has assaulted
me. I have only defended myself against his aggression."

On the forehead of the duty officer a vein swelled up at this
monstrous statement. "You really don't want to assert that Herr
District…, that the gentleman who just walked out, first attacked
you?"

"Yes, I do!"

Now the old gentleman intervened. He identified himself as
Professor Dr. Karl Hesekiel, a citizen here for thirty years, and
residing quite nearby.

He said in a distinct, somewhat lecturing way, as if he were
sitting at his rostrum, "I saw the incident from the very beginning. I am a witness and am ready to swear that the gentleman,

who just walked out, went at this young gentleman, who was quietly standing by me, and grabbed him by the chest, without being provoked by him in the least."

The man taking the protocol looked from one to the other. The atmosphere felt oppressive.

"For what reason should the gentleman have attacked you first?"

And he received the honest-sounding answer: "I have no idea."

He decided to prefer to ask the Herr District Attorney for an explanation before he pressed further into the matter; he conveyed the two present to the side room with the indication that they were to wait there, and sent the policeman out to ask the gentleman waiting outside to come in.

He returned immediately.

"The gentleman is no longer there."

The Sergeant Major sprang up. Impossible! He walked into the street.

When he returned again after a while, his red, full face wore the expression of complete perplexity.

This was indeed a very, a highly remarkable story: a district attorney who was supposed to have undertaken an attack (which, however, he was still not able to believe), and who then withdrew from the interrogation (which he had to believe!). He decided to remove his hand from this mysterious affair and pass it on—up higher. The higher-ups might settle it as they wished.

Since an inquiry by telephone yielded the result that the statements of personal information of the two gentleman in the side room were correct, and that they resided where they were officially registered, they were brought in again and abruptly released. The protocol was closed with their brief statements. The only one who walked home unconcerned and again in the best of moods was Adolf Braun. The Sergeant Major could not make any sense of the story and he racked his brains the whole evening, although he had no direct cause to do so. By no means did he want to talk about it. Many years of service had taught him that holding his tongue was the best means to get ahead. The professor shook his white mane:

the affair did not fit in his learned head either. The young man had looked so decent. But a district attorney—for he had heard the name as its possessor named himself—a district attorney, who commits a sudden attack on a public street—what secret reasons might lie behind it? Since he had more important things to think about, however, and besides, as an old bachelor he had no opportunity to relate the story further, the danger that it would become public was small from his side too. But principal person involved—

2

—District Attorney Sierlin had hardly left the police station and saw himself on the street than he dashed away.

He had completely forgotten that he had just hardly a minute earlier promised to wait here.

He had only the one thought: there now remains for you only the bullet!

You have been struck in the face (and almost to the ground) in a public street—this insult can only be washed away with blood, and this man is not entitled to a challenge!

He rushed away with his longest strides exactly as he had done three weeks earlier. He did not know where he was going, and he only looked up when he found himself in a well-known neighborhood, close to his home.

Only then did it occur to him what he had done: he, a high official, had evaded an interrogation by flight!

He involuntarily threw up the collar of his coat. It seemed to him that everyone passing by must see what he had done.

He turned around and walked on farther, no matter where.

Late in the evening—the children were long since asleep and his wife had been directed to retire with brief and hard words—as he found himself in his room, dirty and falling with fatigue, he closed the door and drew the weapon from his desk.

But as he went to take it up, he saw that his hand was trembling. He had to lay it down again.

Then he gnashed out, "No! First you! You dog! First you!"

He went to the wall cabinet, poured himself a large glass full of cognac, and gulped it down.

Then he sat in his easy chair and stared straight ahead. He sat the whole night like that, the flask beside him, drinking and smoking, and if he spoke to himself, they were always the same words, "First you! First you! You dog! You dog!"

In the morning he rode into the city to a doctor. Not to his family doctor—to another, known to him only by name. He did not need to examine him first, but only to look at him to be able to write with a good conscience the certificate requested: "Severe nervous disturbance—urgently prescribed: immediate, lengthy treatment—abstention from all work—absolute rest—"

At home again, District Attorney Sierlin spent the rest of the morning composing a request for an immediate leave of absence, which he had sent at once—with the certificate and the files he still had—through a special messenger to the appropriate office.

During the following days he hardly spoke a word. At home he hardly left his room. When his wife insisted on coming in, he told her he was sick and had applied for a leave; when she urged him to travel, he rebuked her, saying that all he needed was a couple of days rest, he had been working too hard, and people should leave him in peace.

If he went out, it always happened unexpectedly and at the oddest times. In the middle of a meal he could stand up and hurry out, only to come home at night. Or he left the house when everyone was already asleep and came home only in the morning, without saying where he had been.

He himself did not know. But it was always streets, streets, streets through which he walked. He either self-consciously avoided meeting anyone who came too close to him, or he looked them in the face provocatively and threateningly.

Visitors were not received; telephone calls were not to be answered. For there were such—it leaked out.

He, on whom the drops of rumor were falling, did not sense them.

He varied between bouts of irrational rage and those of a secret, deadly fear.

He was waiting for his enemy.

He was seeking him.

He knew, he would return.

He never went out without a weapon, and he mostly held his hand on the handle of the revolver in the back pocket of his trousers, which gave his shoulders as he walked a curious, contorted appearance.

He was waiting. Why did he not come, the dog, so that he could shoot him down! First him! And then himself!

3

The short and incomplete report of Sergeant Major Groterjahn had gone in and was passed on, further and further on up, until it landed where it could go no higher.

There, in the highest place, it arrived almost at the same time as the application for a leave of absence. They were hardly pleased and at first did not rightly know what to make of the two—in their connection. Only District Attorney Sierlin himself could shed light on this unexplained affair. But District Attorney Sierlin was sick, very sick, and according to the medical certificate of one of the leading authorities, they were not certain if an interrogation was advisable and expedient—the state of his health, or better said, of his temper, was such that it could not be very carefully carried out, would make him much worse, and have disastrous consequences.

Therefore at first they looked around elsewhere, and the choice fell on Examining Magistrate Dr. von Wolfradt. He, a man-of-the-world from the tip of his head to his toes, at the same time one of the most capable among the younger heads, enjoyed the reputa-

KENN]

tion of absolute discretion. He was further known for getting out of the accused whatever there was to get out. In addition he frequented the same social circles as the so suddenly and severely sick man. He was appointed. The conference was serious and ended in complete agreement: this puzzling and highly embarrassing affair must by all means be settled in secret.

Dr. von Wolfradt considered long and thoroughly. He could have personally sought out the district attorney. But he was on leave and was, with his sickness, hardly available and ready for a purely personal statement.

It was better first to make some private inquiries. He looked around. Whom did he know as his friend? They had a lot of common acquaintances. But friends? He really knew only one. Himself a former corps member, he naturally knew that Counselor-at-Law Eberhardt had been his mentor. Such a relationship effectively lasts a lifetime.

Naturally he knew the counselor-at-law. (Who did not know the jovial gentleman?)

He sought him out and knew after the first few words that he had come to the uniquely correct source. His justly famous instinct had once again led him well.

Not that Counselor-at-Law Eberhardt was pleased to hear of this story again, for the third time. It was simply disgusting. (So now it had already come as far as this: a scuffle on a public street, like among street urchins.)

But—released now from his discretion—already in the interest of the honor of his profession, he gave in a short picture the requested information (as far as he thought proper).

Dr. von Wolfradt took notes and only regretted that they were so slight. He hardly became wiser from what he heard.

Here too they were in complete agreement—the affair must be hushed up, however good or bad it turned out.

That could be done, if the victim—Counselor-at-Law Eberhardt did not doubt for a moment that the description of him was correct—for his part did not ask for a prosecution, which he was entitled to.

(And if my old Sierlin, the damned fool, doesn't commit some new stupidity, he added in thought to himself.)

Dr. von Wolfradt had only one more question: "But what does this man want? What is his goal?"

The one questioned smiled and thought: That is for *you* to find out.

Aloud, he said as he pressed the hand of his elegant visitor in a friendly way, "My dear doctor, if one knew *that*! I am only saying this much: This young man is not crazy, and if you believe you will be easily done with him, you may be greatly in error!"

Dr. von Wolfradt smiled back in a superior way—sure of his success.

He would be done with him. He had already been done with very different people.

In addition, his curiosity was aroused to the highest.

He intended to summon this remarkable young man.

4

He resolved to be quite nice in the beginning and only in the course of the interrogation (if it should be necessary) to take other tacks.

Therefore, with a motion of his hand he invited the young man, who entered with a polite, but not obsequious bow and was now standing before him, to take the seat opposite him. It began informally.

The preliminaries were quickly taken care of and the question and answer began:

"You were unjustly sentenced about three years ago, acquitted in the retrial." (Suppressed, tactful regret, yes—almost humane participation in a hard story.)

"Yes, indeed."

ENN]

"The gentleman with whom you had the encounter on the street is the same one who represented the prosecution against you in his capacity as district attorney. You know him therefore?"

"Naturally." (Indifferent.)

"Herr District Attorney Sierlin asserts now that for some time, no, for a long time already you have been—hm—pursuing him."

"Pursuing!" (Astonishment.) Then very politely: "And on what does the gentleman base his assumption?"

A short pause. "On the fact that he meets you uncommonly often and at places where a meeting by chance cannot come into question." (A little bit sharper.)

"At what places, for example?" (Again astonished.)

Leafing in his notes: "In front of his house, for example."

With an even greater astonishment in his tone: "In front of his house? But I don't even know where the gentleman lives."

Still politely, if also again with a slightly sharper nuance: "You don't know where Herr District Attorney Sierlin lives? When you sat so often in front of his house?" (Suburb and street were named.)

"So?—he lives there? I did not know. (Coolly.)

"You know the area?"

"Could be. I often take walks in the environs and sit down when I am tired. I had to restore my health." (A glance at the strong figure, at the tanned face, and the thought from the other side: Well, you have already succeeded in that splendidly.)

Again a short pause. "You have no occupation?"

"Not at the present time. It is very difficult to find work if one has been in prison."

"But—but, you have been rehabilitated. Completely rehabilitated."

A bitter smile. "Nevertheless. People still believe that—"

This time the pause was embarrassing. "But your income does allow you to get by?"

"No. I have no income. I have received a small inheritance and am using it to become capable of working again."

(He reached into his breast pocket, as if for the desired proof.)

Politely waving it away: "Please. We do believe you."

Dr. von Wolfradt was thinking. He was again silent.

It was not going well.

Then he bent over the table, sought to capture the glance of his opposite number confidently with his own, and said, with a light persuasiveness in his voice, "We are here, aren't we, to come to an understanding. It is still possible, even if hardly likely, that the Herr District Attorney is mistaken. All that we want is just only to request an explanation from you for why—"

He did not know how to continue.

But the counter-question was already there. It again sounded entirely innocent and as if astonished: "Explanation? For what?"

"I told you already: explanation of why you came to, so to speak, pursue the gentleman everywhere."

The astonishment in the open face became greater. "Pursue?"

"Yes, pursue! You are in the theater when the Herr District Attorney is there, sitting one row in front of him. You are in the visitor's gallery when he is arguing a case."

"I seldom go to the theater because I lack the means; I have never seen the gentleman there. And, as far as I know, every citizen of good reputation—and I am one again—has the right to go to the public court sessions."

"But always precisely, when Herr District Attorney Sierlin is speaking?"

"I have often been there when the gentleman is not speaking. I just have nothing to do."

Dr. von Wolfradt looked again into his notes. He did not want to lose his patience and should not.

"Last summer you were at a Baltic Sea spa. The end of July. You departed from there on the same day that the Herr District Attorney arrived?"

Now a weak smile came into the features of the one interrogated. "If I really departed when the gentleman arrived, then that rather looks like going out of his way than like pursuing."

Dr. von Wolfradt bit his lip. But he bent even further over and said, "About eight days before that, just in front of the gentleman, you bought a ticket for Kiel and then you did not go?"

The smile became almost amused. "I? Bought a ticket? For Kiel?"

Then a shrug of the shoulders, as if it was impossible even to entertain such nonsense.

The questioner still had more questions ready. He did not want to give up yet.

But to his greatest astonishment he saw how the young man before him suddenly stood up and shoved the chair away. His voice had all at once a quite different sound.

"I understand nothing. I don't know what these questions are supposed to mean. But if something has been put forward against me, then I request to be placed in the position of an accused person and immediately arrested. I am unaware of any injustice. But"— here the voice became bitter—"I have indeed already been in such a position."

Dr. von Wolfradt had likewise stood up, without knowing it. He was so surprised that he could find no words at first. What was he to think of this?

Either this young man with his open, honest face was lying to him in the coarsest way and his whole behavior was the greatest shamelessness that he had ever seen, or—or something was not in order on the other side. One way or the other, it should in no case come to a scandal. Precisely this should be avoided, and he was on the best path for it.

Therefore, with a polite motion, he renewed his invitation to sit down: "But! Arrest? Please, there can be no talk of that. I can only repeat that our wish is simply to bring light into this affair. It almost appears—" as if Herr District Attorney Sierlin looks too much on the dark side of everything, he was about to say.

But he suppressed it, fortunately, just in the nick of time.

He said in as friendly a way as possible (almost with an undertone of heartfelt regret), "You are therefore really not able to help us?"

The expression in the eyes opposite became directly guileless. "I regret having to say that I do not know, in fact, what the gentleman wants from me. I had not seen him when he came up to me and grabbed me in the chest. I naturally had to defend myself."

In a similar way, he added, "If I had known that it was this gentleman, I would not have struck him so roughly. But at first I did not see him."

Dr. von Wolfradt had yet only one thing to do: to fulfill his duty. It was not easy for him to say what he had to say.

He became quite official again. "It—it appears confirmed that you were not the aggressor. You could ask for a prosecution."

Pause. Then politely: "And how would it have to read?"

"For—for assault and battery."

He considered anew. Then: "I renounce it. The gentleman obviously acted in an attack of temporary insanity."

Adolf Braun stood up again.

By the light, almost unnoticeable smile that ran over his face with these last words of his—a quite different smile from earlier—Dr. von Wolfradt knew with undoubted clarity that he had been disgracefully taken for a fool the whole time.

But now—with this magnanimous renunciation—it was too late (and also probably for the best). He only felt: never had an interrogated person been so unassailable, never had he been so helpless.

He could only answer the question "Am I released?" with an affirmative wave of his hand.

He only became conscious of the bow with which he returned that of the released man when it was likewise too late, and his anger did not become less because of it.

There remained only one thing left for him, to form a judgment for himself. He did.

He summed it up in two words as he ejaculated: "My respects!"

5

On the last evening of this week the residents of the street in the quiet suburb witnessed an alarming spectacle.

Drawn to their windows and in front of their doors by a shot, they saw how a man rushed out of the house that belonged to District Attorney Sierlin, crossed over the roadway with long strides, and—yelling furiously—waved a revolver about wildly in the air, firing blindly into an empty bench in the park that lay opposite. When they hurried there, they found sitting on it the owner of the house, District Attorney Sierlin, with glassy eyes, foaming at the mouth, and in complete exhaustion.

They carried him, hardly resisting, back into his house and sent for the doctor.

6

Adolf Braun was thoroughly pleased. This encounter on the street and this ridiculous interrogation by the monkey of an investigating magistrate had been entirely to his liking. The end was near.

It was also time. A year had almost passed and his money had melted down to a small amount.

He was ready for everything. The next thing would probably now be that his enemy would shoot him in a crowd if he met him again in the street. He himself never carried a weapon with him. He did not want to. If the other became his murderer—that too was fulfilled revenge, for the murderer would have to be punished for his act.

He had no fear. If he had ever wanted to be afraid, then his plan might never have been undertaken.

He waited. Either this end came about or—news through Ede.

The news came. On the eighth day after the attack on the street, the third day after the interrogation.

It was astonishing and very satisfactory news.

He learned that he had been seen by his enemy in the neighborhood of his house—although he had no longer been out there for months!

Ede related, "Well, your D.A. has become quite crazy now. He dashed out of his house yesterday evening and shot into the air again and again—nobody knows at whom, for there was no one in the neighborhood. They have taken him to an institution."

Ede concluded, "Now, he would not have wanted to shoot at you, I suppose—you didn't anger him *that* much, did you?"

He looked at his friend with a smile. But he did not smile back. His face wore again the closed, secretive expression that he, Ede, had often seen recently, and which he could never rightly explain—the expression that therefore always seemed a bit uncanny to him. What could he have wanted to keep hidden from him—from him, his best friend?

Their meeting on this evening was shorter than usual.

When Adolf Braun was alone, it seemed to him that a heavy and no longer bearable burden had been lifted from his heart.

7

But it was only entirely lifted from him two days later—when he heard that his enemy had been declared insane and a recovery was no longer to be thought of.

Again his friend Ede brought him the news: "He will never get out again. His old lady bawls the whole day. The villa is to be sold—she will not stay in the house any longer. Kitty goes as the first, of course." Then they intended—and now it came out, the great secret—then they wanted to get married right away. She had something set aside and they would open a little cigar shop. With a sports-betting office, of course. For horse racing was still to have a place, even if now a strongly curtailed place in his heart (in which there was no more room for other things: Kitty came out the victor and looked just like she would tolerate no other rival for him). But he, Adolf, must come to visit them frequently, and naturally he must be godfather to the first, strapping boy (already on the way).

They toasted—again and again: to a happy future.

On parting they shook hands as ever.

————And for ever.

Adolf Braun came home on this evening only after midnight. He had walked a long time through the streets.

In him everything was quiet and peaceful. His work was done. It had been a long and difficult work, tiring and wearing. But it was done, and he had attained what he wanted—what had been present in his mind from the very beginning, at first dim and unclear, then always clearer and more definite. He could be pleased with himself.

But there was also a feeling of emptiness in him such as he had not yet known. It seemed to him as if the goal of his life had been achieved.

To begin again, to start again from where he had been when they had broken him—for that he no longer had the strength. And also no longer the desire.

He had no one in the world, and to live only for the sake of his own life—that did not seem worthwhile enough for him. His money, too, was at an end.

Since he was leaving no debts behind, there was just enough for a decent burial.

And that is what he received, after they had found him several days later on a lonely spot in the woods, with the bullet in his temple and the weapon in his hand.

THE IMAGINED WORLD

A LATE AWAKENING

[KENN]

PROLOGUE

Whoever is accustomed to taking a walk on beautiful days—about noontime and in the vicinity of the lake—in Berlin's Tiergarten, in the view of many the most beautiful park on earth, will probably often meet a gentleman who stands out from the surrounding crowd of strollers not only because of his stateliness and height, but above all also by an inner contentment (so rare today) spread over his whole being. Following him with a glance, he will say either enviously or pleasantly touched, according to his own character, "It appears to be going really well with him."

But if he should then seek, seduced by the good-natured expression on the broad face and the unusual character of his whole appearance—perhaps after sitting down beside him on one of the green rental chairs—to engage him in conversation, he will see only too soon that he is in no way, to be sure, rejected in an unfriendly way, but also that nothing in the brief answers of the stranger encourages the continuance of the acquaintance thus made, so that the only thing left is to withdraw again and go his own way.

Thereby is the one, who was just approached in vain, not at all unsociable. He likes to have contact with people, only they must be people with an artistic disposition or at least interests (such as those with whom he sometimes spends an hour or two in the afternoon in the large café with the hardly flattering nickname).

What they knew of him here—in these circles—was not much: a well-off businessman, Behrendt by name, and, if one was correctly informed, a councilor-of-commerce, who had retired here in Berlin and led a comfortable life of pleasure; who regularly attended the theatre and concerts (it must be said to his honor that they were always the best); who interested himself in everything that was called art in an almost youthful and at times even somewhat comic liveliness, without, however, himself trespassing in any way and therefore harmlessly ("this enthusiasm would quickly die down if he once really looked at what went on backstage"); and who—the main thing—did not show himself averse to occasional attempts to pump him for money (even if he was capable of rejecting them just as abruptly as decisively); and for whom, for all of these reasons finally, a place was cleared for him at one of the reserved tables where, an excellent and mostly silent listener, he never intruded and where, for that matter, he only joined them once a week.

Those who knew nothing of this Herr Behrendt's present life, but who knew all the more about his earlier life, thought and spoke quite differently about him—those from the town in which he was born and had grown up, had lived and worked, and whose honorary citizen he almost would have become, if not—yes, if not—

From those too, his earlier fellow citizens, one or another occasionally came on business or also just for pleasure to the imperial capital. And again probably one or another of them had also made an attempt to look up their earlier fellow citizen in the distinguished pension in the western section, in which he had taken for the time being two comfortable rooms. In vain. For he was dead sure to be turned away with the remark that Herr Councilor-of-Commerce Behrendt regrets that he is unable to receive visits. But if one did see him then by chance on the street or in a restaurant, one was met with all the exterior forms of politeness, yet in such a yawning indifference toward everything that had once been, that one had to utterly give up any further attempt to arrive at the true and ultimate reason for his adventurous flight (as his departure from the town was called) and return to his home grounds no wiser than before. Under these circumstances, they could not be blamed for the fact that they were hardly inclined to contradict the rumors that had still not come to rest.

These rumors had now, in the course of the year—so long it had now been—consolidated to the following assumptions, which were now viewed as "facts" and no longer doubted:

According to them, it was certain that Herr Councilor-of-Commerce Behrendt, the senior owner of the highly respected firm of Behrendt & Spruth, Fruit Preserves, one day, without taking leave of a single person and without leaving behind any kind of explanatory message—except the short one that arrived three days later, saying that he was not returning—was up and away. His intention to go away forever was also confirmed by the fact that in the preceding weeks he had given up all the honorary offices etc. that he held, likewise without any further reasons.

In truth his disappearance by night and fog had been nothing other than a flight—a flight from public opinion. For, to universal horror it had been established with positive certainty that he, probably the most distinguished citizen of the town, had in earlier years on a stay abroad carried out an embezzlement there that had even led him into prison, and which now, after such a long time, had finally been brought to light through the unimpeachable witness of a young friend from that time. This person, who had come here from distant lands to see him one more time, had been so rudely mistreated in one of his well-known fits of rage, that he too had to leave the town so as not to be exposed to further insults, only because he had spoken the truth.

His flight and the disappearance of another person must be connected. For according to the likewise incontestable report of the widowed and crippled wife of Chief Tax Councilor Pinner, who lives on the river bank in Schillerstrasse and who, from her window, was in a position to oversee the region of the city garden through her "spyglass," Councilor-of-Commerce Behrendt had already for weeks before almost daily made his way over the river and up the heights on the other side, returning only after hours, not always, but mostly by the same path. Up there on the summit, however, lay only one single house, that of the wine handler Fürbringer, and in it was only one single female being that for these peculiar walks in a region to which otherwise no decent person came without reason—one would almost say dare come—in this house only the niece of this Fürbringer (who, besides, was never at home during the day) came into consideration. She worked up there in his wine-shop as a kind of waitress, a young thing, still almost a child, judging by her appearance.

She, too, disappeared on exactly the same day—to be sure, as questioning revealed, not secretly, but rather with the consent of her uncle, so as to return to her hometown. Where the two had taken themselves was, unfortunately, unable to be ascertained. Of him, one only knew that he was now living in the imperial capital and there exclusively frequented disreputable, so-called "artistic" circles. No letters, as was said, had been left behind by him, and if he had directed such to here after his flight and had answered questions, then this was done in such a brief and factual way, obviously avoiding every personal explanation, that from them too one did not become wiser about the real reasons that moved him. Visits, however, of earlier acquaintances and business friends were either curtly rejected or shaken off in the same indifferently offensive way that he had also displayed to his fellow citizens so often in recent years.

The only fortunate thing was that his poor family, from whom he had not spared this scandal, did not appear to suffer so very much because of his behavior, which revealed contempt for all morality and all custom. Nor did the business suffer, which his noble father, whose spotless life should have been a model for his only son, had founded and he had taken over. For years already it had been neglected by him, but under the leadership of his partner and his son-in-law it had blossomed and prospered. It was probably earning even much more than earlier. (What was not known: Had he taken his funds out of it or left them there still?)

As for the abandoned wife (was he now really divorced or still not yet?), even she appeared to have consoled herself, for there was talk of a coming remarriage for this still stately, rich, and generally popular woman.

The girl seduced by him, had, of course, been abandoned some-where. No one knew anything more about her or her certainly sad fate.

Thus was the judgment of public opinion about Councilor-of-Commerce Behrendt in his hometown.

That there were also there some who knew what stupid, inso-lent, and mean lies these were about the untouchable honesty of the man whom they had known for a lifetime does not need to be said. But since the true grounds of his indeed very peculiar and strange behavior were closed to them too and they also had other-wise no reason to boast of his special friendship, they let the ru-mors run as they would and did not contradict them very force-fully, not even when an opportunity was offered.

Thus there was really only one single person who would have been able to intervene here—the only one also who had received a letter that, even if it was short, had pointed to the truth—because he at least suspected the reasons that had led to the event that so long and so wildly aroused the feelings of that dear town: a certain Dr. Radewald. But for one thing nothing was to be gotten out of this Dr. Radewald because for years he had gone out of everyone's way, and then too because, according to the general opinion, he did well to keep silent about the affairs of others, since his own were too little pleasing for him to gain him respect and popularity here.

After all this—what is there left over, except to relate the things just as they occurred in reality?

That is about to happen.

[KENN]

CHAPTER ONE

1

The clock on St. Peter's struck nine as Herr Councilor-of-Commerce Ludwig Behrendt, the head of Behrendt & Spruth, Preserved Fruit Producers, punctual as always, entered his office on this first day of the week.

It was a high and light room, but it was unfavorably situated at the end of a long corridor and on the second floor. Yet, only from it did one still have a view into the quiet neighboring garden with its old trees, whereas all the other rooms of the large business house looked over the courtyard and the street.

Before entering to take up the work of the day, he always stepped to the window. He opened it, as wide as possible, and deeply drew in the air of the fresh April day. But even today he looked in vain for the first, longed-for signs of the coming spring. After the extraordinarily long and severe winter the garden appeared dead, and the trunks of its trees reached upward dark and stiff. Nowhere was there any trace of green.

And yet, how he longed for the first warm days, for long, solitary walks in air and light, during which there were no meetings with people as there were here in the streets at every step and turn. How he longed for the end of this winter to pass!

Then those parties would finally end, the last of which was yesterday in his house; according to his wife's claim, it too was quite unavoidable this season. It had again kept him awake long after midnight, so that he now came to his work with insufficient sleep. Sleep, however—what was there better than sleep!

But now it just had to be. It belonged to his position as senior owner of the largest and most respected business house of the town and to his manifold honorary offices, from town councilor all the way to orphanage patron and member of the board of directors of various firms. It also belonged to the program in the vocation of his wife: two big parties with dancing and at least four small ones every winter were the minimum. If one then went everywhere that he was of course invited in turn, that meant offering up two or three evenings of every week to this nonsense. Even if he avoided many under all possible excuses—it was impossible for him to stay away from his own house.

This was now indeed supposed to be the last one until autumn. It was also high time. For if there was anything that he hated, it was this "banding together," as he called it to himself. Always the same faces! Always the same conversations about the indifferent "events" of the day, which were already sufficiently known from the newspapers! Always the same gossip and twaddle about the dear neighbors among the women! And always the same stale dirty jokes of the men, when they were among themselves with their cigars after dinner! It had come so far that, under the terrible boredom of those hours, he was often on the point of getting up and walking away, but then remained anyway.

He lightly yawned behind his hand as he closed the window.

Then, as he was sitting down, his glance morosely ran over the pile of letters from the early mail delivery that lay stacked up before him. He skimmed through it indifferently. The names printed on them of known and unknown firms called to him. What would they be again? Orders, questions, reminders—always the same, always the same here too! As a businessman he should have been pleased with the brisk correspondence. But he was just not at all a businessman. He had known it for a long time.

Then he suddenly started at the sight of a certain handwriting. He drew out a long letter that had come from abroad. As he held it in his hand and turned it over, there ran over his face an expression of almost unbelievable astonishment.

Then he heard the well-known, hasty stride from the hallway. He had just enough time to stick the letter into his breast pocket before, after a quick knock, the door was thrown open and the partner of the firm, Eduard Spruth, stormed in as he did every morning. He always stormed, the whole day from morning to evening; from here to the factory, from the factory to the warehouses, and from them back again, and here from office to office, lurking and spying everywhere, and therefore his appearance was universally disliked.

Disliked also here in the sanctuary of the chief and before him. But he too had to tolerate him. He was the soul of the business. Without him nothing functioned.

Thus the glance of displeasure that, after a quickly spit out "Good morning! How are you?" he likewise threw at the pile of still unopened letters was not indifferent, but rather full of burning curiosity—in his view they should have long since been read and, where possible, half should have already been answered.

But it was the prerogative of the senior head of the firm to receive the incoming post first, a prerogative on which no value at all was placed, so that today too the other man—after a silently inviting wave of a hand toward it—could take possession of the whole stack and with a "Bring everything right back! Will just see—" was allowed to storm out again.

The chief remained behind smiling to himself.

This often repeated little scene amused him today too.

He thought: For what is all this hurry and excitement! We have more orders than we can fill.

He did not understand this greed for money. He had never understood it. No, he was no businessman. He knew that people said he was not. It was the only thing that they said about him and could say about him.

With boredom, he drew the business accounts over from the other side of the desk and began his work.

The morning passed as always. Herr Spruth brought back the letters, which were now opened and arranged, and had to put in a

ENN]

word to one and the other; Fräulein Selma, the stenographer, appeared, radiant as always, and was occupied for a half hour with dictation. Visitors came and went; others were announced and sent away—nothing more was thought about the letter in the breast pocket.

2

After every large party, the whole family assembled the next day for dinner—the leftovers had to be eaten and they had to comment on "how things had gone."

They were sitting there around the heavily laden table. Opposite the head of the house at the other end was his wife: plump, alert, and rosy (a beautiful woman, as she herself believed; a still beautiful woman, as her oldest admirers admitted to her and themselves). But he looked at her entirely without respect, without love. He could not help himself—she looked like a pug.

There was his daughter: like her mother in so many ways, but at all times of an unshakable dullness, which was viewed by some as a sublime indifference to the world, by others as an, in many ways, not really advanced intelligence.

There were her children: two boys (still in their teens) and a small, fat girl—all remarkably similar to the mother, good children, well-behaved children, but somewhat loud and certainly not budding geniuses.

There was the governess (or better said, she was not there, for she possessed the gift of making herself invisible).

Further, there was Karl Lindtner, his son-in-law, at one time the apprentice Karly, with his too short sleeves and his blue-red fists, not to be overlooked now, not only because of the solitaire that flashed over the table from his fat hand, but also as the number one manager of the firm, with many friends and of one heart and soul with the partner, Herr Spruth, restlessly active—a businessman as he should be.

And there was himself, Councilor-of-Commerce Ludwig Behrendt, a head taller than the adults around him, with his resigned, somewhat tired smile, smoothly shaved, his sideburns already lightly turning gray. He did not rightly belong here.

Now he was leaning back—for he was, as in everything, also moderate in his eating—looking over the table and seeking to solve the problem of how they managed to eat and talk at the same time. For, although they were wolfing the food down as if they had gone hungry for twenty-four hours, they were still talking loudly. He gave up.

Yes, here they all were, without a care and content with themselves and their world, a world that obviously had been expressly created only for them.

Finally it appeared that they were all full. They stood up and wished one another on all sides a blessed "Mealtime!" If there was one word in the German language that he hated, it was this. None appeared to him so nonsensical and at the same time so vulgar. Nevertheless he had not succeeded in banning it from his own table. Attempts to do so were regarded as one of his whims, and even if they avoided using it to him directly and the children were reprimanded when they bellowed too loudly, "You are just not to say 'Mealtime!'"—this was still done with the smile of mild indulgence. Everybody said "Mealtime!" Why should they not say it too!

"One again you have said not a word during the whole meal!" complained his wife, as, with a nod of his head, he was withdrawing to his room, and she received as answer, with the same friendly smile that had just gone over the table, "I hardly had an opportunity to say anything." It was again one of those answers that irritated her all the more, since she did not know what to reply.

Alone in his room, the letter in his breast pocket again occurred to him. But he suddenly felt so tired that he stretched out to rest, to have a little nap. But only ten minutes later he was awakened by a messenger from the factory. A fault had been found in one of the new machines and his presence was required.

3

Finally, however, there came for him the hours of the day that he had won by the custom of long years and which he let nothing take from him: the hours of being alone with himself in the late afternoon before the evening meal—spent in long walks, if the weather allowed it in any way, or if that was not possible, in the quiet of his business office after all the employees had left and the extensive building had sunk into stillness until morning. He could become very uncomfortable if he happened to be disturbed under the pretense of pressing business or family matters.

Today, after an hours-long discussion about hard-to-find mistakes, as he stepped before the gates of the factory that lay outside the town, the sky was cloudy. A walk in the open did not seem advisable.

In his office he had hardly opened the window sash, as in the morning, when the storm broke. It swept along the house wall, became entangled in the neighboring garden, and blustered through the dry branches of the trees, so that they split with a crack and whirled around in the air.

A spring storm! he thought, messenger of the new spring, announcing its coming! But why am I looking forward to it? What is it bringing me? It won't rage through and saturate my life, for it lies closed off between these walls in certain quiet!

The wind drove the window sash painfully against his hot hand, which he had stretched out so as to feel the cool drops on it. He had to close it.

The desk was now empty. He sat down and drew out the letter, which he had carried with him unopened since morning.

According to the postmark, it came from Rio de Janeiro.

He knew from whom it came. He knew the handwriting, in spite of not having seen it for many years. It was a handwriting that one never forgets if one had once seen it, and one did not need to be a graphologist to recognize from it the vanity and conceit of the writer.

What did this person want from him? What could he still want from him? Was it not better to throw the letter away unread? Why should he still read it?

But then he read it anyway.

"Dear friend of my youth!

"It has been a long time since I have written you, and we have not grown younger in the meantime. But now I have become aware of you from business friends who are on a visit here—how good things are going for you and how your business is flourishing. Unfortunately I cannot say that of mine. I can indeed live from it, but it is not making a profit. Moreover there has been consuming me more and more from year to year the longing for the dear hometown, which I would like to see once again before I close my eyes. For the time being, however, this cannot be thought of, if a friend or good acquaintance is not found to make the trip possible for me, perhaps one such from earlier days. I have no such friend here.

"I am still alone, which is to say that I am still unmarried. But I hear of you that you are a happy grandfather many times over.

"This time I hope definitely to receive an answer from you—and not again, as with my last letter, to remain without one—as a sign that you remember the earlier, beautiful days, even if they were troubled by that sad event.

"In this expectation, I remain, with many greetings

"Your old friend,

"Eduardo Smith"

He felt repugnance, anger, scorn, disgust, and finally indignation on reading it. Then the letter was rumpled up and torn to pieces.

Was this man mad? How could he dare to write to him! How could he be so bold as to remind him of **that**—now, after thirty, after thirty-one years! Of a forgotten matter, so forgotten as if it had never been.

For who still knew of it? Who could still know of it?

Only one—**he**!

4

Councilor-of-Commerce Behrendt leaned back in his chair and looked up at the white ceiling.

It was deathly still in the empty building. Even the storm outside seemed to have quickly died down, and only isolated heavy drops still pattered against the panes.

How had it happened—how had he been able to do it?! Not a hundred, not a thousand times had he asked himself this in the years since, in the long years since, and always in vain. He never found an answer.

Today he questioned himself no longer. He knew there was no answer. It lay down below, in the inexplicable depths of the soul, and no brooding, no thinking could solve it.

But the facts of that time stood before him again in a downright frightening clarity. There was no forgetting. Nothing erased them. No time was able to fade them and wipe them away.

He, who never knew his mother, was scarcely twenty when he left this town for the first time to obey the wish of his father, which there was no opposing: to go abroad for a year to England in order to prepare himself for his profession as a volunteer there in a large firm of his line of business and at the same time to learn the language, spending the winter in London and the summer in the country.

Very much against his own wishes! They were eager for an artistic occupation, no definite one at first, but rather in the beginning more toward a free living out of his inclinations, which would then lead him onto the right path.

But precisely because he had shown no talent that drove him in a predetermined direction, he had difficulty asserting himself, and when he was asked what he really wanted, it was not easy for him to find an answer.

He gave in, happy for the time being to be allowed to be torn from the narrowness of his home, the strictness of his father's rearing, the bleakness of the town, into the humming life of the world. After a year he would see further.

Thus he then also saw his work as volunteer in the office of the large London firm as rather secondary and the day passed in it more as preparation for the evenings with their pleasures that were still so foreign to him: in the theatres and music halls; the restaurants and dance salons; the bars and clubs.

Naturally "she" came into his life. Naturally he fell in love. Naturally he believed that he could live not a day longer without her. He completely lost his head and, with it, the last remainder of his reason.

Only thus could it happen. Thus it did happen.

On that evening he was to see her alone for the first time—be allowed to take her out, that charming creature of the "Empire," beautiful, beautiful, as only a young Englishwoman can be, of a beauty such as was glorified by the great English painters of the previous generation.

And precisely on that evening, the last of the month, he was almost out of money. His monthly exchange, notified by the post office, could—because of a still unexplained event—only be picked up there the next morning. Under other circumstances unimportant. Today—as he believed—the happiness of his life depended on it.

The only person he knew well enough to ask, asserted that he himself had nothing.

Then he did it. Did it on a sudden impulse, without thinking and without being conscious of it.

He walked back into the office, was let in by the doorman, who knew him by sight, under the pretext of having forgotten something, and from the unlocked desk next to his own he took out a couple of gold pieces—two English sovereigns.

At this desk worked—if this designation was allowed, for he came only when it just suited him, and then only to chat and go away again—a second volunteer, the son of immensely rich parents and a playboy. He had the habit of emptying his purse into this desk—his savings account, as he called it—when it became too full.

He had also done it today—had laughingly thrown a handful of gold pieces into it and in his usual carelessness even neglected to take the key out when he left.

Even if he should come tomorrow—which was entirely unlikely, for he rarely came two days in a row—and even if he should be there before him—which had never before happened—and should actually notice the absence of the two coins, he would attribute it rather to his own negligence than to another.

But these were thoughts that in these moments came only darkly to him who now hastily closed the desk again and hurried out.

He acted, as he later said, when, not wanting to excuse himself and his actions, but only in the torment of finding an explanation for himself for something so entirely incomprehensible—he acted in those moments under the pressure and force of a temporary insanity, which saw, thought, and felt only **one** thing: **her**! Her, whom he must see yet today, if he was to continue living.

Everything else was unimportant compared to **that**.

Just as self-evidently as he took them, tomorrow early when the office was opened the two sovereigns would again lie in their place and the matter would be settled for him (and for that second person). No one would have even the least suspicion of the whole matter.

It happened otherwise.

Whereas he had usually punctually received his money without hesitation on the first of the month at the post office on the basis of the notice already given, there must have been some mistake—not a mistake of his father, his father **never** made mistakes!—probably of the post office in Germany, which hindered the immediate payment. He was asked to come by again at midday.

That and a further, vain inquiry at the office of that acquaintance, where there was still no one, delayed his arrival at his own office by almost three quarters of an hour.

It was too late.

Through a coming together of the most rare circumstances the theft had already been discovered. Precisely today the young Englander had come earlier than usual because he wanted to go to the races; precisely today he knew what he had laid in his desk yesterday, because it had been a round sum; precisely today he was impatient and in a foul mood.

He himself—his late arrival, his turning pale, his confusion betrayed him on the spot. He would also not have lied. He would not have been capable of it.

The police had already been notified. The judge, before whom he was led already the same day, made it quick.

But slowly, in terrible slowness passed the eight days that he "gave" him.

5

When, following them, he came toward midday to his pension (where they believed he was returning from a trip), the chamber maid with the little cap on her head told him on opening the door that an old gentleman had been waiting for him already two hours in his room.

There a motionless figure was sitting in the chair at the window, bent over his walking stick. The figure slowly raised his chin from the knob of the stick at his entrance, and he looked into a face that he did not recognize at first.

But then, as he wanted to hurry toward him, a raised hand and a flash in the stern eyes repelled him. He stood as if in a spell.

Then he heard said—and even the voice that now spoke to him and whose words were to sound in his ears years afterward in every single sound, even the voice that now spoke seemed to him to be that of a stranger. He spoke slowly, as if reciting something exactly considered—and his eyes lay cold and rigid on him, his only son, as if on a stranger.

"The climate of London does not agree you. Your lungs are easily affected. In the opinion of the doctor a warmer climate is to be preferred. You are leaving this very day for Malaga. Your train leaves Charing Cross Station at 2:15 p.m., the ship in Dover leaves the harbor about four-thirty. This evening you will be in Paris; you will travel on immediately and be in Madrid tomorrow. Your arrival in Malaga is to be reported the morning after at the firm with which we are connected, the exporter Garcia Hermanos. You will work with them a year. There on the table lies a ticket for Paris, as well as with what you will need for the next days."

With difficulty and slowly the speaker stood up from the chair at these last words. With another wave of his hand he warded off any approach. He nearly brushed him on going out, but no glance touched him.

He remained behind. The whole affair had lasted no more than three minutes. He himself had not been able to say a word. Now—alone—he cried out. But it was only a rattle and no one heard him.

In the evening he was in Paris, the next day in Madrid, and the day after that in his newly determined place.

His penitence began.

6

It was to be a long penitence.

He was as if broken. He had no other wish for life than the one: to atone!

He atoned. He atoned with his life.

He atoned—even today.

He did penance. He remained down there the prescribed year, but it appeared as if the sun of the south was unable to thaw his heart, frozen forever under a sudden horror.

He returned home. He entered the business as an apprentice, than as helper, only after years as associate.

He did his work, did it patiently, silently, punctually. He did it without any pleasure.

He did it under the eyes of his father, who watched over each of his steps as if only in this way could he keep him from a new mistake.

He married. He took the wife—or better, she took him—whom his father wished him to marry, although he did not love her. The foundation of his own household was in itself already a deliverance, since it took away the necessity of continuing to live with the aging man.

Not a word was mentioned of what had happened. Rarely one that went beyond the business.

Many years passed, until business affairs were also entrusted to him, without which a successful collaboration was no longer possible in the long run. But even then the hard glance still gleamed at the slightest suspicion of insubordination, yes of independence beyond the strictly drawn line, and even the smallest difference of opinion was able to awaken this suspicion.

Only on his death bed was a final hand shake (but even then no word) to indicate to him that he had obtained forgiveness for what he had once committed and for which, for the businessman of the old school, **no** atonement had appeared too great.

He was almost forty when he assumed the position of his father and took over the firm. For twenty years now he had been working in it.

Three years later Herr Eduard Spruth entered it, under considerable capital investment, as partner. He took him in so as to unburden himself and because he felt how an inner fatigue was becoming at times so great that he believed that he was no longer able to bear the burden of so large a business alone.

In addition to this, in his passion to make good what he was lacking, to stand firm in the eyes of his father and in those of his fellow citizens, he let himself be burdened with all possible honorary offices, which unduly took up his time and bored and angered him.

After another two years, his head manager, Karl Lindtner, became his son-in-law. His only daughter married at eighteen. A year later he became a grandfather with the arrival of the twins, and was a grandfather again after another three years when a daughter arrived, who, it appeared, was to be the last.

After the marriage of his daughter he had then built the villa for himself and his wife. Too large for the two of them, but the most beautiful of the town and situated almost at its other end, toward the woods.

Then came yet the title, accompanied by some kind of order "fourth class," which he smilingly laid aside and never wore. With that he appeared to have attained what was attainable for him from his botched life.

Only after the death of his father was he allowed to think about determining things for himself, even if at first only within certain limits. He did it by giving himself a couple of free days from time to time, which he used for visits to the metropolis, to see and hear there the best there was on the stage, in the concert halls, and in the exhibitions. A drop for his unquenched thirst. By reserving these afternoon hours for himself he was allowed to be alone with himself—with his thoughts and his dreams.

His thoughts—oh, they long since went back no more over the forgotten paths of earlier times! The wishes of his youth had vanished; the voices were stilled that had once called to him! The shadowy dreams, which had never become reality, had passed away—and as his only consolation the recognition remained that, so without marked talent, he would still probably not have accomplished anything in any art!

Buried were his dreams and forever! Thus, also away forever with the thoughts, such as they were and which did not let themselves be driven away: whether his penitence had not really been too severe? For then he always immediately felt again that it was too late, that there was no more rebellion, and that nothing would be able to tear his life from its previous tracks—that he had become too apathetic even to try.

Even when here and there he was overcome by rare fits of anger and outrage, say with regard to an all too great injustice that he saw or read about, they went as they had come. The chains had clanked, but they had not loosened, not to say fallen.

They held. They held fast.

They held him here and would hold him here until his death. He was bound with them to what was called his life and for him was no life: to the house that he had built; to his business, which basically was no longer his; to his family, which was his and yet not his; to his friends (which he did not possess) and acquaintances (of whom he had too many); and to this town, in which he was born and grew up, whose most distinguished citizen he was, and which he could not love, which he often could hardly endure!

7

Councilor-of-Commerce Ludwig Behrendt, now almost fifty, slightly gray, tall, and broad-shouldered, alone in his office at the end of the long corridor on the second floor of his large business house, and with his thoughts deep in the past again reached for the letter that had again conjured up these thoughts, and again an expression of anger and disgust came over his features.

What did this letter mean? What did this person want from him? Why did he suddenly write to him again, now after thirty years?

If he still remembered correctly, they had met on the journey, the first great one of his life, and had traveled over the channel together. If he had not been so alone in London (he did not know a human soul), there would probably have been no more contact between them. He would have shaken him off. Thus, however: like little chaps on the same school bench; taken by surprise by the "Du" on meeting one another and brought closer together than he had wished; and, as was said, both alone at that time in the immense, foreign city—they met one another, without coming closer together (for their interests were very different), they met for meals together, again and again, and exchanged their first experiences.

He still remembered him only as a blond, slovenly man with bad teeth and bad manners, who spoke too much and too loudly, made demands on him, and—then in that horrible hour left him in the lurch anyway. For he was deeply convinced of it, then and still today, that the man could have helped him if he had wanted to.

He also remembered indistinctly that on that other day, the most horrible of all, shortly before his departure, when he was paying his bill at the pension, he was also handed a letter from him. In it he regretted that he would not be able to see him again since he had to depart immediately for South America, where a position had just been offered to him. Was that the truth, or was it a lie because he wished to see him no more? And had he not used exactly the same expression in that letter as now, where he spoke of the "sad event"?

He himself at any rate would not have taken his leave of him, even if he had still been able to find time for it in the pressing haste of that day. What was this basically quite strange person to him? If he ever still thought about him at all, it could only have been because in his brooding over the incomprehensibility of his own action, in the torment of seeking some clarity where everything was confused and lay deep under the surface of consciousness, he came again and again to the question, **who** had wanted and was able to notify his father. To question the latter was, of course, never to be thought of, not even in a dream. **Never** was that affair referred to between them, not even with a hint. It could only have been this person, the only one who knew his father and who had naturally immediately heard of his arrest and conviction (which was seen already in the expression in the letter)—only he, the undesired companion of those weeks, could have been the undesired messenger, for it was not to be assumed that the notification had gone to his home from the firm so quickly. That too was not in the English character.

Nevertheless, in the course of the long years with the gradual dying out of his brooding, even the last recollection of him would also have disappeared if he himself had not taken care not to be forgotten. For this letter that lay before him was not the first. Four or five years after his return from Spain and when he was deeply involved in his own business—he had just married—a letter like this one had arrived. Then, again six or seven years later, yet another arrived. Both were rather similar in content and style, and both naturally remained answered just as this one would be.

This one here was, therefore, the third. He was stubborn, this "true friend of my youth"! It was only a pity that this stubbornness gained him nothing!

Perhaps he would write to him again after yet another period of five or six years, if the two of them were still alive. In the meantime he would at any rate have his peace from him. He crumpled the sheet and threw it into the wastepaper basket, but only to immediately bend over to retrieve it and smooth it out. Some sentence or other was there—he wanted to read it yet once again. What did that sentence mean? He did not immediately find it. But the whole! What a style! Slimy and sentimental, mendacious in every word! The "dear home town"—(why did he not write "beloved"?)—that hidden begging: you are rich, I am poor—you could, if you wished!—then the indication of the "sad event"—not tactlessness any more, but rather simply an unheard-of shamelessness! Finally, the signature—that absurd Hispanicizing of an honest German name!

What was he after—this man!

Well, he was far away, and when he saw that he received no answer this time too, he would probably give up bothering him again. He tore the writing into little pieces, smaller and still smaller, before he let them trickle down.

The matter was settled.

He looked at the clock. It was time to leave for home and he wanted to arrive there in time for the evening meal.

But as he was walking home, with quicker steps than usual, he stopped for a moment. How had that passage read? Literally read? He could not recall it now either, but in that second it was as if an inner voice softly whispered in his ear that the matter was far from being at an end, rather it had only just now begun. "Nonsense!" he said out loud. "Nonsense!"—as he walked on again. "I will have it be ended!"

CHAPTER TWO

1

Spring arrived, a splendid spring, with everything that it brings and only it can bring. After a March with storms and rain showers, a capricious April had followed, and now it was May—the trees stood in bloom, the birds rejoiced, and the people committed even more stupidities than usual.

But otherwise everything remained as before, and life continued its accustomed way in the quiet town.

Councilor-of-Commerce Ludwig Behrendt (senior partner of the firm Behrendt & Spruth, Preserved Fruit Producers, which, even if not exactly world renowned, was still known everywhere within the borders of Germany), appeared the same as he had always been—quiet and turned in on himself, a man who never spoke about himself and rarely about others, who only spoke at all when it was necessary and who hardly ever laughed. But who also seldom became angry and let life go by and draw him along with a light indifference.

And yet, he was no longer quite the same. In the last ten years, since his exit from the thirties, yes, really since the death of his father, who had been a constant, living reminder, he had more and more rarely thought of his youth and with it that affair. He wanted to think about it no more. For stronger and stronger became the consciousness in him that what he had done had really not been a mortal sin, but rather hardly more than a youthful thoughtlessness, for which he had then done all too great a penitence and for which he had been punished all too severely. Of this nothing could be changed any longer, as little as of his life. He had to come to terms with it, with this life, just as it was. In the eyes of most people it was a successful and enviable life: well-off, indeed rich; universally respected; and in the bosom of his family—what more did he desire? He often did not know himself. But what he knew was that his life did **not** appear to him enviable.

He had come to terms with it. Everything that he really desired was rest and peace for his final years—a well-deserved rest and a dearly bought peace.

That the two could and would be allowed to be disturbed even for an hour, indeed by a person who had long since so entirely vanished from his horizon, so that he hardly remembered him, a person, besides, whom he hardly knew—that there was a person who dared to disturb his life and remind him of **that**—that was what outraged and upset him interiorly over and over again, so that he no longer found his rest.

For he felt that he could not dismiss it with the movement of his hand and "Nonsense." Something was threatening his security. But what?!

This made him in these spring days even more quiet and with shorter words than he already was, even if days passed in which he completely forgot the impudent letter and its impudent writer.

It was certain that should another letter arrive, he would immediately have it returned with the notice "Return to sender."

2

He was hardly surprised when a letter arrived at the end of May—ten weeks after the first: this time registered and with the notice "Personal Delivery." It was handed to him in person by old Griep, the mail carrier, for an acknowledgment of receipt. He recognized the handwriting of the address immediately and was about to say that the reception of the letter was declined, when his glance fell on the stamps with which it was posted—this time it was the familiar German instead of the foreign ones.

He stopped short and calculated for a moment whether the sender had time in these weeks to make the trip from Brazil over the Atlantic to here. More than enough time, of course! He signed and took receipt of the letter.

Then he pressed the button of the electrical bell on the left side of his desk three times. That was the signal that he wished to see Herr Anker.

Herr Anker, factotum from times immemorial in the house Behrendt, appeared—lean, somewhat bent over, and with the two mighty bushes of hair at the sides of his bald head. (Our business is well "ankered," the punsters among the young gentlemen up front in the accounting section liked to say.)

"Herr Anker, I will be available to no one during the next half hour."

"Very good, Herr Councilor-of-Commerce."

Herr Anker would now station himself for a half hour (not a minute longer) somewhere outside and would keep everyone (even if it was the partner himself) away from his door.

Councilor-of-Commerce Behrendt tore open the letter and read.

"Dear friend of my youth!

"You will be very astonished, as astonished as I was when I saw that my letter remained unanswered. Here I am again in the old homeland. Yes, it is so!! Let me relate to you how it all came about. When I realized that no answer was to be hoped for from you any longer, I gave in to my overpowering longing and cashed in whatever I could. My money has lasted to here, no farther; otherwise I would have rushed directly to you. But now that I am back again, I must make a confession to you, that will astonish you even more, namely that I am not all that happy here. I don't know whether the people have changed or I have, but I feel myself a foreigner here and no longer understand them. Everything seems to me so

ENN]

small and narrow, and even the climate, today warm and tomorrow cold, is not wholesome for my health.

"Thus I have decided on the spot not to remain here longer, but rather to return to the land that, as I only now realize, has become a new, second homeland for me. I can do this now, to be sure, only if you help me thereby, for one thing for the return trip, and then in addition to set up my tent over there again, which I so recklessly took down so as to again see Germany and you, the only friend that I still have here.

"I think a thousand marks, a pittance for you, would let me fulfill my modest and so justified wish.

"I am convinced that you will be all the more glad to fulfill my request, the first that I make of you, since I believe I have noticed from certain indications that my presence in our hometown would not really be comfortable for you, and also probably, as I understand, cannot be comfortable after what happened.

"I therefore await your answer certainly until next Thursday, thus within the next four days, so that I can reserve a place in time on the Columbia, which departs on Saturday.

"In the certain expectation of experiencing no rejection this time, I am

"Your old friend

"Eduard Schmidt

This time Councilor-of-Commerce Behrendt did not throw the letter aside and then pick it up again. After reading one and another sentence again, especially reading repeatedly the final sentence, he carefully put it together and laid it in his briefcase.

Herr Anker was called in.

"Thank you, Herr Anker. I am available again."

The work of the day began.

3

When things ended for the day and he was again alone with himself—in that same room—he drew out the letter again and read it another time—word for word.

He shook his head. If the last letter had been an impudent act that could hardly be surpassed, then this one here surpassed everything in boldness! From the greeting to the end—what shamelessness in every, but really every word! And this style again! How stuffy! One really saw on the face of it how the writer in these last weeks had spoken only German and had improved it on bad German novels!

If—everything was not artificial pretense! Pretense, puffed up for a quite definite goal. A mask behind which to be able to carry out his secret plan.

What until now he only suspected—that behind this apparently stupid twaddle lay a purpose, a quite definite purpose—became almost a certainty for him today. This person must have again been made aware of him over there by some other German and had consequently decided to make up to him again, the "friend of his youth." Since he saw that this did not work with letters, neither the earlier ones nor the latest one, since they were not answered, he had come over here and was now separated from him no longer by the ocean, but rather only by a train trip of one day, was ready here—"to rush to his arms."

He was here and yet wanted to go back immediately, because he did not like it here. Why? Really from the ground given, that he was disappointed and disenchanted? What happened was indeed the rule among those who had lived a long time over there, had become used to freer circumstances, and no longer would and could find their way in the old ways.

But who traveled for this reason immediately back again, after fourteen days? No, here the case was different.

If he wanted to threaten him and through the threat to come here to blackmail him—Councilor-of-Commerce Behrendt pronounced the word quite distinctly to himself—if that was what he wanted, why did he then ask for such a ridiculous small sum, which hardly covered the cost of his trip back—since he indeed had to say to himself that, once more over there, he would receive not a penny more?

No, the requested thousand marks were, of course, only the beginning—when he had them he would stay here all the more and put the screws on!

He tried to read further between the lines, without finding the right answer to his questions. How carefully this time too (as in his earlier letters, if he remembered them correctly) had everything been avoided that could bring the writer in any way under suspicion of blackmail, not to mention anything that could convict him. A master stroke—this pretended stupidity! He read the letter for the third time and his blood began to boil. One thing was certain: This man must not be allowed to come **here**! For if he came here—

He looked up and into the stern eyes of the picture on the wall opposite him.

4

Councilor-of-Commerce Behrendt was accustomed to spend the evening, after dining, in his rooms and to read if there was "nothing happening," that is, if his time was not taken up by parties or meetings. There too he did not like to be disturbed.

These two rooms—his work room and his bedroom with the adjoining bath—in his villa—the most beautiful of the town, built by a foreign architect—lay on the ground floor. Opposite them were the salon and the dining room. Above his were the rooms of his wife and again opposite them the earlier children's rooms, now guest rooms.

Even the furnishings of his two rooms did not come from the local shops. The tall bookcases, the easy chair, the thick carpets of the one room, the bed and the wardrobes of the other were manufactured according to his own specifications by one of the leading firms of the capital, and their expensiveness stood in sharp contrast to the simplicity of the old inherited pieces of his office in town. But he wanted to have at least one thing from his joyless work: rooms in which he could feel himself at home (therefore also his own bedroom), and thus, after the death of his father, he had this house build, sparing nothing on it and its furnishings, although he knew that in the town heads were shaking over such unaccustomed luxury here.

On this evening too he wished to finish reading an engrossing book that he had begun yesterday. He read only the best books and only such as he purchased for himself after careful consideration.

But this curious and unusual feeling of unrest that had not left him throughout the whole day, drove him up and away from his usual place by the large fireplace, where he so gladly sat, even when the logs in it no longer crackled and burned.

In the hall he met his wife.

"You're going out again?" she asked, astonished when she saw him reach for his hat and stick.

"Yes indeed, I'm going out again," was the curt answer she received.

At the garden gate he stopped indecisively. It had been at first his intention to take a walk through the quiet streets of this new villa quarter on the warm May evening and perhaps yet farther into the open, but he gave it up from a sudden, highly unaccustomed wish, to see and speak to people. So he turned toward the town.

There, on the market square, he entered The Elephant, the oldest and best restaurant of the town, in which a company of gentlemen (officials, industrialists, in short, the notables), mostly always the same, were accustomed to talk and drink every evening in a back room that had been renovated in the old German style. His rare visit was greeted with a "Hello!" One of the gentlemen came to meet him. They jumped up and made a place for him at the thickly occupied round table, and Councilor-of-Commerce Behrendt was the center of the evening for a long while. They

talked about all kinds of things, but if he was to be honest, about
nothing that would have interested him, and so he soon became
again the silent listener, which he was known and loved for. (For
what do people like better than to be listened to?)

5

When they broke up it was near midnight, and he, otherwise so
moderate, had drunk a whole bottle of the heavy red wine and was
a bit tipsy.

Only with difficulty did he get rid of the offered company.

It was a mild and clear, starry night.

He did not want to, but still had to think about what had
been lurking in the background of his consciousness all day as also
the whole evening.

But on his way home now scruples and fears were gone.

No, this letter, too, would remain unanswered! Just let this
obviously half-crazy fellow do what he wanted! Let him come here
and relate the truth and all the lies along with it. No one would
believe him! They would laugh at him or shove him aside and pay
no attention to his words.

For, how high he stood in the universal respect of his fellow
citizens—this evening had again given him the proof. No kind of
scamp could come here and question it.

Just let him come! He would know how to keep him from
bothering him. This blackmailer would also get not a red cent
from him!

He awakened toward morning.

An oppressive dream still lay on him, and its nightmarish figures vanished only when he sat up with a jerk.

What was it? The unaccustomed wine?

No.

He knew immediately that this letter—this letter, of which he
had believed yesterday on going to bed that it could remain unan-

swered—**must** be answered—must be answered today and as quickly as possible.

A danger was in the offing—a great danger. A danger that had to be guarded against.

He no longer deluded himself about these dangers, which lurk on all sides and threaten life. Since he had stumbled into one of them in his youth, thoughtlessly and unsuspecting, his eyes had been sharpened, he had been on his guard.

Until today he had not met a serious one. Now it was present and was approaching!

This man could be trusted to do anything: with malice!

A word from him—spoken here, repeated, passed around from mouth to mouth—could tear down everything that he had built up in a long life of penitence and work.

Certainly this life seldom seemed worth living to him. For years already hardly worth the effort. He was not happy. He knew that he was not and, as far as he could see, never would be. Nevertheless it was a life of work and of success (what people call success).

And—it was **his** life. He should not let it be destroyed by some senseless chance.

Precisely because he stood in such high respect here, he must not let his reputation and his honor be touched by even a breath that could tarnish them in public opinion.

What this rascal wanted was clear. If it had not yet been clear to him, the last doubt would have vanished in this morning hour in which, with bare feet and still undressed, he walked back and forth on the soft carpets, gripped the back of a chair to straighten it, sat himself at the desk, grasped the nearest object only to lay it down again, again stood up to walk to the open balcony door, through which the morning air streamed in, fresh and pure—if it had still not been clear to him, in these hours he would have grasped that he was supposed to be a victim.

Something must be done. Only what? He did not yet know. What should he do?

This person wanted money. Money, that's what all blackmailers want. First something, then more and always more. Thus the pretense of this letter. Pretense in its apparently harmless, unctuous style, its mendacious sentimentality, its fresh and at the same time obsequious importunity—precisely thought out pretense, behind which his intention stood out only too clearly between the words. For no reasonable person wrote like that.

What was he to do?

If he did not answer, then after a few days a new letter would come or—he himself. That was certain.

But if he wrote and sent him money, then there remained the one, if only weak possibility that he would really travel back. Then he was free of him. But probably, much more probably he would see from an answer, above all one with money, that his coming here was feared and therefore—without coming here—he would remain in Germany, so as—naturally with all necessary care—to turn the screws tighter and tighter.

The possibility, the weak possibility of traveling back should therefore not be taken from him.

Therefore, write!

But write what, and how?

How impossible all this was!

Even the greeting! To follow his, that of the crude familiarity, even if it was with veiled ridicule—no, he could not do it. To use another way—a strange one—that too would only seen ridiculous! Without any greeting then?

And write what? Send what? Naturally not the amount demanded (although in this hour, even if against his will, he agreed to pay it, if only to get rid of him). By no means more than the trip required. For this five hundred marks was sufficient.

When he had finally decided, it was already so light that he could see what he was writing by the daylight that penetrated in through the high windows.

He took one of his thick visiting cards and wrote in his tall, steep handwriting, after his name: "sends Herr Eduard Schmidt according to his wish the enclosed sum of five hundred marks for the purpose of traveling back to Rio de Janeiro."

But he immediately tore up again what he had written and in place of the last words put: "to make possible his return trip"

That too was not good. That too was false. Everything was impossible. But he found no other way, and the time was pressing him to a decision. He laid the card and five hundred-mark bills in the envelope and addressed it.

He wanted to post the letter that day himself. But not here, rather in one of the small villages in the vicinity, where there was a branch post office. It was neither advisable to put it with the mail at his business nor to take it himself to the local post office, where everyone knew him.

From the garden soft steps sounded over the gravel. It was the old gardener. Councilor-of-Commerce Behrendt called to him with suppressed voice: "Listen, Lutze, I am not quite well and want to lie down until noon. Tell Franz up front to wake me. And inform the office."

6

He slept until noon.

When his wife asked him at the dining table if he did not feel well, he smiled slyly: "No, nothing is wrong—but when one has come home only at six o'clock in the morning—"

She looked at him, once again uncertain whether he was speaking seriously or in jest. For even if jokes of this kind were not entirely unusual with him, they had ceased in recent times. She became angry and found his behavior hardly becoming.

He looked at her from the side—indeed she more and more resembled a pug.

At the close of business he set off on his way.

He avoided the main street and turned through side streets to the town park by the river. The park was rarely visited at this time

KENN]

of day. On the other side of the bridge that he was crossing lay the poorest part of the town—dirty, narrow streets with falling down houses, behind which, when one cut across the highway, there was a rather steep climb uphill through lean vineyards toward the summit, from where the highway, which until there had climbed up in serpentines, ran over unattractive bare fields and meadows into the next village, his goal for today.

It was a path of a quarter hour climbing. He reached it. He did not remember having ever been here, as he seldom came into the town quarter that he had just walked through, except when he was called there on duty as town councilor to inspect one of the dilapidated houses.

As boys, yes as boys, for whom no corner of their town including the surroundings remained unknown, they had certainly also romped around here. But he still remembered it only unclearly. That was so long ago.

It was a stately and still new house, which stood up here on the summit as the only one round about. A sign said that its owner was called Fürbringer and that he was the proprietor of a wine firm. The name was not unknown to him, and he had heard his wine praised. What indeed could have moved him to settle up here, far from all the world, was a puzzle to him, unless it was the wish to be near his vineyard. But that down there was really only a small piece, and besides the wine-growing of this region was not all that famous. The land and the situation could not yet be favorable here, and only farther, above the river, stood the hills with the world-famous names, and only from them could this Fürbringer obtain the wine that he sold. That little bit here, which certainly belonged to him—what could it bring in!

He stood and looked around him. A remarkable idea, to settle up here!

But the letter should be sent, and he did not even know when this small branch post office in the village closed.

So he hurried to reach it, walking a half hour over the bare summit, and after the letter was fortunately and formally dispatched, again a half hour back the same boring path, and he was now standing again in front of the solitary house, not exactly tired, but thirsty from the walk.

Thus his eye was struck just right by the ironwork sign that swung over the entrance and said that the couple of steps led down into a wine-room.

He had to bend down on entering and found himself in the first of two rooms that served as tavern.

Neither was large, but with walls inlaid with light-colored wood, with benches drawn to them, with panels with beautiful old pewter mugs and colorful glass, and above all with their mighty, old, green tiled stove, which connected the two together through the wall, they made such a cozy impression that the man entering looked about him again and again, astonished and delighted.

How could there be such a gem in this good town and no one knew it? That he wanted immediately to—but no, who of them, the gentlemen with whom he had been together with just yesterday, would appreciate it! They would certainly find the horrible artificiality and distortions of their regular tavern much more beautiful than the simplicity of these small rooms. To be sure, who would make their way up to here! But he would keep his discovery to himself. It was only a pity that it was so out of the way! He too would hardly find his way up here again.

But in the meantime he was here and he sat down in the back room.

He sat thus quite a while, as if benumbed by the stillness and the attractiveness of his surroundings, and as if made happy that there was such a thing here.

Then there came the sound of light steps and a young girl, still a child as it appeared to him at first glance, entered, obviously embarrassed that he had had to wait. He ordered a tall glass, received it, and was again alone.

What answer would he probably receive to the letter that he had just sent?

Naturally he could not prevent this man from coming here.

Let him come, only not too near to him! He would get to know him.

Then he became angry with himself. He really wanted to think no more about these matters! With this walk they should just be done with.

He wanted to think about other things, about more pleasant and more beautiful things. But unfortunately there was in his life almost none of either—neither beautiful nor pleasant.

Then he at least took delight in the light wine in the glass before him, which was pure and quite excellent. (Too bad that this attractive tavern was not in the town, but rather so inconvenient, almost unreachable!)

He ordered himself yet another glass.

Again the little girl brought it, and again in the light twilight that prevailed here in this room situated somewhat under the ground she appeared to him to still be a child.

When, on paying, after his change was brought, he shoved back a coin as a tip, it was not taken and he heard softly said, "No thanks. It is not necessary."

He looked up and for the first time directly into a friendly, rounded face with wonderfully beautiful brown eyes, which—as he was now convinced—was really no longer that of a child. He smiled at her. But his smile was not returned. Her face remained serious, while her calm brown eyes attentively and as if searching looked at him for a moment.

She could not be the daughter of the proprietor, who was still young and had lost his wife, as he dimly remembered to have heard, through a curious accident. Even less could she be a wait-ress—anything but that. For this she appeared much too well edu-cated and refined, and the rejection of the tip had taught him what a blunder he had made to offer it. Again a lesson, to open one's eyes before one acts! Perhaps a relative? But he did not want to inquire and only nodded back as he soon walked away.

Outside he stopped.

Actually it was not such a bad thought of this Fürbringer to

build up here. Even if the surroundings were damned unattractive—the view from up here was beautiful. It went across the river
and the town below, over the hills on the other side, far out into
the countryside with its woods and valleys, and ended only where
the bluish lines of the far ridges bounded it. Today, on this late
afternoon in May, everything lay wrapped in a silver mist and
appeared to be suspended in its own atmosphere.

Only, thought Councilor-of-Commerce Behrendt while he was
thus standing and looking at the town lying there, it is not suspended, our good town, it is firmly fixed, like the people in it—
like me!

And then immediately further: But already for the sake of this
view, so as once again to see one's own roofs from above, one should
come up here often. For only from here did one have it.

He sought his own. There they were: rather in the middle of the
panorama was the old, gray, and often repaired roof of the business
house; there the flat roof of his villa, surrounded in green by the
beautiful trees of his garden; and there, at the opposite end, the
broad, multiform buildings of the factory, which appeared to take
up a whole quarter for itself in the middle of the research plantations
that from year to year stretched out farther and farther.

He stood yet a while thus, in the light of the declining evening,
and as he finally pulled himself away and began the climb down,
it was done as if he were taking leave for a long time from a place
which was still easily to be reached again at any time in half an
hour.

CHAPTER THREE

1

When eight days had passed since the sending of his reply without anything happening, Councilor-of-Commerce Behrendt began to wonder; after fourteen he almost began to believe that the "friend of his youth" had really kept his promise and had blessed anew the fatherland of his choice over there with his presence.

He was mistaken. At the beginning of the third week the letter with the well-known, studied handwriting—every letter carefully drawn—lay among the early post and this time it read:

"Dear Friend of my youth!

"Today you receive only a few short words from me. What need is there of words between us! We understand one another, in the memory of what has been, also without it, I should think!

"I have changed my decision once again. In the beginning I was not pleased with the old home country, yet these last weeks have convinced me that I am able to acclimatize myself again to it, if I find a place—a place of refuge, I would prefer to call it—which opens up for me. Here, where I am a stranger, there is naturally no thought of finding a position. But with you, in your large factory, it will be easy for you to make a little place for me, and I have already completely set store by the thought of spending the twilight of my life with you, together with whom I spent a part of my youth, and to end my days under your roof.

"If I also have—not being so favored with luck as you—no other stake to bring with me than a working strength still unbroken in the storms of life, as well as the ability to get along easily and quickly in strange circumstances, there is for me no doubt that the remembrance of common experiences and sufferings outweighs a material stake.

"So I will close then, follow soon after this letter, and am with cordial greetings, your old friend

"Eduard Schmidt."

The letter was read, found its place beside its predecessor in the breast pocket, and the morning passed like all the others: Herr Spruth appeared, to learn what the post had brought, talked about an incredible amount of things in an incredibly short time, and stormed out again; his son-in-law looked in—no longer the shy, young man in the shiny coat with the worn-out sleeves, but rather comfortable and elegant, rings on his finger and pearls in his cravat, but still always full of respect and diligence—and he explained in boring fussiness the epochal advantages of a new lid for conserve bottles; all possible kinds of visitors appeared with questions and requests; Fräulein Selma (actually Anselma), very charmingly smiling, came and was occupied—but the gentleman who "meant to follow hard on his letter," did not appear. Nevertheless, at any moment the door could open and—

Thus Herr Anker, who had come with the briefcase of letters which had to go out this morning with his signature, was already at the door when he was called back: "If a Herr **Eduard Schmidt** should ask for me—I am not in to him."

This was said with the tone that one recognized when Herr Councilor-of-Commerce wanted to see a wish be carried out absolutely.

2

This afternoon, too, passed like so many others.

But Councilor-of-Commerce Behrendt, after the close of business, did not find today his usual rest in his quiet office. The walls of the vast building, now suddenly sunken into silence from one hour to the next, appeared to sink onto him and to close him in even more closely than usual, and even a walk through the empty rooms, with their abandoned desks and chairs, their typewriters and bookcases, made an almost ghostly impression on him today.

He felt that only a walk in the open air could free him from the pressure in his head. But it had to be a strenuous march to get the tension out of the muscles and sinews of his strong body. What if he again sought out the summit on the other side and the house on it? Maybe he should choose another, longer path up to it than the stone's throw route through the vineyard with its detour of the highway.

So he walked through the municipal park and then farther along the river, until he came to the railway bridge, under which a footbridge brought him to the other bank of the river, and then on the other side continued climbing up through woods and under-brush on the poorly maintained, but more comfortable path.

Halfway to the summit, he sat down on a tree limb and read the letter again. At one place he nearly laughed out loud when he pictured to himself the face of his associate—the face of Herr Eduard Spruth—as he said to him that a friend of his youth had offered to enter the firm, and to the greedy question, "With how much?" he replied, "With nothing but his unbroken working strength."

But then he no longer laughed.

So he was here! He was probably already here. He may have come with the train that, ten minutes earlier, had roared over him as he crossed the railway bridge.

He took up the letter again.

Already as he was skimming through it earlier, he had been so startled that it took his breath away, and he had laid the letter aside so as to be able to work.

Even now he was upset.

He knew himself: Impudence, open impudence revolted him wherever he encountered it. He was no longer master of himself if it came too close to him.

But now he was not even revolted. For this here was indeed no longer impudence. It was grotesque, simply grotesque!

Naturally it was the letter of a blackmailer. But it went beyond everything that he had ever seen and heard.

Because this Herr Eduard Schmidt from Rio had sat on the same school bench with him for a short time, had met him again through pure chance after so many years, and then for some weeks had kept up a purely superficial association with him, because he then, through precisely this chance had been the only one to know of his youthful foolishness, he believed he—now, after thirty years!—had him where he wanted him!

Grotesque, simply grotesque!

He read it again, sentence for sentence.

The extortionist intent clearly obvious between the lines. It was recognizable to everyone who was not blind or did not want to be blind. But at the same time, it was still always entirely unassailable. This crafty blackguard further played the role of dolt, so as not immediately to be accused of being a blackmailer.

This time, too, he made no demands for money. He had never openly and frankly made such a demand. He satisfied himself with a position in the business, and—how sweet!—with a little place at his table and under his roof, a further blessed member of his cozy circle, to thus end his days in peace and quiet "at the side of the friend of his youth"!

Crazy, completely crazy!

How could this person have really written this seriously? Could he really believe even for a moment that his crazy wishes would be fulfilled or even be taken into consideration?

Naturally he was conceited and vain beyond all measure. Such insignificant persons do exist. They puff themselves up until they burst. Stubbornly adhering to a fixed idea that they have nourished for years, they often come to the most incredible whims.

Was this Eduard Schmidt one of these half-crazy persons? Or was he—again and again the reader inclined to the opposite view—really rather a clever, superior swindler and this prattle only appeared to be stupid. He constructed every word, so as to attain their desired effect: to drive his victim first to disquiet, then fear. And little by little to make him docile.

But if this was so, if he had to deal with a methodical and therefore very dangerous opponent, was it then wise to reject him on the spot if he came? Was it then not better to receive him and look him over, so as to see whether his assumption was correct, and to determine how far the man would go? He could do this with feigned friendliness and hidden irony. But then, once here and rejected, what would he not tell everyone? Not only the truth, but also what lies—all too gladly believed?

Therefore, should he see him tomorrow and speak with him?

Councilor-of-Commerce Behrendt knew himself. He knew what he was capable of, if this fellow was sitting there before him and in his words—which, as spoken words, could be denied and therefore were far more dangerous than written ones—would be even clearer than in his letters—if he let his mask fall before him.

No, he did not want to take back the rejection, whatever happened. It was indeed hard to say what the other would then do: write new letters and send then through a messenger to his house; stalk him and speak to him in the open street; greet him where possible with a raised voice as the dear friend of his youth; seek to get at him through a third party—

But what purpose did it serve to think over all this!

He must wait for what would happen. The weapon that the rascal had in his hand against him—he would probably be so clever—he would certainly only use when he finally realized that there was nothing for him to hope for. But then—what then?

Sitting there on the tree limb, he was at a loss. But to be at a loss was for him one of the most uncomfortable things of life.

He stood up and shook his head.

All this was really impossible, quite impossible!

He folded the letter, stuck it with its predecessor in his pocket, and walked slowly on. It had grown much later than he wanted.

The woods ended and on leaving it he saw himself almost opposite the house on the summit.

As he did two weeks before, he entered the friendly rooms. He did not need to wait this time. The little girl from the other day was sitting at the window of the front room, occupied with some handwork. She stood up and brought him his wine in the back room.

He drank quickly and did not sit long.

Upon leaving and paying—oh yes, for God's sake do not again give a tip!—as he again saw the friendly and yet so curiously closed face before him, he asked, just to say something (for his thoughts were far away), "Are you related to Fürbringer, the proprietor?"

"Yes, Herr Fürbringer is my uncle."

"Have you been here long?"

"Indeed. Already more than half a year."

The answers were short, like the questions, and given with a soft, somewhat astonished voice.

Outside he stood only a moment with the view over the town.

He felt driven down into it. Again, however, he made the wide detour instead of climbing down the steep, short path that opened up before him. Although he made yet besides a wide arc around the town, before he went home, his strong body did not find the desired fatigue and he slept badly in that night.

3

The next morning—it was nearly midday and had passed like all the others—Herr Anker turned around at the door and in his voice was an obvious disdain: "The gentleman, this Herr Schmidt, was just here. I told him the Councilor-of-Commerce was not in to him."

He sat a while longer at his desk, in the same position, and looked straight ahead.

Then he stood up slowly and walked home, a half hour earlier than usual.

In the entrance hall voices penetrated to his ear from the salon to the right: that of his wife and another—strange one.

He stood still for a moment.

Then he quickly walked in.

As his wife stood up, he saw behind her a small, yellow person in a light-colored suit, hat and walking stick in one hand, who came toward him, holding out his other hand with a lively movement, while a twinkle in the restless, black eyes sought for a secret understanding.

"Just think, Ludwig, an old acquaintance, Herr—Herr Emil Schmid—from Buenos Aires, with whom you were together earlier in England—I did not even know that you were ever in England—"

She stopped short. She saw only how her husband gripped, not the hand that was stretched out to him, but rather the arm of her visitor and more dragged than drew the resisting man to the door, and then also heard how the latter shouted back over his shoulder, "Yes, and in prison too!"

She was still standing on the same spot when her husband returned, outwardly as peaceful as if nothing had happened, only red from suppressed rage. Only then did she break forth: "For God's sake, Ludwig, what did the man do to you—such an attractive person" (in her hunger for people all new acquaintances were attractive persons until, in the case of most of them, she was convinced of the opposite in a short time) "and what does it mean, in prison? He was in prison?"

He looked at her. His face again had its natural color, as he loudly and clearly replied, "No, **I** was in prison!"

But now she became seriously angry. This joke had gone too far. She wanted to tell him how much she disapproved of it, but she did not get to do it. She felt herself held lightly by the arm and led to the sofa. He sat down opposite her on a low and, for his size, much too small, fragile chair, and bent forward as he propped his arms on his knees.

He began: "For one thing, his name is not Emil, but rather Eduard—Eduard Schmidt. Also, he is not from Buenos Aires, but from Rio de Janeiro. But that is beside the point. The matter is this—"

And now he related to her what he thought necessary to tell her.

She looked at him and became more and more upset with every one of his words. When he finished, tears streamed over her face. He was used to this: she was able, on certain occasions, to cry—softly and wordlessly, long and without moving.

He waited patiently, as he always did in such cases. When it ran on too long, he said, "Tell me, Bertha, why are you crying?"

There came out among the sobs: "How horrible! How horrible! Just what will our friends say?"

He kept silent, before he took both her hands, held her so firm that she could not move, and with the voice, against which the was no contradiction and no rejection, emphasizing word for word, said, "You will now stop crying! And we will not come back to this foolishness with a word more! With not one word more—you understand me—yes?"

She swallowed her tears, while he stood up and walked across into his rooms.

Only there did he laugh bitterly! She thought about the others first. She did not think about him. When had she ever thought about him! But then his thoughts returned to the scene just enacted.

What a small, weak fellow he was! He would not have recognized him again among thousands, the—"friend of his youth"! Had he also been so small at that time (and he himself so tall)? They had both been already grown men, but the difference in size had never struck him so much as just now. What a poor observer one really was, when one is young! One saw only oneself and the world and overlooked the next person, without making a comparison. And how he had appeared, this person! Of course he **had** to look like that: this yellow suit, the colored shirt, from which the red tie slipped out when he grabbed him so roughly! He had to laugh, as he again saw him before him and believed he had him

again in his hands, struggling and resisting and squeaking out
unintelligible words—but then he was also already outside, before
the door, chucked out. (Why is it that people with fiery-red hair
always clap poison-green hunter's hats over their round skulls?
And why do lemon-yellow throats, like this one, prefer to wrap
themselves with bright red ties?)

He had gripped him hard, that was true. But as he saw the
impudent, yellow face with the infamous, self-confident smile
around the bluish lips and the decayed, badly filled teeth so suddenly before him—here, in his own house, into which he had
slipped in to his wife behind his back, after he had first been denied access to him at work—when he saw him thus before him,
the rage had come over him, this furious, irrational rage.

These sudden outbreaks of rage were for him the safety valve
of his character, without which he would hardly have been able to
bear these long years of suppressing his dearest wishes. They worked
like bleedings. As, when he, under the tyranny of his father—
naturally never in his presence—took what he happened to have
in his hand and crashed it to the floor—a wash basin, for example.

And later: One time he was in a municipal ordinance meeting, where the prattle and stupidity of the people around him had
brought his patience to a boiling point. He had stood up and left
with a suppressed curse, and on going out had slammed the door
shut so that the walls shook (then, at the next meeting, he excused
himself to the indignant gentlemen with the uncommon amiabil-
ity that he could command when he wanted to).

Another time he got into a scuffle with a brutal driver who was
mishandling his horse and had thrashed him with his own whip,
so that he (the driver) had to be taken to the hospital, and he
himself escaped a charge of bodily injury with difficulty.

Finally, a third time, at a large party, one of those unbearable
windbags had related one of his stories, which everyone already
knew by heart, with a complacency that brought him to rage; he
had lifted him up together with his chair, to then set him so roughly

down on the floor again that everyone around cried out. (That time he did **not** excuse himself.)

He knew himself. He would do what he had done again if he saw this ugly face before him again—even though he was now clear that what he had done had been a great imprudence that could not be repaired, a downright foolishness! He had chucked him out. Now he was out there. But he was still here in the town!

What would happen now? He did not know. But that the word that had gotten to his wife for the first time was now being spread further and further, perhaps already in this minute and to the very next person, to go from mouth to mouth until there was no one left in the whole town who, wherever his name would be named from now on, would not connect his honorable name— even if only in thought—with that word!

And he? What should he do?

What should he do against it?

He felt, as he stood there, how his back ran hot and cold.

4

The days passed and nothing happened. There came neither new letters, nor did Councilor- of-Commerce Behrendt hear or see any- thing of his opponent.

But he had the clear feeling that he was still here, here—in his vicinity, close to him.

But if he was here, he would certainly meet him one day. It was impossible in this small provincial town—for such it was, in spite of the relatively quite considerable number of inhabitants— not to meet.

He could do nothing except await what would happen.

But precisely the fact that he could do nothing made him more unquiet from day to day.

Even if there was nothing remarkable outwardly—his voice

was as calm and his walk as firm as ever—it bored into him and whispered—one person knew about it already—who else?

He was not certain of his wife, but it was impossible for him to speak with her about this matter again. She was restrained with regard to him, that he saw. But what about the others?

Yesterday, at the midday Sunday meal, which brought the family together as usual—had they not all too quickly become silent when the talk had by chance turned to England? He himself had naturally acted as if he noticed nothing. But he could not rid himself of the thought: Did they not wish to spare him with their silence?

And like yesterday at table, he asked himself at almost every meeting, by every encounter with acquaintances: Do they already know?

He asked himself and did not understand himself.

In the course of years the persons among whom he lived and was forced to live had indeed lost their importance for him more and more. The past five years especially, in which he felt old age nearing, had taught him how little it was worth occupying himself with them and their judgment.

He hated none of them. He was far from that. There was also no occasion for it, for he let no one come near him. The friendly indifference he brought without exception to all with whom he had anything to do, held everyone at a certain distance, and thus he was, even in his own family, if not a stranger, then still basically not someone who really belonged there.

Mostly silent and turned in on himself (as his father, even if in a completely different way and from completely other traits of character, had also been), he had no need to pour out his heart before others, to confide in others, to open his soul to others.

He was not really liked. Honest persons were not liked these days. He knew how little he was liked. Not even by his employees. It had never happened that he said an unfriendly word to any of them. They knew that he was always on their side if they made demands that they thought justified (and which **he** mostly held to be only all too justified—to the greatest displeasure of his partners and his son-in-law).

They, those employees, also saw that he always silently helped, as often as he heard of emergencies (but they had to be suggested to him, of himself he did not see them). When, however, it came to personal negotiations, they preferred to turn, not to him but to Herr Lindtner, who had come from their circle and was, in spite of his present outward elegance, of a rough and kindred nature. Indeed, they preferred to turn to the other owner of the firm rather than to him, even though they knew they would be showered by him with a flood of accusations and be dealt with by empty phrases.

If he was thus more respected than liked, there were and had always been persons who would have given much to be allowed to approach him closer, who revered him and more or less openly sought his friendship. But they were certainly never able to get rid of the feeling that he did not even see them.

Thus, how did it happen that suddenly, from one day to the next, from that day on in which this person had popped up here, his surroundings to a certain extent existed again for him, that they again had validity, even importance for him, and that their judgments again were of importance to him?

He did not understand himself.

But did it not show that his life and work, on which he had long since set no more value, still possessed some value for him, and possessed it in a measure that he himself would no longer have held to be possible?

He scolded himself.

What did it matter to him if people here knew or not? On whom was he dependent? Who had anything to say to him? Who could harm him?

Whoever was so stupid and mean as to change his judgment about him—good, let him do it! But he should just refrain from letting it be noticed even with a twitch of an eye! Then he would have him to deal with!

But that was precisely what made him more and more unsure

these days. He was not questioned; nowhere even an allusion; nowhere even the shadow of evidence that one "knew." And yet the feeling became stronger and stronger in him that a net was drawing together over him, woven from a thousand fine threads, threads of gossip, of talebearing, of whispering.

The feeling increased in many hours to a downright physical torment that he believed he could no longer bear. In such hours he wished to meet him. Then he would at least have a physical enemy opposite, a being of flesh and blood that he could seize with his large and strong hands, instead of, as now, helplessly grasping with them into empty air after unreal shadows, which slipped away from him and dissolved when he approached. Shadows perhaps—he also told himself again and again—which only he had created in his overexcitement, and which in the long hours of the night, in which he lay sleepless, still came again and again and bent over him. The meeting—when would it finally happen?

He wanted it here now, and he no longer walked out of the house and over the street without expecting it.

5

It took place on a shiny summer morning at the end of June—in the middle of the town, on the main street, and after precisely fourteen days.

Councilor-of-Commerce Behrendt was walking down it about midday, so as to carry out an errand before his meal, greeted as always every twenty steps, to greet in return—old acquaintances by raising his hand, others by raising his hat—when at a lessening of the street traffic he saw two gentlemen approaching him from the other side. Who the one was, he did not know at first glance, until it later occurred to him; the other he recognized immediately—it was he!

He it was and—he greeted him! Greeted him across the way, while a smile distorted the yellow face and exposed the bad teeth, greeted just as if not the least thing had taken place between them, greeted as one greets a good, old acquaintance.

He stood still. He felt how the blood was shooting into his face. He hand gripped his stick more firmly, and for a second it seemed as if he intended to cross over the roadway. But there was only a short, vehement movement of his shoulders, and already in the next moment he continued his way, with his long, firm strides, and without seeing the astonished looks on those he passed by, without noticing them.

The errand was not carried out. He was immediately called for after his meal and until the close of business he was so overrun with visitors and questions that he did not have three minutes to be alone with himself.

Only then could he be free, now animated only by the one wish, to be alone with himself and to hear and see no more of other people.

To be alone, but not here in this room, over which the sweat of these long working hours lay. It must be outside.

He had to get away.

He spontaneously chose once again the lonely path over the river and then through the woods up to the summit.

He walked, as in the morning after his meeting, with his broad, stretching strides, only now he went forward more quickly, since he no longer needed to give way, but rather had free room on both sides.

The rage that had been suppressed for long hours broke out of him and gave vent to disjointed, projected words and hard blows of his stick.

He knew himself. If the meeting of today at noon repeated itself, he was no longer sure of himself. He was capable, if he saw this person before him again, of seizing him by the throat and slamming him against the nearest wall, so that his skull would break, or choking him with his fingers. With his enormous physical strength, which surprised even himself when he once had occasion to apply it, for example, by raising heavy objects (he had no

KENN]

other comparison, for he did not go in for sports and hated them)—
with his strength this wretch of a man could remain under his
hands like nothing, but then—he would be a murderer. He had
absolutely no desire to spend the rest of his life behind bars.

It should, therefore, come to no new meeting, nor indeed to a
scandal in the open street.

It had been fortunate today that the street lay between them.
Otherwise he would perhaps already no longer be walking here,
breathing free air.

There was no other possibility: either this fellow must leave
the town, or he himself.

But how could **he** go away from here!

6

How beautiful it really was up here and how cool after the rapid
walk in these quiet rooms with bright tables, which no other guest
appeared to enter except him, as if they were his own, which he
had established for himself here. No waiter, only this silent little
spirit—the wine was already before him as he sat down, and the
glass was placed there as if by an invisible hand. He pressed himself firmly into the corner and leaned his head back against the
green, cool tiles of the stove, before he took the first draught. He
was not really tired, but he felt now the aftermath of his day—
with its meeting; the long, enervating business transactions precisely today; the rapid walk just now.

But this was no time to be tired and to dream. It was a matter
of making a decision, an immediate decision.

Tomorrow already, yes already this evening, on returning home
he could again meet this ugly face and there could occur what had
just now, on his climb, had stood so clearly before his eyes, as if it
had already happened.

Who had the other actually been, who had been with him and
also greeted him? Right: the lottery collector Türschmann—also

an evil guy. So that was his acquaintance. Naturally. What decent person would otherwise want to have anything to do with him!

What was he actually still doing here? The long days? The money that he had sent him, the five hundred marks, must have gradually come to an end. So what was he living on? Had he found other acquaintances from earlier days who were helping him, happy with the great news he brought them, and greedy to spread it and perhaps even to take a share of the fat booty?

Or was he preparing a new chess move against him? But of what kind? He just could not take many more steps now without coming out of his reserve, exposing himself, and bringing himself into danger.

No matter what, he had to leave. And there was only one way to do it: to settle the matter with him.

But how?

Even the thought of a personal conversation with him was upsetting.

He, usually so calm and collected, who had learned with countless persons to treat them and take them as they were, not as they should be, he knew clearly that in this case he would fail. His nerves—and he had nerves, in many regards very sensitive ones—he would lose control of them.

Accordingly, it could only take place through the mediation of a third party. But through whom?

Friends whom he might trust in this matter and on whom he might depend, he did not have. The only one whom he might call such, the old, retired schoolmaster—or, as one said now, councilor-of-instruction—did not come into question. Even if he would face the matter completely unprejudiced (as he faced most things in life) and at most would smile his soft, ironic smile over a youthful foolishness, which was nothing but such, in the practical treatment of the case—and it was matter of this alone here—he would still fail. He was no match for such a wily guy as this Eduard Schmidt.

Thus there remained only a paid person—an attorney. Here,

for the same reasons, the longtime counsel of the firm and his family, the old counselor and notary Habermann, did not come into question. Besides it seemed to him simply impossible to make such a confession to him, who already knew him as a child and who had seen him grow up. This was all the more impossible since he did not know at all how this old gentleman—a friend of his father, not quite as harsh and one-sided in his thinking as he, but still one of the old school—would receive his admission and judge it. No, he must not think of going to him. So he, too, was eliminated.

Who of the remaining attorneys of the town, all of whom he knew more or less, came into question? Basically speaking, none of them. He did not rightly trust any of them to handle this matter with the necessary tactfulness, even if they would be able, one way or another, to take care of it.

Then a certain Jarchow occurred to him. He was, to be sure, not a "certified" attorney, but rather only a consulting lawyer without any academic education, what one called a shyster, and yet was not really one. At any rate, an extraordinarily clever person and an entirely cunning advisor, as his own firm, in one of those processes that every large house is forced to carry out from time to time, even against its own wishes, had to experience once years ago, much to its sorrow. For it had flatly lost the process, although it had been in the right. How it stood with his tactfulness, he indeed did not know. But in that process, in which he had admired the dexterity of this mind, he had the feeling that this man defended the interests of a client so well precisely because he understood so well how to keep an eye on his own. He was certainly not a gossip. Otherwise one would have heard of it.

Naturally he would thoroughly take advantage of him and try to get out of the curious and extraordinary case as much as possible for himself. But that did not matter so much here. The task was, to get the person away from here, and indeed as quietly as possible and forever. For this he trusted this Jarchow more than any other, and so he again considered turning to him, something he had rejected in the first moment.

Jarchow would not let himself be confounded by any, however great, insolence in the appearance of this Schmidt, would oppose it with his own, certainly not lesser insolence, and would speak to him in his own language. It occurred to him how outrageously bold this small fellow had been in that process with a certain line of argumentation, so impudent that everyone in the hall simply became speechless.

Certainly—he would keep silent, because it lay in his interest to keep silent.

There was, therefore, no danger for himself in turning to him.

But—how degrading this would be!

He, the Councilor-of-Commerce Behrendt, in transactions with a person whom he could not once seek out by day, so as not to risk the possibility of being seen, for then the whole town would know about it the next day and would naturally bring the two into some kind of invented connection!

In his indecision—he did not lightly decide on this step—he could no longer bear his place behind the heavy table. Shoving it back with a movement of his hand, he stood up and walked back and forth in the two small rooms. In the front one, the little girl was sitting somewhat elevated at a window bent over a book. He only noticed her when she stood up.

As if to explain his restless walking about, he ordered a new glass and drank the first empty in quick draughts. How thirsty he was today!

Then he sat down again and made his decision.

If he still wanted to meet him today, this counseling lawyer Jarchow, then he must make an appointment immediately and immediately go down into the town. For up here there was just no connection. Or was there? He called to the other room.

The young girl appeared in the doorway.

How friendly she could smile, when she wanted to!

Yes, certainly they had a telephone.

He had the book brought to him and made the call outside in the entrance hall.

A female voice answered his call.

"Is the Herr Attorney available?"

"In what matter, please, a business affair?"

"Yes."

"But the office hours of my husband are over."

"I would still like to request—"

"One moment, please."

Then, after a couple of seconds, another voice, this time a man's, short and firm: "I regret that my office hours are until six o'clock."

Then, after a brief pause, when he received no reply: "With whom am I actually speaking then?"

Councilor-of-Commerce Behrendt gave his name distinctly, and clear astonishment rang from the voice, as if suddenly changed, at the other end. He was asked almost incredibly, "Not indeed Herr Councilor-of-Commerce personally?"

"Yes indeed, Herr Attorney, he himself. Could I speak with you, and indeed this evening?"

The answer came immediately. "But of course, Herr Councilor-of-Commerce."

"It's all right this very evening?"

"I'll be at home the whole evening."

"Good! I'll be at your place in a half hour, around seven-thirty."

"Very good, Herr Councilor-of-Commerce."

He made a second call, this time to his own house. The servant Franz answered.

"I'm not coming home this evening, Franz. Notify my wife." (He never said "my lady.")

On occasion he was away evenings, but very seldom. When he sometimes had to ask a visitor to dinner, whom he did not want to see at his own table and therefore invited to The Elephant or another restaurant.

He looked at his watch.

He had mistaken the time. It was already past seven.

He took yet a quick draught, reached for his hat and stick, and hurried out.

7

It was growing dark as he arrived down there, again heated by the quick climb down on the shortest path through the vineyard.

A heavy mist lay over the town, which he felt as oppressive. The sky was covered with dark clouds, through which the red-yellow rays of a light streamed, which seemed to have left this earth for ever.

From St. Peter's the clock struck seven-thirty.

He was now on the other side, but still outside the town walls.

He sat himself on the low, stone parapet, which here bordered the river down to the railway bridge, keeping his left foot on the ground so as to give his body support.

This would not do, no, it would not do, that he, as he was—heated and out of breath—burst in on this stranger, only in order to be there on time, as if he in fact was in flight before a pursuer. He could just wait. He had indeed said that he was at home the whole evening.

If all this was already impossible—he still found no other word for this affair and thus he repeated it to himself again and again—if all this was already impossible for him, then he wanted at least not to let it be noticed. So he sat then for a half hour, in his thoughts already at the coming conference. It was still here. Only the soft flowing of the river, the rattle of a late truck on the highway opposite, and from the town now and then a lost sound, a call, and a dog's howl.

What was he to say? He had to introduce himself: explain his visit at this time, the reason why he had come—even if he was not to be interrogated about all particulars (he was convinced ahead of time that he would be spared no question). It was painful. It was more than painful.

He decided to leave as much as possible to the other and only to indicate what drove him here. If this Jarchow was the clever man, concerned about his own interests, that he held him to be, he would be able to think of the rest; if he was not, if he was clumsy and insinuating, there was still always time to stand up, bring out his wallet, and leave.

But he must first be calm so as to be master of the situation. He had always been so up to now and everywhere.

So he sat and calmed himself.

Only once did someone come by him—an old woman who, startled by the tall, dark figure on the parapet who popped up before her, sprang to one side to then quickly continue her way to the town.

It was dark when Councilor-of-Commerce Behrendt stood up.

8

In five minutes he reached the town gate and a few minutes later he was standing before the house he sought in the street that was well known to him. (There was no street in the town that he did not know, even if he entered most of them only occasionally, as today—once every couple of years.)

He had resolved, if he should be recognized here and greeted in spite of the darkness, to leave the greeting unnoticed and to pass by whoever it was. But no one that he knew met him.

S. Jarchow (without specification of a profession) was on a name-plate on the still almost new house. S.—that could mean a number of things—he wanted to take it for Siegfried, Siegfried, who would slay the dragon for him, he thought smiling, as he climbed up the quiet steps, empty of people, to the third floor. At his ringing the door was opened for him almost immediately.

He was standing opposite a middle-aged woman with sharp,

dark eyes in a black dress, who, before he could even ask a question, invited him with a movement of her hand to enter the room on the right. (If she had been standing here behind the door the whole time since seven-thirty, she must have waited a long time, thought Councilor-of-Commerce Behrendt as he went in.)

Only now did he hear her say, "My husband will appear directly, Herr Councilor-of-Commerce. May I ask you in the meantime to take a seat?" The woman spoke with a remarkably deep and pleasant voice.

The room in which he found himself was obviously the waiting room for clients, but was distinguished in the most advantageous way from such purgatories. On the nicely covered table there were no scraps of well-read issues of old magazines. The few pictures on the wall—good reproductions—were certainly known to none of those who waited here except him. The only book on the table was, appropriately, the penal code book. Everything, down to the white curtains on the window (which could not have just been hung in his honor), was shining clean.

The view, too, through the open door into the next room, the actual office, convinced him that he found himself anywhere but in the den of a shyster full of dusty case files with crumpled edges, under whose burden warped shelves were falling together. Rather, he was in a room kept in meticulous order, lighted to the furthest corner, in which there were no files to be seen at all. The large desk was cleared, the typewriter reposing after the day's work under its usual cover, the bright bookcases were firmly closed—in his own office it did not look more orderly (and he was himself very orderly).

Everything here seemed to say to the one seeking advice and help, "Have confidence! Everything that you ever confide to these walls remains confidential."

Here was missing, also by day, His Majesty, the arrogant Herr Chief Clerk, with his self-satisfied air, likewise the constant rushing here and there of the female typist. The two surely did everything alone, without foreign help, let no one see into their files, and certainly did only good thereby.

Councilor-of-Commerce Behrendt heard spoken behind him, "Jarchow. May I ask the Herr Councilor-of-Commerce to come in?" and he turned around to the one who had soundlessly entered: a thick-set man with smooth, lean face, with a prominent nose, and, behind large, horn-rim glasses, black eyes like those that had just now examined him in the entrance hall. They otherwise also resembled one another, this man and this woman, only that his voice did not have the melodious sound of hers at all.

They sat at a small, round table, in low, comfortable club chairs, one with his legs crossed over one another, the other quite upright and expectant.

The door to the waiting room (at every other consultation certainly closed and made soundproof by the heavy curtain drawn before it) remained open, as if to show that they were not being listened to.

Councilor-of-Commerce Behrendt began in the slow, calm, and thoughtful tone that he used in all his business transactions that from the beginning assured him of a superiority.

"There is present here," he said, "for several weeks a person whom I earlier knew fleetingly and who believes he can now harass me."

He hesitated a moment. then went on: "Since I will have nothing at all to do with him, I would like to have your advice, in what way—"

Now the questions would come, the questions of how and why, and he would have to answer them. He knew that he wanted to say, and yet the words, as general as they were to be kept, came only with difficulty.

He did not have time to express them. He was interrupted. "I believe I may anticipate Herr Councilor-of-Commerce, if I assume what it is about."

He looked up astonished, but his astonishment was to become even greater.

"Surely it's about Herr Eduard Schmidt, who has been staying here for some time and alleges that he had been friends with Herr Councilor-of-Commerce as a young man. He is staying in the Hotel Schwanen, and—"

Councilor-of-Commerce Behrendt was just about to bend forward and complete what the man was saying: "and is telling everyone that I stole and was imprisoned."

But of course he did not do it.

He heard further: "and who is spreading rumors here that, in and of themselves are too untenable to be taken seriously by anyone, to which, however, it would be better to put an end."

It was only a short glance with which the eyes of the two men at the small table in the bright, sober room of meticulous order and barrenness met, but in this second one of them knew that he had done the right thing in coming here, and he experienced a feeling of respect, which was rare with him, for the superior cleverness and the tact—yes, the tact—with which this "consulting lawyer" spared him an explanation, which—according to what he already knew—was unnecessary.

He suppressed the question of how the man opposite him had come by this knowledge.

Then, as if his thoughts were guessed, he heard further (and now there passed over the face there before him an expression that he little liked, liked not at all): "Men like me must keep their eyes and ears open everywhere."

At the same time, however, as if he saw that he had shown a weak spot, Jarchow continued: "If I have correctly understood Herr Councilor-of-Commerce, he wishes to prepare a quick end to the presence of this gentleman here in town, because it is troublesome to him. May I ask, whether there is any kind of evidence available that could give justified occasion for an action against this man?"

Councilor-of-Commerce Behrendt decided to put an end to the matter. He gave a brief account: he spoke of the letters received and brought out the two that he still possessed; also about the way he had answered the next to the last of them, and what reception he had given the writer, when the latter dared to intrude upon him.

The dark eyes behind the round horn glasses sparkled at his explanation. The two writings were carefully read, word for word, many sentences several times. They too appeared to give the reader an obviously great pleasure, as proved by a repeated twitch around his lips.

"Very sly," was then his opinion, as he gave the sheets back with a light bow. "Very refined. Everything of course only bluff, presumption. But unfortunately these letters—in and of themselves, of course, an unheard-of molestation and unexampled impudence—do not allow one to construe a regular extortion."

("Construe … my God," thought Councilor-of-Commerce Behrendt to himself and he listened further.)

"The only possibility of reaching the goal of getting rid of him lies, therefore, only in the line of a friendly agreement. I said already that I know this Herr Schmidt, know him by sight. He was sitting near me one evening and I had the occasion to observe him. I will surely be finished with him. With people who talk so much, one is easily finished. Certainly—he must have a definite sum in hand for the return trip and—as he says—so as to make a new existence for himself over there."

A small pause ensued. Then Councilor-of-Commerce Behrendt saw himself suddenly addressed no longer in the third person, but rather directly (as if they had now come to the point that mattered and which made further ceremony unnecessary). "How high were you thinking to go, Herr Councilor-of-Commerce?"

And on the dismissive, motion of his hand: "Blackmailers are like flies. They come again and again, as often as one chases them away. In this case, of course, it must be made impossible. May I, Herr Councilor-of-Commerce, in the worst case go up to—let us say now—ten thousand?"

The questioner saw how the tall, heavy figure unexpectedly quickly rose from the chair, which was much too narrow for him.

"I leave all that to your judgment, Herr Attorney. I only wish that the affair, if at all possible, may be concluded by tomorrow. I would like to avoid yet another meeting with this gentleman."

He saw how the eyes behind the glasses still greenly glistened, as if the impudence just now so indignantly rejected by him was entirely according to his heart and he himself was now still capable of such. He saw the experienced trace around mouth and nose, the not quite clean and badly cut fingernails, and he heard, "I understand completely, Herr Councilor-of-Commerce, and will deal with the gentleman tomorrow. Le me think it over. May I, perhaps tomorrow evening, look you up to give you a report, or would a meeting at a third place—?"

He was interrupted. "I will transmit to you tomorrow morning through a messenger the sum of ten thousand marks and tomorrow evening about this time be here again."

"Just as it pleases Herr Councilor-of-Commerce."

He was again in the third person, while the man leading him out was completely obsequious.

9

Before Councilor-of-Commerce Behrendt entered his business office on the next morning, he collected ten thousand marks from his private account at his bank, had them sealed, and handed them over to "Number One," the old messenger Krause, who since time immemorial had his stand on the northwest corner of the market square, to take care of the errand.

The man did not speak about the tasks given him, since he said almost nothing at all, unless it was a yes or no or a number. He was commissioned to get a receipt, and he delivered it twenty minutes later.

In the evening about eight Councilor-of-Commerce Behrendt, for the second time in twenty-four hours, climbed up the steps to Counseling Attorney Jarchow and was received by him at the door.

He also began, when they were hardly seated: "I hope everything has been carried out to the satisfaction of Herr Councilor-of-Commerce. I sought out the gentleman this morning, immediately after I received your delivery and after I had thought over everything yesterday evening and drafted a plan. He was not to be met with. He was never at home, the landlord told me, with whom he was already deeply in debt, but rather spent the whole day and half the night hanging around in all kinds of bars. But he would likely come to the noon meal. I left a message that I would expect him at my place around two. He appeared punctually."

Here the speaker stopped, and over his face went something like a laugh—he cannot really laugh at all, thought the listener—before he continued: "It is really very much to be regretted that Herr Councilor-of-Commerce could not see the scene that was then played out here. Naturally I did not let myself be drawn into any discussion, but rather after a couple of words without more ado laid before him this written document to be signed—the amount in the draft read seven thousand—of which Herr Councilor-of-Commerce will first kindly take notice."

He read:

"I, the undersigned, declare hereby that in the course of this year I have written letters to Herr Councilor-of-Commerce Behrendt for the express purpose of extortion. I further declare that I will refrain from any further attempt at such extortion from now on and within twenty-four hours will depart from here and return to South America.

"I acknowledge at the same time the receipt of eight thousand marks."

He continued, "He leaped up, shouted that he could not and would not sign in his lifetime. He spoke of misunderstanding and force and so on. Good, said I, Herr Councilor-of-Commerce is also satisfied with this second document here. But then you receive only four thousand."

The second written document read:

"I, the undersigned, declare hereby that I will refrain from any further harassing of Herr Councilor-of-Commerce Ludwig

Behrendt and within the next eight days will begin a return trip to South America.

"I acknowledge at the same time the receipt of four thousand marks."

"Now, Herr Councilor-of-Commerce should have seen the torment in which the choice set him. He turned this way and that, talked and talked, until I threatened to put an end to any further negotiation and explained to him that we would also know how to arrest him for slander. Finally we agreed on the eight thousand and he signed the first document, which naturally puts him entirely in our hands in case he should make even the slightest attempt to molest Herr Councilor-of-Commerce further. Besides, he has already departed this afternoon with the five-thirty train. My wife, who knows him by sight, was at the train station and saw him get aboard."

Attorney Jarchow became silent and looked at his client, who was listening without uttering a word.

Now came the great moment for him. "As I already said, and as results from this document, from the ten thousand received I expended eight. As to the remainder, may I—?"

He hesitantly unfolded two notes, which he had held the whole time in his hand, and laid the one, then also the other on the small table between them.

Councilor-of-Commerce Behrendt appeared not to see them. He took the undersigned written document and the draft of the first, shoved both into his breast pocket, and stood up.

"May I request that for your efforts you accept the remainder for your account."

And once again, as if his thoughts had been guessed this time too, the other anticipated his question. "The two written documents, which Herr Councilor-of-Commerce has just now taken, are the only evidence in this matter. There exist no others. Not even a file has been made."

Now would have been the time to say a word of thanks for the quick and doubtless very skillful settlement of the affair, which

-KENN]

had been accomplished entirely in his sense, and to give his hand to this small, black-haired man, who was accompanying him as he turned to leave.

But he was unable to do it. He just could not bring himself to it. A "Good evening" from his side, a deep bow from the other was all.

Outside, in the quiet and empty street, however (it was entirely indifferent to him whether he was now seen here or not), he stopped and dried his forehead.

For all this, as he again said to himself, was just impossible, was just completely impossible!

CHAPTER FOUR

1

He was gone. Councilor-of-Commerce Ludwig Behrendt could again walk through the streets of his town without having to fear seeing that impudent, yellow face suddenly pop up before him and losing his self-composure.

It was as before: he had to return greetings from the left and the right, he was spoken to, stopped, and walked on, only to be greeted again and be stopped anew.

If he had already often found this greeting and being spoken to so troublesome that, on these hurried walks, he had avoided the main street as much as possible, he now no longer avoided it. It was as if he wished to convince himself that these greetings that were directed at him were still just as respectful and friendly, still just as unprejudiced as before.

If they had earlier been returned by him mostly indifferently and mechanically, he now begin to think about them: Had City Councilor Hauschild not looked at him as if he had discovered something new about him? Had Pastor Lutze of St. Peter's not glanced to the side (even if not obviously), as if he were ashamed of him? And why had Bertram, the pharmacist, all of a sudden become so obviously nice when he shopped at his place (which, as a rule, he usually was not)?

When Councilor-of-Commerce Behrendt spoke with people now, it could happen that abruptly, in the middle of a conversation, the thought came: Does he know? Has he also heard of it?— so that he examined the speaker more sharply or he himself broke off in the middle of a sentence, and only an astonished look brought him to his senses.

Was it possible, then, that his relationship with people had changed so much in these couple of days?

He felt it more than he saw it. He sensed it in the answers he received—they were often too premeditated for him. In the glances that met his—they seemed to rest on him in a reserved curiosity or to avoid his.

He felt a change in the conduct of the others.

Perhaps, however, he was also only imagining all this—they knew nothing, they behaved exactly the same way to him as earlier. It was only **he**, who now suddenly saw others in a new light, from one day to the next.

If this rascal in his helpless rage had spread gossip around here—they just had to see how mendacious this person was, who had disappeared again just as quickly as he had popped up! Who could believe him? Who would?

The bad part was just that he himself no longer knew how he should conduct himself.

His unaffectedness was in danger of forsaking him.

He just could not go up to every individual who seemed to him suspicious, take him by the coat button, and say, "Listen, my good man, I know very well what you are thinking—I see it in you. You have heard that once I—well now, we know what it is— but I would only like to tell you that it is indeed literally true, but basically it is perfect nonsense. For one thing, it was so long ago that it is already no longer real, and then it is a matter of a long forgotten and long ago expiated youthful stupidity, on which an honest person—which you surely are—does not touch with one thought more. So please—"

It was just impossible for him to speak like that.

To his face, however—to himself—no one said what he was thinking. Some did not do so out of regard for the highly respected reputation of his firm and because they rightly valued him; the others, because in some way or other they were dependent on him.

251

Let one just do it once—he thought. Say to me to my face what is now being talked about in the streets and houses, and tell me the plain truth! I would then see more clearly and could grasp it. But for that they are all too considerate and—too cowardly!

He, who was usually such a calm, self-assured, and superior man, became inwardly more restless from day to day. He felt that he had got rid of the cause of his unrest, but with this the unrest itself had in no way left.

It did not help that he told himself: Whether one knows it or not is indifferent. You never did place much value on the judgment of these people! Who, then, can do anything to you? What can bring harm to you? Certainly not to the business and its reputation, whose growth over the decades you promoted in spotless honesty!

Nothing could change even in your position here. And if it did! He would indeed be only happy if they again took away all these honorary offices—burdens and trouble, one like the other—which they had loaded on him in the course of time, and which only the attempt to make good what he had once failed in he had later, in indifference and good nature, let be loaded on him!

It did not help that he told himself again and again: At the base of your being this whole town and your dear fellow men and what they think about you don't mean a fig to you (for you lived here physically, to be sure, but never in spirit). He was here, lived in the town, and had become a hundredfold overgrown with it and its interests. And—everyone knew him here, every cat and every child!

No, he was no longer the same. He felt it, and it tormented him that he felt it.

That person was gone. He was free of him and forever. He was already swimming now in the water over there from where he had come.

But he had sown his seed. It had grown up and was raining down on him with a thousand fine needle pricks.

2

The days became hotter and hotter, and the time of the long vacation was approaching.

One Sunday, at midday, when the Behrendt and Lindtner families were gathered around the dining table, as every Sunday, the question was discussed, where did they wish to go this year. The family head surprised its members with the notice that he was not going away, but rather would spend the six weeks here. That he had spend the vacation without them had already happened if not recently. Then he had been alone somewhere in the mountains and had hiked (to be sure, without any inclination for mountain sports).

But that he wanted to remain here and not allow himself any recreation at all was a surprise and caused universal astonishment.

They made only weak attempts, however, to dissuade him from his intention. For one thing, they knew that such attempts were just completely pointless. He simply did not agree with them or at most silently smiled at them, as if he agreed with them, and then still did as he wished.

Then, too, because they (as he, whom it centered around, not entirely incorrectly believed) were precisely this time inwardly quite satisfied not to have him among them for a couple of weeks and to be allowed to leave him to himself.

Thus the expressions of regret did not sound completely honest, and probably only genuine was the pouting of his youngest grandchild, little Erna: "Grandpa should come too." For she was truly attached to him and gladly came to his mouth and his knees.

When, after a few days, the whole company was off and away in the coach that drove up to take Frau Councilor-of-Commerce to the train station, and he was alone in the quiet house that he was to inhabit for a while with the servant Franz and the old cook, he uttered a sigh of relief.

Why did he remain here?

He himself was probably not entirely clear about the real reasons for his decision—again found really curious by everyone.

He had no desire to sit around for weeks with the whole family in some overfilled resort on the North Sea (with too narrow a bed and too rich meals) and this precisely the whole day, instead of as here, where he only had to bear it at mealtimes; nor did he have a desire to wander from one place to another or, on rainy days, to perch crowded into the corner of some tavern. This was certainly one of the reasons.

But not the true one.

The true reason why he remained here was that he **could** not go away now!

For it was as if a secret enemy had suddenly arisen here in this town, who must be defied and brought to silence at any price, and as quickly as possible.

If he went away now, it would look as if he were fleeing from it. Then this enemy would become bolder and more powerful from day to day, and when he returned after six weeks, it would have conquered and the whole town would be against him.

He could not go away. Not now.

He stayed here although the stay in these hot streets was no pleasure.

His personal enemy, in the figure of this yellow, little scoundrel from overseas, was gone, out of his sight and rendered harmless, but the other, the immaterial, creeping, invisible, and intangible enemy was here; it would grow and grow, if he did not succeed in grasping it and choking it to death—the other enemy: rumor!

He must not go away.

3

It was lovely to be alone, and he enjoyed his freedom every hour of the day.

Really for the first time there came into his life hours that he did not rightly know what to do with. The business affairs that he now had to take care of alone (for his partner, too, was on holiday), in this slack time, hardly claimed him in the mornings; and as lovely as the evening hours with his books always were for him, those of the afternoon stretched out, since it was too hot for long walks.

On one of these afternoons the house on the summit came to mind and at the same time, in the same moment—dear God, yet again!—it occurred to him that, on his last visit (since he was in such a hurry to keep the appointment with that legal consultant), he had completely forgotten to pay for his drinks (and for the two telephone calls)!

He laughed angrily within himself—what must that little girl think of him? He now also remembered that she had stood there and calmly let him go by without saying a word—simple goose that she was!

Now, after all, if she naturally also did not know who he was— how was she to find out, up there, cut off from all life and the town? She would probably not consider him a bilker, and the matter was not so bad that it could not easily be made good.

Only irritating. Was he already so old and senile that this could happen to him! But here too that damned story all alone was at fault, which had brought him so entirely out of his tracks!

He wanted to go up there today, to say a friendly word to her and perhaps also, as one does with a child, pat her on the cheeks, but at any rate bring along a box of pralines for her. (For she did not accept tips, the little thing, and he had no desire at all to hear again that cool, "No thanks, it is not necessary.")

Thus in the afternoon he entered the confectionery shop of the Sisters Süßkind in the market. "Sisters" was no longer the correction designation, since one of the two sisters had died. For love had agreed badly with Suzy, the beautiful Susanne. After a romantic elopement, which kept the town in suspense for weeks, she had returned home after a couple of years, sick and tired, and then withered like a faded flower. (For her pining away of a "broken heart" there was really no more appropriate designation, as crude as this might sound). Molly, her twin, who was constantly ignored over her beaming sister, had cared for her until her death and then had taken the business into her hands alone—how she had done that earned her the highest respect. She it was then, who, with a smile as sweet as her chocolate, now greeted the old acquaintance of her youth with "Surely for the dear, little Erna," as she tied the box in a silk wrapper.

But Councilor-of-Commerce Behrendt was not disposed to any conversation today, and so he only thanked her in a friendly way as he shook hands and left.

As with almost every person with whom he now came into contact, there arose in him, as if from a deep darkness, the question: "Did she already know?" Besides, there was the fact that Molly was one of the few here who—if she had an especially sharp memory—would be able to remember that he had once spent a couple of weeks in England. But then, even if she knew it—that must have happened at the same time that her sister so suddenly disappeared and she had other things to think about than him (about him, as he knew, so many of her thoughts had indeed been concerned).

If she had heard of it now, she just did not show it. His suspicion had been in the end once again only a product of his imagination, which now saw everywhere nothing but accomplices and conspirators, and while Molly looked after him (as she always did, for he had been her silent and oh so hopeless love), his anxiety about his own mental state gripped him more and more, and again with full force.

No, things could not go on like this!

4

The words that he had figured out as he arrived up there remained unspoken. He met her outside in the front garden.

Just where were eyes! For as he saw her now, not in the twilight of the inside rooms, but rather for the first time in the clear light of day, he recognized how very much he had deceived himself when he believed that she was still a child.

Childish about her was the small, even if altogether not tender, but rather healthy and symmetrical figure and the slenderness of her limbs, probably also the reserved—if by no means shy—attitude toward him, the strange guest, of whom she certainly did not comprehend what drove him up here as the only one around this time of day. But otherwise nothing else. It was an adult woman who now stepped back so as to let him go by her.

Where were his eyes!

Thus the box of sweets that Molly had so nicely bound with a gold ribbon remained in his pocket and he only said, "What must you think of me, dear Fräulein!"

He received no answer. But from the glance with which she looked at him, a somewhat astonished look, he saw that from the first moment she did not at all know what he meant or at most, if it occurred to her, thought that such a small forgetfulness was not worth speaking about; he would soon come back again and then take care of the small debt.

Thus there was nothing left for him than to let the matter rest until afterwards and to seat himself in his old place.

This he did, and once again enjoyed the next two hours of calm and peace in the cool, dim corner of the back room so much that he decided, often from now on, yes every day—why not?—to come up here and forget here everything that down there below angered him, made him uneasy, and was beginning to torment him. For no breath of the poisonous cloud intruded up here, while down below they threateningly rose up around and over him—as he believed. Here he was alone. Where could he have it better than here?

For an hour he thus dreamed to himself—how everything had happened in his life and how everything would really have become entirely different and would have had to become so, if not—yes, if not—

When he then left and wanted to pay, the forgotten amount, without his having to remember it again, was added on, but indifferently, as if it did not matter whether it was paid or not. Again he now saw how very much he had deceived himself about her age. But also how friendly this face was with its brown eyes and full cheeks. One had to look at it gladly. How lovely it would only be, if she would once laugh.

He could not really say that her attitude was in any way unfriendly. Only indifferent, as before, when he asked her what she must think of him. In her short answers usually lay an undertone of astonishment, as if she did not like his questions—and probably questions altogether—and feared further ones. Now, as he was departing, he turned and said back to her, "And how may I call you, Fräulein?"

She had to answer, and she did. But again it sounded quite short.

"I'm called Marie."

That sounded as if she wanted to say, "Yes, I'm called that. But what is it to you how I am called? And what do you really always want up here?"

Well, in the end it was better than if she, like other waitresses (and a waitress she actually was, in spite of her kinship with the proprietor), would believe herself obliged to sit down with him and entertain him with her chatter.

Besides, he did not come up here for her sake, but rather to be alone with himself and his thoughts.

5

Thus day after day, in this hot summer and vacation time, he climbed the wooded path up to the summit, to drink his wine there and inwardly to come to terms with himself and people.

But, since it won't do that people see one another daily without in the long run learning various things about one another,
even if they speak ever so little to one another, thus **he** at least—in
spite of the few questions and the hesitant, short answers—learned
about her (for apart from the fact that she was the niece of this ever
invisible wine-handler Fürbringer and was called Marie, until now
he hardly knew anything about her) that she was here not so much
to help with the business—for this was taken care of by another,
stone-deaf female relative and an elderly servant (both likewise
invisible)—as to serve guests in the tavern; that her uncle was out
of the house on business the whole day and always returned home
only in the evenings, when probably also one or another of his
business friends still came up here; that this business was getting
along well, but this little tavern, to which guests came only on
Sundays, but then often and in whole families, was only an appendage, more a wine-tasting cellar than a bar; and that she was
from the region of Württemberg, thus more from "down there," to
where she would return as soon as her uncle found another helper;
and finally, that she, so alone up here, did not feel lonely at all and
was not afraid (because she was never afraid of anything).

Beyond this, however, she did not appear inclined to make
further admissions, and so he finally gave up questioning, greeted
her in a friendly way on arriving and departing, enjoyed his rest
and the coolness of his corner, and forgot that in the next room, at
the window, mostly bent over a piece of handwork, yet another
person besides him was sitting, until the glass and carafe before
him were empty and he stood up to stretch out his long limbs that
had become stiff, but also because he did not like to call, but
rather preferred to stand in the doorway and ask if he might have
another glass. He could not bring himself to treat this young girl
like a waitress.

When she brought him the new wine and just as quietly went
again to her place—and he back to his—he did think for a moment: Has she already had unpleasant experiences with men? And
had she therefore become like this?

But she just did not need to be afraid of him. Ridiculous! He could quite easily be her father!

Now—importunity was the last thing he could be accused of, and if she was abrupt, he could be too.

But why did she have such a darling face, into which he would have been happy to look often and long—a child's face, in this he had not deceived himself. There were so few human faces he was happy to look at. Pity!

6

On Sundays he dared not think of walking over the river.

He could be seen on these days (and that would have been to him like giving away a secret). Then, too, on Sundays other guests were there and the two small rooms certainly full of noise and smoke (and that would also seem to him like a desecration of his quiet corner, if he had to witness it).

Precisely on this third Sunday of the vacation, however, a feeling came over him that he otherwise did not know—that of being alone. His house appeared to him curiously deserted. Franz, the servant, was on leave and the cook was also away visiting relatives.

He wondered about himself. Usually it could not be quiet enough around him and he had always been alone with himself, however many people were around him.

Why was it that he felt himself forsaken today? Surely not a late and suddenly awakened longing for people?

He had never longed for them.

He longed for life. For the great, wide life there outside, the life of the big cities. There, even if he knew not a human soul, he would never feel lonely.

Today he would have liked to stroll down the Linden in Berlin, a stranger and unknown, in no personal relationship to the people around him and yet among them—one of them, the countless many.

He longed for a strong, intellectual stimulus that would tear him out of these stupid thoughts that always circled around one point, these thoughts so little worthy of him. He longed for a walk through the silent halls of a museum (what was called such here, the scanty rooms on the upper floor of the middle school, he knew by heart, for it was really his own creation, wrested from dullness and indifference in a years-long struggle), for a good performance on one of the leading stages (hidden in the corner of a box)—a play was being given now in Berlin whose authorship was vehemently disputed—it was supposed to be good, but was not yet available in print (which aroused curiosity all the more). A mood like today's, however, would not have brought him into the local theatre, even if they were playing now—for, as everywhere in art, he could tolerate only the highest in human presentations.

There remained only his books in these high, serious shelves behind the panes shining in the summer sun. But today they failed him, which almost never happened and never should, if he wanted to live at all. Today he felt himself unworthy of their company— not even one of them.

He had a longing—for what he did not know himself.

Out—out from this town and away from its people!

Already the daily, secret walks to the house on the summit were a small liberation, even if only for hours. For he must still return again to his yoke.

But that was indeed his own fault. He could have gone away. For Spruth or his son-in-law would just have stayed here.

He could still go away from here, at least for a couple of days. The business here would get along without his supervision for that long. But basically he did not want to go away.

In autumn, when they were all here again, then—and as long as he wished. He had indeed brought it to this, that he no longer needed to ask anyone.

But he was no longer able even to look forward to this.

Those weeks in the big city—they no longer satisfied his thirst.

They were drops on his dried up soul, which was no longer

able to revive under them. He was becoming old. This, too, he felt more and more.

His modest excursions into the distant realm of art—they would soon cease of themselves. He felt that too.

But today he could no longer remain here in his empty house.

Irresolutely he stepped out into the sultry dampness and turned toward the town.

He did not know where or what he wanted there.

But again, as he came closer and closer to its houses, he caught himself with the thought that had more and more taken possession of him in these weeks and now no longer left him: Whom will you meet? With whom will you speak? And will he, whom you directly meet—know about it?

He stopped.

No, it could not go on like this any longer!

Precisely because he was not vain or conceited, he had always been a good observer of his own ego, as far as he had taken the trouble at all to reflect on himself.

With the great sharpness of his thinking he saw in this moment clearly, inexorably clearly what was creeping over him and was gradually threatening to gain control over him and his will: the beginning of paranoia—a mental illness, of which he had once seen an example. It would have the saddest and most fearful consequences. When it broke out, it could end in no other way than in madness.

No, it should not come to that with him!

These first signs were already serious enough: Every time he went out he wondered, as just now, about whom he would meet. He avoided meetings. If he had to speak to someone because he was spoken to, he suspected a hidden meaning behind every harmless word. Instead of listening—and he had always been a very good, patient listener, even if seldom an interested one—he only thought about the fact that at any moment a thoughtless and harmful word could fall. He himself often answered without being asked, just so as not to let the other come to this word. Finally, he spoke more than usual. In a word, he was no longer the superior one, as everywhere until now, but rather had become the unsure one.

All these were signs of paranoia and could mean nothing else. Something must be done about it, and indeed quickly.

He wanted and had to find out what and how much they knew. He had to know, because he wanted to see what kind of condition he was in.

Until now he was aware of only two persons who certainly knew about it. One was his wife, whom he himself had told (for if he had not told her, she would have thought of murder and manslaughter). The other, this small legal counselor Jarchow, had hinted about it to him. In addition he was rather sure his family knew. It was more than probable that his wife, under tears and oaths "only to keep it secret," had immediately passed it on.

With all the other people there were only guesses, which could just as well be correct as that they were the products of his overheated imagination.

Was there then in the whole town no one with whom he could discuss the whole matter calmly and from whom he could expect an unbiased judgment?

There were few people in it with whom one could carry on a rational conversation. Perhaps they existed. No, they did not. If they did, he would have known them.

Dr. Radewald occurred to him.

With him one could carry on a conversation, and he saw him from time to time.

If the rumor had also reached him, who lived so much for himself and apart from everyone, then **everyone** knew it! He decided to go to him.

7

Dr. Radewald was a senior assistant schoolmaster, retired due to his eternal conflicts with his superiors on the administrative board,

who had remained here for no other reason than that he was now
a resident.

He was—in the view of everyone—not at all a proper acquaintance for a man like Councilor-of-Commerce Behrendt. But in the
latter's view, he was the only one here with whom one could talk
about something other than the local interests and the questions
of the day. About a book, not even known here by title; about
pictures and the theatre; about a matter of which the newspapers
only wrote in order to suppress it and which only those readers
found out about who were able to think independently; and now
and again also about a question that was better not discussed here
at all.

Thus he wanted to talk with him today also about **his** question and hear his judgment—not directly, but rather in the course
of the conversation and as if it were the story of a third party
(which in the course of long years it had also almost become for
him).

To be sure, he knew this judgment ahead of time. With his
sarcastic smile, Dr. Radewald would make the most malicious remarks about his dear fellow citizens, who were shameless enough
to bear a grudge against such a youthful stupidity, instead of stick-
ing their noses into their own foul-smelling affairs, and then, without any transition, begin speaking about a new book and probably
also about its author.

So, to Dr. Radewald.

He would be at home. He was always at home.

He would be genuinely pleased to see him. He was always
pleased when he visited him.

He would not disturb him. He did not let himself be disturbed.

For him, he was not the Councilor-of-Commerce Behrendt,
the most prominent personality of the town, the rich businessman
in offices and honors, but rather simply a man, more rational than
most of the others here, with whom one could talk as one should
(and who sometimes brought along a book that he longed for, but

which was not within the means of the thin wallet of a retired senior assistant schoolmaster).

Dr. Radewald was at home, was clearly delighted, and was ready for any conversation as well as any controversy.

He made a place on one of the chairs by simply sweeping off a pile of books, so that they rolled over one another onto the floor, and invited him to sit. Everything was suffocating here under books, which lay together everywhere in heaps and piles. But this disorder was only apparent. It was astonishing with what absolute certainty their owner reached into the chaos, as soon as there was talk of a book sought, found it, and drew it out.

Without first asking how he was and how it was going, they were immediately so immersed in a conversation about a new book that Councilor-of-Commerce Behrendt soon gave up any hope of being able to interest him today in such a personal matter as his. He also became conscious now really for the first time that they were never in a relation to one another in such a way that personal things had ever been touched on between them. This Dr. Radewald would probably also have been highly astonished to be taken now as a confidant and advisor.

So he then listened for two hours (without this time really understanding what the other related in clever flashes of wit) and left as he had arrived.

Twilight was falling as he entered the street, and the restless and tormenting thoughts of midday immediately became master of him again. Again he did not know where he should go. And yet he must get finished with this matter—must do it soon, today even!

As he turned into the market, the tavern sign of The Elephant and its reserved table occurred to him, and he knew immediately what he had to do. He wanted to show that he defied public opinion if it had already turned on him. At the same time his visit was to be the decisive test for him: how they presented themselves to him, how he had to present himself from now on.

He decided calmly, carefully, and as objectively as possible to observe and draw his conclusions.

For this reason, before he entered, he stood a few minutes before the display of the jeweler Zandtke, which was also lighted today on Sunday, and felt more than he saw the simple beauty of a necklace with a splendid stone; he wondered at the carelessness with which tiny Zandtke so little guarded his show-window against a break-in (in a big city such a window would have been covered by two or three grills); he considered whether a break-in was not possible here, or were all the people truly as honest as they acted and looked. Then he entered.

The table in the side room was now, in high summer and in the middle of the vacations, naturally not so thickly occupied as usual, but a number of unswerving men, who appeared unable to pass up their daily evening place in spite of the summer heat and the stuffy air, were sitting around it—all, of course, more or less well known faces.

They stood up, greeted him, but—as it seemed to him—somewhat embarrassedly, as if they did not rightly know what to make of his visit today and how to present themselves to him.

Councilor-of-Commerce Behrendt returned the greetings, avoided the handshakes where possible, and sat down.

Pharmacist Bertram had just returned from ten days in Berlin.

These gentlemen, too—all in well-paying positions or proprietors of profitable businesses—went out, made their trips, and saw a bit of the world.

But when they returned and related what they had seen out there—remarkably, it was always something he had not seen and about which he could not speak with them: the newest revue with five hundred naked legs and a text of unsurpassable idiocy; the dance halls with the most refined thrills; in short—the "hits of the season."

On the other hand, they had no idea of what had appeared to him as the most valuable, and he took care not to speak of it, except when a mention escaped him, which each time showed him how foreign what he spoke of was to them. But they had indeed all, in addition to their respect for the rich industrialist, the greatest of the town, always shown a certain shyness before his intellectual superiority, which was expressed in the fact that in his—**so** rare—presence they were not as loud and self-satisfied in their conduct as when they were among themselves.

Today however this shyness appeared to have given way. As if they wished to take revenge for such a long practiced regard, each related with little wit and much delight their not always entirely clean adventures and there were loud horselaughs again about the round table. He felt himself to a certain extent excluded and was no longer, as at the last time, the declared center of the company.

He of course let this be noticed by no expression, silently listened and obligingly smiled and—kept quiet. But although he listened, yet only isolated words of what was spoken, without connection and meaning, penetrated to his consciousness. He heard words, words, word—from across, from the right, from the left. They had no content for him, but they began to offend him. Each of them offended him, he who had now for so many years already had always listened to the same ones.

They upset him—in their satisfied tone, in their oily commonness, in their—yes, in their measureless insolence!

If they had to get them out at all, then—damn it!—they should be said with discretion, discreet in the consciousness of one's own unworthiness, but not be howled around a table full of people, as if they were newly discovered truths!

Above all not when **he** was present and gave them the honor of listening! Councilor-of-Commerce Behrendt was certainly not conceited and even less overbearing, but he demanded absolute respect for himself and his name—demanded it above all now.

This respect was wounded today—here—and for the first time openly.

They did not express it—cowards that they were—but they thought it (how he saw that they were thinking it!): "You are—no, you were indeed the most esteemed one among us, but your superiority is past. For if we are also outwardly the same toward you, we now know what you are!"

Was he only imagining all this again? Was he again seeing only ghosts?

Whatever—he felt how rage was rising up from the anger surging within him, this rage that he feared so much because it could drive him to deeds whose consequences were now much more to be feared than earlier.

He sought to suppress it. He tried to remain calm and to understand what and whereof they were speaking.

In vain. The more effort he made, the stronger it became.

He looked into the faces around him, into the faces all more or less reddened by the heat and the drink, all of whom he knew, many for years. He looked into the faces of these good citizens, pillars of the community like him, and of whom not one had committed an offense against the sacred foundation of such a community—property—as he had!

He felt that any second could bring catastrophe.

He forced himself with a last, a superhuman effort.

He attacked none of those sitting around. He took up no chair to break on the floor. He did not break one glass—he only stood up quite unexpectedly, without having finished his drink, and walked out with such an icy "Good evening, gentlemen!" that they all sat there like stones, to then smile at one another meaningfully: "So it really is true."

No one sprang up to hold him back from departing as he threw the waiter a coin. No one offered him today his undesired accompaniment.

8

On the way home his rage increased even more.

He had condemned himself, not to eight days, like that mild English judge, but rather to a life-long penitentiary.

He had done penance. He had done penance beyond all human strength.

ENN]

Who was allowed to dare to sit in judgment over him anew? But they were transgressing against the first principle of every administration of judicial punishment: Ne bis in idem—Not twice in the same case!

He was defenseless—defenseless, as he had been just now!

He could do nothing but sit there and smile, as just now, smile, stand up, and—leave.

In his room he walked out onto the veranda, from which a few steps led down into the garden.

His fists gripped the warm iron of the railing of the balustrade as if he had under his hands what tormented him and what he hated.

The iron rails gave way under the pressure of his hands.

He stooped down and saw by the light of the moon that he had bent them together. Disconcerted at his own tremendous strength, he wiped the blood from the inner side of his right index finger and then walked back into the room, so as to wash his hands and face.

Then he took off his clothes. He sat with his naked feet propped against the brass bar of the fireplace, hour after hour, leaning deeply back in the wide leather chair.

Once more he laughed out, so bitter and loud that his wife upstairs would have heard it if she were not away on a trip. But no one could have heard it. For Franz was certainly off on one of his little escapades and the cook was asleep upstairs at the other side of the garden.

Then the attack was over.

The blood ebbed back to his heart and he was again able to think calmly.

He looked the truth in the face and recognized—the fault lay not with the others, but with himself.

He should not have excused himself (as many a time) with the old "what people had made of him," but rather he should have made of himself what he wanted—in spite of them and everything!

He should have revolted, revolted from the very beginning. Even at that time.

He should have stepped in his path, stopped him, and defied the orders of this man who so disdainfully shoved him aside as if he were no longer his son and as if he had not committed an excusable youthful prank, but rather a damnable crime.

He should have then, perhaps expelled and avoided by his former acquaintances (for he had no friends), built up his own life in his own work, following his own inclinations, whether hungry or in want—regardless!

He should never ever have taken the wife whom he did not love, with whom he lived without loving her, deceiving her and defrauding himself of all the happiness of love.

He should not have drudged for thirty years in this business, which was his own and which was then still wrested from his hand, because he was too tired and too uninterested to keep it longer in his hands. To all these vexations and worries, he should not have let himself be burdened by those of other people who did not concern him.

Yes, he should—he should not have stayed here in this town, but rather should have sought his own path—certainly not an assured one, a difficult and steep one, but also one certainly not **entirely** without happiness.

He had not done it.

Why, therefore, was he accusing others? What fault was he seeking in them? He should accuse himself, himself—his cowardice and his weakness!

His father was unable to act otherwise than just as his character and his views were.

And the others—well, he knew them. They allowed themselves to be driven and ended where they were driven (as he had let himself be driven).

And now it was too late!

It was too late. If he were twenty years, yes even only ten years younger, perhaps he might still possess the strength to break the chains, but at fifty one no longer started a new life.

It was a matter of continuing the old one, until it was at an end, as well or as badly as it went, whether it gave him joy or not—not to ask whether it was hard or not.

But the people, the people should no longer disturb him as they had done in these weeks and this evening. They must again be for him what they had been.

Once already—weeks before—he believed he had made himself free of them. He had deceived himself. They had still occupied him, made him uneasy, and tormented him—they and their judgment.

But now he was truly free of them. Entirely free and for ever.

One day he would escape from them—to where they could not longer follow him.

He was free of them.

As in a film—naturally there were cinemas here and among them one that even now and then showed a film that one could watch without throwing up—as in a film the figures on the screen often suddenly move to the foreground and appear to step out of the frame and come at the audience—thus had the people of this town suddenly closed in on him in these weeks and he had given them a significance that they had never before possessed for him.

And as in a film the same figures just as abruptly draw back again, to become smaller and smaller and finally disappear, so for him (in the hours of this night) the people of this town became again small and smaller and disappeared back into their nothingness.

They were again as indifferent for him as they had always been for him. Indifferent also from now on was what they knew about him and what they thought about him.

He was finished with them.

He was finished with this foolish story, as he had become finished so smoothly and quickly with the fellow who had caused it.

But he—this too he clearly felt—was also finished with himself. In his life there could be no more transformation, like that which had just taken place—it was concluded, this his life, before it had really ended.

Everything would be as before: He would wake up, go into his office, see and speak with many people during the day, not one of whom interested him; he would sit down to a meal and hear (or also not hear) what his wife said to him; he would—perhaps—still make some short trip or other, read some book, which might anger or please him; and he would lie down every evening to sleep—never without the wish not to wake again.

He would continue living, as well or poorly as it went, and whether it was easy or difficult for him, no one asked. That was thoroughly in order and right.

Why should anyone ask about him? Did he ask about the others?

It was the truth, and the truth was bitter.

But one final consolation they could not take from him: once—somewhere and sometime!—

9

Whoever would have seen Councilor-of-Commerce Ludwig Behrendt the next day in his office (but no one saw him, because it was after the business was closed), would probably have thought that something was no longer quite right with him.

Yet what happened there was not the inspiration of a sudden decision, but rather to a certain extent the result of the previous long and sleepless night.

He drew up a chair, placed it under the picture of his father, which from that day when he had taken him in had thus hung opposite, so that the strict, cold eyes looked into his every time he looked up. He climbed onto the chair and, in the absence of a hammer, struck with his heavy paperweight so long and so strongly on the nail from which the picture was hanging that it gave way and, with a rattle, fell to earth between the wall and the chair, on whose edge it struck sharply. Frame and glass shattered at his feet.

It remained lying where it lay.

Early in the morning instruction would be given to reframe what had fallen down during the night. But it would nevermore take it old place.

CHAPTER FIVE

1

As he had done for many years, Councilor-of-Commerce Behrendt again strode through the streets of his hometown with his long, firm strides, avoided no one anymore, was greeted (always first) and returned the greeting; was addressed, remained a while standing and walked further—and had in the next moment forgotten with whom he had just spoken and had been with.

His days passed as they had gone by all these years, and what alone distinguished them from the earlier ones was these afternoon hours in the corner of the back room in his accustomed place in the small wine tavern on the summit.

The most beautiful thing about them was that he was so sure of not being disturbed there by any guest (for even the couple of drivers, one every couple of days, did not come in now because of the heat, but rather drank down their liter outside in the front garden while they watered their horses; and never by this quiet, little Fräulein Marie, who now already knew when he was coming, for when he entered carafe and glass were always already standing at his seat by the oven. He sat here and she sat there, always at her accustomed place by the low window near the entrance, often occupied with handwork, but at times also with nothing but her thoughts, which she let be drawn out through the vine-covered panes—to where? He had no idea and carefully guarded himself from asking her with even a single word.

For if she was also never unfriendly, this small, remarkable Fräulein, and not really dismissive, there was still nothing in her behavior to invite him into a little conversation, as would have been only natural between two people who had now already seen one another daily for weeks and always alone. He found her silence not quite natural. Even if she certainly had further thoughts about this curious guest, who was the only one from the town to take the troublesome path up here daily, to sit here for hours in the corner brooding to himself and drinking wine that he could just as well find down below; even if she certainly often wished him gone to the devil, the man for whom she had to sit here and wait on until he had drunk as it pleased him—even if all this was true, he could not have had such an intimidating effect that she couldn't give an account of herself; such a young thing, who obviously had no other human relation than perhaps her uncle. (What kind of a person he was, he did not know, for he had never seen him.) She sat out her godforsaken days up here between a stone-deaf old woman and a cretin of a servant, and must surely have a need to talk a bit, even if it was only with an old fellow like him.

But it appeared as if, in her opinion, he now knew enough about her and this place and no longer needed to learn more. He also indeed had what he wanted: rest from people and from her.

Nevertheless he still could not bring himself to treat her as a waitress. She was no waitress. Not according to her nature and conduct. Thus he took care now that he always carried enough small change with him to be able to leave the small charge for his drinks each time counted out (and without a tip), before he went, as he also, when he had drunk up and wanted yet another glass, preferred to stand and show himself at the middle door, instead of knocking on his table or calling out. When she then set down before him what he wished with a brief, soft "Please!" he gave an equally brief glance into her pleasant, but unmoving face, nodded his thanks, and believed that he had never seen such an attractive face, or one that, at the same time, seemed in such opposition to her cool nature.

She can certainly also be quite different, he thought in such moments.

Of which other face did this one remind him now in its goodness and friendliness? It must have been a long time ago, but finally he did remember it: the face of that young Englishman who had worked beside him in London (or better, had not worked), and from whom he—well, had taken the small loan that cost him his life. That young Englishman who then, as he returned as soon as possible the sum lend, had written the nice letter in which he repeated again how "awfully sorry" he was and what a "damned ass" he had been to have made a great fuss about the stupid story and brought him into that embarrassment—yes, he had had the same smile, however much they were otherwise so different from one another. For he had seen her smile, not often, but still once or twice while she was standing outside with the tired horses, shooing the flies away and speaking with their masters. But whoever could smile **thus** must be a good-natured, humane person, like that young Englishman had been.

She could, therefore, certainly be quite different than she was with him.

Why was she so against him? He had done nothing to her.

But this question was as quickly forgotten as it was posed on his coming and going, among the many, heavy, and gloomy thoughts of the many hours that he thus passed in this corner by the stove—his legs stretched out on the bench, his head bent over against the cool tiles, and staring before him.

For these thoughts told him more and more clearly that he could not much longer endure his life as it was. But how was he to change it?

He was afraid of it, and it often appeared to him as if there were only just one escape for him—to here, in this lonely corner!

2

No, such as it was and would be, it appeared to him no longer worth living, his life that he himself had destroyed for the sake of a delusion, and which was no life anymore.

It would continue on thus—ten, perhaps even twenty years yet—for he was descended, at least on his father's side, from a thoroughly healthy family, had never been sick, and his mighty body could resist the approaching old age for a long time yet.

But how was he to endure this life longer, if, as in the recent time, his inner weariness increased and at the same time his strength to resist it decreased?

He felt that one day, when his strength was used up, he would end it. For why and for whom should he continue to live?

He had always found that people took themselves and their little, unimportant existence much too importantly. Who and what was important and indispensable in the end?

Who, for example, would miss him? Where would they miss him?

Certainly not in the business. There least of all where he was only in the way. The two, his partner and his son-in-law, one heart and one soul, would, as soon as his authority no longer represented the principles through which his father and he after him had developed the business and had given the name of the firm the good reputation that it possessed, those two would only too quickly throw these principles overboard. Inferior fruit, unhealthy, because oversweetened, goods, and the improper use of coloring, which indeed gave them an attractive appearance, would make possible cheaper production and therefore a lower price, and likewise the old reputation of the firm would suffer more and more as the unavoidable result, until nothing more was left of it. He—he would no longer be there—that was all.

His wife would at most be touched by the social scandal, but with the auto, against which he had—as almost the only thing—successfully resisted up to now, and which she—still in widow's weeds—would soon acquire, she would soon comfort herself.

His daughter, so similar to her in many things, to him in none, was entirely absorbed by her own family and was, in her wonderful dullness and with her intellectual modesty, to be shaken by nothing. She had gotten the husband she sought, and he satisfied her in every respect.

Of the two boys, it was not to be expected that their pretensions would ever go beyond satisfied commonplace fellows. They might one day become first-rate citizens of this town, and they did not need him for that. The little girl, however, was still too little—she would probably ask about him a couple of times and then forget him.

Friends? If he had such here, he did not know them. Certainly some would regret his passing, without realizing it, but miss him? No one would miss him.

Why, then, did he still hesitate?

The vacations would soon end now. Everything would go in its old pace: work and business; so-called "social entertainments" (unbearable); evenings among people or alone with himself and his books—and in between, in the afternoon hours, what recently had become his only pleasure, these walks up here—they too must end sometime, for he just could not constantly take the path over the river without the whole town soon learning about it and seeking for motives.

Motives—oh, what others did he have than to flee here from his own life and—he admitted it to himself—to look for a fleeting moment into a pleasant and good little face—a moment only, for he could never sustain it.

3

One day it would happen—somewhere and sometime.

One day he would do it—sometime and somewhere.

It just did not have to be today. When the nausea and the weariness became too great—then!

He had no fear. Only people who still have something to lose are afraid. What had he still to lose?

KENN]

The hard thing was not death. The hard thing was the dying—the transition.

Why did this not exist (an old thought recurred to him):

Before the gates of the town, in a broad park surrounded by walls, stand the low buildings arranged like rays from the center.

To there pilgrims come—walking or driving—who are fed up with their lives.

At the entrance they pay their coin and are led to the pavilion that they themselves choose.

For here everyone can pay his last tribute to life in whatever way he will: alone or with his fellow travelers who take the last walk with him.

He can die as he has lived: loud, with the glass in his hand, a song and a laugh on his lips. Or—silently.

He can do it among the sounds that he loved most. He can do it in quietness.

He can come—prepared. He can come in the inspiration of a moment.

And he can still turn back, so long as he has not emptied the glass with the soporific that stands before him.

Then no longer.

For then, after a while, the couch on which he has sunk in sleep will be shoved by an invisible force into a side room, where the gases change the temporal sleep dreamlessly and without pain into eternal sleep—to roll farther through the long hall down to the furnace in the middle of the building where the flames do their last work on the lifeless shell of his body.

Why did it not exist?

Stupid question! Because the human being of today still did not possess any right of self-determination, but rather in life as in dying was delivered to the favor and disfavor of others—that's why not!

How they all—no, not all, but yet many, all too many—would rage against it and would call forth all the arguments of morality, of faith, of reason (their reason)! And as the final argument: humankind would die out if dying were made so easy for them.

Would that really be so bad, he asked himself.

Would the next unavoidable war with gas and poison from above not depopulate this earth anyhow?

Was it really so important whether this particle of earth flew through space with or without the conscious knowledge of these creatures?

In any case, how much easier it would be to endure life, with its sufferings, its endless sufferings, with the certain prospect of the possibility of such a departure and at any time!

But these were chimeras that the day destroyed.

4

On one of those days, about eight before the end of the vacation, Councilor-of-Commerce Behrendt was detained by a business friend. Business friend—what a hideous expression! Either they were friends and so did no business together; or they did it and therefore were far from being friends. Thus, to receive and deal with business friends had, since his entry into the firm, been the affair of his partner, Herr Eduard Spruth, whose whole delight it was. He could talk and talk, eat and drink with them, and talk them into something, for he let no one go without an order. For himself, on the other hand, those visits had been from the very beginning a horror. But Spruth was away and he could not send away today's visitor, who was in addition an old acquaintance of his father.

It was late, too late for his usual walk. But it seemed to him that the day was lost if he had not drunk his wine up there, had sat a while in his corner, and had given a fleeting, even if unreturned, glance into a certain face.

There was no longer time for the roundabout way through the woods, if he did not wish to expose himself to the danger of meeting up with one or another guest. That he preferred to avoid by all means. Thus he took, as he had not done in a long time, the direct climb up, by cutting across the serpentine of the roadway, and thus arrived on the other side of the house at the side gate to the small front garden.

As he entered it, he saw her. She was standing with her back to him, and looking in the direction of the woods, where the footpath opened onto the roadway. Thus, without being seen herself, she was able to recognize who was coming from there up to the house.

She had not heard his coming.

She stood without moving, as if she had long been standing there, in the somewhat bend forward attitude of waiting.

Longing waits thus, he told himself—as he stood still himself.

But for whom was she waiting? Whom could she be waiting for?

She started when he stepped closer. She became neither red nor embarrassed, but her greeting appeared to him more indifferent than usual, as she now let him go by and enter.

It would now have been the most simple and natural thing— and every other person would have done it—to make a harmless joke about the fact that she had been caught.

He did not do it.

He seated himself as always in his place, where his wine was already standing.

For whom had she been waiting there just now? For whom could she have been waiting except for him, her daily, only guest at this time? The thought came only to be immediately rejected again.

For him? Ridiculous! Downright ridiculous! He was ashamed of himself, old fool that he was! He, an old man; she, the young thing!

But he longed so much to see her face.

He did not want to do it at first, but then did it anyway. He quietly moved away from his place at the stove and around the table to its other end, so that he could observe the front room on its window side through the open middle door.

She was sitting there as always in her accustomed place at the window and was unoccupied. Her hands lay folded in her lap and she was looking out through the low panes of the window into the greenery, entirely lost in thought.

He sat and looked at her.

He did not move.

But nevertheless she must have felt that she was being watched. She looked up and a touch of displeasure crossed her forehead as she quickly stood up and walked out.

In this moment Councilor-of-Commerce Behrendt would have given much not to have behaved like a stupid boy. For he must have seemed so in her eyes. But it was too late. The only thing he could do was to quickly empty his glass and, when he heard her enter again, stand up and ask for a new one.

They looked past one another when she brought it.

They looked past one another also when he then left after a short while.

In the next days they avoided looking at one another, and no word was exchanged between them but the short greeting on arriving and departing.

He did not want to come anymore.

But then he came anyway.

He sat, as always, in his corner. But she no longer sat in her place at the window from which he had driven her.

Yet she was always present nearby.

It was so quiet in the two small rooms that—had she paid attention to it—and **he** at least paid attention—one would have be able to hear the breathing of the other.

5

Councilor-of-Commerce Behrendt felt more strongly every day how little joy he still had in life (if he had ever had it). One day it would be—sometime and somewhere.

But he did not want to go unprepared.

From a love for order in his affairs, often reaching to the point of pedantry, he wanted to tidy up before it got too bad.

He tidied up.

In his business it was quickly done. In the hours that he spent there daily and in which there was now little more to do than dictate a number of letters and confer with Herr Anker on what was most necessary. There he was long since dispensable and everything would go on without him.

But what they had hung around his neck in the course of years and what he had let be thrust upon him in his stupid good nature and indifference—those "honors and titles"—he wanted to take care of yet.

He pleaded neither age nor condition. He countered the weak attempts to persuade him with his usual silence. The mayor himself came and sought to induce him ("for the good of the town"); people came from the poorhouse and the orphans' home; and replies came from the companies on whose board of directors he sat.

A couple of weeks earlier he would have brooded over whether these replies were coming all too quickly and too willingly, because they—well, because they had changed their opinion of him. Today he gave not the least thought to it, but rather took pleasure in recognizing how smoothly and how quickly he was again free of them all.

Already after a couple of days he was able to convince himself that what was still outstanding could just as easily also be put aside in writing.

There still remained only his personal affairs.

These he took care of for himself in the long hours of these hot nights in which he just could not sleep, but always got up again and walked about, thinking about his life, about his failed life.

Then he saw how little there basically was that he had to take care of. A couple of letters could be burned, but nothing would also be harmed, if they were to be found. His sketches were better destroyed, so as not to fall into incompetent hands. The drafts, too, of his first works, on which he had once set such great hopes and of which he now, reading them over again after decades, would have to say that they would not have attained what he had dreamed—very full of talent, but inadequate.

How quickly all that was also taken care of! Nothing finally that other eyes could not have been allowed to read! None of those small and yet so charming secrets that just give life the right spice!

For what was a life without secrets—without secrets from others?

6

He was finished with everything.

Now there only remained one farewell—that from a place he had grown fond of.

For he did not want to wait for this until the time had come.

He wanted to go up there one more time, then no more.

That should happen today.

Yesterday had been Sunday. Its hours had stretched out very painfully through the day. No book brought him peace, no thought brought him repose. (If his "Death Park" had been a reality—he would hardly have been able to resist it!)

Yet another couple of days and the vacations would end and everyone would return.

It should happen today.

He would not be able to go out for his daily walk much longer. Autumn was gently announcing itself. The weather had changed. Yesterday—to make his affliction complete—it had rained the whole day, and today there was a biting coolness. The forest path would be a morass.

But suddenly to stay away—that just would not do.

For one thing, he wanted to sit again in his corner, drink wine, look into those brown eyes, and say a friendly word of farewell—even if she had clearly enough shown how indifferent, even unlikable he was to her, no, he did not want to be unfriendly.

He was up there, wet and muddy.

They had greeted one another as always.

Now she was sitting nearby, but he could not see her, even if he had tried to and had changed his place. She must be away in back, busying herself at the little bar.

Did he hear her breathing? Why then was he so uneasy?

For hardly had he taken his place than he had to get up again.

It seemed to him that he had to see her. See her right away—and then leave immediately! Otherwise—well, what then, otherwise?

He could not remain here.

He had to leave. Otherwise—

So he quickly finished his drink, laid down the amount, as he had always done of late, and walked over, ready to leave.

She appeared and looked at him as if in astonishment over this sudden departure. But she said nothing.

For him, too, the word that he wanted to say, stuck in his throat.

Then it came out, forced and unclear: "Now the vacations are almost over. I don't know if I will still be able to come up here so often, Fräulein—"

He was standing close in front of her.

She looked up at him and smiled, as one smiles when one wants to break out the next moment into tears (and her voice, too, sounded embarrassed and forced): "Yes," she said, but he did not understand what she was saying, "Yes, I too must leave now—to return home."

When two flames join together—who can say which one of the two first reaches out for the other?

Thus they held one another and their lips lay bound together as if they would never again release one another.

It was he who first released himself.

She grasped for his hands and it sounded fearful: "But tomorrow I will still be here."

She saw that he still did not hear what she was saying. She only felt herself drawn anew onto this broad chest.

She had to repeat it—urgently, in order to be understood: "But tomorrow I will still be here."

He held her back and looked at her.

"Tomorrow?" he said, as if waking from a dream, and looked at her as if he were really seeing her for the first time.

"Tomorrow," he repeated and was unaware that he answered, "Of course I will come tomorrow."

She followed him outside into the rain, which had set in again, and saw how he was hurrying through the wood in long strides (as if he wanted to escape the rain) and disappeared.

He was reeling like a drunken man.

7

At home, he looked himself over; he was dripping wet and was spattered up over his knees. Had it rained then? Just now, on his return? Rained?

He waved off help from Franz and sent him away. He had to be alone. Then, having changed clothes, he lit a fire in the large fireplace, which Franz had prepared as a precaution when the weather changed, since he knew how his master liked to sit by it on cool days.

Now he rested there, somewhat quieter, in the deep chair before the crackling wood and the leaping flames.

What had just now happened—it was so improbable that he was still unable to really grasp it. And yet it was quite natural. Had he not loved her from the first day on and had he not gone up there only for her sake—day after day—only for her sake?

But she? Did she love him, an old man? Was she able to love

him? Why? Since when? Incredible. But she was no longer a child. Her kisses had proved it.

Love—it sounded so curious.

Love—had he ever known love then?

That time, with the young English girl, beautiful and cold, as only an Englishwoman can be, for whom he had done what destroyed his life—it had not been love, but rather passion, one that was not even satisfied.

His wife—he had never loved her, and never, not even for a moment, pretended to love her. She had not once been unhappy in her marriage, and he had remained—as they say—true to her, without really knowing why. For the couple of little adventures on his trips, which did not even deserve this name, what meaning did they have?

But that other one, here in this town, with that dreadful woman who had run after him for years, had pursued him and had thrown herself around his neck, he had ended it before it became a public scandal.

She was not the only one who had offered herself to him and whom he could have taken. He had hardly paid attention to them all and none left any memory in him.

Love—he had not known it and yet had grown old.

Love—did he love this little girl up there, with the brown eyes and the full lips, who knew how to kiss so well?

If love was happiness, then he loved her. For it was happiness that did not let him sleep in the hours of this night and thrilled through him with an unexpected strength.

Love—it had also come to him. Late. But it was there.

Now it was up to him to keep it.

He gave himself over to his dreams, without defending himself, gave himself to them as one does in order to flee in them from a reality that is no longer bearable in its tedium and emptiness.

Where were the tiredness and the aversion to life of these last weeks?

Had he really ever thought of putting an end to his life?

It had just now begun.

It had just begun!

Tomorrow he would climb up there once again, take her in his arms, and talk over with her how everything was to be now.

They would go away from here, as soon as only possible, the day after tomorrow already, and then travel at first—to foreign lands that she did not know, which he would show her, and among other people than these people here—to lands where the winter was short and the summer long. They would travel, travel far and ever farther until, tired of roaming about, they would build their nest, so as to live in it till the end of their—no, till the end of *his* days.

He suddenly shivered.

The fire had burned down. From outside the light of a damp and cool day penetrated.

8

The sun was shining hotly again, but the air, cooled off by the rain, was fresh and clear as he arrived up there.

Along the whole way he had sought to smile at himself—was he not going with roses in hand like a young puppy, who secretly goes to his first love? He did not quite succeed.

She was standing at the gate of the front garden, and as if he had come for the first time and as if she had to show him the way, she took him by the hand and drew him down the steps.

Below, they kissed, not like yesterday, impassioned and in rapture, but rather intimately and long, as if they were only now quite sure of their love.

Then she sat down beside him, laid her arm around his neck and her head against his broad chest, and listened to him. He talked and talked, and when he was silent he pressed his mouth again and again on the brown skin of this slender throat under him and drank in her scent.

KENN]

He spoke as he had never spoken in his life to another person. It seemed to him as if he had to tell her everything, and he told her everything: who he was and how his life had been—what he had done wrong and how he had paid for it—what he had suffered and what he thought about when he had sat here. And then, how everything should be different now and would be.

The dreams of the night were supposed to come alive under his words, and did not. For the more he spoke and the longer, the less he believed his own words; and they became more and more faint, until they became silent.

She listened to him and did not move, but only lightly stroked again and again the spot behind his ear where her hand was lying.

She did not interrupt him. She interrupted him with not a word. She only smiled now and then at his words, not scornfully, oh no, but sadly, like a mother smiles over the wishes of her child, which she would so gladly like to fulfill and yet is unable to fulfill, since their fulfillment is so entirely impossible.

When he fell silent and his mouth lay on her neck, she spoke. She did not comment on what he had just said, as if she had heard it and yet not heard it, and what she said was this: that she was returning now to her hometown, since she was no longer needed here, and that there, very soon, she would marry the man who was waiting for her, whom she had known from childhood and who loved her, who was a good man and an honest man, the man to whom she belonged.

And then she took the little book that she had been holding the whole time in her other hand, and took a picture out of it and showed it to him—it was the picture of a young man with firm features and clear eyes that one could well trust.

Finally, however, it was the turn of the little book itself, and it turned out to be a timetable. She opened it to the page where the picture had been, loosed her arm from his neck, took his large hand in both of hers (and they still hardly encompassed his) and led his index finger down to a place in the row of numbers.

"But first I will have a free day for myself," she said, "and a good one. With this train, 11:26, I will depart from here tomorrow and at 2:20 I will be here" (he read the name of the old capital Heinrichslust, and there rose up in his memory an old castle in an old park), "and if another person has already departed with the train here at 7:52"—the finger was led one column to the left. But she got no further.

CHAPTER SIX

1

As Councilor-of-Commerce Behrendt in the morning, from a good night's sleep and fresh as not for a long time, came out of his room and saw the astonished glance of Franz, the servant, fall on the bag in his hand, which he always took when he went on a short trip, he said casually, "I'm going away for a couple of days, Franz."

At this the man found the courage to ask, "Will Herr Councilor-of-Commerce be back at the end of the week, when Madam—"

He received just as indifferently the answer: "Could be, Franz, or maybe not. But everything is in order?"

That was quickly affirmed, and he asked whether he was allowed to carry the bag to the train.

Yes, he was, and he was to wait at the station gate.

On the main street that led from the market to the train station, Councilor-of-Commerce Behrendt entered the shop of the jeweler Zandtke, who had just raised his shutters, had the necklace that he had seen in the show window a short time before displayed to him, and bought it without further ado. Little Herr Zandtke was just as startled as he was highly pleased. For in the first place this was by far the best sale that he had made since opening his shop seventeen years ago, and in the second place, he had never hoped, here in this town, to sell this piece, the most valuable of his whole stock, which by a rare occasion he had acquired far under its worth. If he had nonetheless put it in his show window, it was only to show that he, too, could if he wished. But who here was at all in a position to evaluate the choice beauty of this jewelry? Who? Except for him, who had just bought it, and whom, with a broad grin, he now gazed after—this remarkable Councilor-of-Commerce Behrendt, who, in the early morning on his way to the train station—his servant had just gone by with his luggage—had entered his shop and, without batting an eyelash, had simply laid down the thousand mark bill—a very remarkable and doubtless very important man. What had they been saying about him recently? What kind of nonsense? Naturally once again only the mischievous prattle of this nest of gossips!

But Herr Zandtke knew that discretion was not only the duty of doctors and pastors, but was also the first law of wisdom of his own profession, and he would take care not to transgress this law.

Franz was waiting at the gate with yet another question on his heart: "May I not make up the room of Herr Councilor-of-Commerce in the next days? The whole house would then be in order?"

"Do whatever you can't leave undone," was his reply. But this time the voice sounded not only friendly, as always, but so youthful, almost (if he had dared to think it) cocky. Did his master look forward so much to this short trip? Well now, it had been a long time since he had gone away, besides he had been here the whole vacation—it was time that he also thought about himself.

2

It was a local train, stopping at every station, and the single passenger in second class arrived in Heinrichslust only at noon.

The highway forked in front of the train station: it led on the right to the village that lay farther back, which was therefore not visible from here; on the left, it led in a gentle rise through an avenue of old chestnuts up to the castle, whose towers one could see standing out. Next to the castle, however, was supposed to be the Crown Prince Hotel.

How did she just know everything so exactly? Well, in the first

[ENN]

days of her arrival she had been brought here by her uncle, who had business in the vicinity, and then had walked around here alone a whole afternoon. She had liked it here so much, especially the park, that she had decided to come here once again before she traveled on to her home.

Thus Councilor-of-Commerce Behrendt walked with his bag in his hand (for at the train station there were neither hotel porters nor baggage carriers) up toward the castle. The Crown Prince was the only house in its vicinity. It was situated on a badly paved street and close to the edge of the forest, in the shadow of the most splendid old oaks and beeches.

He received a gigantic room with a gigantic bed and heavy, old furniture, and then sat at one of the tables in front of the house under the trees. For she had told him that he was to eat before she arrived—she would already have done so in the car of her express train and she wanted to waste no time, but go right away into the park.

An old waiter in a worn-out, but very clean tailcoat served him. It took a long time, as if everything had to be fetched from the village, but what he was served was outstanding.

There was more than enough time for him to reach the train station again.

He did not recognize her at first as she stepped out, for he was seeing her for the first time in coat and hat. But how attractive she looked! He had to pull himself together so as not to take her immediately into his arms.

He gave her his hand. "You here, Fräulein Marie? What a surprise!"

She immediately entered into his tone. "And you, Herr Councilor-of-Commerce—yes, what are you doing here?"

They laughed. They laughed very much altogether on this afternoon, as had been planned: "Then we want to be really cheerful and leave dumb thoughts behind."

At the castle they stopped.

"Now I will go ahead," she said, "to take a room for myself. But I will be back here soon."

In going, she turned back once more. "What room number does the Herr Councilor-of-Commerce have then?"

"Eight!" he called, laughing.

He stayed behind and waited on the stone bench by the basin, into which certainly no water had run for a long time. A Triton over it was blowing into his shell and a properly voluptuous nymph looked up at him longingly and with an indescribably dumb expression. The castle, a gigantic box with firmly closed and nailed shut windows stood there, as boring outside as inside, he thought.

She returned sooner than he expected, and they walked through the famous park, which—at least at this time of year—appeared to attract no more visitors, for far and wide there was not a human being.

It was different from other parks, and what was first of all surprising about it was the wide distance between its trees and their groups from one another. They stood in the broad, green meadows, each tree and each group by itself, and it was the work of an artistic-creative spirit, which placed these here and those there, to allow each its importance. Each of the trees, however, was a choice example of its species, and what was still able to flourish in this climate had been transplanted here. Thus the whole park had something uncommonly free and grand about it, and nowhere was the view hemmed in or obscured.

But it must be said that the two of them had eyes less for it and its quiet beauty than for themselves.

Not that they talked much. On the contrary—they walked often silently next to one another, as if it were enough for them to be together. But they often stopped still, to look at one another: she at him somewhat from the side, and he at her a bit from above, since he was so much taller than she, and if their glances met then, they laughed (when they did not kiss).

She laughed much on that afternoon.

The park was vast, but when they reached its high point, where the bench was, from where its green waves rolled down to the gray walls of the castle, there was still enough time to walk toward a forest pub that—as a sign promised—was supposed to be no farther than a half hour distant in the woods.

There they drank their coffee and this time walked back through the same valley as before, only on the other and more beautiful side of the small river.

On the bench again—the first twilight of the evening was sinking—he took her in his arms and wrapped the chain with the bright stone around her brown neck.

She did not say, "You should not give me anything," and "That is just much too beautiful for me." She looked at him, long and earnestly. "I will enjoy it, when I am alone."

He saw how the beauty of his gift pleased her, but also that she had no idea of its true value.

"If she should ever be in need—may her destiny preserve her from such—it can help her sometime," he thought.

They sat beside one another for a long time yet, until the first, light fog arose from the valley.

It was no longer summer and it was not yet autumn. It was one of those lovely days that do not know if they should return once more to warm ones or already take their farewell from them.

Then, as he again drew her close to him (for she was never close enough), he saw how a tear was hanging on her eyelash.

Alarmed, he asked, "You are crying? Why are you crying?"

"I'm in need of nothing. But you—you must not be sad any longer—as you so often were, at my place up there. Look, people are just not worth being sad about. You must be cheerful, from now on—promise me?"

He wanted to say, "How can I be cheerful without you?" But he did not say it.

He only said, "I will try to be because you want it."

They stood up. Now he took her under her two elbows and lifted her up high. He held her so that her face was quite near his, and looked into the brown eyes a long while. She was so light.

"Such a great man," her mouth said on his, "having everything that he wants, and yet not be cheerful—"

As they reached the first streets of the little town—for in fact, besides the castle and the park there was also a town with the same name Heinrichslust, even if it was only a superfluous appendage of them—they saw the first people.

Farther on they found a wine tavern, not so beautiful and clean as their wine tavern, but still quite cozy, in whose side room they were alone.

They ordered and laughed again over everything and everyone:

Over the comical, little Schnauzer that stuck its shaggy head through the door, looked at them with its hair-covered eyes, as if it thoroughly disapproved of their presence ("he rumpled his nose at us," she maintained); over the wine list with its pompous names, which did not even exist (but what they drank was truly good); over the old gentleman at his regular table, the only one they were able to look out at; and over the solemn composure with which he stuffed his long pipe.

But they laughed the most when she said to him as they were getting ready to leave, "Say, don't forget to pay."

"What did you think at that time?"

"No, I'm not telling!"

"Do, please! If I tell you first what I thought—will you tell me then?"

"Well, alright. But you first."

He hardly got it out for laughing. "There she stands, the dumb goose, and says not a word. But now you!"

She, too, almost choked. "Me? There he goes, the old gyp!"

They were still laughing as they walked through the old narrow streets that were slipping here from day into night.

Then there suddenly rose up before them the mighty walls of the castle as if produced by magic.

"Now you go ahead," she softly asked.

He was inwardly alarmed for a second.

But when he still heard her laughingly ask, "I still do not know what room number the Herr Councilor-of-Commerce has," he called back so loudly, "It's still eight!" that the white nymph in the shimmering moonlight shuddered and seemed to press closer to her protector.

The Crown Prince was brightly lit, as if it were waiting for more and more guests. Its door stood wide open and from the hall and lobby the light streamed over the tables and trees before the house.

But no one was in sight, not even the old waiter, and no one met him as he climbed up the broad stairway with the wonderful banisters and the soft carpet, walked through the totally quiet corridor, and sought and found his room.

He left the door ajar and sat so that he had it in view.

Thus he sat and did not take his eyes away from it until she quietly opened it a quarter hour later.

3

When Councilor-of-Commerce Behrendt awoke in the morning, he was alone and it was late. But it was still dark in the high room

Was it the trees before his window that cut off the light?

He opened it and saw that it was the fog, which hung between the branches.

He turned back and only now saw the sheet of paper that lay on the table beside his things.

He picked it up. "Goodbye! I thank you!" was on it.

The words were written with pencil and in a child's steep handwriting. The "I" was underlined once, the "you" twice.

They were the answer to his words—to the only ones he still remembered to have stammered out in the unconscious intoxication of that night and always repeated anew. "I thank you! I **thank** you! I THANK you!"

He read it and only then understood.

Then came the pain, sharp and stinging. He staggered and had to brace himself.

How was he to live without her? How was he to live without her?

But then he banished it. After the happiness of this night, this inconceivable happiness, there should be no more pain.

Every happiness was short. If it lasted longer, it was happiness no more.

He should not ask, "How can I live without her?" He must ask, "How could I live with her?"

(For loving and living together are two separate things—she knew it, clever, naturally sensitive, and unsentimental as she was.)

Be cheerful—he had promised it to her.

Everything that he did on this day was done quietly and slowly as if he now expected nothing more.

He dressed, packed his bag, and in the empty, large room—for the tables in front of the house were still not set, due to the dampness—took a plentiful breakfast. (It was the time when he was used to having his midday meal.)

He asked that his bag be taken to the train station, settled his bill, and was more strongly touched than he was accustomed to be by the expression of joy that went over the careworn face of the old waiter at the extraordinarily large tip.

He spoke a couple of words with him.

"Yes, almost no strangers come here anymore. Earlier it was different. Today a young lady also stayed overnight with us, but she has already departed."

He still had to go once more up to his room, although he was certain that nothing had been forgotten. It was still not made up. He threw himself on the bed and pressed the pillow to himself.

Then in the park he wandered from tree to tree, from bench to bench, until he came to the one situated highest up.

Everything, every leaf and every blade, was lightly moistened by a silver breath and now shone, where the sun broke forth from a white sky, in a trembling glitter.

He sat down on the bench, on which they had stayed so long yesterday.

Before him the ridges and meadows rolled out like green carpets, and suddenly it seemed to him as if the world here around him had become unreal—**as if he only imagined it**!

4

What had she just said yesterday, here on this same bench, this little girl who knew so wonderfully how to laugh and (long since no longer a child) so wonderfully how to kiss?

"When anything makes me angry and sad, I only have to think about it no more and it is no longer there."

Was she not right again? Was she not mostly right, in her unspoiled sensitivity, in her healthy understanding?

He thought of her words again. Was it not so?

My thoughts create the world. My thoughts let it sink back again into its nothingness.

I live and the world is there—it exists. I am dead and it is gone—it exists no more.

I think and I am. I cease to think and I am no more.

My thoughts are everything—they are my happiness; they are my unhappiness.

If I am their master, then I am master over my life and my death. If I am their slave, then I am the plaything of my fate.

He wanted to become master of his thoughts and remain so from then on.

He wanted to be happy by ruling in his thoughts.

He made it his intention in this hour.

He knew—and knew it from today on: he possessed an immense power to be happy when he wanted to be.

He wanted to be. He wanted to be the master of his will.

He wanted to subdue his thoughts, when they rebelled; to

train them, so that they obeyed his word; to shoo them away, when they wanted to gnaw at him with "remembering."

He wanted to build himself a world, a new, a different one than the old one was from which he came. And it should be beautiful and light, this world, making him cheerful and happy.

He still had ten, twenty years before him. He could still catch up on what he had missed. Not everything, but much. Was it not so?

Certainly these thoughts that thus came to him, here on the bench and while the day was slowly dying, were not new and also probably not especially deep. Many may have thought them already, but it seemed to him that not too many were living according to them.

Perhaps they had already been put into a philosophical system. But that was all the same to him.

He was satisfied that he had found them for himself—those according to which he would now live in this world, this only **imagined world.**

The sun had wiped the silver gleam from branch and blade, and the dying day was becoming gray as he arose.

5

So completely unthinkable was the thought of returning back there that it never even occurred to him.

As something self-evident, after a long wait, he boarded the train that was going in the opposite direction, shook the conductor's hand, and was alone.

He threw himself down and crossed his arms behind his head. But he did not sleep for a long time.

He had worked much in his life—now he wanted to enjoy himself, as well and as long as he could, and make for himself a good day, a good day and—a long one!

He thought about her and how everything had turned out.

Everything so different—so entirely different.

He thought about her—he would always think about her. For she was the most beautiful thing in his life, which had been so poor until then. But he also thought about that little, yellow blackmailer from Rio for a moment; he had to be thankful to him too. Without him he would never have written the letter that then led him over the hill to the village post office; without him he would not have known about the wine tavern of the—still unknown to him—Herr Fürbringer; and without him—nothing of **her**! Without him everything would have remained as it was: he would still be sitting today in the good town (senior partner of the firm Behrendt & Spruth, Fruit Preserves, family father, city father, orphan father), would still be sitting there, year after year and from year to year older, wearier, and more bitter.

His thoughts came more slowly and he fell asleep.

The imagined world sank.

When he awoke and it arose anew in his consciousness, the train was rushing through the suburbs of Berlin.

Now he would soon be in the city that never sleeps.

EPILOG

Whoever on beautiful days in the Tiergarten—
— But the story has been told.

AFTERWORD

John Henry Mackay's novel *Die Menschen der Ehe* (*The People of Marriage*, 1892) is, as he himself noted, "decidedly propagandistic." He said twenty years later that writing it was for him a "kind of liberation." Its theme of free love was very much "in the air" at the time, a theme that was also—in a somewhat different context—close to Mackay the boy-lover. Some anarchists were much more vehement than Mackay in their condemnation of the institution of marriage. Emma Goldman, for example, wrote strongly about it shortly afterwards in her "Marriage and Love" (in *Anarchism and Other Essays*, 1910) and concluded: "Thus Dante's motto over Inferno applies with equal force to marriage: 'Ye who enter here leave all hope behind.'" And in a review of Mackay's novel, Emma Heller Schumm (wife of George Schumm, who translated Mackay's *The Anarchists* into English) faulted Mackay for not being sweeping enough in his condemnation of marriage:

"It is only because literature is still so poor in novels that have stamped marriage with the label 'failure' that I feel at all grateful to him for the little he has given us. Perhaps I would be less disappointed if the title of the book had not misled me to expect more, and if I did not know Mr. Mackay's condemnation of marriage to be absolute, and not confined to merely 'bad marriages.'…

"Mr. Mackay has not, as his American friends, who knew of the forthcoming book, had fondly hoped he would, dealt a deathblow to marriage. Where is the great artist and psychologist who will, by giving to the world *the* novel of free love?" (*Liberty*, 21 January 1893, Whole No. 255, p. 3).

Mackay did not publicly comment on the review, but near the end of his life he recalled the novel in his *Abrechnung* (1932):

"It was a disappointment. One had—I know not why—expected a voluminous discussion of the problem of marriage.

"I am sorry. I feel myself quite incompetent here, although, many years later, in 1930, I once more dared that dangerous field with a small one-acter, the 'Scene': Ehe [Marriage].

"All that I wanted, there and here, was to show in an example how very much more beautiful and pure the—even then!—so much slandered 'free love' was than the—even today!—so vehemently defended institution of marriage, and how much more correct it is to separate than to remain together if one no longer loves" (*John Henry Mackay: Autobiographical Writings*, Xlibris, 2001, p. 48).

Like the central character of *The Anarchists*, the protagonist of *The People of Marriage*, Franz Grach, is the spokesman for Mackay's own views and so may be identified with him. His opposite number, the strong woman Dora Syk, is, I believe, patterned after Mackay's good friend Gabriele Reuter (1859–1941). Certainly Reuter believed in free love. As Jeannine Blackwell wrote in her Ph.D. dissertation "Bildungsroman mit Dame: The Heroine in the German Bildungsroman from 1770 to 1900" (1982): "Reuter herself willingly had a child out of wedlock, and lived for a short period with German anarchist poet John Henry Mackay." The two were part of the group of writers that spent summers in the mountain village of Schreiberhau (today, Szklarska Poreba, Poland). Reuter may have stayed with Mackay there. Margarete Hauptmann wrote to Hedwig Fischer (wives of the well-known writer and publisher, respectively) on 25 September 1904:

"Yesterday evening John Henry Mackay had a party in his Schreiberhau cabin, to which we also went. It was very successful and entertaining. Frau Bölsche had prepared the cold buffet and Frau Gabriele Reuter did the honors. In the low, narrow room moved an elegant, wittily conversing crowd, drinking champagne—all gave a fantastic effect, as if from another world and time" (quoted in Peter de Mendelssohn, *S. Fischer und sein Verlag*, Frankfurt/Main: S. Fischer Verlag, 1970, p. 311).

In Mackay's correspondence with Benjamin R. Tucker, however, there is no mention of Reuter. Instead, from the first remaining letter of 28 February 1905, Mackay several times mentions only one woman visitor in Schreiberhau, the Dresden actress Luise Firle (1865–1942). (See *John Henry Mackay: Autobiographical Writings*, Xlibris, 2001.)

Although Reuter had begun publishing early, she was still not well known when Mackay's book appeared. That changed only a few years later, however, when she published *Aus guter Familie* (*From a Good Family*, 1895), the novel that made her famous—and financially independent. At first she had difficulty finding a publisher for it. Then she sent the manuscript to Mackay to examine. She related the result in her autobiography:

"He recommended it to his own publisher S. Fischer so warmly that Fischer decided to print it. And it was Mackay too who suggested the title 'Aus guter Familie.' I had titled it only 'Agathe Heidling.' The changed title contributed not immaterially to its success" (Gabriele Reuter, *Vom Kinde zum Menschen: Die Geschichte meiner Jugend*, Berlin: S. Fisher Verlag, 1921, p. 471).

If, as I believe, the character Dora Syk in *The People of Marriage* is modeled after Reuter, she repaid him in kind in *Aus guter Familie*. For the character Martin Greffinger in that novel is clearly intended to be Mackay. Mackay's American biographer, Thomas A. Riley, suggested much too mildly that Greffinger "seems to be a portrait of Mackay" (*Germany's Poet-Anarchist John Henry Mackay: A Contribution to the History of German Literature at the Turn of the Century, 1880–1920*, New York: The Revisionist Press, 1972, p. 102). Lynne Tatlock stated that Mackay served "as prototype for the final development of Martin" (introduction to *From a Good Family*, by Gabriele Reuter, translated by Lynne Tatlock, Rochester, NY: Camden House, 1999, p. xii). There is even an echo of *The People of Marriage* in Reuter's novel when Agathe, the central character, thinks her friend Eugenie wants to marry Martin. Eugenie replies reproachfully: "A Social Democratic student? But Agathe—one doesn't marry such! And besides, he really hates marriage!"

KENN]

Contemporary readers of *The People of Marriage* would have had no difficulty in identifying an unnamed personage in the novel, the owner of the iron works, whom Mackay described thus: "From one of these dark knolls the narrow turrets of a modern castle towered into the sun-hot sky. There dwelt the king of the region. He knew that's what he was: he talked down to his workers (using the familiar pronoun 'Ihr') and cared for them like 'a father for his children.' Things went well for him doing it; less so for his 'children.' Never mind!"

This was Carl Ferdinand Freiherr von Stumm-Halberg (1858–1906), who owned the leading iron works in Saarland. Here is an excerpt from his speeches to his workers in the years 1889–1895, i.e., around the time of Mackay's novel. In it the "you" addressed to the workers is in fact the familiar pronoun "Ihr" as Mackay pointed out ("Ihr" is the plural of "Du", the pronoun used to address intimates, children, and inferiors):

"I for my part would stay not a moment longer as your head, if in place of my personal relationship to each of you I had to place coming to terms with a workers' organization under independent leadership.... Such a relationship to an independent power is forbidden me already by my sense of moral duty and my Christian conviction.... If this should ever change and I would in fact be hindered from supervising and rectifying the worker also in his relations outside the mill, then I would not remain a day longer at the head of the business, for I would then no longer be in a position to fulfill the moral duty that my conscience prescribes for me before God and my fellow men. An employer for whom it is indifferent how his workers conduct themselves outside the mill violates, in my opinion, his most important duty.... I could name a whole series of workers' activities outside the mill where I hold it to be the absolute duty of an employer, who is permeated by his moral duty, to interfere and not withdraw to the comfortable standpoint and say: what the worker does outside the mill is indifferent to me, I am interested only in the work done in the mill.... I state all this not to claim a merit for myself, for I do it only as my duty as a human being, a Christian, and as head of the great Neunkirchen family of workers.... I believe I may say with a good conscience that I am in no way inferior to my professional comrades in the direction of social welfare, at least not in the effort to care for your material and spiritual welfare, to the best of my knowledge and belief, and to manifest practical Christianity, for which I feel myself responsible to God. In this way I hope to take care that, far beyond the days of my own life, you will remain unreceptive to the enticements of the Social Democrats and other false prophets. That is the best direction of social welfare that I can grant and leave to you. Remain firm for all time in the old, unshakable loyalty to our exalted monarch, remain firm in Christian neighborly love and the genuine fear of God, whichever confession you belong to. Then it will continue to go well for you according to human judgment." (This excerpt is from the Internet – Datenbank zur Unterrichtsvorbereitung im Fach Geschichte, Bremerhaven, 10.06.2001.)

Mackay was not a Social Democrat, but as an anarchist he surely qualified as one of the false prophets castigated by "King Stumm"—and at any rate the distinction between anarchist and Social Democrat was not as clear then as it is now. Indeed, Lynne Tatlock informs us in a footnote to her translation of Reuter's *Aus guter Familie*: "In the Germany of the 1880s at least two anarchist movements grew out of and subsequently separated themselves from the Social Democratic party" (Gabriele Reuter, *From a Good Family*, translated by Lynne Tatlock, Rochester, NY: Camden House, 1999, p. 220, n. 87).

In his memoirs Mackay commented: "I quite certainly have no weakness for the military. On the contrary! But—unmusical as I am—for military music." But he did note the popular music of his day and mentioned several songs in his writings. Already in *The Anarchists* (1891) he recalled the song "Two Lovely Black Eyes" that the cockney comedian Charlie Coburn had introduced in London in 1886. Later, in the poem "Pfingsten" in his boy-love poetry collection *Am Rande des Lebens* (1909), he recalled an outing with a boy to Grunewald (Berlin), where everyone sang "Im Grunewald ist Holzauktion" and "Donna Theresa." The first of these was the hit dance song of Berlin in 1892 and continues to be popular; the second is also still on the nostalgia repertoire.

Another German evergreen is the song "Nur einmal blüht im Jahr der Mai" (May blooms only once in the year), which Franz Grach and Dora Syk in *The People of Marriage* hear and then join in singing. The music is by Wilhelm Heiser, the text by Johann Gabriel Seidl. It begins:

Es streuet Blüten jedes Jahr der Lenz auf allen Wegen, bringt Rosen dir zur Gabe dar und liebereichen Segen.

Da laßt die Sorgen all' vorbei und schütze die zarten Triebe!

Nur einmal blüht im Jahr der Mai, nur einmal im Leben die Liebe, nur einmal blüht im Jahr der Mai, nur einmal im Leben die Liebe.

Every year spring strews blossoms on every path

Brings roses to you for a gift and loving blessing.

Then all cares are left behind and tender inclinations protected!

May blooms only once in the year, love only once in life,

May blooms only once in the year, love only once in life.

Another reference that would have resonated with contemporary readers of Mackay's novel is in the passage in which Grach recalls an event from his youth. The scene is in the back room of a tavern where the students had taken the waitress. One of them played the piano, another "in a dim memory of 'Nana,' emptied his beer into the piano." Emile Zola's novel *Nana* had been published in 1880. The scene the student recalls occurs near the beginning of the novel at a drunken all-night party where the characters are trying to think how to liven things up:

"Then the little fair-haired fellow, the man who bore one of the greatest names in France and had reached his wit's end and was desperate at the thought that he could not hit upon something really funny, conceived a brilliant notion: he snatched up his bottle of champagne and poured its contents into the piano. His allies were convulsed with laughter.

"'Hey! Why's he putting champagne into the piano?' asked Tatan Nene in great astonishment as she caught sight of him.

"'What, my lass, you don't know why he's doing that?' replied Labordette solemnly. 'There's nothing so good as champagne for pianos. It gives 'em tone.'

"'Ah,' murmured Tatan Nene sounding convinced."

In *Die Menschen der Ehe*, the student's memory—or at least his wit—was dim indeed!

All together *Die Menschen der Ehe* is a scathing portrait of Saarbrücken, where Mackay lived briefly in the home of his stepfather, building inspector Dumreicher, at Pestelstrasse 4. His character Franz Grach even refers to the town as Abdera: "Dora Syk— and teacher of the second class in the girls' school of Abdera! Now if that is not a joke one may laugh at, then I don't know what is!" The real Abdera is a maritime city in northeast Greece. The air of the region was thought in ancient times to cause people to become dull, and from this came a folk belief among the ancient Greeks that all Abderites were stupid.

A century later the population of Saarbrücken—at least some of them—had come to terms with Mackay's novel. On 16 November 1995 the Saarländischer Rundfunk broadcast a one-hour discussion of it in their series "Literatur im Gespräch" and gave a nice overview of various aspects of Mackay's life. It may be doubted, however, if many there had actually read the novel. This is illustrated by the poem "SAGITTA oder: 'Salü Saarbrücken'" that Hans Arnfried Astel wrote about the same time for his series "Sand am Meer—poetische Geheimkorrespondenz":

Narrowly and secretly
Saarbrücken honors its great son
John Henry Mackay.
Scotch on his father's side, but German was his mother tongue.
From Hamburg his mother followed her second husband to the dull town of businessmen, officials, and military.

This town, and what's worse, its citizens, by Mackay, who wanted his name pronounced

Mak-kai in good German, this town was pictured by the fugitive in the "Pictures of a Small Town" with the title

"The People of Marriage."

No one here knows the book, and that hardly surprises me, for here, where every native wind is caught in a butterfly net, the old Maoist will remain a leftist before the anarchist J.H.M. will be sold as a "gift book."

Narrowly and secretly they honor him by the wind arrow over the globe at the main railway station on the Saar.

Mackay as "Sagitta," which is Latin for arrow, published the first hustler novel of the Weimar Republic.

The covering of dust on the window pane here: a curtain.

I see the woman next door, but she cannot see me.

(Reprinted in *Espero,* nos. 6/7, March 1996. From 1967 to 1998 Hans Arnfried Amstel was director of the literature department of the Saarländischer Rundfunk.)

(As an aside I note that the mention of Mackay's insistence on the "German" pronunciation of his name is based on a misunderstanding of Erich Mühsam—expressed in his *Namen und Menschen: Unpolitische Erinnerungen.* Mühsam apparently did not realize that the pronunciation insisted on by Mackay was in fact the ordinary Scottish pronunciation.)

In 1911 Mackay invested most of the money he had inherited from his mother in a lifetime annuity, which he expected to give him an income sufficient to live on the rest of his life without having to be concerned about the sale of his books. But the runaway inflation of 1923 wiped out the value of the annuity, so that Mackay was dependent on those sales—which were never very large. He looked for a topic that would suit the popular taste—and pay immediately. Crime is always popular and serialization in a newspaper brought immediate reward. Mackay wrote his American friend Benjamin R. Tucker on 15 August 1926: "Could you give me the names of some American weeklies, which contain 'fascinating sto-

ries' and *pay well*? I have written one. Who could translate it?—
Schumm?" (See *John Henry Mackay: Autobiographical Writings*,
Xlibris, 2001.) This story must be his thriller *Staatsanwalt Sierlin:
Die Geschichte einer Rache* (*District Attorney Sierlin: The Story of a
Revenge*), which was serialized the following year in the *Vossische
Zeitung* (Berlin).

When things seemed bleakest, a millionaire patron appeared
on the scene in 1927, enabling Mackay to found the Stirner Verlag.
It was the Stirner Verlag that first published Mackay's thriller in
book form in 1928. Mackay dedicated the book edition to his
patron, the Russian émigré Michel Davidowsky. Alas, following
the publication by the Stirner Verlag of Mackay's *Werke in einem
Band* (1928), Davidowsky withdrew his support and Mackay's
plans for a "Great Stirner Edition" had to be abandoned. Nor did
Mackay receive the lifetime pension he had been promised.

District Attorney Sierlin reflects Mackay's lifetime interest in
crime. Not that Mackay himself was a criminal—far from it. But
he enjoyed fantasizing about it. His friend Friedrich Dobe later
recalled:

"Mackay loved to let his fantasy play and invent situations
and events in which the seemingly impossible is to be made possible. Thus I remember an evening in one of the Pilsner Urquell
bars mentioned earlier, I believe it was Stallman's. On the wall
opposite on a plaster base stood a life-sized bust of one of the
Caesars that often drew our glances. Suddenly Mackay asked me,
'How would you go about it if you had to steal this bust?' 'Why
should I steal it?' 'That doesn't matter. Assume that you are in love
with it or know that it hides a secret treasure—enough that it is a
life and death matter that you have this bust. How would you go
about it?' And we made suggestions to one another, each more
fantastic than the other, how we would manage to steal the bust
from the pub without being noticed. Some of Mackay's stories—
and not the worst—arose from such playful games of fantasy"
(Friedrich Dobe, *John Henry Mackay als Mensch*, Koblenz: Edition
Plato, 1987, p. 26).

KENN]

Dobe mentions the short stories "Herkulische Tändeleien," "Der Stärkere," and "Der große Coup" as products of Mackay's "playful games of fantasy." (These and other short stories and novellas mentioned here are in English in the volume *John Henry Mackay: Shorter Fiction*, Xlibris, 2000.) But surely *District Attorney Sierlin* is the most successful and original result of these plays of fantasy. This "Story of a Revenge" (the subtitle) builds and sustains a tension that is gripping indeed. And although here as elsewhere Mackay uses the technique of the "omniscient author," by concentrating on the different actors in repeating the scenes of the story he is able to display a fine psychological insight into individual actions.

A reviewer for the *Vossische Zeitung* (in which the novel had first been serialized, nota bene) used the phrases: "a book so surely resting on its own foundation, such convincing, humanly gripping treatment ... such cool consistency ... what artistic sureness ... what absolute psychological force." Other reviewers were not quite as kind. Wilhelm von Scholz (1874–1969), a prolific author of poems, plays, novels, and memoirs, wrote in *Das literarische Echo* (1930, 33: 9–10): "This tale begins excitingly and also holds the tension until about the middle of the book. Then the interest of the reader slackens, for the tale develops all too consequently and programmatically—one can also certainly say: the tension heightens all too programmatically. But the heightening in a straight, unbroken line, without new diversions from the already anticipated, almost foreseen path, loses its essence and quickly awakens the impression of constant uniformity."

This description reminds one immediately of Maurice Ravel's famous orchestral work "Boléro"—which was composed the same year as the publication of Mackay's book. Scholz continued: "To be sure, the book is lacking in any kind of aftereffect beyond its conclusion." (And did Ravel not say something similar about his own "Boléro"?) "But on the other hand it is undoubtedly a serious literary accomplishment and the work of a clever, significant person, in which life is reflected above all in its shadows, and it deserves attention."

The reviewer (von Hentig) for the *Monatsschrift für Kriminalpsychologie und Strafrechtsreform* (Monthly for Criminal Psychology and Penal Reform; 1928, 19: 768) took a more "professional" view: "At times a certain paranoid undertone of the book awakens a strong interest. Many features of this district attorney, who ambitiously envisions a place for himself in the Supreme Court of Justice in Leipzig, are seen in a sharp, caricaturized way and are dazzlingly presented. But since one does not see why a talented and healthy person chooses as his only goal in life this crude and unproductive kind of revenge and loses himself in a private vendetta, we experience the book as a technical solution, as a deluded system that has by chance a rational starting point, not as a work of art that also has something to suggest to science."

Mackay thought the book did not have the fate it deserved. He added: "This, too, among my books cries out for filming; its effect, as I have been told, with correct treatment, would have to be just as uncanny as that of the book itself" (in *Abrechnung*; in English in *John Henry Mackay: Autobiographical Writings*, Xlibris, 2001, p. 60). (He had earlier written of his sports novel *Der Schwimmer,* "What an artistically beautiful film could be made of it!")

Kurt Zube, Mackay's German biographer (under the pseudonym K. H. Z. Solneman), agreed that *District Attorney Sierlin* was "downright material for a film." I agree with his description of the novel:

"The revenge of an innocently sentenced man on the responsible district attorney is described with constantly increasing tension in a masterly composed construction. The protagonist proceeds so methodically and cleverly in doing it that none of the actions with which he pursues and encircles the attorney, who becomes ever more nervous, offer any means against himself. He applies a tactic of wearing him down, the model example of passive resistance, which puts the bad conscience of the attorney under ever harder pressure. It becomes so unbearable for him that it finally leads him to an actual attack on his pursuer, who averts it with pleasure so as also to have the means to allow the so-called 'state of laws' to act against him. Sierlin finally lands in a mental hospital for the rest of his life. This is a truly anarchist story" (K. H. Z. Solneman, *Der Bahnbrecher John Henry Mackay: Sein Leben und sein Werk*, Freiburg/Br.: Verlag der Mackay-Gesellschaft, 1979, p. 256).

Zube finds only the ending of the story "somewhat unsatisfying," for "someone who summons up such energy to demand an accounting for the time in his life that was spoiled by another, should also find his life still worth living for other goals and not end it in suicide." Perhaps. But it is part of Mackay's honest insight into the human condition that he also shows how difficult it is to live an anarchist life. Once again (as the poet Browning suggested) a man's reach exceeded his grasp.

An amusing note in *District Attorney Sierlin* is presented by Assistant Judge Kreidewien, who coined the term "somewhat too human" and applied it to D. A. Sierlin. It is, of course, a parody of Nietzsche's "Human, All Too Human" and may be a tip of the hat to the contemporary cult of Nietzsche. What Mackay really thought of Nietzsche was forcefully expressed in his comparison of Nietzsche and Stirner: "No one admires more than I the defiant courage of this thinker [Nietzsche], his proud disdain of all traditional authority, and the power at times of his language; but wanting to compare this eternally vacillating spirit, who is always anew self-contradictory, almost helplessly tumbling from truth to error, with the deep, clear, calm, and superior genius of Stirner is an absurdity, not worth serious refutation" (from the introduction to Mackay's biography *Max Stirner: Sein Leben und sein Werk*, 3rd ed., 1914—more on Stirner below).

Die gedachte Welt (*The Imagined World*) was not published in Mackay's lifetime. Edited by Edward Mornin, it first appeared in 1989 along with a few other unpublished works of Mackay. If *District Attorney Sierlin* is a "true anarchist story," as Zube remarked, then *The Imagined World* is a true egoist story. As Mornin commented: "In *Die gedachte Welt* Mackay carries his liberation ideas to their ultimate conclusion. Through the love and example of a simple, devoted girl, Ludwig Behrendt is rescued from self-destruction and led to the conviction that everyone can form his own life and create his own world through his readiness to be happy or unhappy" (Edward Mornin, editor, *Die gedachte Welt* by John Henry Mackay, Frankfurt am Main: Verlag Peter Lang, 1989, p. 24). Mornin then quotes the lines near the end of the novel:

"He thought of her words again. Was it not so?

"My thoughts create the world. My thoughts let it sink back again into its nothingness.

"I live and the world is there—it exists. I am dead and it is gone—it exists no more.

"I think and I am. I cease to think and I am no more.

"My thoughts are everything—they are my happiness; they are my unhappiness.

"If I am their master, then I am master over my life and my death. If I am their slave, then I am the plaything of my fate.

"He wanted to become master of his thoughts and remain so from then on.

"He wanted to be happy by ruling in his thoughts."

"These ideas," Mornin concludes, "were taken by Mackay from the writings of Stirner. *Die gedachte Welt*, his last large work, leads to a point beyond which there can be no more real development. This point, at which the human being creates his own world ('the imagined world') through his will, presents an existential conclusion and negates in the final analysis the importance of the outside world" (p. 25).

Mornin references several very apt pages from the egoist philosopher Max Stirner's *Der Einzige und sein Eigentum* (1844). (All quotations from Stirner here are in the brilliant English translation of Steven T. Byington. This was published in 1907 by Benjamin R. Tucker, who gave the book the title *The Ego and His*

Own.) These include, for example, the passages in which Stirner compares "freedom" and "ownness":

"What a difference between freedom and ownness! One can get *rid* of a great many things, one yet does not get rid of all; one becomes free from much, not from everything…. Ownness, on the contrary, is my whole being and existence, it is I myself. I am free from what I am *rid* of, owner of what I have in my *power* or what I *control*. My *own* I am at all times and under all circumstances, if I know how to have myself and do not throw myself away on others. To be free is something that I cannot truly *will*, because I cannot make it, cannot create it: I can only wish it and—aspire toward it, for it remains an ideal, a spook….

"Freedom teaches only: Get yourselves rid, relieve yourselves of everything burdensome; it does not teach you who you yourselves are. Rid, rid! so rings its rallying-cry, and you, eagerly following its call, get rid even of yourselves, 'deny yourselves.' But ownness calls you back to yourselves, it says 'Come to yourself!' Under the aegis of freedom you get rid of many kinds of things, but something new pinches you again: 'you are rid of the Evil One; evil is left.' As *own* you are *really rid of everything*, and what clings to you you *have accepted*; it is your choice and your pleasure. The *own* man [der *Eigene*] is the *free*-born, the man free to begin with; the free man, on the contrary, is only the *eleutheromaniac*, the dreamer and enthusiast."

We see these ideas well illustrated by Ludwig Behrendt in *The Imagined World*. With the arrival of the blackmailer he is awakened to a sense of how very much he has lost his freedom. He tries to regain it by getting rid of the blackmailer. But even though he achieves this, he realizes that he is still not free. Nor does his achievement of ridding himself of his concern for the opinions of his fellow citizens satisfy him. He is consequently led to consider suicide as the path to final freedom. Then, as Mornin has pointed out, the young girl (whom Behrendt has fallen in love with without realizing it) suggests to him something else altogether: that he can will to own himself—and in so doing create his own world. This he does, and it is the very choice proposed by Stirner.

(As an aside here, I note that I have put the original German of what Byington translated as "the *own* man" in square brackets above, namely, "der *Eigene*." This term was taken from Stirner's book to be the title of the first "gay" journal in the world, *Der Eigene*, which began as an anarchist journal in the direction of Stirner in 1896, but was openly homosexual from 1898. With interruptions—mostly due to interference by the police—it continued until 1932. To try to be explicit and non-sexist, I have elsewhere translated the journal's title "The Self-Owner.")

Stirner's ideas appear in many of Mackay's writings, of course. He prided himself on being the rediscoverer of Stirner and was (and remains) *the* biographer of Stirner. There is surely a reference to Stirner's book in *The Imagined World* when Behrendt's acquaintance Dr. Radewald is described as "the only one here with whom one could talk about something other than the local interests and the questions of the day. About a book, not even known here by title." (Two other topics are also mentioned: "about a matter of which the newspapers only wrote in order to suppress it and which only those readers found out about who were able to think independently; and now and again also about a question that was better not discussed here at all." Mornin has suggested that the second is "probably an allusion to pederasty." The first is perhaps homosexuality in general; I am assuming that "pederasty" is a synonym for "boy-love" here.)

Some further passages from Stirner (also referenced by Mornin) help illuminate the ending of Mackay's novel:

"Exertions to 'form' all men into moral, rational, pious, human, 'beings' (training) were in vogue from of yore. They are wrecked against the indomitable quality of I, against own nature, against egoism. Those who are trained never attain their ideal, and only profess with their *mouth* the sublime principles, or make a *profession*, a profession of faith. In fact of this profession they must in *life* 'acknowledge themselves sinners altogether,' and they fall short of their ideal, are 'weak men,' and bear with them the consciousness of 'human weakness.'

"It is different if you do not chase after an *ideal* as your 'destiny,' but dissolve yourself as time dissolves everything. The dissolution is not your 'destiny,' because it is present time.

"Yet the *culture*, the religiousness, of men has assuredly made them free, but only free from one lord, to lead them to another. I have learned by religion to tame my appetite, I break the world's resistance by the cunning that is put in my hand by *science*; I even serve no man; 'I am no man's lackey.' But then it comes. You must obey God more than man. Just so I am indeed free from irrational determination by my impulses, but obedient to the master *Reason*....

"Without doubt culture has made me *powerful*. It has given me power over all *motives*, over the impulses of my nature as well as over the exactions and violences of the world.... From religion (culture) I do learn the means for the 'vanquishing of the world,' but not how I am to subdue *God* too and become master of him; for God 'is the spirit.' And this same spirit, of which I am unable to become master, may have the most manifold shapes; he may be called God or National Spirit, State, Family, Reason, also—Liberty, Humanity, Man.

"*I* receive with thanks what the centuries of culture have acquired for me; I am not willing to throw away and give up anything of it: I have not lived in vain. The experience that I have *power* over my nature, and need not be the slave of my appetites, shall not be lost to me; the experience that I can subdue the world by culture's means is too dear-bought for me to be able to forget it. But I want still more."

Although Behrendt has been "rescued from self-destruction" by the girl's "love and example" (Mornin), Mackay makes it quite clear in *The Imagined World*, with his description of the "Death Park," that suicide is part of everyone's right to self-determination. In fact, this is one of the recurring themes in Mackay's writings, and already in one of his earliest publications, the narrative poem

Helene (1888), it is central to the title character's motivation (as I pointed out in "No Good Deed Goes Unpunished: John Henry Mackay's *Helene*," *Germanic Notes*, 1986, 17: 6–8).

On a lighter note may be mentioned Behrendt's dislike of the greeting "Mealtime!" (in German, "Mahlzeit!"). Mackay had already satirized this greeting in his short story "Nausea":

"'Me-e-a-l-time ... Me-e-a-l-time ...' Oh how I hate that word! Whether stated or not, from dawn to dusk, the whole people bellow out that greasy, slimy, self-satisfied word, in which there is no sense and no reason. I hear it always. I cannot avoid it.

"Even when I lie dying, I will have to hear it: 'Me-e-a-l-time! Me-e-a-l-time'—yes, for the worms!" (*John Henry Mackay: Shorter Fiction* , Xlibris, 2000, p. 65).

I experienced this ridiculous greeting firsthand during the academic year 1974–75, which I spent as guest of the Institute for the History of Science (University of Munich), where I shared lunch with colleagues in the canteen of the German Museum.

In *The Imagined World* the young girl Marie deserves a closer look. Her "child's face" reminded Behrendt of "the face of that young Englishman who had worked beside him in London." Edward Mornin noted: "That the girl who attracts Behrendt reminds him of a young man is perhaps to be ascribed to Mackay's homosexuality." I believe that much more is going on here with this girl who "was never afraid of anything." There are several indications that Mackay is really describing an affair with a boy and has only used the well-known device of changing the pronoun to disguise the fact and make the novel acceptable to the public. The first indication is indeed that noted by Mornin, but the whole one-night stand has all the elements of a typical man-boy encounter down to the showing of the photo of the lad's real girlfriend. Despite the prevalent anti-boylove, anti-homosexual, anti-sex propaganda, many (heterosexual) boys welcome the interest of an older man, even as they are basically interested in girls. This was as true in Mackay's time as it is today. Of course they show their photos. And then as now boy-lovers are pleased to see them, among other

-KENN]

reasons, to reassure themselves that they are not "seducing" the boy into becoming a homosexual as the denouncers of pederasty all say now—and said in Mackay's Berlin.

In his "Books of the Nameless Love," written under the pseudonym Sagitta, Mackay was more explicit. But homosexuality was never explicitly part of any story written under his real name—or almost never: it appears in an unexpectedly matter-of-fact way in the novella *Der Unschuldige* (The Innocent, 1931), his last published fiction. But there are hints of boy-love in several short stories and poems, where it is mostly hidden by the lack of any pronouns, thus allowing the reader to assume the gender at will—and, of course, the heterosexual assumption has prevailed. Already in *Helene* (1888) the title character appears to be patterned after a boy who appears in the "Sagitta" novel *Fenny Skaller*, which is largely autobiographical. The short short story "Ein Abschied: Ein später Brief" (A Farewell: A Late Letter, 1903) is an unusual example in which the gender of the older lover of a young man is unstated. All prior critics have assumed that person is a woman, but I read the character as a man.

Whatever the sources for Mackay's literary figures—whether Gabriele Reuter for Dora Syk in *The People of Marriage* or a boy for Marie in *The Imagined World*—the two can be read on several levels with enjoyment. The third novel here, *District Attorney Sierlin*, is more superficial in this regard. Yet it too has depths in its psychological insights and unrelenting anarchistic treatment even as it remains on the surface a gripping thriller. All together, the three novels presented here reveal many sides of the Scotch-German writer—anarchist, boy-lover, his own man—the unique John Henry Mackay.

Hubert Kennedy